Critical acclaim for Ian Rankin

'Arguably no Scottish novelist since Sir Walter Scott has had the commercial .... ss that Ian Rankin .... d to have invente................................ modern Edinbu.... .... readers, just as Scott did in his time . . . Rebus lives. So does Rankin's Edinburgh' Allan Massie, *Spectator*

'Rankin captures, like no one else, that strangeness that is Scotland at the end of the twentieth century. He has always written superb crime fiction . . . but what he's also pinning down is instant history'
Literary Review

'Rankin writes laconic, sophisticated, well-paced thrillers' *Scotsman*

'Rankin strips Edinburgh's polite façade to its gritty skeleton' *The Times*

'The real strength of Ian Rankin's work . . . is that it's a good deal more than a crime novel. The genre is simply the wrapper in which a complex story of human flaws and frailty is contained' *Herald*

'Rankin proves himself the master of his own milieu . . . There cannot be a better crime novelist writing' *Daily Mail*

'Arguably Scotland's finest living writer' *The Times*

'The internal police politics and corruption in high places are both portrayed with bone-freezing accuracy. This novel should come with a wind-chill factor warning' *Daily Telegraph*

Born in the Kingdom of Fife in 1960, Ian Rankin graduated from the University of Edinburgh and has since been employed as grape-picker, swineherd, taxman, alcohol researcher, hi-fi journalist and punk musician. His first Rebus novel, *Knots & Crosses*, was published in 1987 and the Rebus books have now been translated into 26 languages. Ian Rankin has been elected a Hawthornden Fellow, and is a past winner of the prestigious Chandler-Fulbright Award, as well as two CWA short-story 'Daggers' and the 1997 CWA Macallan Gold Dagger for Fiction for *Black & Blue*, which was also shortlisted for the Mystery Writers of America 'Edgar' award for Best Novel. *Black & Blue*, *The Hanging Garden*, *Dead Souls* and *Mortal Causes* have been televised on ITV, starring John Hannah as Inspector Rebus. *The Falls* and *Fleshmarket Close* have also been shown on ITV, starring Ken Stott as Rebus. *Dead Souls*, the tenth novel in the series, was shortlisted for the CWA Gold Dagger Award in 1999. An Alumnus of the Year at Edinburgh University, he has also been awarded four honorary doctorates, from the University of Abertay Dundee in 1999, from the University of St Andrews in 2001, in 2003 from the University of Edinburgh and in 2005 from the Open University. In 2002 Ian Rankin was awarded an OBE for services to literature. In 2004 *Resurrection Men* won the Edgar Award for Best Novel. In 2005 *Fleshmarket Close* won the Crime Thriller of the Year award at the British Book Awards. Ian is the winner of the Crime Writers' Association Diamond Dagger 2005. In 2005 he was also awarded the Grand Prix du Littérature Policier (France), the Deutsche Krimi Prize (Germany) and the Icons of Scotland award. He lives in Edinburgh with his wife and two sons. Visit his website at www.ianrankin.net.

By Ian Rankin

The Inspector Rebus series
Knots & Crosses
Hide & Seek
Tooth & Nail
Strip Jack
The Black Book
Mortal Causes
Let It Bleed
Black & Blue
The Hanging Garden
Death Is Not The End (*novella*)
Dead Souls
Set in Darkness
The Falls
Resurrection Men
A Question of Blood
Fleshmarket Close

Other novels
The Flood
Watchman
Westwind

Writing as Jack Harvey
Witch Hunt
Bleeding Hearts
Blood Hunt

Short stories
A Good Hanging and Other Stories
Beggars Banquet

Non-fiction
Rebus's Scotland

All Ian Rankin's titles are available on audio. Also available:
Jackie Leven Said by Ian Rankin and Jackie Leven.

Ian Rankin

The Black Book

An Orion paperback

First published in Great Britain in 1993
by Orion
This paperback edition published in 1994
by Orion Books Ltd,
Orion House, 5 Upper St Martin's Lane,
London WC2H 9EA

Reissued 2005

23

ISBN-13 978-0-7528-7724-2
ISBN-10 0-7528-7724-0

Printed and bound in Great Britain by
Clays Ltd, St Ives plc

The Orion Publishing Group's policy is to use papers that
are natural, renewable and recyclable products and
made from wood grown in sustainable forests. The logging
and manufacturing processes are expected to conform to
the environmental regulations of the country of origin.

www.orionbooks.co.uk

INTRODUCTION

Late on in *The Black Book*, I mention a town in the USA called Bar Harbor. The reference may be fleeting, but it reminds me that a lot of the plotting of my novel was actually done in North America. Nineteen ninety-two for me comprised two momentous events. In February, my son Jack was born. And three months later, almost to the day, the family Rankin headed to the USA for an unforgettable six-month stay, made possible by America's most famous crime writer, Raymond Chandler.

Flashback: early summer the previous year. A letter arrives at our dusty farmhouse in south-west France. We'd been living there full-time for just over a year – refugees from corporate London – and the place was beginning to take shape. I'd only nearly killed myself half a dozen times, falling off roofs, slicing into my boot with a chainsaw, electrocuting myself while rewiring the mains, and going head-over-heels in a bramble patch with a weed-whacker aiming to strip the skin off my face. But the house now had things like ceilings and a bath and rudimentary heating. The broken windows had been mended and the woodworm treated. We even had a sofa, so no longer had to haul the back seat out of the Citroën and into the living room of an evening.

We deserved a break.

It came – of sorts – in the shape of that letter, telling me I'd won the Chandler-Fulbright Fellowship in Detective Fiction. The reward was a chunk of money (courtesy of

Raymond Chandler's estate), with the stipulation that it be spent during the course of a six-month stay in the United States. This was fine with me. I showed my wife Miranda the letter, and she showed me a little strip of card and asked me if I thought the tip was a blueish sort of colour. I said I thought it was, and she said she thought she was pregnant. And so it came to pass that my short-lived dream of a drug-and-drink-fuelled orgy of classic car-driving across America was replaced with something more wholesome. In May 1992, with Jack three months old (the minimum age at which British Airways would carry him), we set out for Seattle. We had friends there, and they gave us time (and space) to get acclimatised. Eventually, with the purchase of a 1969 VW camper van, we were ready for a drive which would last for the next five months and put another 15,000 miles on the VW's already well-worn clock.

It was as I drove through the USA (and bits of Canada), that I started thinking of my next Rebus novel. *The Black Book* was the result. In it, there's an Elvis-themed restaurant, situated near Edinburgh's Haymarket Station. I would find the real thing, however, in a New Orleans backstreet. That place was a dive, but I liked the idea of it, and had a lot of fun thinking up menu items such as the *Love Me Tenderloin*. I also had the opportunity to do a lot of thinking about the series. I was sure in my mind now that it *was* a series, and there were changes I wanted to make. At the end of the previous Rebus novel, *Strip Jack*, I had burned down the fictitious police station where my hero had been based since book one. In *The Black Book*, I moved him to a real-life station on St Leonard's Street. I also, for the first time, mentioned where he lived – a real street – and took him to the site of the authentic Edinburgh mortuary.

I had also learned lessons in economy. If there was a need for a certain character type in the story, and such a character had been used in one of the previous books, then why not bring them back to life, rather than go to the trouble of inventing some brand-new personality? So it is that people like Matthew Vanderhyde and Jack Morton come back into Rebus's life. Rebus's brother Michael reappears, sleeping at Rebus's flat while Rebus himself has moved in with Dr Patience Aitken. However, I also had room for a new character, a foil for Rebus: Detective Constable Siobhan Clarke. Rebus already had a sidekick of sorts in the shape of Detective Sergeant Brian Holmes, and Siobhan entered the book as just another of Rebus's colleagues, and someone who might work well beside Holmes. By story's end, however, and by sheer force of character, she had usurped Holmes. I had found Rebus's perfect working partner: someone who respected him but could still be infuriated by his reluctance to stick to the rules; someone confident enough in their own abilities to be able to give as good as they got. It was not in Siobhan's nature to remain 'just another colleague'; she seemed to have other ideas entirely.

Another, different kind of foil for Rebus had already announced his readiness in a previous book. Morris Gerald Cafferty – Big Ger – was Edinburgh's premier gangster. Having existed for the length of a cameo in *Tooth & Nail*, Cafferty was to emerge in *The Black Book* as a fully formed presence, the epitome of moral and spiritual corruption. He may not enter proceedings until halfway through, but the effect is chilling. What I find most intriguing about Cafferty is the ambiguity he brings with him. He is very like Rebus in some ways, something he can acknowledge but Rebus never will. Both men are ageing fast, finding the changing landscape unsympathetic. They remind me of Cain and Abel, or two sides of the same coin.

Or Jekyll and Hyde.

In previous books, I had made copious use of Robert Louis Stevenson's dark masterpiece, going so far as to use Hyde's surname as a pun in the title of my novel *Hide & Seek*. However, it seems to me now that *The Black Book* owes a greater debt to another Scots gothic chiller: James Hogg's *Confessions of a Justified Sinner*. In that book, an innocent is cajoled and seduced and psychologically cudgelled into committing a murder. Is his tormentor the Devil, or a cruel and devious psychopath? Maybe the malevolent voice is his own, the ravings of a man possessed. The issue is never settled: it's left to the reader to decide.

I'll leave readers of *The Black Book* to decide how closely I follow my predecessor's course.

One last thing: you need to know that 'lum' is a Scottish word for a chimney. It'll help you get one of my favourite bad puns in the series . . .

April 2005

'To the wicked, all things are wicked; but to the just, all things are just and right.'

James Hogg, *The Private Memoirs and Confessions of a Justified Sinner*

Acknowledgements

The author wishes to acknowledge the assistance of the Chandler-Fulbright Award in the writing of this book.

Prologue

There were two of them in the van that early morning, lights on to combat the haar which blew in from the North Sea. It was thick and white like smoke. They drove carefully, being under strict instructions.

'Why does it have to be us?' said the driver, stifling a yawn. 'What's wrong with the other two?'

The passenger was much larger than his companion. Though in his forties, he kept his hair long, cut in the shape of a German military helmet. He kept pulling at the hair on the left side of his head, straightening it out. At the moment, however, he was gripping the sides of his seat. He didn't like the way the driver screwed shut his eyes for the duration of each too-frequent yawn. The passenger was not a conversationalist, but maybe talk would keep the driver awake.

'It's just temporary,' he said. 'Besides, it's not as if it's a daily chore.'

'Thank God for that.' The driver shut his eyes again and yawned. The van glided in towards the grass verge.

'Do you want me to drive?' asked the passenger. Then he smiled. 'You could always kip in the back.'

'Very funny. That's another thing, Jimmy, the *stink*!'

'Meat always smells after a while.'

'Got an answer for everything, eh?'

'Yes.'

'Are we nearly there?'

'I thought you knew the way.'

1

'On the main roads I do. But with this mist.'

'If we're hugging the coast it can't be far.' The passenger was also thinking: if we're hugging the coast, then two wheels past the verge and we're over a cliff face. It wasn't just this that made him nervous. They'd never used the east coast before, but there was too much attention on the west coast now. So it was an untried run, and *that* made him nervous.

'Here's a road sign.' They braked to peer through the haar. 'Next right.' The driver jolted forwards again. He signalled and pulled in through a low iron gate which was padlocked open. 'What if it had been locked?' he offered.

'I've got cutters in the back.'

'A bloody answer for everything.'

They drove into a small gravelled car park. Though they could not see them, there were wooden tables and benches to one side, where Sunday families could picnic and do battle with the midges. The spot was popular for its view, an uninterrupted spread of sea and sky. When they opened their doors, they could smell and hear the sea. Gulls were already shrieking overhead.

'Must be later than we thought if the birds are up.' They readied themselves for opening the back of the van, then did so. The smell really was foul. Even the stoical passenger wrinkled his nose and tried hard not to breathe.

'Quicker the better,' he said in a rush. The body had been placed in two thick plastic fertiliser sacks, one pulled over the feet and one over the head, so that they over-lapped in the middle. Tape and string had been used to join them. Inside the bags were also a number of breeze blocks, making for a heavy and awkward load. They carried the grotesque parcel low, brushing the wet grass. Their shoes were squelching by the time they passed the sign warning about the cliff face ahead. Even more difficult

2

was the climb over the fence, though it was rickety enough to start with.

'Wouldn't stop a bloody kid,' the driver commented. He was peching, the saliva like glue in his mouth.

'Ca' canny,' said the passenger. They shuffled forwards two inches at a time, until they could all too clearly make out the edge. There was no more land after that, just a vertical fall to the agitated sea. 'Right,' he said. Without ceremony, they heaved the thing out into space, glad immediately to be rid of it. 'Let's go.'

'Man, but that air smells good.' The driver reached into his pocket for a quarter-bottle of whisky. They were halfway back to the van when they heard a car on the road, and the crunch of tyres on gravel.

'Aw, hell's bells.'

The headlights caught them as they reached the van.

'The fuckin' polis!' choked the driver.

'Keep the heid,' warned the passenger. His voice was quiet, but his eyes burned ahead of him. They heard a handbrake being engaged, and the car door opened. A uniformed officer appeared. He was carrying a torch. The headlights and engine had been left on. There was no one else in the car.

The passenger knew the score. This wasn't a set-up. Probably the copper came here towards the end of his night shift. There'd be a flask or a blanket in the car. Coffee or a snooze before signing off for the day.

'Morning,' the uniform said. He wasn't young, and he wasn't used to trouble. A Saturday night punch-up maybe, or disputes between neighbouring farmers. It had been another long boring night for him, another night nearer his pension.

'Morning,' the passenger said. He knew they could bluff this one, if the driver stayed calm. But then he thought, *I'm* the conspicuous one.

'A right pea-souper, eh?' said the policeman.

The passenger nodded.

'That's why we stopped,' explained the driver. 'Thought we'd wait it out.'

'Very sensible.'

The driver watched as the passenger turned to the van and started inspecting its rear driver-side tyre, giving it a kick. He then walked to the rear passenger-side and did the same, before getting down on his knees to peer beneath the vehicle. The policeman watched the performance too.

'Got a bit of trouble?'

'Not really,' the driver said nervously. 'But it's best to be safe.'

'I see you've come a ways.'

The driver nodded. 'Off up to Dundee.'

The policeman frowned. 'From Edinburgh? Why didn't you just stick to the motorway or the A914?'

The driver thought quickly. 'We've a drop-off in Tayport first.'

'Even so,' the policeman started. The driver watched as the passenger rose from his inspection, now sited behind the policeman. He was holding a rock in his hand. The driver kept his eyes glued to the policeman's as the rock rose, then fell. The monologue finished mid-sentence as the body slumped to the ground.

'That's just beautiful.'

'What else could we do?' The passenger was already making for his door. 'Come on, vamoose!'

'Aye,' said the driver, 'another minute and he'd have spotted your ... er ...'

The passenger glowered at him. 'What you mean is, another minute and he'd've smelt the booze on your breath.' He didn't stop glowering until the driver shrugged his agreement.

They turned the van and drove out of the car park. The gulls were still noisy in the distance. The police car's engine was turning over. The headlights picked out the prone unconscious figure. But the torch had broken in the fall.

1

It all happened because John Rebus was in his favourite massage parlour reading the Bible.

It all happened because a man walked in through the door in the mistaken belief that any massage parlour sited so close to a brewery and half a dozen good pubs had to be catering to Friday night pay packets and anytime drunks; and therefore had to be bent as a paper-clip.

But the Organ Grinder, God-fearing tenant of the set-up, ran a clean shop, a place where tired muscles were beaten mellow. Rebus was tired: tired of arguments with Patience Aitken, tired of the fact that his brother had turned up seeking shelter in a flat filled to the gunwales with students, and most of all tired of his job.

It had been that kind of week.

On the Monday evening, he'd had a call from his Arden Street flat. The students he'd rented to had Patience's number and knew they could reach him there, but this was the first time they'd ever had reason. The reason was Michael Rebus.

'Hello, John.'

Rebus recognised the voice at once. 'Mickey?'

'How are you, John?'

'Christ, Mickey. Where are you? No, scratch that, I know where you are. I mean –' Michael was laughing softly. 'It's just I heard you'd gone south.'

'Didn't work out.' His voice dropped. 'Thing is, John,

7

can we talk? I've been dreading this, but I really need to talk to you.'

'Okay.'

'Shall I come round there?'

Rebus thought quickly. Patience was picking up her two nieces from Waverley Station, but all the same ... 'No, stay where you are. I'll come over. The students are a good lot, maybe they'll fix you a cup of tea or a joint while you're waiting.'

There was silence on the line, then Michael's voice: 'I could have done without that.' The line went dead.

Michael Rebus had served three years of a five-year sentence for drug dealing. During that time, John Rebus had visited his brother fewer than half a dozen times. He'd felt relief more than anything when, upon release, Michael had taken a bus to London. That was two years ago, and the brothers had not exchanged a word since. But now Michael was back, bringing with him bad memories of a period in John Rebus's life he'd rather not remember.

The Arden Street flat was suspiciously tidy when he arrived. Only two of the student tenants were around, the couple who slept in what had been Rebus's bedroom. He talked to them in the hallway. They were just going out to the pub, but handed over to him another letter from the Inland Revenue. Really, Rebus would have liked them to stay. When they left, there was silence in the flat. Rebus knew that Michael would be in the living room and he was, crouched in front of the stereo and flipping through stacks of records.

'Look at this lot,' Michael said, his back still to Rebus. 'The Beatles and the Stones, same stuff you used to listen to. Remember how you drove dad daft? What was that record player again ...?'

'A Dansette.'

'That's it. Dad got it saving cigarette coupons.' Michael stood up and turned towards his brother. 'Hello, John.'

'Hello, Michael.'

They didn't hug or shake hands. They just sat down, Rebus on the chair, Michael on the sofa.

'This place has changed,' Michael said.

'I had to buy a few sticks of furniture before I could rent it out.' Already Rebus had noticed a few things – cigarette burns on the carpet, posters (against his explicit instructions) sellotaped to the wallpaper. He opened the taxman's letter.

'You should have seen them leap into action when I told them you were coming round. Hoovering and washing dishes. Who says students are lazy?'

'They're okay.'

'So when did this all happen?'

'A few months ago.'

'They told me you're living with a doctor.'

'Her name's Patience.'

Michael nodded. He looked pale and ill. Rebus tried not to be interested, but he was. The letter from the tax office hinted strongly that they knew he was renting his flat, and didn't he want to declare the income? The back of his head was tingling. It did that when he was fractious, ever since it had been burned in the fire. The doctors said there was nothing he or they could do about it.

Except, of course, not get fractious.

He stuffed the letter into his pocket. 'What do you want, Mickey?'

'Bottom line, John, I need a place to stay. Just for a week or two, till I can get on my feet.' Rebus stared stonily at the posters on the walls as Michael ran on. He wanted to find work ... money was tight ... he'd take any job ... he just needed a chance.

'That's all, John, just one chance.'

Rebus was thinking. Patience had room in her flat, of course. There was space enough there even with the nieces staying. But no way was Rebus going to take his brother back to Oxford Terrace. Things weren't going that well as it was. His late hours and her late hours, his exhaustion and hers, his job involvement and hers. Rebus couldn't see Michael improving things. He thought: I am not my brother's keeper. But all the same.

'We might squeeze you into the box room. I'd have to talk to the students about it.' He couldn't see them saying no, but it seemed polite to ask. How *could* they say no? He was their landlord and flats were hard to find. Especially good flats, especially in Marchmont.

'That would be great.' Michael sounded relieved. He got up from the sofa and walked over to the door of the box room. This was a large ventilated cupboard off the living room. Just big enough for a single bed and a chest of drawers, if you took all the boxes and the rubbish out of it.

'We could probably store all that stuff in the cellar,' said Rebus, standing just behind his brother.

'John,' said Michael, 'the way I feel, I'd be happy enough sleeping in the cellar myself.' And when he turned towards his brother, there were tears in Michael Rebus's eyes.

On Wednesday, Rebus began to realise that his world was a black comedy.

Michael had been moved into the Arden Street flat without any fuss. Rebus had informed Patience of his brother's return, but had said little more than that. She was spending a lot of time with her sister's girls anyway. She'd taken a few days off work to show them Edinburgh. It looked like hard going. Susan at fifteen wanted to do all the things which Jenny, aged eight, didn't or couldn't. Rebus felt almost totally excluded from this female tri- umvirate, though he would sneak into Jenny's room at night just to re-live the magic and innocence of a child asleep. He also spent time trying to avoid Susan, who seemed only too aware of the differences between women and men.

10

He was kept busy at work, which meant he didn't think about Michael more than a few dozen times each day. Ah, work, now there was a thing. When Great London Road police station had burnt down, Rebus had been moved to St Leonard's, which was Central District's divisional HQ.

With him had come Detective Sergeant Brian Holmes and, to both their dismays, Chief Superintendent 'Farmer' Watson and Chief Inspector 'Fart' Lauderdale. There had been compensations – newer offices and furniture, better amenities and equipment – but not enough. Rebus was still trying to come to terms with his new workplace. Everything was so tidy, he could never find anything, as a result of which he was always keen to get out of the office and onto the street.

Which was why he ended up at a butcher's shop on South Clerk Street, staring down at a stabbed man.

The man had already been tended to by a local doctor, who'd been standing in line waiting for some pork chops and gammon steaks when the man staggered into the shop. The wound had been dressed initially with a clean butcher's apron, and now everyone was waiting for a stretcher to be unloaded from the ambulance outside.

A constable was filling Rebus in.

'I was only just up the road, so he couldn't have been here more than five minutes when somebody told me, and I came straight here. That's when I radioed in.'

Rebus had picked up the constable's radio message in his car, and had decided to stop by. He kind of wished he hadn't. There was blood smeared across the floor, colouring the sawdust which lay there. Why some butchers still scattered sawdust on their floors he couldn't say. There was also a palm-shaped daub of blood on the white-tiled wall, and another less conclusive splash of the stuff below this.

The wounded man had also left a trail of gleaming drips

11

outside, all the way along and halfway up Lutton Place (insultingly close to St Leonard's), where they suddenly stopped kerbside.

The man's name was Rory Kintoul, and he had been stabbed in the abdomen. This much they knew. They didn't know much more, because Rory Kintoul was refusing to speak about the incident. This was not an attitude shared by those who had been in the butcher's at the time. They were outside now, passing on news of the excitement to the crowd who had stopped to gawp through the shop window. It reminded Rebus of Saturday afternoon in the St James Centre, when pockets of men would gather outside the TV rental shops, hoping to catch the football scores.

Rebus crouched over Kintoul, just a little intimidatingly.

'And where do you live, Mr Kintoul?'

But the man was not about to answer. A voice came from the other side of the glass display case.

'Duncton Terrace.' The speaker was wearing a bloodied butcher's apron and cleaning a heavy knife on a towel. 'That's in Dalkeith.'

Rebus looked at the butcher. 'And you are ...?'

'Jim Bone. This is my shop.'

'And you know Mr Kintoul?'

Kintoul had turned his head awkwardly, seeking the butcher's face, as if trying to influence his answer. But, slouched as he was against the display case, he would have required demonic possession to effect such a move.

'I ought to,' said the butcher. 'He's my cousin.'

Rebus was about to say something, but at that moment the stretcher was trolleyed in by two ambulancemen, one of whom almost skited on the slippery floor. It was as they positioned the stretcher in front of Kintoul that Rebus saw something which would stay with him. There were two signs in the display cabinet, one pinned into a side of corned beef, the other into a slab of red sirloin.

Cold Cuts, one said. The other stated simply, Fleshing. A large fresh patch of blood was left on the floor as they lifted the butcher's cousin. Cold Cuts and Fleshing. Rebus shivered and made for the door.

On the Friday after work, Rebus decided on a massage. He had promised Patience he'd be in by eight, and it was only six now. Besides, a brutal pummelling always seemed to set him up for the weekend.

But first he wandered into the Broadsword for a pint of the local brew. They didn't come more local than Gibson's Dark, a heavy beer made only six hundred yards away at the Gibson Brewery. A brewery, a pub and a massage parlour: Rebus reckoned if you threw in a good Indian restaurant and a corner shop open till midnight he could live happily here for ever and a day.

Not that he didn't like living with Patience in her Oxford Terrace garden flat. It represented the other side of the tracks, so to speak. Certainly, it seemed a world away from this disreputable corner of Edinburgh, one of many such corners. Rebus wondered why he was so drawn to them.

The air outside was filled with the yeasty smell of beer-making, vying with the even stronger aromas from the city's other much larger breweries. The Broadsword was a popular watering hole, and like most of Edinburgh's popular pubs, it boasted a mixed clientele: students and low lifes with the occasional businessman. The bar had few pretensions; all it had in its favour were good beer and a good cellar. The weekend had already started, and Rebus was squeezed in at the bar, next to a man whose immense alsatian dog was sleeping on the floor behind the barstools. It took up the standing room of at least two adult men, but nobody was asking it to shift. Further along the bar, someone was drinking with one hand and keeping another proprietorial hand on a coatstand which

13

Rebus assumed they'd just bought at one of the nearby secondhand shops. Everyone at the bar was drinking the same dark brew.

Though there were half a dozen pubs within a five-minute walk of here, only the Broadsword stocked draught Gibson's, the other pubs being tied to one or other of the big breweries. Rebus started to wonder, as the beer slipped down, what effect it would have on his metabolism once the Organ Grinder got to work. He decided against a refill, and instead made for O-Gee's, which was what the Organ Grinder had called his shop. Rebus liked the name; it made the same sound customers made once the Grinder himself got to work – 'Oh Jeez!' But they were always careful not to say anything out loud. The Organ Grinder didn't like to hear blasphemy on the massage table. It upset him, and nobody wanted to be in the hands of an upset Organ Grinder. Nobody wanted to be his monkey.

So, there he was sitting with the Bible in his lap, waiting for his six-thirty appointment. The Bible was the only reading matter on the premises, courtesy of the Organ Grinder himself. Rebus had read it before, but didn't mind reading it again.

Then the front door burst open.

'Where's the girls, eh?' This new client was not only misinformed, but also considerably drunk. There was no way the Grinder would handle drunks.

'Wrong place, pal.' Rebus was about to make mention of a couple of nearby parlours which would be certain to offer the necessary Thai assisted sauna and rub-down, but the man stopped him with a thick pointed finger.

'John bloody Rebus, you son of a shite-breeks!'

Rebus frowned, trying to place the face. His mind flipped through two decades of mug shots. The man saw Rebus's confusion, and spread his hands wide. 'Deek Torrance, you don't remember?'

Rebus shook his head. Torrance was walking determinedly forward. Rebus clenched his fists, ready for anything.

'We went through parachute training together,' said Torrance. 'Christ, you must remember!'

And suddenly Rebus did remember. He remembered everything, the whole black comedy of his past.

They drank in the Broadsword, swopping stories. Deek hadn't lasted in the Parachute Regiment. After a year he'd had enough, and not too long after that he'd bought his way out of the Army altogether.

'Too restless, John, that was my problem. What was yours?'

Rebus shook his head and drank some more beer. 'My problem, Deek? You couldn't put a name to it.' But a name *had* been put to it, first by Mickey's sudden appearance, and now by Deek Torrance. Ghosts, both of them, but Rebus didn't want to be their Scrooge. He bought another round.

'You always said you were going to try for the SAS,' Torrance said.

Rebus shrugged. 'It didn't work out.'

The bar was busier than ever, and at one point Torrance was jostled by a young man trying to manoeuvre a double bass through the mêlée.

'Could you no' leave that outside?'

'Not around here.'

Torrance turned back to Rebus. 'Did you see thon?'

Rebus merely smiled. He felt good after the massage. 'No one brings anything small into a bar around here.' He watched Deek Torrance grunt. Yes, he remembered him now, all right. He'd gotten fatter and balder, his face was roughened and much fleshier than it had been. He didn't even sound the same, not exactly. But there was that one characteristic: the Torrance grunt. A man of few words, Deek Torrance had been. Not now, though, now he had plenty to say.

'So what do you do, Deek?'

Torrance grinned. 'Seeing you're a copper I better not say.' Rebus bided his time. Torrance was drunk to the point of slavering. Sure enough, he couldn't resist. 'I'm in buying and selling, mostly selling.'

'And what do you sell?'

Torrance leaned closer. 'Am I talking to the polis or an old pal?'

'A pal,' said Rebus. 'Strictly off-duty. So what do you sell?'

Torrance grunted. 'Anything you like, John. I'm sort of like Jenners department store ... only I can get things they can't.'

'Such as?' Rebus was looking at the clock above the bar. It couldn't be that late, surely. They always ran the clock ten minutes fast here, but even so.

'Anything at all,' said Torrance. 'Anything from a shag to a shooter. You name it.'

'How about a watch?' Rebus started winding his own. 'Mine only seems to go for a couple of hours at a stretch.'

Torrance looked at it. 'Longines,' he said, pronouncing the word correctly, 'you don't want to chuck that. Get it cleaned, it'll be fine. Mind you, I could probably part-ex it against a Rolex ...?'

'So you sell dodgy watches.'

'Did I say that? I don't recall saying that. *Anything*, John. Whatever the client wants, I'll fetch it for him.' Torrance winked.

'Listen, what time do you make it?'

Torrance shrugged and pulled up the sleeve of his jacket. He wasn't wearing a watch. Rebus was thinking. He'd kept his appointment with the Grinder, Deek happy to wait for him in the anteroom. And afterwards they'd still had time for a pint or two before he had to make his way home. They'd had two ... no, three drinks so far.

16

Maybe he was running a bit late. He caught the barman's attention and tapped at his wrist.

'Twenty past eight,' called the barman.

'I'd better phone Patience,' said Rebus.

But someone was using the public phone to cement some romance. What's more, they'd dragged the receiver into the ladies' toilet so that they could hear above the noise from the bar. The telephone cord was stretched taut, ready to garotte anyone trying to use the toilets. Rebus bided his time, then began staring at the wall-mounted telephone cradle. What the hell. He pushed his finger down on the cradle, released it, then moved back into the throng of drinkers. A young man appeared from inside the ladies' toilet and slammed the receiver hard back into its cradle. He checked for change in his pocket, had none, and started to make for the bar.

Rebus moved in on the phone. He picked it up, but could hear no tone. He tried again, then tried dialling. Nothing. Something had obviously come loose when the man had slammed the receiver home. Shite on a stick. It was nearly half past eight now, and it would take fifteen minutes to drive back to Oxford Terrace. He was going to pay dearly for this.

'You look like you could use a drink,' said Deek Torrance when Rebus joined him at the bar.

'Know what, Deek?' said Rebus. 'My life's a black comedy.'

'Oh well, better than a tragedy, eh?'

Rebus was beginning to wonder what the difference was.

He got back to the flat at twenty past nine. Probably Patience had cooked a meal for the four of them. Probably she'd waited fifteen minutes or so before eating. She'd have kept his meal warm for another fifteen minutes, then dumped it. If it was fish, the cat would have eaten it. Otherwise its destination would be the compost heap in the garden. This had happened before, too many times, really. Yet it kept on happening, and Rebus wasn't sure the excuses of an old friend or a broken watch would work any kind of spell.

The steps down to the garden flat were worn and slippery. Rebus took them carefully, and so was slow to notice the large sports holdall which, illuminated by the orange street-lamp, was sitting on the rattan mat outside the front door of the flat. It was his bag. He unzipped it and looked in. On top of some clothes and a pair of shoes there was a note. He read it through twice.

Don't bother trying the door, I've bolted it. I've also disconnected the doorbell, and the phone is off the hook for the weekend. I'll leave another load of your stuff on the front step Monday morning.

The note needed no signature. Rebus whistled a long breathy note, then tried his key in the lock. It didn't budge. He pressed the doorbell. No sound. As a last resort, he crouched down and peered in through the letterbox. The hall was in darkness, no sign of light from any of the rooms.

'Something came up,' he called. No response. 'I tried phoning, I couldn't get through.' Still nothing. He waited a few more moments, half-expecting Jenny at least to break the silence. Or Susan, she was a right stirrer of trouble. And a heartbreaker too, by the look of her. 'Bye, Patience,' he called. 'Bye, Susan. Bye, Jenny.' Still silence. 'I'm sorry.'

He truly was.

'Just one of those weeks,' he said to himself, picking up the bag.

On Sunday morning, in weak sunshine and a snell wind, Andrew McPhail sneaked back into Edinburgh. He'd been away a long time, and the city had changed. Everywhere and everything had changed. He was still jetlagged from several days ago, and poorer than he should have been due to London's inflated prices. He walked from the bus station to the Broughton area of town, just off Leith Walk. It wasn't a long walk, but every step seemed heavy, though his bags were light. He'd slept badly on the bus, but that was nothing new: he couldn't remember when he'd last had a good night's sleep, sleep without dreams.

The sun looked as though it might disappear at any minute. Thick clouds were pushing in over Leith. McPhail tried to walk faster. He had an address in his pocket, the address of a boarding house. He'd phoned last night, and his landlady was expecting him. She sounded nice on the phone, but it was difficult to tell. He wouldn't mind, no matter what she was like, so long as she kept quiet. He knew that his leaving Canada had been in the Canadian newspapers, and even in some of the American ones, and he supposed that journalists here would be after him for a story. He'd been surprised at slipping so quietly into Heathrow. No one seemed to know who he was, and that was good.

He wanted nothing but a quiet life, though perhaps not as quiet as a few of the past years.

He'd phoned his sister from London and asked her to check directory enquiries for a Mrs MacKenzie in the Bellevue area. (Directory enquiries in London hadn't gone out of their way to help.) Melanie and her mother had lodged with Mrs MacKenzie when he'd first met them, before they moved in together. Alexis was a single parent, a DSS case. Mrs MacKenzie had been a more sympathetic landlady than most. Not that he'd ever visited Melanie and her mum there – Mrs MacKenzie wouldn't have liked it.

She didn't take lodgers much these days, but she was a good Christian and McPhail was persuasive.

He stood outside the house. It was a plain two-storey construction finished off in grey pebbledash and ugly double glazing. It looked just the same as the houses either side of it. Mrs MacKenzie answered the door as though she'd been ready for him for some time. She fussed about in the living room and kitchen, then led him upstairs to show him the bathroom, and then finally his own bedroom. It was no larger than a prison cell, but had been nicely decorated (sometime in the mid-1960s, he'd guess). It was fine, he'd no complaints.

'It's lovely,' he told Mrs MacKenzie, who shrugged her shoulders as if to say, of course it is.

'There's tea in the pot,' she said. 'I'll just go make us a cuppy.' Then she remembered something. 'No cooking in the room, mind.'

Andrew McPhail shook his head. 'I don't cook,' he said. She thought of something else and crossed to the window, where the net curtains were still closed.

'Here, I'll open these. You can open a window too, if you want some fresh air.'

'Fresh air would be nice,' he agreed. They both looked out of the window down onto the street.

'It's quiet,' she said. 'Not too much traffic. Of course, there's always a wee bit of noise during the day.'

McPhail could see what she was referring to: there was an old school building across the road with a black iron fence in front of it. It wasn't a large school, probably primary. McPhail's window looked down onto the school gates, just to the right of the main building. Directly behind the gates was the deserted playground.

'I'll get that tea,' said Mrs MacKenzie. When she'd gone, McPhail placed his cases on the springy single bed. Beside the bed was a small writing desk and chair. He lifted the chair and placed it in front of the window, then sat down. He moved a small glass clown further along the sill so that he could rest his chin where it had been. Nothing

20

obscured his view. He sat there in a dream, looking at the playground, until Mrs MacKenzie called to him that the tea was in the living room. 'And a Madeira cake, too.' Andrew McPhail got up with a sigh. He didn't really want the tea now, but he supposed he could always bring it up to his room and leave it untouched till later. He felt tired, bone tired, but he was home and something told him that tonight he would sleep the sleep of the dead.

'Coming, Mrs MacKenzie,' he called, tearing his gaze away from the school.

2

On Monday morning word went around St Leonard's police station that Inspector John Rebus was in an impressively worse mood than usual. Some found this hard to believe, and were almost willing to get close enough to Rebus to find out for themselves ... almost.

Others had no choice.

DS Brian Holmes and DC Siobhan Clarke, seated with Rebus in their sectioned-off chunk of the CID room, had the look of people who were resting their backsides on soft-boiled eggs.

'So,' Rebus was saying, 'what about Rory Kintoul?'

'He's out of hospital, sir,' said Siobhan Clarke.

Rebus nodded impatiently. He was waiting for her to put a foot wrong. It wasn't because she was English, or a graduate, or had wealthy parents who'd bought her a flat in the New Town. It wasn't because she was a she. It was just Rebus's way of dealing with young officers.

'And he's still not talking,' said Holmes. 'He won't say what happened, and he's certainly not pressing any charges.'

Brian Holmes looked tired. Rebus noticed this from the corner of his eye. He didn't want to make eye-contact with Holmes, didn't want Holmes to realise that they now had something in common.

Both had been kicked out by their girlfriends.

It had happened to Holmes just over a month ago. As Holmes revealed later, once he'd moved in with an aunt in Barnton, it was all to do with children. He hadn't realised how strongly Nell wanted a baby, and had started to joke about it. Then one day, she'd blown up – an awesome sight – and kicked him out, watched by most of the female neighbours in their mining village south of Edinburgh. Apparently the women neighbours had applauded as Holmes scurried off.

Now, he was working harder than ever. (This also had been a cause of strife between the couple: her hours were fairly regular, his anything but.) He reminded Rebus of a frayed and faded pair of work denims, not far from the end of their life.

'What are you saying?' Rebus asked.

'I'm saying I think we should drop it, sir, with all respect.'

'"With all respect", Brian? That's what people say when they mean "you fucking idiot".' Rebus still wasn't looking at Holmes, but he could feel the young man blushing. Clarke was looking down at her lap.

'Listen,' said Rebus, 'this guy, he staggers a couple of hundred yards with a two-inch gash in his gut. Why?' No answer was forthcoming. 'Why,' Rebus persisted, 'does he walk past a dozen shops, only stopping at his cousin's?'

'Maybe he was making for a doctor's, but had to stop,' Clarke suggested.

'Maybe,' said Rebus dismissively. 'Funny that he can make it into his *cousin's* shop, though.'

'You think it's something to do with the cousin, sir?'

'Let me ask the both of you something else.' Rebus stood up and took a few paces, then retraced his steps, catching Holmes and Clarke exchanging a glance. It set Rebus wondering. At first, there had been sparks between them, sparks of antagonism. But now they were working well together. He just hoped the relationship didn't go further than that. 'Let me ask you this,' he said. 'What do we know about the victim?'

'Not much,' said Holmes.

'He lives in Dalkeith,' Clarke offered. 'Works as a lab technician in the Infirmary. Married, one son.' She shrugged.

'That's it?' asked Rebus.

'That's it, sir.'

'Exactly,' said Rebus. 'He's nobody, a nothing. Not one person we've talked to has had a bad word to say about him. So tell me this: how did he end up getting stabbed? And in the middle of a Wednesday morning? If it had been a mugger, surely he'd tell us about it. As it is, he's clammed up as tight as an Aberdonian's purse at a church collection. He's got something to hide. Christ knows what, but it involves a car.'

'How do you work that out, sir?'

'The blood starts at the kerb, Holmes. Looks to me like he got out of a car and at that point he was already wounded.'

'He drives, sir, but doesn't own a car at present.'

'Smart girl, Clarke.' She prickled at 'girl', but Rebus was talking again. 'And he'd taken a half day off work without telling his wife.' He sat down again. 'Why, why, why? I want the two of you to have another go at him. Tell him we're not happy with his lack of a story. If he can't think of one, we'll pester him till he does. Let him know we mean business.' Rebus paused. 'And after that, do a check on the butcher.'

'Chop chop, sir,' commented Holmes. He was saved by the phone ringing. Rebus picked up the receiver. Maybe it would be Patience.

'DI Rebus.'

'John, can you come to my office?'

It wasn't Patience, it was the Chief Super. 'Two minutes, sir,' said Rebus, putting down the phone. Then, to Holmes and Clarke: 'Get onto it.'

'Yes, sir.'

'You think I'm making too much of this, Brian?'

'Yes, sir.'

'Well, maybe I am. But I don't like a mystery, no matter how small. So bugger off and satisfy my curiosity.'

As they rose, Holmes nodded towards the large suitcase which Rebus had placed behind his desk, supposedly out of view. 'Something I should know about?'

'Yes,' said Rebus. 'It's where I keep all my graft payments. Yours still probably fit in your back pooch.' Holmes didn't look like budging, though Clarke had already retreated to her own desk. Rebus expelled air and lowered his voice. 'I've just joined the ranks of the dispossessed.' Holmes' face became animated. 'Not a bloody word, mind. This is between you and me.'

'Understood.' Holmes thought of something. 'You know, most evenings I eat at the Heartbreak Cafe ...'

'I'll know where to find you then, if I ever need to hear any early Elvis.'

Holmes nodded. 'And Vegas Elvis too. All I mean is, if there's anything I can do ...'

'You could start by disguising yourself as me and trotting along to see Farmer Watson.'

But Holmes was shaking his head. 'I meant anything within reason.'

Within reason. Rebus wondered if it was within reason to be asking the students to put up with him sleeping on the sofa while his brother slept in the box room. Maybe he should offer to lower the rent. When he'd arrived at the flat unannounced on Friday night, three of the students and Michael had been sitting cross-legged on the floor rolling joints and listening to mid-period Rolling Stones. Rebus stared in horror at the cigarette papers in Michael's hand.

'For fuck's sake, Mickey!' So at last Michael Rebus had elicited a reaction from his big brother. The students at least had the grace to look like the criminals they were. 'You're lucky,' Rebus told them all, 'that at this exact second I don't give a shit.'

'Go on, John,' said Michael, offering a half-smoked cigarette. 'It can't do any harm.'

'That's what I mean.' Rebus drew a bottle of whisky out of the carrier-bag he was holding. 'But this can.'

He had proceeded to spend the final hours of the evening sprawled across the sofa supping whisky and singing along to any old record that was put on the turntable. He'd spent much of the weekend in the same spot, too. The students hadn't seemed to mind, though he'd made them put away the drugs for the duration. They cleaned the flat around him, with Michael pitching in, and everyone trooped out to the pub on Saturday night leaving Rebus with the TV and some cans of beer. It didn't look as though Michael had told the students about his prison record; Rebus hoped he'd keep it that way. Michael had offered to move out, or at least give his brother the box room, but Rebus refused. He wasn't sure why.

On Sunday he went to Oxford Terrace, but there didn't seem to be anyone home, and his key still wouldn't open the door. So either the lock had been changed or Patience was hiding in there somewhere, going through her own version of cold turkey with the kids for company.

Now he stood outside Farmer Watson's door and looked down at himself. Sure enough, when he'd gone to Oxford Terrace this morning Patience had left a suitcase of stuff for him outside the door. No note, just the case. He'd changed into the clean suit in the police station toilets. It was a bit crumpled but no more so than anything he usually wore. He hadn't a tie to match, though: Patience had included two horrible brown ties (were they really *his*?) along with the dark blue suit. Brown ties don't make it. He knocked once on the door before opening it.

'Come in, John, come in.' It seemed to Rebus that the

Farmer too was having trouble making St Leonard's fit his ways. The place just didn't feel right. 'Take a seat.' Rebus looked around for a chair. There was one beside the wall, loaded high with files. He lifted these off and tried to find space for them on the floor. If anything, the Chief Super had less space in his office than Rebus himself. 'Still waiting for those bloody filing cabinets,' he admitted. Rebus swung the chair over to the desk and sat down.

'What's up, sir?'

'How are things?'

'Things?'

'Yes.'

'Things are fine, sir.' Rebus wondered if the Farmer knew about Patience. Surely not.

'DC Clarke getting on all right, is she?'

'I've no complaints.'

'Good. We've got a bit of a job coming up, joint operation with Trading Standards.'

'Oh?'

'Chief Inspector Lauderdale will fill in the details, but I wanted to sound you out first, check how things are going.'

'What sort of joint operation?'

'Money lending,' said Watson. 'I forgot to ask, do you want coffee?' Rebus shook his head and watched as Watson bent over in his chair. There being so little space in the room, he'd taken to keeping his coffee-maker on the floor behind his desk, where twice so far to Rebus's knowledge he'd spilt it all across the new beige carpet. When Watson sat up again, he held in his meaty fist a cup of the devil's own drink. The Chief Super's coffee was a minor legend in Edinburgh.

'Money lending with some protection on the side,' Watson corrected. 'But mostly money lending.'

The same old sad story, in other words. People who wouldn't stand a chance in any bank, and with nothing

27

worth pawning, could still borrow money, no matter how bad a risk. The problem was, of course, that the interest ran into the hundreds per cent and arrears could soon mount, bringing more prohibitive interest. It was the most vicious circle of all, vicious because at the end of it all lay intimidation, beatings and worse.

Suddenly, Rebus knew why the Chief Super had wanted this little chat. 'It's not Big Ger, is it?' he asked.

Watson nodded. 'In a way,' he said.

Rebus sprang to his feet. 'This'll be the fourth time in as many years! He always gets off. You know that, I know that!' Normally, he would have recited this on the move, but there was no floorspace worth the name, so he just stood there like a Sunday ranter at the foot of The Mound. 'It's a waste of time trying to pin him on money lending. I thought we'd been through all this a dozen times and decided it was useless going after him without trying another tack.'

'I know, John, I know, but the Trading Standards people are worried. The problem seems bigger than they thought.'

'Bloody Trading Standards.'

'Now, John ...'

'But,' Rebus paused, 'with respect, sir, it's a complete waste of time and manpower. There'll be a surveillance, we'll take a few photos, we'll arrest a couple of the poor saps who act as runners, and nobody'll testify. If the Procurator Fiscal wants Big Ger nailed, then they should give us the resources so we can mount a decent size of operation.'

The problem, of course, was that nobody wanted to nail Morris Gerald Cafferty (known to all as Big Ger) as badly as John Rebus did. He wanted a full scale crucifixion. He wanted to be holding the spear, giving one last poke just to make sure the bastard really was dead. Cafferty was scum, but clever scum. There were always flunkies around to go to jail on his behalf. Because Rebus had failed so often to put the man away, he would rather not think of him at all. Now the Farmer was telling him that there was to be an 'operation'. That would mean long days and nights of surveillance, a lot of paperwork, and the arrests of a few pimply apprentice hardmen at the end of it all.

'John,' said Watson, summoning his powers of character analysis, 'I know how you feel. But let's give it one more shot, eh?'

'I know the kind of shot I'd take at Cafferty given half a chance.' Rebus turned his fist into a gun and mimed the recoil.

Watson smiled. 'Then it's lucky we won't be issuing firearms, isn't it?'

After a moment, Rebus smiled too. He sat down again. 'Go on then, sir,' he said, 'I'm listening.'

At eleven o'clock that evening, Rebus was watching TV in the flat. As usual, there was no one else about. They were either still studying in the University library, or else down at the pub. Since Michael wasn't around either, the pub seemed an odds-on bet. He knew the students were wary, expecting him to kick at least one of them out so he could claim a bedroom. They moved around the flat like eviction notices.

He'd phoned Patience three times, getting the answering machine on each occasion and telling it that he knew she was there and why didn't she pick up the phone?

As a result, the phone was on the floor beside the sofa, and when it rang he dangled an arm, picked up the receiver, and held it to his ear.

'Hello?'

'John?'

Rebus sat up fast. 'Patience, thank Christ you –'

'Listen, this is important.'

29

'I know it is. I know I was stupid, but you've got to believe –'

'Just listen, will you!' Rebus shut up and listened. He would do whatever she told him, no question. 'They thought you'd be here, so someone from the station just phoned. It's Brian Holmes.'

'What did he want?'

'No, they were phoning *about* him.'

'What about him?'

'He's been in some sort of . . . I don't know. Anyway, he's hurt.'

Still holding the receiver, Rebus stood up, hauling the whole apparatus off the floor with him. 'Where is he?'

'Somewhere in Haymarket, some bar . . .'

'The Heartbreak Cafe?'

'That's it. And listen, John?'

'Yes?'

'We will talk. But not yet. Just give me time.'

'Whatever you say, Patience. Bye.' John Rebus dropped the phone from his hand and grabbed his jacket.

Rebus was parking outside the Heartbreak Cafe barely seven minutes later. That was the beauty of Edinburgh when you could avoid traffic lights. The Heartbreak Cafe had been opened just over a year before by a chef who also happened to be an Elvis Presley fan. He had used some of his extensive memorabilia to decorate the interior, and his cooking skills to come up with a menu which was almost worth a visit even if, like Rebus, you'd never liked Elvis. Holmes had raved about the place since its opening, drooling for hours over the dessert called Blue Suede Choux. The Cafe operated as a bar too, with garish cocktails and 1950s music, plus bottled American beers whose prices would have caused convulsions in the Broadsword pub. Rebus got the idea that Holmes had become friends with the owner; certainly, he'd been spending a lot of time there since the split from Nell, and had put on a fair few pounds as a result.

From the outside, the place looked nothing special: pale cement front wall with a narrow rectangular window in the middle, most of which was filled with neon signs advertising beers. And above this a larger neon sign flashing the name of the restaurant. The action wasn't here, however. Holmes had been set on around the back of the place. A narrow alley, just about able to accommodate the width of a Ford Cortina, led to the patrons' car park. This was small by any restaurant's standards, and was also where the overflowing refuse bins were kept. Most clients, Rebus guessed, would park on the street out front. Holmes only parked back here because he spent so much time in the bar, and because his car had once been scratched when he'd left it out front.

There were two cars in the car park. One was Holmes', and the other almost certainly belonged to the owner of the Heartbreak Cafe. It was an old Ford Capri with a painting of Elvis on its bonnet. Brian Holmes lay between the two cars. So far no one had moved him. He would be moved soon, though, after the doctor had finished his examination. One of the officers present recognised Rebus and came over.

'Nasty blow to the back of the head. He's been out cold for at least twenty minutes. That's how long ago he was found. The owner of the place – that's who found him – recognised him and called in. Could be a fractured skull.'

Rebus nodded, saying nothing, his eyes on the prone figure of his colleague. The other detective was still talking, going on about how Holmes' breathing was regular, the usual reassurances. Rebus walked towards the body, standing over the kneeling doctor. The doctor didn't even glance up, but ordered a uniformed constable, who was holding a flashlight over Brian Holmes, to move it a bit to the left. He then started examining that section of Holmes' skull.

Rebus couldn't see any blood, but that didn't mean much. People died all the time without losing any blood over it. Christ, Brian looked so at peace. It was almost like staring into a casket. He turned to the detective.

'What's the owner's name again?'

'Eddie Ringan.'

'Is he inside?'

The detective nodded. 'Propping up the bar.'

That figured. 'I'll just go have a word,' said Rebus.

Eddie Ringan had nursed what was euphemistically called a drinking problem for several years, long before he'd opened the Heartbreak Cafe. For this reason, people reckoned the venture would fail, as other ventures of his had. But they reckoned wrong, for the sole reason that Eddie managed to find a manager, a manager who not only was some kind of financial guru but was also as straight and as strong as a construction girder. He didn't rip Eddie off, and he kept Eddie where Eddie belonged during working hours – in the kitchen.

Eddie still drank, but he could cook and drink; that wasn't a problem. Especially when there were one or two apprentice chefs around to do the stuff which required focused eyes or rock steady hands. And so, according to Brian Holmes, the Heartbreak Cafe thrived. He still hadn't managed to persuade Rebus to join him there for a meal of King Shrimp Creole or Love Me Tenderloin. Rebus wasn't persuaded to walk through the front door ... until tonight.

The lights were still on. It was like walking into some teenager's shrine to his idol. There were Elvis posters on the walls, Elvis record covers, a life-size cut-out figure of the performer, even an Elvis clock, with the King's arms pointing to the time. The TV was on, an item on the late news. Some oversized charity cheque was being handed over in front of Gibson's Brewery.

There was no one in the place except Eddie Ringan slumped on a barstool, and another man behind the bar, pouring two shots of Jim Beam. Rebus introduced himself and was invited to take a seat. The bartender introduced himself as Pat Calder.

'I'm Mr Ringan's partner.' The way he said it made Rebus wonder if the two young men were more than merely business partners. Holmes hadn't mentioned Eddie was gay. He turned his attention to the chef.

Eddie Ringan was probably in his late twenties, but looked ten years older. He had straight, thinning hair over a large oval-shaped head, all of which sat uneasily above the larger oval of his body. Rebus had seen fat chefs and fatter chefs, and Ringan surely was a living advertisement for *some*body's cooking. His doughy face was showing signs of wear from the drink; not just this evening's scoop, but the weeks and months of steady, heavy consumption. Rebus watched him drain the inch of amber fire in a single savouring swallow.

'Gimme another.'

But Pat Calder shook his head. 'Not if you're driving.' Then, in clear and precise tones: 'This man is a police officer, Eddie. He's come to talk about Brian.'

Eddie Ringan nodded. 'He fell down, hit his head.'

'Is that what you think?' asked Rebus.

'Not really.' For the first time, Ringan looked up from the bartop and into Rebus's eyes. 'Maybe it was a mugger, or maybe it was a warning.'

'What sort of a warning?'

'Eddie's had too many tonight, Inspector,' said Pat Calder. 'He starts imagining –'

'I'm not bloody imagining.' Ringan slapped his palm down on the bartop for emphasis. He was still looking at Rebus. 'You know what it's like. It's either protection money – insurance, they like to call it – or it's the other restaurants ganging up because they don't like the business you're doing and they're not. You make a lot of enemies in this game.'

Rebus was nodding. 'So do you have anyone in mind, Eddie? Anyone in particular?'

But Ringan shook his head in a slow swing. 'Not really. No, not really.'

'But you think maybe *you* were the intended victim?'

Ringan signalled for another drink, and Calder poured. He drank before answering. 'Maybe. I don't know. They could be trying to scare off the customers. Times are hard.'

Rebus turned to Calder, who was staring at Eddie Ringan with a fair amount of revulsion. 'What about you, Mr Calder, any ideas?'

'I think it was just a mugging.'

'Doesn't look like they took anything.'

'Maybe they were interrupted.'

'By someone coming up the alley? Then how did they escape? That car park's a dead end.'

'I don't know.' Rebus kept watching Pat Calder. He was a few years older than Ringan, but looked younger. He'd drawn his dark hair back into what Rebus supposed was a fashionable ponytail, and had kept long straight sideburns reaching down past his ears. He was tall and thin. Indeed, he looked like he could use a good meal. Rebus had seen more meat on a butcher's pencil. 'Maybe,' Calder was saying, 'maybe he did fall after all. It's pretty dark out there. We'll get some lighting put in.'

'Very commendable of you, sir.' Rebus rose from the uncomfortable barstool. 'Meantime, if anything *does* come to mind, and especially if any *names* come to mind, you can always call us.'

'Yes, of course.'

Rebus paused in the doorway. 'Oh, and Mr Calder?'

'Yes?'

'If you let Mr Ringan drive tonight, I'll have him pulled over before he reaches Haymarket. Can't you drive him home?'

'I don't drive.'

'Then I suggest you put your hand in the till for cab fare. Otherwise Mr Ringan's next creation might be Jailhouse Roquefort.'

As Rebus left the restaurant, he could actually hear Eddie Ringan starting to laugh.

He didn't laugh for long. Drink was demanding his attention. 'Gimme another,' he ordered. Pat Calder silently poured to the level of the shot-glass. They'd bought the glasses on a trip to Miami, along with a lot of other stuff. Much of the money had come out of Pat Calder's own pockets, as well as those of his parents. He held the glass in front of Ringan, then toasted him before draining the contents himself. When Ringan started to complain, Calder slapped him across the face.

Ringan looked neither surprised nor hurt. Calder slapped him again.

'You stupid bugger!' he hissed. 'You stupid, stupid bugger!'

'I can't help it,' said Ringan, proffering his empty glass. 'I'm all shook up. Now give me a drink before I do something *really* stupid.'

Pat Calder thought about it for a moment. Then he gave Eddie Ringan the drink.

The ambulance took Brian Holmes to the Royal Infirmary.

Rebus had never been persuaded by this hospital. It seemed full of good intentions and unfilled staff rosters. So he stood close by Brian Holmes' bed, as close as they'd let him stand. And as the night wore on, he didn't flinch; he just slid a little lower down the wall. He was crouching with his head resting against his knees, arms cold against the floor, when he sensed someone towering over him. It was Nell Stapleton. Rebus recognised her by her very height, long before his eyes had reached her tear-stained face.

'Hello there, Nell.'

'Christ, John.' And the tears started again. He pulled himself upright, embracing her quickly. She was throwing words into his ear. 'We talked only this evening. I was horrible. And now this happens ...'

'Hush, Nell. It's not your fault. This sort of thing can happen anytime.'

'Yes, but I can't help remembering, the last time we spoke it was an argument. If we hadn't argued ...'

'Sshh, pet. Calm down now.' He held her tight. Christ, it felt good. He didn't like to think about how good it felt. It felt good all the same. Her perfume, her shape, the way she moulded against him.

'We argued, and he went to that bar, and then ...'

'Sshh, Nell. It's not your fault.'

He believed it, too, though he wasn't sure whose fault it was: protection racketeers? Jealous restaurant owners? Simple neds? A difficult one to call.

'Can I see him?'

'By all means.' Rebus gestured with his arm towards Holmes' bed. He turned away as Nell Stapleton approached it, giving the couple some privacy. Not that the gesture meant anything; Holmes was still unconscious, hooked up to some monitor and with his head heavily bandaged. But he could almost make out the words Nell used when she spoke to her estranged lover. The tone she used made him think of Dr Patience Aitken, made him half-wish *he* were lying unconscious. It was nice to think people were saying nice things about you.

After five minutes, she came tiredly back. 'Hard work?' Rebus offered.

Nell Stapleton nodded. 'You know,' she said quietly, 'I think I've an idea why this happened.'

'Oh?'

She was speaking in a near-whisper, though the ward was quiet. They were the only two souls about on two legs. She sighed loudly. Rebus wondered if she'd ever taken drama classes.

'The black book,' she said. Rebus nodded as though understanding her, then frowned.

'What black book?' he asked.

'I probably shouldn't be telling you, but you're not just someone he works with, are you? You're a friend.' She let out another whistle of air. 'It was Brian's notebook. Nothing official, this was stuff he was looking into on his own.'

Rebus, wary of waking anyone, led her out of the ward. 'A diary?' he asked.

'Not really. It was just that sometimes he used to hear rumours, bits of pub gossip. He'd write them down in the black book. Then he might take things further. It was sort of a hobby with him, but maybe he thought it was also a way to an early promotion. I don't know. We used to argue about that, too. I was hardly seeing him, he was so busy.'

Rebus was staring at the wall of the corridor. The overhead lighting stung his eyes. He'd never heard Holmes mention any kind of notebook.

'What about it?'

Nell was shaking her head. 'It was just something he said, something before we ...' Her hand went to her mouth, as though she were about to cry. 'Before we split up.'

'What was it, Nell?'

'I'm not sure exactly.' Her eyes met Rebus's. 'I just know Brian was scared, and I'd never seen him scared before.'

'Scared of what?'

She shrugged. 'Something in the book.' Then she shook her head again. 'I'm not sure what. I can't help feeling ... feeling I'm somehow responsible. If we'd never ...'

Rebus pulled her to him again. 'There there, pet. It's not your fault.'

'But it *is*! It *is*!'

'No it isn't.' Rebus made his voice sound determined. 'Now, tell me, where did Brian keep this wee black book of his?'

About his person, was the answer. Brian Holmes' clothes and possessions had been removed when the ambulance delivered him to the Infirmary. But Rebus's ID was enough to gain access to the hospital's property department, even at this grim hour. He plucked the notebook out of an A4 envelope's worth of belongings, and had a look at the other contents. Wallet, diary, ID. Watch, keys, small change. Stuff without personality, now that it had been separated from its owner, but strengthening Rebus's conviction that this was no mere mugging.

Nell had gone home still crying, leaving no message to be passed along to Brian. All Rebus knew was that she suspected the beating was something to do with the notebook. And maybe she was right. He sat in the corridor outside Holmes' ward, sipping water and skipping through the cheap leatherette book. Holmes had employed a kind of shorthand, but the code was not nearly complex enough to puzzle another copper. Much of the information had come from a single night and a single action: the night an animal rights group had broken into Fettes HQ's records room. Amongst other things, they'd uncovered evidence of a rent-boy scandal among Edinburgh's most respectable citizens. *This* didn't come as news to John Rebus, but some other entries were intriguing, and especially the one referring to the Central Hotel.

The Central Hotel had been an Edinburgh institution until five years ago, when it had been razed to the ground. An insurance scam was rumoured, and £5,000 had been hoisted by the insurance company involved as a reward for proof that just such a scam had really taken place. But the reward had gone uncollected.

The hotel had once been a traveller's paradise. It was sited on Princes Street, no distance at all from Waverley Station, and so had become a travelling businessman's home-from-home. But in its latter years, the Central had seen business decline. And as genuine business declined, so disingenuous business took over. It was no real secret that the Central's stuffy rooms could be hired by the hour or the afternoon. Room service would provide a bottle of champagne and as much talcum powder as any room's tenants required.

In other words, the Central had become a knocking-shop, and by no means a subtle one. It also catered to the town's shadier elements in all shapes and forms. Wedding parties and stag nights were held for a spread of the city's villains, and underage drinkers could loll in the lounge bar for hours, safe in the knowledge that no honest copper would stray inside the doors. Familiarity bred further contempt, and the lounge bar started to be used for drug deals, and other even less savoury deals too, so that the Central Hotel became something more than a mere knocking-shop. It turned into a swamp.

A swamp with an eviction order over its head.

The police couldn't turn a blind eye forever and a day, especially when complaints from the public were rising by the month. And the more trash was introduced to the Central, the more trash was produced by the place. Until almost no real drinkers went there at all. If you ventured into the Central, you were looking for a woman, cheap drugs, or a fight. And God help you if you weren't.

Then, as had to happen, one night the Central burnt

down. This came as no surprise to anyone; so much so that reporters on the local paper hardly bothered to cover the blaze. The police, of course, were delighted. The fire saved them having to raid the joint.

But the next morning there was a solitary surprise: for though all the hotel's staff and customers had been accounted for, a body turned up amongst the charred ceilings and roofbeams. A body that had been burnt out of all recognition.

A body that had been dead when the fire started.

These scant details Rebus knew. He would not have been a City of Edinburgh detective if he *hadn't* known. Yet here was Holmes' black book, throwing up tantalising clues. Or what looked like tantalising clues. Rebus read the relevant section through again.

Central fire. El was there! Poker game on 1st floor. R. Brothers involved (so maybe Mork too??). Try finding.

He studied Holmes' handwriting, trying to decide whether the journal said El or E1; the letter l or the number 1. And if it was the letter l, did he mean El to stand as the phonetic equivalent of a single letter l? Why the exclamation mark? It seemed that the presence of El (or L or E-One) was some kind of revelation to Brian Holmes. And who the hell were the R. Brothers? Rebus thought at once of Michael and him, the Rebus brothers, but shook the picture from his mind. As for Mork, a bad TV show came to mind, nothing else.

No, he was too tired for this. Tomorrow would be time enough. Maybe by tomorrow Brian would be up and talking. Rebus decided he'd say a little prayer for him before he went to sleep.

3

A prayer which went unanswered. Brian Holmes had still not regained consciousness when Rebus phoned the Infirmary at seven o'clock.

'Is he in a coma or something, then?'

The voice on the other end of the phone was cold and factual. 'There will be tests this morning.'

'What sorts of tests?'

'Are you part of Mr Holmes' immediate family?'

'No, I'm bloody not. I'm ...' A police officer? His boss? Just a friend? 'Never mind.' He put down the receiver. One of the students put her head around the living-room door.

'Want some herbal tea?'

'No thanks.'

'A bowl of muesli?'

Rebus shook his head. She smiled at him and disappeared. Herbal tea and muesli, great God almighty. What sort of way was that to start the day? The door of the box room opened from within, and Rebus was startled when a teenage girl dressed only in a man's shirt came out into the daylight, rubbing at her eyes. She smiled at him as she passed, making for the living-room door. She walked on tiptoe, trying not to put too much bare foot on the cold linoleum.

Rebus stared at the living-room door for another ten seconds, then walked over to the box room. Michael was lying naked on the narrow single bed, the bed Rebus had bought secondhand at the weekend. He was rubbing a hand over his chest and staring at the ceiling. The air inside the box room was foetid.

'What the hell do you think you're doing?' Rebus asked.

'She's eighteen, John.'

'That's not what I meant.'

'Oh? What did you mean?'

But Rebus wasn't sure any more. There was just something plain ugly about his brother sharing a box room bed with some student while he slept on the sofa not eight feet away. It was all ugly, all of. it. Michael would have to go. Rebus would have to move into a hotel or something. None of it could go on like this much longer. It wasn't fair on the students.

'You should come to the pub more often,' Michael offered. 'That's what's wrong you know.'

'What?'

'You just don't see life, John. It's time you started to live a little.'

Michael was still smiling when his brother slammed the door on him.

'I've just heard about Brian.'

DC Siobhan Clarke looked in some distress. She had lost all colour from her face except for two dots of red high on her cheeks and the paler red of her lips. Rebus nodded for her to sit down. She pulled a chair over to his desk.

'What happened?'

'Somebody hit him over the head.'

'What with?'

Now *that* was a good question, the sort of question a detective would ask. It was also a question Rebus had forgotten to ask last night. 'We don't know,' he said. 'Nor do we have any motive, not yet.'

'It happened outside the Heartbreak Cafe?'

Rebus nodded. 'In the car park out back.'

'He kept saying he was going to take me there for a meal.'

'Brian always keeps his word. Don't worry, Siobhan, he'll be all right.'

She nodded, trying to believe this. 'I'll go see him later.'

'If you like,' said Rebus, not sure quite what his tone was supposed to mean. She looked at him again.

'I like,' she said.

After she'd gone, Rebus read through a message from Chief Inspector Lauderdale. It detailed the initial surveillance plans for the money lending operation. Rebus was asked for questions and 'useful comments'. He smiled at that phrase, knowing Lauderdale had used it hoping to deter Rebus from his usual basic critique of anything put in front of him. Then someone delivered a hefty package, the package he had been waiting for. He lifted the flaps of the cardboard box and started to pull out bulging files. These were the notes referring to the Central Hotel, its history and final sorry end. He knew he had a morning's reading ahead of him, so he found Lauderdale's letter, penned a large OK on it, scrawled his signature beneath, and tossed it into his out tray. Lauderdale wouldn't believe it, wouldn't believe Rebus had accepted the surveillance without so much as a murmur. It was bound to perplex the Chief Inspector.

Not a bad start to the working day.

Rebus sat down with the first file from the box and started to read.

He was filling a second page with his own notes when the telephone rang. It was Nell Stapleton.

'Nell, where are you?' Rebus continued writing, finishing a sentence.

'I'm at work. Just thought I'd call and see if you'd found anything.'

He finished the sentence. 'Such as?'

'Well, what happened to Brian.'

'I'm not sure yet. Maybe he'll tell us when he wakes up. Have you talked to the hospital?'

'First thing.'

'Me too.' Rebus started writing again. There was a nervous silence on the other end of the line.

'What about the black book?'

'Oh, that. Yes, I had a wee read of it.'

'Did you find whatever Brian was afraid of?'

'Maybe and maybe not. Don't worry, Nell, I'm working on it.'

'That's good.' There was genuine relief in her voice. 'Only, when Brian wakes up, don't tell him I told you, will you?'

'Why not? I think it's ... it shows you care about him.'

'Of course I care!'

'That didn't stop you chucking him out.' He wished he hadn't said it, but he had. He could hear her anguish, and imagined her in the University library, trying not to let any of the other staff see her face.

'John,' she said at last, 'you don't know the whole story. You've only heard Brian's side.'

'That's true. Want to tell me yours?'

She thought it over. 'Not like this, on the telephone. Maybe some other time.'

'Any time you like, Nell.'

'I'd better get back to work. Are you going to see Brian today?'

'Maybe tonight. They're running tests all morning. What about you?'

'Oh yes, I'll drop by. It's only two minutes away.'

So it was. Rebus thought of Siobhan Clarke. For some reason, he didn't want the two women to meet at Brian's bedside. 'What time are you thinking of going?'

'Lunchtime, I suppose.'

'One last thing, Nell.'

'Yes?'

'Does Brian have any enemies?'

It took her a little while to answer. 'No.'

Rebus waited to see if she had anything to add. 'Well, take care, Nell.'

'You too, John. Bye.'

After he'd put down the receiver, Rebus started back to his note-taking. But after half a sentence he stopped, tapping his pen thoughtfully against his mouth. He stayed that way for a considerable time, then made some phone calls to his contacts (he didn't like the word 'grasses'), telling them to keep ears open regarding an assault behind the Heartbreak Cafe.

'A colleague of mine, which means it's serious, okay?'

He'd ended up saying 'colleague' but had meant to say 'friend'.

At lunchtime, he walked over to the University and paid his respects at the Department of Pathology. He had called ahead and Dr Curt was ready in his office, wearing a cream-coloured raincoat and humming some piece of classical music which Rebus annoyingly could recognise but not name.

'Ah, Inspector, what a pleasant surprise.'

Rebus blinked. 'Really?'

'Of course. Usually when you're pestering me, it's because of some current and pressing case. But today ...' Curt opened his arms wide. 'No case! And yet you phone me up and invite me to lunch. It can't be very busy along at St Leonard's.'

On the contrary, but Rebus knew the workload was in good hands. Before leaving, he'd loaded enough work onto Siobhan Clarke that she wouldn't have time for a

45

lunch-break, beyond a sandwich and a drink from the cafeteria. When she'd complained, he'd told her she could take time off later in the afternoon to visit Brian Holmes.

'How have you settled in there, by the way?'

Rebus shrugged. 'It doesn't matter to me where they put me. Where do you want to eat?'

'I've taken the liberty of reserving a table at the University Staff Club.'

'What, some sort of canteen?'

Curt laughed, shaking his head. He had ushered Rebus out of his office and was locking the door. 'No,' said Curt. 'There *is* a canteen, of course, but as you're buying I thought we'd opt for something a little bit more refined.'

'Then lead on to the refinery.'

The dining-room was on the ground floor, near the main door of the Staff Club on Chambers Street. They'd walked the short walk, talking about nothing in particular when they could hear one another above the traffic noise. Curt always walked as though he were late for some engagement. Well, he was a busy man: a full teaching load, plus the extra duties heaped on him at one time or another by most of the police forces in Scotland, and most onerously by the City of Edinburgh Police.

The dining-room was small but with plenty of space between the tables. Rebus was pleased to see that the prices were reasonable, though the tally was upped when Curt ordered a bottle of wine.

'My treat,' he said. But Rebus shook his head.

'The Chief Constable's treat,' he corrected. After all, he had every intention of claiming it as a legitimate expense. The wine arrived before the soup. As the waitress poured, Rebus wondered when would be the right moment to open the *real* conversation.

'Slainte!' said Curt, raising his glass. Then: 'So what's this all about? You're not the kind for lunch with a friend,

46

not unless there's something you want, and can't get by buying pints and bridies in some smoky saloon.'

Rebus smiled at this. 'Do you remember the Central Hotel?'

'A dive of a place on Princes Street. It burnt down six or seven years ago.'

'Five years ago actually.'

Curt took another sip of wine. 'There was a smouldering body as I recall. "Crispy batter" we call those.'

'But when you examined the corpse, he hadn't died in the fire, had he?'

'Some new evidence has come to light?'

'Not exactly. I just wanted to ask what you remember about the case.'

'Well, let's see.' Curt broke off as the soup arrived. He took three or four mouthfuls, then wiped a napkin around his lips. 'The body was never identified. I know that we tried dental checks, but to no avail. There was no external evidence, of course, but people stupidly believe that a burned body tells no tales. I cut the deceased open and found, as I'd known I would, that the internal organs were in pretty good shape. Cooked on the outside, raw within, like a good French steak.'

A couple at a nearby table were soundlessly chewing their food, and staring hard at their tabletop. Curt seemed either not to notice or not to mind.

'DNA fingerprinting had been around for four years, but though we got some blood from the heart, we were never given anything to match it against. Of course, the heart was the clincher.'

'Because of the bullet wound.'

'Two wounds, Inspector, entrance and exit. That set you lot scurrying back to the scene, didn't it?'

Rebus nodded. They'd searched the immediate vicinity of the body, then widened the search until a cadet found the bullet. Its calibre was eight millimetre, matching the

47

wound to the heart, but it offered no other clues.

'You also found,' said Rebus, 'that the deceased had suffered a broken arm at some time in the past.'

'Did I?'

'But again it didn't get us any further forward.'

'Especially,' said Curt, mopping his bowl with bread, 'bearing in mind the reputation of the Central. Probably every second person in the place had been in a fight and suffered *some* breakages.'

Rebus was nodding. 'Agreed, yet he was never identified. If he'd been a regular, or one of the staff, surely someone would have come forward. But nobody ever did.'

'Well, it was a long time ago. Are you about to start dusting off some ghosts?'

'There was nothing ghostly about whoever brained Brian Holmes.'

'Sergeant Holmes? What happened?'

Rebus was hoping to spend some of the afternoon reading through more of the case-notes. He'd thought it would take half a day; but this had been optimistic from the start. He was now thinking in terms of half a week, including some evening reading in the flat. There was so much stuff. Lengthy reports from the fire department, the council's building department, news clippings, police reports, interview statements . . .

But when he got back to St Leonard's, Lauderdale was waiting. He had received Rebus's hasty comment on the money-lending surveillance, and now wanted to push things on. Which meant that Rebus was trapped in the Chief Inspector's office for the best part of two hours, an hour of it head-to-head stuff. For the other hour, they were joined by Detective Inspector Alister Flower, who had worked out of St Leonard's since its opening day back in September 1989 and bragged continually that when he had shaken hands with the main dignitary at the occasion, they had both turned out to be Masons, with Flower's being the older clan.

Flower resented the incomers from Great London Road. If there were friction and factions within the station, you could be sure Flower was at the back of them somewhere. If anything united Lauderdale and Rebus it was a dislike of Flower, though Lauderdale was slowly being drawn into the Flower camp.

Rebus, however, had contempt even for the funny way the man spelt his first name. He called him 'Little Weed' and thought probably Flower had something to do with the taxman's sudden inquiries.

In the operation against the money lenders, Flower was to lead the other surveillance team. Typically, in an effort to appease the man, Lauderdale offered him the pick of the surveillances. One would be of a pub where the lenders were said to hang out and take payments. The other would be of what looked like the nominal HQ of the gang, an office attached to a mini-cab firm on Gorgie Road.

'I've okayed the Gorgie surveillance with Divisional HQ West,' said Lauderdale, as ever efficient behind a desk. Take him out onto the streets, Rebus knew, and he was about as efficient as pepper on a vindaloo.

'Well,' said Flower, 'if it's okay with Inspector Rebus, I think I'd prefer the watch on the pub. It's a bit closer to home.' And Flower smiled.

'Interesting choice,' said Rebus, his arms folded, legs stretched out in front of him.

Lauderdale was nodding, his eyes flitting between the two men. 'Well, that's settled then. Now, let's get down to details.'

The same details, in fact, that Rebus and he had gone through in the hour prior to Flower's arrival. Rebus tried to concentrate but couldn't. He was desperate to get back to the Central Hotel records. But the more agitated he grew, the slower things moved.

The plan itself was simple. The money lenders worked out of the Firth Pub in Tollcross. They picked up business there, and generally hung around waiting for debtors to come and pay the weekly dues. The money was taken at some point to the office in Gorgie. This office also was used as a drop-off point by debtors, and here the leading visible player could be found.

The men working out of the Firth were bit-parts. They collected cash, and maybe even used some verbal persuasion when payment was late. But when it came to the crunch, everyone paid dues to Davey Dougary. Davey turned up every morning at the office as prompt as any businessman, parking his BMW 635CSi beside the battered mini-cabs. On the way from car to office, if the weather was warm he would slip his jacket off and roll up his shirt-sleeves. Yes, Trading Standards had been watching Davey for quite some time.

There would be Trading Standards officers involved in both surveillances. The police were really only there to enforce the law; it was a Trading Standards operation in name. The name they had chosen was Moneybags. Another interesting choice, thought Rebus, so original. Keeping surveillance in the pub would mean sitting around reading newspapers, circling the names of horses on the betting sheet, playing pool or the jukebox or dominoes. Oh yes, and drinking beer; after all, they didn't want to stand out in the crowd.

Keeping surveillance on the office meant sitting in the window of a disused first floor room in the tenement block across the road. The place was without charm, toilet facilities, or heating. (The bathroom fittings had been stolen during a break-in earlier in the year, down to the very toilet-pan.) A happy prospect, especially for Holmes and Clarke who would bear the burden of the surveillance, always supposing Holmes recovered in time. He thought of his two junior officers spending long days huddling for warmth in a double sleeping-bag. Hell's bells. Thank God Dougary didn't work nights. And thank God there'd be some Trading Standards bodies around too.

Still, the thought of nabbing Davey Dougary warmed Rebus's heart. Dougary was bad the way a rotten apple was. There was no repairing the damage, though the surface might seem untainted. Of course, Dougary was one of Big Ger Cafferty's 'lieutenants'. Cafferty had even turned up once at the office, captured on film. Much good would it do; he'd have a thousand good reasons for that visit. There'd be no pinning him in court. They might get Dougary, but Cafferty was a long way off, so far ahead of them they looked like they were pushing their heap of a car while he cruised in fifth gear.

'So,' Lauderdale was saying. 'We can start with this as of next Monday, yes?'

Rebus awoke from his reverie. It was clear that much had been discussed in his spiritual absence. He wondered if he'd agreed to any of it. (His silence had no doubt been received as tacit consent.)

'I've no problem with that,' said Flower.

Rebus moved again in his seat, knowing that escape was close now. 'I'll probably need someone to fill in for DS Holmes.'

'Ah yes, how is he doing?'

'I haven't heard today, sir,' Rebus admitted. 'I'll call before I clock off.'

'Well, let me know.'

'We're putting together a collection,' Flower said.

'For Christ's sake, he's no' deid yet!'

Flower took the explosion without flinching. 'Well, all the same.'

'It's a nice gesture,' Lauderdale said. Flower shrugged his shoulders modestly. Lauderdale opened his wallet and dug out a reluctant fiver, which he handed to Flower.

Hey, big spender, thought Rebus. Even Flower looked startled.

'Five quid,' he said, unnecessarily.

Lauderdale didn't want any thanks. He just wanted Flower to take the money. His wallet had disappeared back into its cave. Flower stuck the note in his shirt pocket and rose from his chair. Rebus stood too, not looking forward to being in the corridor alone with Flower. But Lauderdale stopped him.

'A word, John.'

Flower sniffed as he left, probably thinking Rebus was to receive a dressing down for his outburst. In fact, this wasn't what Lauderdale had in mind.

'I was passing your desk earlier. I see you've got the files on the Central Hotel fire. Old news, surely?' Rebus said nothing. 'Anything I should know about?'

'No, sir,' said Rebus, rising and making for the door. He reckoned Flower would be on his way by now. 'Nothing you should know about. Just some reading of mine. You could call it a history project.'

'Archaeology, more like.'

True enough: old bones and hieroglyphs; trying to make the dead come to life.

'The past is important, sir,' said Rebus, taking his leave.

4

The past was certainly important to Edinburgh. The city
fed on its past like a serpent with its tail in its mouth.
And Rebus's past seemed to be circling around again too.
There was a message on his desk in Clarke's handwriting.
Obviously she'd gone to visit Holmes, but not before taking
a telephone call intended for her superior.

> DI Morton called from Falkirk. He'll try again another
> time. He wouldn't say what it's about. Very cagey. I'll be
> back in two hours.

She was the sort who would make up the two hours
by staying late a few nights, even though Rebus had
deprived her of a reasonable lunch-break. Despite being
English, there was something of the Scottish Protestant
in Siobhan Clarke. It wasn't her fault she was called
Siobhan either. Her parents had been English Literature
lecturers at Edinburgh University back in the 1960s.
They'd lumbered her with the Gaelic name, then moved
south again, taking her to be schooled in Nottingham and
London. But she'd come back to Edinburgh to go to
college, and fallen in love (her story) with Edinburgh.
Then she'd decided on the police as a career (alienating
her friends and, Rebus suspected, her liberal parents). Still,
the parents had bought her a New Town flat, so it couldn't
be all strife.

Rebus suspected she'd do well in the police, despite

people like him. Women did have to work harder in the force to progress at the same pace as their male colleagues: everyone knew it. But Siobhan worked hard enough, and by Christ did she have a memory. A month from now, he could ask her about this note on his desk, and she'd remember the telephone conversation word for word. It was scary.

It was slightly scary too that Jack Morton's name had come up at this particular time. Another ghost from Rebus's past. When they'd worked together six years ago, Rebus wouldn't have given the younger Morton more than four or five years to live, such was his steady consumption of booze and cigarettes.

There was no contact phone number. It would have taken only a few minutes to find the number of Morton's nick, but Rebus didn't feel like it. He felt like getting back to the files on his desk. But first he phoned the Infirmary to check on Brian Holmes' progress, only to be told that there wasn't any, though there was also no decline.

'That sounds cheery.'

'It's just an expression,' the person on the phone said.

The test results wouldn't be known until next morning. He thought for a moment, then made another call, this time to Patience Aitken's group practice. But Patience was out on a call, so Rebus left a message. He got the receptionist to read it back so he could be sure it sounded right.

' "Thought I'd call to let you know how Brian's doing. Sorry you weren't in. You can call me at Arden Street if you like. John." '

Yes, that would do. She'd have to call *him* now, just to show she wasn't uncaring about Brian's condition. With a speck of hope in his heart, Rebus went back to work.

He got back to the flat at six, having done some shopping en route. Though he'd proposed taking the files home, he really couldn't be bothered. He was tired, his head ached, and his nose was stuffy from the old dust which rose from their pages. He climbed the flights of stairs wearily, opened the door, and took the grocery bags into the kitchen, where one of the students was spreading peanut butter onto a thick slice of brown bread.

'Hiya, Mr Rebus. You got a phone call.'

'Oh?'

'Some woman doctor.'

'When?'

'Ten minutes ago, something like that.'

'What did she say?'

'She said if she wanted to find out about . . .'

'Brian? Brian Holmes?'

'Aye, that's it. If she wanted to find out about him, she could call the hospital, and that's exactly what she'd done twice today already.' The student beamed, pleased at having remembered the whole message. So Patience had seen through his scheme. He should have known. Her intelligence, amongst other things, had attracted him to her. Also, they were very much alike in many ways. Rebus should have learned long ago, never try to put one over on someone who knows the way your mind works. He lifted a box of eggs, tin of beans, and packet of bacon out of the bag.

'Oh my God,' said the student in disgust. 'Do you know just how intelligent pigs *are*, Mr Rebus?'

Rebus looked at the student's sandwich. 'A damned sight more intelligent than peanuts,' he said. Then: 'Where's the frying-pan?'

Later, Rebus sat watching TV. He'd nipped over to the Infirmary to visit Brian Holmes. He reckoned it was quicker to walk rather than driving around The Meadows. So he'd walked, letting his head clear. But the visit itself had been depressing. Not a bit of progress.

55

'How long can he stay conked out?'

'It can take a while,' a nurse had consoled.

'It's *been* a while.'

She touched his arm. 'Patience, patience.'

Patience! He almost took a taxi to her flat, but dropped the idea. Instead, he walked back to Arden Street, climbed the same old weary stairs, and flopped onto the sofa. He had spent so many evenings deep in thought in this room, but that had been back when the flat was his, only his.

Michael came into the living room, fresh from a shave and a shower. He wore a towel tight around his flat stomach. He was in good shape; Rebus hadn't noticed before. But Michael saw him noticing now, and patted his stomach.

'One thing about Peterhead, plenty of exercise.'

'I suppose you've got to get fit in there,' Rebus drawled, 'so you can fight back when someone's after your arse.'

Michael shook off the remark like it was so much water. 'Oh, there's plenty of that too. Never interested me.' Whistling, he went into the box room and started to dress.

'Going out?' Rebus called.

'Why stay in?'

'Seeing that wee girl again?'

Michael put his head around the door. 'She's a consenting adult.'

Rebus got to his feet. 'She's a wee girl.' He walked over to the box room and stared at Michael, forcing him to stop what he was doing.

'What, John? You want me to stop going out with women? If you don't like it, tough.'

Rebus thought of all the remarks he could make. This is my flat ... I'm your big brother ... you should know better ... He knew Mickey would laugh – quite rightly – at any and all of them. So he thought of something else to say.

'Fuck you, Mickey.'

Michael Rebus recommenced dressing. 'I'm sorry I'm such a disappointment, but what's the alternative? Sit here all night watching you stew or sulk or whatever it is you do inside your head? Thanks but no thanks.'

'I thought you were going to look for a job.'

Michael Rebus grabbed a book from the bed and threw it at his brother. 'I'm looking for a fucking job! What do you think I do all day? Just give it a rest, will you?' He picked up his jacket and pushed past Rebus. 'Don't wait up for me, eh?'

That was a laugh: Rebus was asleep, and alone in the flat, before the ten o'clock news. But it wasn't a sound sleep. It was a sleep filled with dreams. He was chasing Patience through some office block, always just losing her. He was eating in a restaurant with a teenage girl while the Rolling Stones entertained unnoticed on the small stage in the corner. He was watching a hotel burn to the ground, wondering if Brian Holmes, still unaccounted for, had gotten out alive ...

And then he was awake and shivering, the room illuminated only by the street-lamp outside, burning through a chink in the curtains. He'd been reading the book Michael had thrown at him. It was about hypnotherapy and still lay in his lap, beneath the blanket someone had thrown over him. There were noises nearby, noises of pleasure. They were coming from the box room. Some therapy, no doubt. Rebus listened to them for what seemed like hours until the light outside grew pale.

5

Andrew McPhail sat beside his bedroom window. Across
the road, the children were being lined up two by two
outside the school doors. The boys had to hold hands with
the girls, the whole thing supervised by two female staff
members, looking hardly old enough to be parents, never
mind teachers. McPhail sipped cold tea from his mug and
watched. He paid very close attention to the children.
Any one of the girls might have been Melanie. Except, of
course, that Melanie would be older. Not much older, but
older. He wasn't kidding himself. He knew the odds were
Melanie wouldn't be at this school, probably wasn't even
in Edinburgh any more. But he watched all the same, and
imagined her down there, her hand touching the cool
wet hand of one of the boys. Small delicate fingers, the
beginning of fine lines on the palm. One girl was really
quite similar: short straight hair curling in towards her
ears and the nape of her neck. The height was familiar,
too, but the face, what he could see of the face, was
nothing like Melanie. Really, nothing like her. And besides,
what did it matter to McPhail?

They were marching into the building now, leaving
him behind with his cold tea and his memories. He
could hear Mrs MacKenzie downstairs, washing dishes
and probably chipping and breaking as much crockery as
she got clean. Not her fault, her eyesight was failing.
Everything about the old woman was failing. The house
was bound to be worth £40,000, as good as money in

the bank. And what did he have? Only memories of the way things had been in Canada and before Canada.

A plate crashed onto the kitchen floor. It couldn't go on like this, really it couldn't. There'd be nothing left. He didn't like to think about the budgie in the living-room ...

McPhail drained the strong tea. The caffeine made him slightly giddy, sweat breaking out on his forehead. The playground was empty, the school doors closed. He couldn't see anything through the building's few visible windows. There might be a late-arriving straggler, but he didn't have time to waste. He had work to do. It was good to keep busy. Keeping busy kept you sane.

'Big Ger,' Rebus was saying, 'real name Morris Gerald Cafferty.'

Dutifully, and despite her good memory, DC Siobhan Clarke wrote these words on her notepad. Rebus didn't mind her taking notes. It was good exercise. When she lowered her head to write, Rebus had a view of the crown of her head, light-brown hair falling forward. She was good looking in a homely sort of way. Indeed, she reminded him a bit of Nell Stapleton.

'He's the prime mover, and if we're offered him we'll take him. But Operation Moneybags will actually be focusing on David Charles Dougary, known as Davey.' Again, the words went onto the paper. 'Dougary rents office space from a dodgy mini-cab service in Gorgie Road.'

'Not far from the Heartbreak Cafe?'

The question surprised him. 'No,' he said, 'not too far.'

'And the restaurant owner hinted at a protection pay-off?'

Rebus shook his head. 'Don't get carried away, Clarke.'

'And these men are involved in protection money too, aren't they?'

'There's not much Big Ger Cafferty *isn't* involved in: money laundering, prostitution. He's a big bad bastard, but that isn't the point. The point is, this operation will concentrate on loan-sharking, period.'

'All I'm saying is maybe Sergeant Holmes was attacked by mistake instead of the Cafe's owner.'

'It's a possibility,' said Rebus. And if it's true, he thought, I'm wasting a lot of time and effort on an old case. But as Nell said, Brian was frightened of something in his black book. And all because he'd started trying to track down the mysterious R. Brothers.

'But to get back to business, we'll be setting up a surveillance across the road from the taxi firm.'

'Round the clock?'

'We'll start with working hours. Dougary has a fairly fixed routine by all accounts.'

'What's he supposed to be doing in that office?'

'The way he tells it, everything from basic entrepreneurship to arranging food parcels for the Third World. Don't get me wrong, Dougary's clever. He's lasted longer than most of Big Ger's "associates". He's also a maniac, it's worth bearing that in mind. We once arrested him after a pub brawl. He'd torn the ear off another man with his teeth. When we got there, Dougary was chomping away. The ear was never recovered.'

Rebus always expected some reaction from his favourite stories, but all Siobhan Clarke did was smile and say, 'I love this city.' Then: 'Are there files on Mr Cafferty?'

'Oh aye, there are files. By all means, plough through them. They'll give you some idea what you're up against.'

She nodded. 'I'll do that. And when do we start the surveillance, sir?'

'First thing Monday morning. Everything will be set up on Sunday. I just hope they give us a decent camera.' He noticed Clarke was looking relieved. Then the penny dropped. 'Don't worry, you won't miss the Hibs game.'

She smiled. 'They're away to Aberdeen.'

'And you're still going?'

'Absolutely.' She tried never to miss a game.

Rebus was shaking his head. He didn't know that many Hibs fans. 'I wouldn't travel that far for the Second Coming.'

'Yes you would.'

Now Rebus smiled. 'Who's been talking? Right, what's on the agenda for today?'

'I've talked to the butcher. He was no help at all. I think I'd have more chance of getting a complete sentence out of the carcases in his deep freeze. But he does drive a Merc. That's an expensive car. Butchers aren't well known for high salaries, are they?'

Rebus shrugged. 'The prices they charge, I wouldn't be so sure.'

'Anyway, I'm planning to drop in on him at home this morning, just to clear up a couple of points.'

'But he'll be at work.'

'Unfortunately yes.'

Rebus caught on. 'His wife will be home?'

'That's what I'm hoping. The offer of a cup of tea, a little chat in the living room. Wasn't it terrible about Rory? That sort of thing.'

'So you can size up his home life, and maybe get a talkative wife thrown in for good measure.' Rebus was nodding slowly. It was so devious he should have thought of it himself.

'Get tae it, lass,' he said, and she did, leaving him to reach down onto the floor and lift one of the Central Hotel files onto his desk.

He started reading, but soon froze at a certain page. It listed the Hotel's customers on the night it burnt down. One name fairly flew off the page.

'Would you credit that?' Rebus got up from the desk and put his jacket on. Another ghost. And another excuse to get out of the office.

The ghost was Matthew Vanderhyde.

6

The house next to Vanderhyde's was as mad as ever. Owned by an ancient Nationalist, it sported the saltire flag on its gate and what looked like thirty-year-old tracts taped to its windows. The owner couldn't get much light, but then the house Rebus was approaching had its curtains drawn closed.

He rang the doorbell and waited. It struck him that Vanderhyde might well be dead. He would be in his early-to mid-seventies, and though he'd seemed healthy enough the last time they'd met, well, that was over two years ago.

He had consulted Vanderhyde in an earlier case. After the case was closed, Rebus used to drop in on Vanderhyde from time to time, just casually. They only lived six streets apart, after all. But then he'd started to get serious with Dr Patience Aitken, and hadn't found time for a visit since.

The door opened, and there stood Matthew Vanderhyde, looking just the same as ever. His sightless eyes were hidden behind dark green spectacles, above which sat a high shiny forehead and long swept-back yellow hair. He was wearing a suit of beige cord with a brown waistcoat, from the pocket of which hung a watch-chain. He leaned lightly on his silver-topped cane, waiting for the caller to speak.

'Hello there, Mr Vanderhyde.'

'Ah, Inspector Rebus. I was wondering when I'd see you. Come in, come in.'

From Vanderhyde's tone, it sounded like they'd last met two weeks before. He led Rebus through the dark hallway and into the darker living room. Rebus took in the shapes of bookshelves, paintings, the large mantelpiece covered in mementoes from trips abroad.

'As you can see, Inspector, nothing has changed in your absence.'

'I'm glad to see you looking so well, sir.'

Vanderhyde shrugged aside the remark. 'Some tea?'

'No thanks.'

'I'm really quite thrilled that you've come. It must mean there's something I can do for you.'

Rebus smiled. 'I'm sorry I stopped visiting.'

'It's a free country, I didn't pine away.'

'I can see that.'

'So what sort of thing is it? Witchcraft? Devilment in the city streets?'

Rebus was still smiling. In his day, Matthew Vanderhyde had been an active white witch. At least, Rebus hoped he'd been white. It had never been discussed between them.

'I don't *think* this is anything to do with magic,' Rebus said. 'It's about the Central Hotel.'

'The Central? Ah, happy memories, Inspector. I used to go there as a young man. Tea dances, a very acceptable luncheon – they had an excellent kitchen in those days, you know – even once or twice to an evening ball.'

'I'm thinking of more recent times. You were at the hotel the night it was torched.'

'I don't recall arson was proven.'

As usual, Vanderhyde's memory was sharp enough when it suited him. 'That's true. All the same, you were there.'

'Yes, I was. But I left several hours before the fire started. Not guilty, your honour.'

'Why were you there in the first place?'

'To meet a friend for a drink.'

'A seedy place for a drink.'

'Was it? You'll have to remember, Inspector, I couldn't *see* anything. It certainly didn't *smell* or *feel* particularly disreputable.'

'Point taken.'

'I had my memories. To me, it was the same old Central Hotel I'd lunched in and danced in. I quite enjoyed the evening.'

'Was the Central your choice, then?'

'No, my friend's.'

'Your friend being ...?'

Vanderhyde considered. 'No secret, I suppose. Aengus Gibson.'

Rebus sifted through the name's connotations. 'You don't mean Black Aengus?'

Vanderhyde laughed, showing small blackened teeth. 'You'd better not let him hear you calling him that these days.'

Yes, Aengus Gibson was a reformed character, that much was public knowledge. He was also, so Rebus presumed, still one of Scotland's most eligible young men, if thirty-two could be considered young in these times. Black Aengus, after all, was sole heir to the Gibson Brewery and all that came with it.

'Aengus Gibson,' said Rebus.

'The same.'

'And this was five years ago, when he was still ...'

'High spirited?' Vanderhyde gave a low chuckle. 'Oh, he deserved the name Black Aengus then, all right. The newspapers got it just right when they came up with *that* nickname.'

Rebus was thinking. 'I didn't see his name in the records. Your name was there, but his wasn't.'

'I'm sure his family saw to it that his name never appeared in any records, Inspector. It would have given the media even more fuel than they needed at the time.'

Yes, Christ, Black Aengus had been a wild one all right, so wild even the London papers took an interest. He'd looked to be spiralling out of control on ever-new excesses, but then suddenly all that stopped. He'd been rehabilitated, and was now as respectable as could be, involved in the brewing business and several prominent charities besides.

'The leopard changed its spots, Inspector. I know you policemen are dubious about such things. Every offender is a potential repeat offender. I suppose you have to be cynical in your job, but with young Aengus the leopard really *did* change.'

'Do you know why?'

Vanderhyde shrugged. 'Maybe because of our chat.'

'That night in the Central Hotel?'

'His father had asked me to talk to him.'

'You know them, then?'

'Oh, from long ago. Aengus regarded me more as an uncle than anything else. Indeed, when I heard that the Central had been razed to the ground, I saw it as symbolic. Perhaps he did too. Of course I knew the reputation it had garnered – an altogether unsavoury reputation. When it happened to burn down that night, well, I thought of the phoenix Aengus rising cleansed from its ashes. And it turned out to be true.' He paused. 'Yet now here you are, Inspector, asking questions about long forgotten events.'

'There was a body.'

'Ah yes, never identified.'

'A murdered body.'

'And somehow you've reopened that particular investigation? Interesting.'

'I wanted to ask you what you remembered from that night. Anyone you met, anything that seemed at all suspicious.'

Vanderhyde tilted his head to one side. 'There were many people in the hotel that night, Inspector. You have a list of them. Yet you choose to come to a blind man?'

'That's right,' said Rebus. 'A blind man with a photographic memory.'

Vanderhyde laughed. 'Certainly, I can give ... impressions.' He thought for a moment. 'Very well, Inspector. For you, I'll do my best. I only ask one thing.'

'What's that?'

'I've been stuck here too long. Take me out, will you?'

'Anywhere in particular?'

Vanderhyde looked surprised that he needed to ask. 'Why, Inspector, to the Central Hotel, of course!'

'Well,' said Rebus, 'this is where it used to stand. You're facing it now.' He could feel the stares of passers-by. Princes Street was lunchtime busy, office workers trying to make the most of their limited time. A few looked genuinely annoyed at having to manoeuvre past two people *daring* to stand still on the pavement! But most could see that one man was blind, the other his helper in some way, so they found charity in their souls and didn't complain.

'And what has it become, Inspector?'

'A burger joint.'

Vanderhyde nodded. 'I thought I could smell meat. Franchised, doubtless, from some American corporation. Princes Street has seen better days, Inspector. Did you know that when Scottish Sword and Shield was started up, they used to meet in the Central's ballroom? Dozens and dozens of people, all vowing to restore Dalriada to its former glory.'

Rebus remained silent.

'You don't recall Sword and Shield?'

'It must have been before my time.'

'Now that I think of it, it probably was. This was in the 1950s, an offshoot of the National Party. I attended a couple of the meetings myself. There would be some furious call to arms, followed by tea and scones. It didn't last long. Broderick Gibson was the president one year.'

'Aengus's father?'

'Yes.' Vanderhyde was remembering. 'There used to be a pub near here, famous for politics and poetry. A few of us went there after the meetings.'

'I thought you said you only went to two?'

'Perhaps a few more than two.'

Rebus grinned. If he looked into it, he knew he would probably find that a certain M. Vanderhyde had been president of Sword and Shield at some time.

'It was a fine pub,' Vanderhyde reminisced.

'In its day,' said Rebus.

Vanderhyde sighed. 'Edinburgh, Inspector. Turn your back and they change the name of a pub or the purpose of a shop.' He pointed behind him with his stick, nearly tripping someone up in the process. 'They can't change that though. *That's* Edinburgh too.' The stick was wavering in the direction of the Castle Rock. It rapped someone against their leg. Rebus tried to smile an apology, the victim being a woman.

'Maybe we should go sit across the road,' he suggested. Vanderhyde nodded, so they crossed at the traffic lights to the quieter side of the street. There were benches here, their backs to the gardens, each dedicated to someone's memory. Vanderhyde got Rebus to read the plaque on their bench.

'No,' he said, shaking his head. 'I don't recognise either of those names.'

'Mr Vanderhyde,' said Rebus, 'I'm beginning to suspect you got me to bring you here for no other reason than the outing itself.' Vanderhyde smiled but said nothing. 'What time did you go to the bar that night?'

'Seven sharp, that was the arrangement. Of course, Aengus being Aengus, he was late. I think he turned up at half past, by which time I was seated in a corner with a whisky and water. I think it was J and B whisky.' He seemed pleased by this small feat of memory.

'Anyone you knew in the bar?'

'I can hear bagpipes,' Vanderhyde said.

Rebus could too, though he couldn't see the piper. 'They play for the tourists,' he explained. 'It can be a big earner in the summer.'

'He's not very good. I should imagine he's wearing a kilt but that the tartan isn't correct.'

'Anyone in the bar you knew?' Rebus persisted.

'Oh, let me think . . .'

'With respect, sir, you don't *need* to think. You either know or you don't.'

'Well, I think Tom Hendry was in that night and stopped by the table to say hello. He used to work for the newspapers.'

Yes, Rebus had seen the name on the list.

'And there was someone else . . . I didn't know them, and they didn't speak. But I recall a scent of lemon. It was very vivid. I thought maybe it was a perfume, but when I mentioned it to Aengus he laughed and said it didn't belong to a woman. He wouldn't say any more, but I got the feeling it was a huge joke to him that I'd made the initial comment. I'm not sure any of this is relevant.'

'Me neither.' Rebus's stomach was growling. There was a sudden explosion behind them. Vanderhyde slipped his watch from his waistcoat pocket, opened the glass, and felt with his fingers over the dial.

'One o'clock sharp,' he said. 'As I said, Inspector, some things about our precipitous city remain immutable.'

Rebus nodded. 'Such as the precipitation, for instance?' It was beginning to drizzle, the morning sun having disappeared like a conjurer's trick. 'Anything else you can tell me?'

'Aengus and I talked. I tried to persuade him that he was on a very dangerous path. His health was failing, and so was the family's wealth. If anything, the latter argument was the more persuasive.'

'So there and then he renounced the bawdy life?'

'I wouldn't go that far. The Edinburgh establishment has never bided too far from the stews. When we parted he was setting off to meet some woman.' Vanderhyde was thoughtful. 'But if I do say so myself, my words had an effect on him.' He nodded. 'I ate alone that evening in The Eyrie.'

'I've been there myself,' said Rebus. His stomach growled again. 'Fancy a burger?'

After he'd dropped Vanderhyde home he drove back to St Leonard's – not a lot wiser for the whole exercise. Siobhan sprang from her desk when she saw him. She looked pleased with herself.

'I take it the butcher's wife was a talker,' Rebus said, dropping into his chair. There was another note on his desk telling him Jack Morton had called. But this time there was also a number where Rebus could reach him.

'A right little gossip, sir. I had trouble getting away.'

'And?'

'Something and nothing.'

'So give me the something.' Rebus rubbed his stomach. He'd enjoyed the burger, but it hadn't quite filled him up. There was always the canteen, but he was a bit worried about getting a 'dough-ring', as he termed the gut policemen specialised in.

'The something is this.' Siobhan Clarke sat down. 'Bone won the Merc in a bet.'

'A bet?'

Clarke nodded. 'He put his share of the butcher's business up against it. But he won the bet.'

'Bloody hell.'

'His wife actually sounded quite proud. Anyway, she told me he's a great one for betting. Maybe he is, but it doesn't look like he's got a winning formula.'

'How do you mean?'

She was warming to her subject. Rebus liked to see it, the gleam of successful detection. 'There were a few things not quite right in the living room. For instance, they'd videotapes but no video, though you could see where the machine used to sit. And though they had a large unit for storing the TV and video, the TV itself was one of those portable types.'

'So they've got rid of their video and their big television.'

'I'd guess to pay off a debt or debts.'

'And your money would be on gambling dues?'

'If I were the betting kind, which I'm not.'

He smiled. 'Maybe they had the stuff on tick and couldn't keep up the payments.'

Siobhan sounded doubtful. 'Maybe,' she conceded.

'Okay, well, it's interesting so far as it goes, but it doesn't go very far ... not yet. And it doesn't tell us anything about Rory Kintoul, does it?' She was frowning. 'Remember him, Clarke? He's the one who was stabbed in the street then wouldn't talk about it. *He's* the one we're interested in.'

'So what do you suggest, sir?' There was a tinge of ire to that 'sir'. She didn't like it that her good detection had not been better rewarded. 'We've already spoken to him.'

'And you're going to speak to him again.' She looked ready to protest. 'Only this time,' Rebus went on, 'you're going to be asking about his cousin, Mr Bone the butcher. I'm not sure what we're looking for exactly, so you'll have to feel your way. Just see whether anything hits the marrow.'

'Yes, sir.' She stood up. 'Oh, by the way, I got the files on Cafferty.'

'Plenty of reading in there, most of it x-rated.'

'I know, I've already started. And there's no x-rating nowadays. It's called "eighteen" instead.'

Rebus blinked. 'It's just an expression.' As she was turning away, he stopped her. 'Look, take some notes, will you? On Cafferty and his gang, I mean. Then when you're finished you can refresh my memory. I've spent a long time shutting that monster out of my thoughts; it's about time I opened the door again.'

'No problem.'

And with that she was off. Rebus wondered if he should have told her she'd done well at Bone's house. Ach, too late now. Besides, if she thought she were pleasing him, maybe she'd stop trying so hard. He picked up his phone and called Jack Morton.

'Jack? Long time no hear. It's John Rebus.'

'John, how are you?'

'No' bad, how's yourself?'

'Fine. I made Inspector.'

'Aye, me too.'

'So I heard.' Jack Morton choked off his words as he gave a huge hacking cough.

'Still on the fags, eh, Jack?'

'I've cut down.'

'Remind me to sell my tobacco shares. So listen, what's the problem?'

'It's your problem, not mine. Only I saw something from Scotland Yard about Andrew McPhail.'

Rebus tried the name out in his head. 'No,' he admitted, 'you've got me there.'

'We had him on file as a sex offender. He'd had a go at the daughter of the woman he was living with. This was about eight years back. But we never got the charge to stick.'

Rebus was remembering a little of it. 'We interviewed him when those wee girls started to disappear?' Rebus shivered at the memory: his own daughter had been one of the 'wee girls'.

'That's it, just routine. We started with convicted and suspected child offenders and went on from there.'

'Stocky guy with wiry hair?'

'You've got him.'

'So what's the point, Jack?'

'The point is, you really have got him. He's in Edinburgh.'

'So?'

'Christ, John, I thought you'd know. He buggered off to Canada after that last time we hassled him. Set himself up as a photographer, doing shots for fashion catalogues. He'd approach the parents of kids he fancied. He had business cards, camera equipment, the works, rented a studio and used to take shots of the children, promising they'd be in some catalogue or other. They'd get to dress up in fancy dresses, or sometimes maybe just in under-wear ...'

'I get the picture, Jack.'

'Well, they nabbed him. He'd been touching the girls, that was all. A lot of girls, so they put him inside.'

'And?'

'And now they've let him out. But they've also deported him.'

'He's in Edinburgh?'

'I started checking. I wanted to find out where he'd ended up, because I knew if it was anywhere near my patch I'd pay him a visit some dark night. But he's on your patch instead. I've got an address.'

'Wait a second.' Rebus found a pen and copied it down.

'How did you get his address anyway? The DSS?'

'No, the files said he had a sister in Ayr. She told me he'd had her get a phone number for him, a boarding house. Know what else she said? She said we should lock him in a cellar and forget about the key.'

'Sounds like a lovely lass.'

'She's my kind of woman, all right. Of course, he's probably been rehabilitated.'

That word – rehabilitated. A word Vanderhyde had used about Aengus Gibson. 'Probably,' said Rebus, believing it about as much as Morton himself. They were professional disbelievers, after all. It was a policeman's lot.

'Still, it's good to know about. Thanks, Jack.'

'You're welcome. Any chance we'll be seeing you in Falkirk some day? It'd be good to have a drink.'

'Yes, it would. Tell you what, I might be over that way soon.'

'Oh?'

'Dropping McPhail off in the town centre.'

Morton laughed. 'Ya shite, ye.' And with that he put down the phone.

Jack Morton stared at the phone for the best part of a minute, still grinning. Then the grin melted away. He unwrapped a stick of chewing gum and started gnawing it. It's better than a cigarette, he kept telling himself. He looked at the scribbled sheet of notes in front of him on the desk. The girl McPhail had assaulted was called Melanie Maclean these days. Her mother had married, and Melanie lived with the couple in Haddington, far enough from Edinburgh so that she probably wouldn't bump into McPhail. Nor, in all probability, would McPhail be able to find her. He'd have to know the stepfather's name, and that wouldn't be easy for him. It hadn't been *that* easy for Jack Morton. But the name was here. Alex Maclean. Jack Morton had a home address, home phone number, and work number. He wondered . . .

He knew too that Alex Maclean was a carpenter, and Haddington police were able to inform him that Maclean had a temper on him, and had twice (long before his marriage) been arrested after some flare-up or other. He wondered, but he knew he was going to do it. He picked up the receiver and punched in the numbers. Then waited.

'Hello, can I speak to Mr Maclean please? Mr Maclean? You don't know me, but I have some information I'd like to share with you. It concerns a man called Andrew McPhail ...'

Matthew Vanderhyde too made a telephone call that afternoon, but only after long thought in his favourite armchair. He held the cordless phone in his hand, tapping it with a long fingernail. He could hear a dog outside, the one from down the street with the nasal whine. The clock on the mantelpiece ticked, the tick seeming to slow as he concentrated on it. Time's heartbeat. At last he made the call. There was no preamble.

'I've just had a policeman here,' he said. 'He was asking about the night the Central Hotel caught fire.' He hesitated slightly. 'I told him about Aengus.' He could pause now, listening with a weary smile to the fury on the other end of the line, a fury he knew so well. 'Broderick,' he interrupted, 'if any skeletons are being uncloseted, *I* don't want to be the only one shivering.'

When the fury began afresh, Matthew Vanderhyde terminated the call.

7

Rebus noticed the man for the first time that evening. He thought he'd seen him outside St Leonard's in the afternoon. A young man, tall and broad-shouldered. He was standing outside the entrance to Rebus's communal stairwell in Arden Street. Rebus parked his car across the street, so that he could watch the man in his rearview mirror. The man looked agitated, pumped up about something. Maybe he was only waiting for his date. Maybe.

Rebus wasn't scared, but he started the car again and drove off anyway. He'd give it an hour and see if the man was still there. If he was, then he wasn't waiting on any date, no matter how bonny the girl. He drove along the Meadows to Tollcross, then took a right down Lothian Road. It was slow going, as per. The number of vehicles needing to get through the city of an evening seemed to grow every week. Edinburgh in the twilight looked much the same as any other place: shops and offices and crowded pavements. Nobody looked particularly happy.

He crossed Princes Street, cut into Charlotte Square, and began the crawl along Queensferry Street and Queensferry Road until he could take a merciful (if awkward) right turn into Oxford Terrace. But Patience wasn't home. He knew Patience's sister was expected this week, staying a few days then taking the girls home. Patience's cat, Lucky, sat outside, demanding entry, and Rebus for once was almost sympathetic.

'Nae luck,' he told it, before starting back up the steps.

When he got back to Arden Street, there was no sign of the skulking hulk. But Rebus would recognise him if he saw him again. Oh yes, he'd know him, all right.

Indoors, he had another argument with Michael, the two of them in the living room, everyone else in the kitchen. That was another thing: how many tenants did he have? There seemed to be a shifting population of about a dozen, where he'd rented to three with a possible fourth. He could swear he saw different faces every morning, and as a result could never remember anyone's name.

So there was another row about that, this time with the students in the kitchen while Michael sat in the box room, at the end of which Rebus said, 'Away to hell,' and proceeded to follow his own instructions by getting back in his car and making for one of the city's least respectable quarters, there to dine on pies and pints while staring at a soundless TV. He spoke with a few of his contacts, who had nothing to report regarding the assault on Brian Holmes.

So it was just another evening, really.

He got back purposely late, hoping everyone else would have gone to bed. He fumbled with the door-catch of the tenement and let the door swing shut loudly behind him, searching in his pockets for the flat key, eyes to the ground. So he didn't see the man, who must have been sitting on the bottom step of the stairs.

'Hello there.'

Rebus looked up, startled, recognised the figure, and sent small change and keys scattering as he threw a punch. He wasn't that drunk, but then his target was stone cold sober and twenty years younger. The man palmed the punch easily. He looked surprised at the attack, but also somehow excited by it. Rebus cut short the thrill of it all by sharply raising his knee into unprotected groin. The man expelled air noisily, and started to double over, which gave Rebus the opportunity to punch down onto the back of his neck. He felt his knuckles crackle with the force of the blow.

'Jesus,' the man gasped. 'Stop it.'

Rebus stopped it and wagged his aching hand. But he wasn't about to offer help. He kept his distance, and asked 'Who are you?'

The man managed to stop retching for a moment. 'Andy Steele.'

'Nice to meet you, Andy. What the fuck do you want?'

The man looked up at Rebus with tears in his eyes. It took him a while to catch his breath. When he spoke, Rebus either couldn't understand the accent or else just didn't believe what he was saying. He asked Steele to repeat himself.

'Your auntie sent me,' said Steele. 'She's got a message for you.'

Rebus sat Andy Steele down on the sofa with a cup of tea, including the four sugars Steele himself had requested.

'Can't be good for your teeth.'

'They're not my own,' Steele replied, huddled over the hot mug.

'Then whose are they?' asked Rebus. Steele gave the flicker of a smile. 'You've been following me all day.'

'Not exactly. Maybe if I had a car, but I don't.'

'You don't have a car?' Steele shook his head. 'Some private detective.'

'I didn't say I was a private detective exactly. I mean, I *want* to be one.'

'A sort of trainee, then?'

'Aye, that's right. Testing the water, so to speak.'

'And how's the water, Andy?'

Another smile, a sip of tea. 'A bit hot. But I'll be more careful next time.'

'I didn't even know I had an aunt. Not up north.' Steele's accent was a giveaway.

Andy Steele nodded. 'She lives next door to my mum and dad, just across the road from Pittodrie.'

'Aberdeen?' Rebus nodded to himself. 'It's coming back to me. Yes, an uncle and aunt in Aberdeen.'

'Your dad and Jimmy – that's your uncle – fell out years ago. You're probably too young to remember.'

'Thanks for the compliment.'

'It's just what Ena told me.'

'And now Uncle Jimmy's dead?'

'Three weeks past.'

'And Aunt Ena wants to see me?' Steele nodded. 'What about?'

'I don't know. She was just talking about how she'd like to see you again.'

'Just me? No mention of my brother?'

Steele shook his head. Rebus had checked to see if Michael was in the box room. He wasn't. But the other bedrooms seemed to be occupied.

'Right enough,' said Rebus, 'if they argued when I was wee, maybe it was before Michael was born.'

'They might no' even know about him,' Steele conceded. Well, that was families for you. 'Anyway, Ena kept harping on about you, so I told her I'd come south and have a look. I got laid off from the fishing boats six months ago, and I've been going up the wall ever since. Besides, I told you I've always fancied being a private eye. I love all those films.'

'Films don't get you a knee in the balls.'

'True enough.'

'So how *did* you find me?'

Steele's face brightened. 'I went to the address Ena gave me, where you and your dad used to live. All the neighbours knew was that you were a policeman in Edinburgh. So I got the directory out and phoned every station I could find, asking for John Rebus.' He shrugged and returned to his tea.

'But how did you get my home address?'

'Someone in CID gave it to me.'

'Don't tell me, Inspector Flower?'

'A name like that, aye.'

Seated on the sofa, Andy Steele looked to be in his mid-twenties. He had the sort of large frame which could be kept in shape only through hard work, such as that found on a North Sea fishing boat. But already, deprived of work for six months, that frame was growing heavy with disuse. Rebus felt sorry for Andy Steele and his dreams of becoming a private eye. The way he stared into space as he drank the tea, he looked lost, his immediate life without form or plan.

'So are you going to go and see her?'

'Maybe at the weekend,' said Rebus.

'She'd like that.'

'I can give you a lift back.'

But the young man was shaking his head. 'No, I'd like to stay in Edinburgh for a bit.'

'Suit yourself,' said Rebus. 'Just be careful.'

'Careful? I could tell you stories about Aberdeen that would make your hair stand on end.'

'And could they thicken it a bit at the temples while they're at it?'

It took Andy Steele a minute to get the joke.

The next day, Rebus paid a visit to Andrew McPhail. But McPhail wasn't home, and his landlady hadn't seen him since the previous evening.

'Usually he comes down at seven sharp for a wee bitty breakfast. So I went upstairs and there was no sign of him. Is he in any trouble, Inspector?'

'No, nothing like that, Mrs MacKenzie. This is a lovely Madiera by the way.'

'Ach, it's a few days since I made it, it's probably a bit dry by now.'

Rebus shook his head and gulped at the tea, hoping to wash the crumbs down his throat. But they merely formed into a huge solid lump which he had to force down by degrees, and without a public show of gagging.

There was a bird-cage standing in one corner of the room, boasting mirrors and cuttle-fish and millet spray. But no sign of any bird. Maybe it had escaped.

He left his card with Mrs MacKenzie, telling her to pass it on to Mr McPhail when she saw him. He didn't doubt that she would. It had been unfair of him to introduce himself as a policeman to the landlady. She would probably become suspicious, and might even give McPhail a week's notice on the strength of those suspicions. That would be a terrible shame.

Actually, it didn't look to Rebus as though Mrs MacKenzie would twig. And McPhail would doubtless come up with some reason for Rebus's visit. Probably the City of Edinburgh Police were about to award him a commendation for saving some puppies from the raging torrents of the Water of Leith. McPhail was good at making up stories, after all. Children just loved to hear stories.

Rebus stood outside Mrs MacKenzie's house and looked across the road. It had to be coincidence that McPhail had chosen a boarding house within ogling distance of a primary school. Rebus had seen it on his arrival; it had been enough to decide him on identifying himself to the landlady. After all, he didn't believe in coincidence.

And if McPhail couldn't be persuaded to move, well, maybe the neighbours would find out the true story of Mrs MacKenzie's lodger. Rebus got into his car. He didn't always like himself or his job.

But some bits were okay.

Back at St Leonard's, Siobhan Clarke had nothing new to

report on the stabbing. Rory Kintoul was being very cagey about another interview. He'd cancelled one arranged meeting, and she'd not been able to contact him since.

'His son's seventeen and unemployed, spends most of the day at home, I could try talking to him.'

'You could.' But it was a lot of trouble. Maybe Holmes was right. 'Just do your best,' said Rebus. 'After you've talked with Kintoul, if we're no further forward we'll drop the whole thing. If Kintoul wants to get himself stabbed, that's fine with me.'

She nodded and turned away.

'Any news on Brian?'

She turned back. 'He's been talking.'

'Talking?'

'In his sleep. I thought you'd know.'

'What's he been saying?'

'Nothing they can make out, but it means he's slowly regaining consciousness.'

'Good.'

She started to turn away again, but Rebus thought of something. 'How are you getting to Aberdeen on Saturday?'

'Driving, why?'

'Any room in the car?'

'There's just me.'

'Then you won't mind giving me a lift.'

She looked startled. 'Not at all. Where to?'

'Pittodrie.'

Now she looked even more surprised. 'I wouldn't have taken you for a Hibs fan, sir.'

Rebus screwed up his face. 'No, you're all alone in that category. I just need a lift, that's all.'

'Fine.'

'And on the way, you can tell me what you've learned from the files on Big Ger.'

8

By Saturday, Rebus had argued three times with Michael
(who was talking about moving out anyway), once with
the students (also talking about moving), and once with
the receptionist at Patience's surgery when she wouldn't
put Rebus through. Brian Holmes had opened his eyes
briefly, and it was reckoned by the doctors that he was
on his way to recovery. None of them, however, hazarded
the phrase 'full recovery'. Still, the news had cheered
Siobhan Clarke, and she was in a good mood when she
arrived at Rebus's Arden Street flat. He was waiting for
her at street level. She drove a two-year-old cherry-red
Renault 5. It looked young and full of life, while Rebus's
car (parked next to it) looked to be in terminal condition.
But Rebus's car had been looking like this for three or
four years now, and just when he'd determined to get rid
of it it always seemed to go into remission. Rebus had the
feeling the car could read his mind.

'Morning, sir,' said Siobhan Clarke. There was pop
music coming from the stereo. She saw Rebus cringe as
he got into the passenger seat, and turned the volume
down. 'Bad night?'

'People always seem to ask me that.'

'Now why could that be?'

They stopped at a bakery so Rebus could buy some
breakfast. There had been nothing in the flat worth the
description 'food', but then Rebus couldn't really complain.
His contribution to the larder so far had filled a single

shopping basket. And most of that had been meat, something the students didn't touch. He noticed Michael had gone vegetarian too, at least in public.

'It's healthier, John,' he'd told his brother, slapping his stomach.

'What's that supposed to mean?' Rebus had snapped.

Michael had merely shaken his head sadly. 'Too much caffeine.'

That was another thing, the kitchen cupboards were full of jars of what looked like coffee but turned out to be 'infusions' of crushed tree bark and chicory. At the bakery, Rebus bought a polystyrene beaker of coffee and two sausage rolls. The sausage rolls turned out to be a bad mistake, the flakes of pastry breaking off and covering the otherwise pristine car interior – despite Rebus's best attempts with the paper bag.

'Sorry about the mess,' he offered to Siobhan, who was driving with her window conspicuously open. 'You're not vegetarian, are you?'

She laughed. 'You mean you haven't noticed?'

'Can't say I have.'

She nodded towards a sausage roll. 'Well, have you heard of mechanically recovered meat?'

'Don't,' warned Rebus. He finished the sausage rolls quickly, and cleared his throat.

'Anything I should know about between you and Brian?'

The look on her face told him this was not the year's most successful conversational gambit. 'Not that I know of.'

'It's just that he and Nell were ... well, there's still a good chance –'

'I'm not a monster, sir. And I know the score between Brian and Nell. Brian's just a nice guy. We get along.' She glanced away from the windscreen. 'That's all there is to it.' Rebus was about to say something. 'But if there *was* more to it than that,' she went on, 'I don't see that it would be any of your business, with respect, sir. Not unless it was interfering with our work, which I wouldn't let happen. I don't suppose Brian would either.'

Rebus stayed silent.

'I'm sorry, I shouldn't have said that.'

'What you said was fair enough. The problem was the *way* you said it. A police officer's never off duty, and I'm your boss – even on a jaunt like this. Don't forget that.'

There was more silence in the car, until Siobhan broke it. 'It's a nice part of town, Marchmont.'

'Almost as nice as the New Town.'

She glared at him, her grip on the steering-wheel as determined as any strangler's.

'I thought,' she said slyly, 'you lived in Oxford Terrace these days, sir.'

'You thought wrong. Now, what about turning that bloody music off? After all, we've got a lot to talk about.'

The 'lot', of course, being Morris Gerald Cafferty.

Siobhan Clarke hadn't brought her notes with her. She didn't need them. She could recite the salient details from memory, along with a lot of detail that might not be salient but was certainly interesting. Certainly she'd done her homework. Rebus thought how frustrating the job could be. She'd swotted up on Big Ger as background to Operation Moneybags, but Operation Moneybags almost certainly wouldn't trap Cafferty. And she'd spent a lot of hours on the Kintoul stabbing, which might also turn out to be nothing.

'And another thing,' she said. 'Apparently Cafferty's got a little diary of sorts, all of it in code. We've never been able to crack his code, which means it must be highly personal.'

Yes, Rebus remembered. Whenever they brought Big Ger into custody, the diary would be collected along with his other possessions. Then they'd photocopy the pages of the diary and try to decipher them. They'd never been successful.

'Rumour has it,' Siobhan was saying, 'the diary's a record of bad debts, debts Cafferty takes care of personally.'

'A man like that garners a lot of rumours. They help make him larger than life. In life, he's just another witless gangster.'

'A code takes wits.'

'Maybe.'

'In the file, there's a recent clipping from the *Sun*. It's all about how bodies keep washing up on the coastline.'

Rebus nodded. 'On the Solway coast, not far from Stranraer.'

'You think it's Cafferty's doing?'

Rebus shrugged. 'The bodies have never been identified. Could be anything. Could be people pushed off the Larne ferry. Could be some connection with Ulster. There are some weird currents between Larne and Stranraer.' He paused. 'Could be anything.'

'Could be Cafferty, in other words.'

'Could be.'

'It's a long way to go to dispose of a body.'

'Well, he's not going to shit in his own nest, is he?'

She considered this. 'There was mention in one of the papers of a van spotted on that coastline, too early in the morning to be delivering anything.'

Rebus nodded. 'And there was nowhere along the road for it to be delivering *to*. I read the papers sometimes, Clarke. The Dumfries and Galloway Police have patrols along there now.'

Siobhan drove for a while, gathering her thoughts. 'He's just been lucky so far, hasn't he, sir? I mean, I can understand that he's a clever villain, and clever villains are harder to catch. But he has to delegate, and usually even though a villain's clever his underlings are so stupid or lazy they *would* shit in the nest.'

85

'Language, Clarke, language.' He got a smile from her. 'Point taken, though.'

'Reading all about Cafferty's "associates" I didn't get an impression of many "O" Grades. They've all got names like Slink and Codge and the Radiator.'

Rebus grinned. 'Radiator McCallum, I remember him. He was supposed to be descended from a family of Highland cannibals. He did research and everything, he was so proud of his ancestors.'

'He disappeared from the scene, though.'

'Yes, three or four years ago.'

'Four and a half, according to the records. I wonder what happened to him.'

Rebus shrugged. 'He tried to doublecross Big Ger, got scared and ran off.'

'Or didn't get the chance to run off.'

'That too, of course. Or else he just got fed up, or had another job offer. It's a very mobile profession, being a thug. Wherever the work is ...'

'Cafferty certainly gets through the personnel. McCallum's cousins disappeared from view just before McCallum himself did.'

Rebus frowned. 'I didn't know he had any cousins.'

'Known colloquially as the Bru-head Brothers. Something to do with a penchant for Irn-Bru.'

'Altogether understandable. What were their real names, though?'

She thought for a moment. 'Tam and Eck Robertson.'

Rebus nodded. 'Eck Robertson, yes. I didn't know about the other one, though. Hang on a minute ...'

Tam and Eck Robertson. The R. Brothers. Which would mean that Mork was ...

'Morris bloody Cafferty!' Rebus slapped the dashboard. Brian shortened the name and used a k for the c. Christ ... If Brian Holmes was on to something involving Cafferty and his gang, no wonder he was scared. Something to do

86

with the night the Central Hotel caught fire. Did they start the blaze because the hotel hadn't been paying its protection dues? What about the body, maybe it'd been some debtor or other. And soon afterwards, Radiator McCallum and his cousins left the scene. Bloody hell.

'If you're going to have a seizure,' said Siobhan, 'I'm trained in cardiac resuscitation.'

Rebus wasn't listening. He stared at the road ahead, one fist around the coffee cup, the other pounding his knee. He was thinking of Brian's note. He hadn't said for sure that Cafferty was there that night, only that the brothers were. And something about a poker game. He was going to try to find the Robertson brothers; that was his final comment. After which, someone came along and hit him on the head. Maybe it was beginning to come together.

'I'm not sure I can deal with catatonia though.'

'What?'

'Was it something that I said?'

'Yes, it was.'

'The Bru-Head Brothers?'

'The very same. What else can you tell me about them?'

'Born in Niddrie, petty thieves from the time they left the pram –'

'They probably stole the pram, too. Anything else?'

Siobhan knew that she'd hit some nerve. 'Plenty. Both had long records. Eck liked flashy clothes, Tam always wore jeans and a T-shirt. The funny thing is, though, Tam kept scrupulously clean. He even took his own soap everywhere with him. I thought that was strange.'

'If I were the gambling kind,' said Rebus, 'I'd bet the soap was lemon-scented.'

'How did you know that?'

'Instinct. Not mine, someone else's.' Rebus frowned. 'How come I never heard of Tam?'

'He moved to Dundee when he left school, or rather

when he was *asked* to leave school. He only came back to Edinburgh years later. The records have him down as working for the gang for about six months, maybe even less.' She waited. 'Are you going to tell me what this is all about?'

'It's all about a hotel fire.'

'You mean those files on the floor behind your desk?'

'I mean those files on the floor behind my desk.'

'I couldn't help taking a peek.'

'They might tie in with the attack on Brian.' She turned to him. 'Keep your eyes on the road. You concentrate on the driving, and I'll tell you a story. It might even keep us going till Aberdeen.'

And it did.

'In ye come, Jock. My, my, I wouldn't have recognised ye.'

'I was in shorts the last time you saw me, Auntie Ena.'

The old woman laughed. She used a zimmer frame to walk back through the narrow musty hall and into a small back room. The room was crammed with furniture. There would be a front room, too, another lounge kept for the most special occasions. But Rebus was family, and family were greeted in the back room.

She was frail-looking and hunch-backed and wore a shawl over her angular shoulders. Her silver hair had been pulled back severely and pinned tight against her head, and her eyes were sunken dots in a parchment face. Rebus couldn't remember her at all.

'You must have been three when we were last in Fife. You could talk the hind legs off a donkey, but with such a thick accent, I could hardly make out a word of it. Always wanting to tell a joke or sing a song.'

'I've changed,' Rebus said.

'Eh?' She had dumped herself into a chair beside the

fireplace, and craned her head forward. 'My hearing's not so good, Jock.'

'I said, nobody calls me Jock!' Rebus called. 'It's John.'

'Oh aye, John. Right you are.' She pulled a travel-rug over her legs. In the fireplace stood an electric fire, the kind with fake coals, fake flames, and, so far as Rebus could tell, fake heat. There was one pale orange bar on, but he couldn't feel anything.

'Danny found you, then?'

'You mean Andy?'

'He's a good laddie. Such a shame he got made redundant. Did he come back with you?'

'No, he's still in Edinburgh.' She was resting her head against the back of the chair. Rebus got the impression she was about to drift off to sleep. The walk to the front door and back had probably exhausted her.

'His parents are nice folk, always so kind to me.'

'You wanted to see me about something, Auntie Ena?'

'Eh?'

He crouched down in front of her, resting his hands on the side of the chair. 'You wanted to see me.' Well, she could see him . . . and then she couldn't, as her eyes glazed over and, mouth wide open, she started to snore.

Rebus stood up and gave a loud sigh. The clock over the mantelpiece had stopped, but he knew he had at least two hours to kill. Talking over the Central Hotel case with Siobhan had made him agitated. He wanted to get back to work on it. And here he was, trapped in this miniature museum. He looked around, wrinkling his nose at a chrome commode in one dark corner. There were photos inside a glass-fronted china cabinet. He went over and examined them. He recognised a picture of his grandparents on his father's side, but there were no photos of his father. The feud, or whatever it had been, had seen to that.

The Scots never forgot. It was a burden and a gift. The

living-room led directly onto a small scullery. Rebus looked in the antique fridge and found a piece of brisket, which he sniffed. There was bread in a large tin in the pantry, and butter in a dish on the draining-board. It took him ten minutes to make the sandwiches, and five minutes to find out which of the many caddies contained the tea.

He found a radio beside the sink and tried to find commentary on a football game, but the batteries were weaker than his tea. So he tiptoed back through to where Auntie Ena was still sleeping and sat down in the chair opposite her. He hadn't come up here expecting an inheritance, exactly, but he had bargained for more than this. A particularly loud snore brought Auntie Ena wriggling towards consciousness.

'Eh? Is that you, Jimmy?'

'It's John, your nephew.'

'Gracious, John, did I nod off?'

'Just forty winks.'

'Isn't that terrible of me, with a visitor here and everything.'

'I'm not a visitor, Auntie Ena, I'm family.'

'Aye, son, so you are. Now, listen to me. There's some beef in the fridge. Shall I go and –?'

'They're already made.'

'Eh?'

'The sandwiches. I've made them up.'

'You have? You always were a bright one. Now what about some tea?'

'Sit where you are, I'll make some fresh.'

He made a pot of tea and brought the sandwiches through on a plate, setting them in front of her on a footstool. 'There we are.' He was about to hand her one, when she made a grab for his wrists, nearly toppling the plate. He saw that her eyes were shut, and though she looked frail enough her grip was strong. She'd started speaking before Rebus realised she was saying grace.

'Some hae meat and cannae eat, and some hae nane that want it. But we hae meat and we can eat, so let the Lord be thankit.'

Rebus almost burst out laughing. Almost. But inside, he was touched too. He handed her a smile along with her sandwich, then went to fetch the tea.

The meal revived her, and she seemed to remember why she'd wanted to see him.

'Your faither and my husband fell out very many years ago. Maybe forty or more years ago. They never exchanged a letter, a Christmas card, or a civil word ever again. Now, don't you think that's stupid? And do you know what it was about? It was about the fact that though we invited your faither and mither to our Ishbel's wedding, we didn't invite you. We'd decided there would be no children, you see. But then a friend of mine, Peggy Callaghan, brought her son along uninvited, and we could hardly turn him away, since there was no way for him to get back home on his own. When your faither saw this, he argued with Jimmy. A real blazing row. And then your faither stormed out, leaving your mither to follow him. A sweet woman she was. So that's that.'

She sat back in her chair, breadcrumbs prominent on her lower lip.

'That was all?'

She nodded. 'Doesn't seem like much, does it? Not from this distance. But it was enough. And the both of them were too stubborn ever to make it up.'

'And you wanted to see me so you could tell me this?'

'Partly, yes. But also, I wanted to give you something.' She rose slowly from her chair, using the zimmer-frame for support, and leaned up towards the mantelpiece. Rebus half-rose to help her, but she didn't need his help. She found the photograph and handed it down to him. He looked at it. In fading black and white, it showed two grinning schoolboys, not exactly dressed to the nines.

91

They had their arms casually slung around one another's necks, and their faces were close together. Best friends, but more than that: brothers.

'He kept that, you see. He told me once that he'd thrown out all the photos of your faither. But when we were going through his things, we found that in the bottom of a shoebox. I wanted you to have it, Jock.'

'It's not Jock, it's John,' said Rebus, his eyes not entirely dry.

'Of course it is,' said his Auntie Ena. 'Of course it is.'

Earlier that afternoon, Michael Rebus had lain along the couch asleep and unaware that he was missing one of his favourite films, *Double Indemnity*, on BBC2. He'd gone to the pub for a lunchtime drink: alone, as it turned out. The students weren't into it. Instead, they'd gone shopping, or to the launderette, or home for the weekend to see parents and friends. So Michael drank only two lagers topped with lemonade and returned to the flat, where he promptly fell asleep in front of the TV.

He'd been thinking about John recently. He knew he was imposing on his big brother, but didn't reckon on doing so much longer. He had spoken on the phone to Chrissie. She was still in Kirkcaldy with the kids. She'd wanted nothing to do with him after the bust, and was especially disgusted that his own brother had given evidence against him. But Michael didn't blame John for that. John had principles. And besides, some of the evidence had worked – deliberately, he was sure – in Michael's favour.

Now Chrissie was talking to him again. He'd written to her all through his incarceration, then had written from London too; not knowing whether she'd received any of his letters. But she had. She told him that when they spoke. And she didn't have a boyfriend, and the kids were fine, and did he want to see them some time?

'I want to see you,' he'd told her. It sounded right.

He was dreaming about her when the doorbell went. Well ... her and Gail the student, if truth be told. He staggered to his feet. The bell was insistent.

It took a second to turn the snib-lock, after which Michael's world imploded.

With another Hibernian defeat behind her, Siobhan Clarke was quiet on the way home, which suited Rebus. He had some thinking to do, and not about work, for a change. He thought about the job too much as it was, gave himself to it the way he had never given himself to any *person* in his life. Not his ex-wife, not his daughter, not Patience, not Michael.

He'd come into the police prematurely weary and cynical. Then he watched recruits like Holmes and Clarke and saw their best intentions thwarted by the system and the public's attitude. There were times you'd feel more welcome if you were painting plague markers on people's doors.

'A penny for them,' said Siobhan Clarke.

'Don't waste your money.'

'Why not? Look how much I've wasted already today.'

Rebus smiled at that. 'Aye,' he said, 'I keep forgetting, there's always someone in the world worse off than yourself ... Unless you're a Hibs supporter.'

'Ha bloody ha.'

Siobhan Clarke reached for the stereo and tried to find a station that didn't run the day's classified results.

9

Full of good intentions, Rebus opened the door of the flat, sensing immediately that nobody was home. Well, it was Saturday night, after all. But they might at least have turned the TV off.

He went into the box room and placed the old photograph on Michael's unmade bed. The room smelt faintly of perfume, reminding Rebus of Patience. He missed her more than he liked to admit. When they'd first started seeing one another, they'd agreed that they were both too old for anything that could be called 'love'. They'd also agreed that they were more than ready for lashings of sex. Then, when Rebus had moved in, they'd talked again. It didn't really mean commitment, they were agreed on that; it was just handier for the moment. Ah, but when Rebus had rented out his own flat ... *that* had meant commitment, commitment to sleeping on the sofa should Patience ever kick him out.

He lay along the sofa now, noticing that he had all but annexed what had been the flat's main communal space. The students tended to sit around in the kitchen now, talking quietly with the door closed. Rebus didn't blame them. It was all a mess in here, and all *his* mess. His suitcase lay wide open on the floor beside the window, ties and socks trickling from it. The holdall was tucked behind the sofa. His two suits hung limply from the picture-rail next to the box room, partially blocking out a psychedelic poster which had been making Rebus's eyes hurt. The place had a feral smell from lack of fresh air. The smell suited it, though. After all, wasn't this Rebus's lair?

He picked up the telephone and rang Patience. Her taped voice spoke to him; the message was new.

'I'm going with Susan and Jenny back to their mother's. Any messages, leave them after the tone.'

Rebus's first thought was how stupid Patience had been. The message let any caller – *any* caller – know she wasn't home. He knew that burglars often telephoned first. They might even go through the phone book more or less at random, finding phones that rang and rang, or answering machines. You had to make your message vague.

He guessed that if she'd gone to her sister's, she wouldn't be back until tomorrow night at the earliest, and might even stay over on the Monday.

'Hi, Patience,' he said to the machine. 'It's me. I'm ready to talk when you are. I ... miss you. Bye.'

So, the girls had gone. Maybe now things could get back to normal. No more smouldering Susan, no more gentle Jenny. They weren't the cause of the rift between Rebus and Patience, but maybe they hadn't helped. No, they definitely hadn't helped.

He made himself a cup of 'coffee substitute', all the time thinking of wandering down to the late-opening shop at the corner of Marchmont Road. But their coffee was instant and expensive, and besides, maybe this stuff would taste okay.

It tasted awful, and was absolutely caffeine-free, which was probably why he fell asleep during a dreary mid-evening movie on the television.

And awoke to a ringing telephone. Someone had switched the TV off, and perhaps that same person had thrown the blanket over him. It was getting to be a regular thing. He was stiff as he sat up and reached for the receiver. His watch told him it was one-fifteen a.m.

'Hello?'

'Is that Inspector Rebus?'

'Speaking.' Rebus rubbed at his hair.

'Inspector, this is PC Hart. I'm in South Queensferry.'

'Yes?'

'There's someone here claims he's your brother.'

'Michael?'

'That's the name he gave.'

'What's up? Is he guttered?'

'Nothing like that, sir.'

'What is it then?'

'Well, sir, we've just found him ...'

Rebus was very awake now. 'Found him where?'

'He was hanging from the Forth Rail Bridge.'

'What?' Rebus felt his hand squeezing the telephone receiver to death. *'Hanging?'*

'I don't mean like that, sir. Sorry if I ...' Rebus's grip relaxed.

'No, I mean he was hanging by his feet, sort of suspended, like. Just hanging in mid-air.'

'We thought it was some sort of joke gone wrong at first. You know, bungee jumper, that kind of thing.' PC Hart was leading Rebus to a hut on the quayside at South Queensferry. The Firth of Forth was dark and quiet in front of them, but Rebus could make out the rail bridge lowering far above them. 'But that's not the story he gave us. Besides, it was clear he hadn't taken the dive on his own.'

'How clear?'

'His hands were tied together, sir. And his mouth had been taped shut.'

'Christ.'

'Doctor says he'll be all right. If they'd tipped him over the side, his legs could've come out of the sockets, but the doc reckons they must have lowered him over.'

'How did they get onto the bridge in the first place?'

'It's easy enough, if you've a head for heights.'

Rebus, who had no head for heights, had already declined the offer of a visit to the spot where Michael had been found, up on the ochre-coloured iron construction.

'Looks like they waited till they knew there'd be no trains about. But a boat was going under the bridge, and the skipper thought he saw something, so he radioed in. Otherwise, well, he could have been up there all night.' Hart shook his head. 'A cold night, I can't say I'd fancy it.'

They were at the hut now. There was only enough room inside for two men. One of these, seated with a blanket over his shoulders, was Michael. The other was a local doctor, called from his bed by the look of him. Other men stood around: police, the proprietor of a hotel on the waterfront, and the boat skipper who might just have saved Michael's life, or at the very least his sanity.

'John, thank Christ.' Michael was trembling, and seemed to have no colour in him at all. The doctor was holding a hot cup of something, from which he was coaxing Michael to drink.

'Drink up, Mickey,' said Rebus. Michael looked pathetic, like the victim of some terrible tragedy. Rebus felt a tremendous sadness overwhelm him. Michael had spent years in jail, where God knows what had happened to him. Then, released, he'd had no luck at all until he'd come to Edinburgh. The bravado, the nights out with the students – Rebus suddenly saw it for what it really was, a front, an attempt to put behind him all that Michael had feared these past few years. And now this had happened, reducing him to the crouched shivering animal in the hut.

'I'll be back in a second, Mickey.' Rebus pulled Hart

around the side of the hut. 'What has he told you?' He was trying to control the fury inside him.

'He said he was in your flat, sir, on his own.'

'When?'

'This afternoon, about four. There was a ring at the doorbell, so he answered, and three men pushed their way in. The first thing they did was put a cloth bag over his head. Then they held him down and tied him up, took the bag off and taped shut his mouth, then put the bag back.'

'He didn't see them?'

'They kept his face against the hall carpet. He just got the quick glimpse of them when he opened the door.'

'Go on.' Rebus was trying not to look up at the rail bridge. Instead, he focused on the flashing red lights on top of the more distant road bridge.

'They seem to have wrapped something like a carpet around him and taken him downstairs and into a van. It was pretty cramped in there, according to your brother. Narrow, like. He reckoned there were boxes either side of him.' Hart paused. He didn't like the look of concentration on the Inspector's face.

'Well?' Rebus snapped.

'He says they drove around for hours, not saying anything. Then he was lifted out of the van and taken into something like a cellar or a storeroom. They never took the bag off his head, so he can't be sure.' Hart paused. 'I didn't want to question him too closely, sir, in his present condition.'

Rebus nodded.

'Anyway, finally they brought him up here. Tied him to the side of the bridge, and lowered him over it. They still hadn't said anything. But when they started to lower away, they finally took the bag off his head.'

'Christ.' Rebus screwed shut his eyes. It brought back the grimmest memories of his own SAS training, the way they'd tried to get him to hand over information. Taking him up in a helicopter with a bag over his head, then threatening to drop him out, and carrying out their threat ... But only eight feet off the ground, not the hundreds of feet he'd visualised. Horrible, all of it. He pushed past Hart, pulled the doctor out of the way, and bent down to hug Michael, keeping him close against his chest as he heard Michael start to bawl. The crying lasted for many minutes, but Rebus wasn't about to let go.

And then at last, it was over. Racking dry coughs, the breathing slowing, and a sort of calm. Michael's face was a mess of tear tracks and mucus. Rebus handed him a handkerchief.

'The ambulance is waiting,' the doctor said quietly. Rebus nodded. Michael was obviously in shock; they'd keep him in the Infirmary overnight.

Two patients to visit, thought Rebus. What was more, he suspected similar motives behind the attacks. Very similar motives, if it came down to it. The rage began in him all over again, and his scalp prickled like hell. But he calmed a little as he helped Michael over to the ambulance.

'Do you want me to come with you?' he asked.

'Absolutely not,' said Michael. 'Just go home, eh?'

Part of the way to the ambulance, Michael's legs gave way, his knees refusing to lock. They carried him instead, like taking an injured player off the field, closed the door on him, and took him away. Rebus thanked the doctor, the skipper, and Hart.

'Hellish thing to happen,' Hart said. 'Any idea why it did?'

'A few,' said Rebus.

He went home to brood in his darkened living room. His whole life seemed shot to hell. Someone had been sending him a message tonight. They'd either decided to send it *via* Michael, or else they'd simply mistaken Michael for him. After all, people said they looked alike. Since the men had come to Arden Street, they were either working on very old information, or else they knew all about his separation from Patience, which meant they were very well-informed indeed. But Rebus suspected the former. The name on the doorbell still said Rebus, though it also listed on a scrap of paper four other names. That must have confused them for a minute. Yet they'd decided to attack anyway. Why? Did it mean they were desperate? Or was it just that any hostage would do to get the message across?

Message received.

And almost understood. Almost. This was serious, deadly serious. First Brian, now Michael. He had so few doubts that the two were connected. It felt like it was time to do something, not just wait for their next move. He knew what he wanted to do, too. That one phrase had brought it to mind: *shot to hell*. A part of him wanted to be holding a gun. A gun would even the odds very nicely indeed. He even knew where he could get one, didn't he? *Anything from a shag to a shooter*. He found that he'd been pacing the floor in front of the window. He felt caged, unwilling to sleep and unable to act against his invisible foe. But he had to do *some*thing ... so he went for a drive.

He drove to Perth. It didn't take long on the motorway in the middle of the night. In the city itself, he got lost once or twice (with no one about to ask directions of, not even a policeman) before finding the street he wanted. It was sited on a ridge of land, with houses on the one side only. This was where Patience's sister lived. Rebus spotted Patience's car and found a parking space two cars away from it. He turned off his lights and engine and reached into the back seat for the blanket he'd brought, pulling the blanket over as much of him as it would cover. He sat for a while, feeling more relaxed than in ages. He'd thought of bringing some whisky with him, but knew the kind of head it would give him in the morning. And tomorrow he wanted to be clear-headed if nothing else. He thought of Patience asleep in the spare room, just through the wall from Susan. She slept soundly, the moon lighting her forehead and her cheeks. It seemed a long way from Edinburgh, a long way from the shadow of the Forth Rail Bridge. John Rebus drifted into sleep, and slept well for once.

When he awoke, it was six-thirty on Sunday morning. He threw aside the blanket and started the car, turning the heating all the way up. He felt chilled but rested. The street was quiet, except for a man walking his ugly white poodle. The man seemed to find Rebus's presence there curious. Rebus smiled steadily at him as he shifted the gearstick into first and drove away.

10

He went straight to the Infirmary where, despite the early hour, pre-breakfast tea was being served. Michael was sitting up in bed with the cup on the tray in front of him. He seemed like a statue, staring at the surface of the dark brown liquid, his face blank. He didn't move as Rebus approached, pulled a chair noisily from a pile beside one wall, and sat down.

'Hiya, Mickey.'

'Hello, John.' Michael continued to stare. Rebus hadn't seen him blink yet.

'Going through it again and again, eh?' Michael didn't answer. 'I've been there myself, Mickey. Something terrible happens, you play it over in your mind. Eventually it fades. You might not believe that just now.'

'I'm trying to understand who did it, *why* they did it.'

'They wanted you scared, Mickey. I think it was a message for me.'

'Couldn't they have written instead? They got me scared all right. I could have shit through a Polo mint.'

Rebus laughed loudly at this. If Michael was getting back a sense of humour, the rest couldn't be far behind. 'I brought you this,' he said.

It was the photograph from Aberdeen. Rebus placed it on the tray beside the untouched tea.

'Who are they?'

'Dad and Uncle Jimmy.'

'Uncle Jimmy? I don't remember an Uncle Jimmy.'

'They fell out a long time ago, never spoke again.'

'That's a shame.'

'Uncle Jimmy died a few weeks ago. His widow – Auntie Ena – wanted us to have this photo.'

'Why?'

'Maybe because we're blood,' Rebus said.

Michael smiled. 'You wouldn't always know it.' He looked up at Rebus with wet shining eyes.

'We'll know it from now on,' said Rebus. He nodded towards the cup. 'Can I have that tea if you're not drinking it? My tongue feels like a happy hour's welcome-mat.'

'Help yourself.'

Rebus drank the tea in two swallows. 'Jesus,' he said, 'I was doing you a favour, believe me.'

'I know all about the tea they serve in institutions.'

'You're not as daft as you look then.' Rebus paused. 'You didn't see much of them, eh?'

'Who?'

'The men who grabbed you.'

'I saw bodies coming through the door. The first one was about my height, but a lot broader. The others, who knows. I never saw any faces. Sorry.'

'No problem. Can you tell me *any*thing?'

'No more than I told the constable last night. What was his name again?'

'Hart.'

'That's it. He thought I'd been bungee-jumping.' Michael gave a low laugh. 'I told him, no, I was just hanging around.'

Rebus smiled. 'But thankfully not at a loose end, eh?'

But Michael had stopped laughing. 'I had a nightmare about it. They had to give me something to make me sleep. I don't know what it was, but I still feel doped.'

'Get them to give you a prescription, you can sell tabs to the students.'

'They're good kids, John.'

'I know.'

'It'd be a shame if they moved out.'

'I know that, too.'

'You remember Gail?'

'The girl you've been seeing?'

'I've seen every inch of her. Strictly past tense now. But she has a boyfriend in Auchterarder. You don't suppose he's the jealous type?'

'I don't think he's behind last night.'

'No? Only, I've not been around Edinburgh long enough to make any enemies.'

'Don't worry,' said Rebus. 'I've got enemies enough for both of us.'

'That's very reassuring. Meanwhile . . .'

'Yes?'

'What about getting a spyhole for your door? Just think if one of the lassies had answered.'

Oh, Rebus had thought about it. 'And a chain,' he said. 'I'm getting them this afternoon.' He paused. 'Hart said something about the van.'

'When they pushed me in, it was like I was fitting into a narrow space. Yet I got the feeling the van itself was a decent size.'

'So it had stuff in the back then?'

'Maybe. Bloody solid, whatever it was. I bruised both knees.' Michael shrugged. 'That's about it.' Then he thought of something. 'Oh yes, and it had a bad smell. Either that or something had died in the carpet they wrapped me in . . .'

They sat talking for another quarter of an hour or so, until Michael closed his eyes and went to sleep. He wouldn't be asleep for long: they were starting to serve breakfast. Rebus got up and moved the chair back, then placed the photograph on Michael's bedside cabinet. He had another call to pay, while he was here.

But there were doctors with Brian Holmes, and the nurse didn't know how long they'd be. She only knew that Brian had woken again in the night for almost a minute. Rebus wished he'd been there: a minute would be long enough for the question he wanted to ask. Brian had also been talking in his sleep, but his words had been mumbled at best, and no one had any record of what he'd said. So Rebus gave up and went off to do some shopping. If he phoned around noon they'd let him know when Michael was likely to be getting home.

He went back to the flat by way of the corner shop, where he bought a week's worth of groceries. He was finishing breakfast when the first student wandered into the kitchen and drank three glassfuls of water.

'You're supposed to do that *before* you go to bed,' Rebus advised.

'Thank you, Sherlock.' The young man groaned. 'Got any paracetamol?' Rebus shook his head. 'Definitely a bad keg of beer last night. I thought the first pint tasted ropey.'

'Aye, but I'll bet the second tasted better and the sixth tasted great.'

The student laughed. 'What're you eating?'

'Toast and jam.'

'No bacon or sausages?'

Rebus shook his head. 'I've decided to lay off meat for a while.'

The student seemed unnaturally pleased.

'There's orange juice in the fridge,' Rebus continued. The student opened the fridge door and gave a gasp.

'There's enough stuff in here to feed a lecture hall!'

'Which is why,' said Rebus, 'I reckon it'll do us for at least a day or two.'

The student lifted a letter from the top of the fridge. 'This came for you yesterday.'

It was from the Inland Revenue. They were thinking of coming to check on the flat.

'Remember,' Rebus told the student, 'anyone asks, you're my nephews and nieces.'

'Yes, uncle.' The student recommenced rummaging in the refrigerator. 'Where did Mickey and you get to last night?' he asked. 'I crept in at two and there was no sign of life.'

'Oh, we were just ...' But Rebus couldn't find any words. So the student supplied them for him.

'Shooting the breeze?'

'Shooting the breeze,' agreed Rebus.

He drove to a DIY superstore on the edge of the city and bought a chain for the door, a spy-hole, and the tools a helpful assistant suggested would be needed for both jobs. (A lot more tools than Rebus used, as it turned out.) Since there was a supermarket nearby, Rebus did a bit more grocery shopping, by which time the pubs were open for business. He looked in a few places, but couldn't find who he was looking for. But he was able to put word out with a couple of useful barmen, who said they would pass the message along.

Back at the flat, he called the Infirmary, who told him Michael could come home this afternoon. Rebus arranged to pick him up at four. He then got to work. He drilled the necessary hole in the door, only to find he'd drilled it too high for the girl student, who had to stand on tiptoe even to get close. So he drilled another hole, filled in the first with wood putty, and then fitted the spy-hole. It was a bit askew, but it would work. Fitting the sliding chain was easier, and left him with two tools and a drill-bit unused. He wondered if the DIY store would take them back.

Next he tidied the box room and put Michael's stuff into the washing machine, after which he shared the macaroni cheese which the students had prepared for lunch. He didn't quite apologise to them for the past week, but he insisted they use the living room whenever they liked, and he told them also that he was reducing their rent – news they took unsurprisingly well. He didn't say anything about Michael; he didn't reckon Michael would want them to know. And he'd already explained away the extra security on the door by citing several recent burglaries in the locality.

He brought Michael and a large bottle of sleeping tablets back from the hospital, having first bribed the students to be out of the flat for the rest of the afternoon and evening. If Michael needed to cry again, he wouldn't want an audience.

'Look, our new peephole,' said Rebus at the door of the flat.

'That was quick.'

'Protestant work ethic. Or is it Calvinist guilt? I can never remember.' Rebus opened the door. 'Please also note the security chain on the inside.'

'You can tell it's a rush job, look where the paint's all scored.'

'Don't push your luck, brother.'

Michael sat in the living room while Rebus made two mugs of tea. The stairwell had seemed full of menace for both brothers, each sensing the other's disquiet. And even now Rebus didn't feel completely safe. This was not, however, something he wished to share with Michael.

'Just the way you like it,' he said, bringing the tea in. He could see Michael was weepy again, though trying to hide it.

'Thanks, John.'

The phone rang before Rebus could say anything. It was Siobhan Clarke, checking details of the following morning's surveillance operation.

Rebus assured her that everything was in hand; all she

had to do was turn up and freeze her bum off for a few hours.

'You're a great one for motivation, sir,' was her final comment.

'So,' Rebus asked Michael, 'what do you want to do?'

Michael was shaking a large round pill out of the brown bottle. He put it on his tongue with a wavering hand, and washed it down with tea.

'A quiet night in would suit me fine,' he said.

'A quiet night in it is,' agreed Rebus.

11

Operation Moneybags began quietly enough at eight-thirty on Monday morning, thirty minutes before Davey Dougary's BMW bumped its way into the pot-holed parking lot of the taxi-cab firm. Alister Flower and his team, of course, wouldn't be starting work till eleven or a little after, but it was best not to think about that, especially if, like Siobhan Clarke, you were already cold and stiff by opening time, and dreading your next visit to the chemical toilet which had been installed, for want of any other facilities, in a broom closet.

She was bored, too. DC Peter Petrie (from St Leonard's) and Elsa-Beth Jardine from Trading Standards appeared to be nursing post-weekend hangovers and resultant blues. She got the feeling that Jardine and her might actually have a lot to talk about – both were women fighting for recognition in what was perceived as a male profession – but the presence of Petrie ruled out discussion.

Peter Petrie was one of those basically intelligent but not exactly perceptive officers who climbed the ladder by passing the exams (though never with brilliant marks) and not getting in anyone's way. Petrie was quiet and methodical; she didn't doubt his competence, it was just that he lacked any spark of inspiration or instinct. And probably, she thought, he was sitting there with his thermos summing her up as an over-talkative smart-arse with a university degree. Well, whatever he was he was no John Rebus.

She had accused her superior of not exactly motivating those who worked for him, but this was a lie. He could draw you into a case, and into his way of thinking about a case, merely by being so narrow-minded about the investigation. He was secretive – and that drew you in. He was tenacious – and that drew you in. Above all, though, he had the air of knowing exactly where he was going. And he wasn't all that bad looking either. She'd learned a lot about him by sticking close to Brian Holmes, who had been only too willing to chat about past cases and what he knew of his boss's history.

Poor Brian. She hoped he was going to be all right. She had thought a lot last night about Brian, but even more about Cafferty and his gang. She hoped she could be of help to Inspector John Rebus. She already had a few ideas about the fire at the Central Hotel ...

'Here comes someone,' said Petrie. He was squatting behind the tripod and busily adjusting the focus on the camera. He fired off half a dozen shots. 'Unidentified male. Denim jacket and light-coloured trousers. Approaching the office on foot.'

Siobhan took up her pad and copied down Petrie's description, noting the time alongside.

'He's entering the office ... now.' Petrie turned away from the camera and grinned. 'This is what I joined the police for: a life of adventure.' Having said which, he poured more hot chocolate from his thermos into a cup.

'I can't use that loo,' said Elsa-Beth Jardine. 'I'll have to go out.'

'No can do,' said Petrie, 'it would attract too much attention, you tripping in and out every time you needed a piss.'

Jardine turned to Siobhan. 'He's got a way with words, your colleague.'

'Oh, he's a right old romantic. But it's true enough about going to the toilet.' The bathroom had flooded

110

during the previous year's break-in, leaving the floor unsafe. Hence the broom closet.

Jardine flipped over a page of her magazine. 'Burt Reynolds has seven bathrooms in his home,' she commented.

'One for every dwarf,' muttered Petrie.

Rebus might, in Siobhan's phrase, have an air of knowing exactly where he was going, but in fact he felt like he was going round in circles. He'd visited a few early-opening pubs (near the offices of the daily newspaper; down towards the docks at Leith), social clubs and betting shops, and had asked his question and left his message in all of them. Deek Torrance was either keeping a low profile, or else he'd left the city. If still around, it was unfeasible that he wouldn't at some point stagger into a bar and loudly introduce himself and his thirst. Few people, once introduced, could forget Deek Torrance.

He'd also opened communications with hospitals in Edinburgh and Dundee, to see if either of the Robertson brothers had received surgery for a broken right arm, the old injury found on the Central Hotel corpse.

But now it was time to give up and go check out Operation Moneybags. He'd left Michael still asleep this morning, and likely to remain asleep for quite some time if those pills were anything to go by. The students had tiptoed in at a minute past midnight, 'well kettled' as one of them termed it, having spent Rebus's thirty quid on beverages at a local hostelry. They too had been asleep when Rebus had let himself out of the flat. He hardly dared admit to himself that he liked sleeping rough in his own living-room.

The whole weekend seemed like a strange bad dream now. The drive to Aberdeen, Auntie Ena, Michael . . . then the drive to Perth, the lock-fitting, and too much spare time (even after all that) in which to brood. He wondered

111

how Patience's weekend had gone. She'd be back later today for sure. He'd try phoning again.

He parked in one of the many side streets off Gorgie Road and locked his car. This was not one of the city's safest areas. He hoped Siobhan hadn't worn a green and white scarf to work this morning ... He walked down onto Gorgie Road, where buses were spraying the pavement with some of the morning's rainwater, and was careful not to pause outside the door, careful not to glance across the street at the cab offices. He just pushed the door open and climbed the stairs, then knocked at another door.

Siobhan Clarke herself opened it. 'Morning, sir.' She looked cold, though she had wrapped up well enough. 'Coffee?'

The offer was from her thermos, and Rebus shook his head. Normally during a surveillance, drinks and food could be brought in, but not to *this* surveillance. There wasn't supposed to be any activity in the building, so it would look more than a mite suspicious if someone suddenly appeared at the door with three beakers of tea and a home-delivery pizza. There wasn't even a back entrance to the building.

'How's it going?'

'Slow.' This from Elsa-Beth Jardine, who didn't look at all comfortable. There was an open magazine on her lap. 'Thank God I'm relieved at one o'clock.'

'Think yourself lucky, then,' commented DC Petrie.

Ah, how Rebus liked to see a happy crew. 'It's not supposed to be fun,' he told them. 'It's supposed to be work. If and when we nab Dougary and Co., *that's* when the party begins.' They had nothing to add to this, and neither did Rebus. He walked over to the window and peered out. The window itself was so grimy he doubted anyone could see them through it, and especially not from across the street. But a square had been cleaned off just a little, enough so that any photos would be recognisable.

'Camera working okay?'

'So far,' said Petrie. 'I don't really trust these motorised jobs. If the motor goes, you're buggered. You can't wind on by hand.'

'Got enough batteries?'

'Two back-up sets. They're not going to be a problem.'

Rebus nodded. He knew Petrie's reputation as a solid detective who might climb a little higher up the ladder yet. 'How about the phone?'

'It's connected, sir,' said Siobhan Clarke.

Usually, there would be radio contact between any stake-out and headquarters, but not for Moneybags. The problem was the cab company. The cabs and their home base were equipped with two-way radios, so it was possible that communications from Moneybags to HQ could actually be picked up across the road. There was the added complication, too, that the cab radios might interfere with Moneybags' transmissions.

To avoid these potential disasters, a telephone line had been installed early on Sunday morning. The telephone apparatus sat on the floor near the door. So far it had been used twice: once by Jardine to make a hairdresser's appointment; and once by Petrie to make a bet after he'd checked the day's horse-racing tips in his tabloid. Siobhan intended using it this afternoon to check on Brian's condition. But now Rebus was actually using it to phone St Leonard's.

'Any messages for me?' He waited. 'Oh? That's interesting. Anything else? *What?* Why the hell didn't you tell me that first?' He slammed the phone down. 'Brian's awake,' he said. 'He's sitting up in bed eating chicken soup and watching daytime TV.'

'Either of which could give him a relapse,' said Siobhan. She was wondering what the other message had been.

*

'Hello, Brian.'

'Hello, sir.' Holmes had been listening to a personal hi-fi. He switched it off and slipped the headphones down around his neck. 'Patsy Cline,' he said. 'I've been listening to a lot of her since Nell booted me out.'

'Where did the tape come from?'

'My aunt brought it in, bless her. She knows what I like. It was waiting for me when I woke up.'

Rebus had a sudden thought. They played music to coma victims, didn't they? Maybe they'd been playing Patsy Cline to Holmes. No wonder he'd been a long time waking up.

'I'm finding it hard to take in, though,' Holmes went on. 'I mean, whole days of my life, just gone like that. I wouldn't mind, I mean I like a good sleep. Only I can't remember a bloody thing I dreamt about.'

Rebus sat down by the bedside. The chair was already in place. 'Been having visitors?'

'Just the one. Nell looked in.'

'That's nice.'

'She spent the whole time crying. My face isn't horribly scarred and no one's telling me?'

'Looks as ugly as ever. What about amnesia?'

Holmes smiled. 'Oh no, I remember the whole thing, not that it'll help.'

Holmes really did look fine. It was like the doctors said, the brain shuts all systems down, thinks what damage has been done, effects repairs, and then you wake up. Policeman heal thyself.

'So?'

'So,' said Holmes, 'I'd spent the evening in the Heartbreak Cafe. I can even tell you what I ate.'

'Whatever it was, I'll bet you finished with Blue Suede Choux.'

Holmes shook his head. 'They'd none left. Like Eddie said, it's the fastest mover since the King himself.'

114

'So what happened after you ate?'

'The usual, I sat at the bar drinking and chatting, wondering if any gorgeous young ladies were going to slip onto the stool beside mine and ask if I came there often. I talked with Pat for a while. He was on bar duty that night.' Holmes paused. 'I should explain, Pat is –'

'Eddie's business partner, and maybe a *sleeping* partner too.'

'Now now, no homophobia.'

'Some of my best friends know gays,' Rebus said. 'You've mentioned Calder in the past. I can also tell you he doesn't drive.'

'That's right, Eddie does.'

'Even when he's shit-faced.'

Holmes shrugged. 'I've never made it my business.'

'You will when he knocks some poor old lady down.'

Holmes smiled. 'That car of his might look like a hot-rod, but it's in terrible shape. It barely does forty on the open road. Besides, Eddie's the most, if you will, *pedestrian* driver I know. He's so slow I've seen him overtaken by a skateboard – and that was being carried under somebody's arm at the time.'

'So it was just you and Calder at the bar?'

'Until Eddie joined us, after he'd finished cooking. I mean, there were other people in the place, but no obvious villains.'

'Pray continue.'

'Well, I went to go home. Someone must have been waiting behind the dustbins. Next thing I knew there was a draught up my kilt. I opened my eyes and saw these two nurses washing my tadger.'

'What?'

'That's what woke me up, I swear.'

'It's a medical miracle.'

'The magic sponge,' said Holmes.

115

'So who thumped you, any ideas?'

'I've been mulling it over. Maybe they were after Eddie or Pat.'

'And why would that be?'

Holmes shrugged.

'Don't keep secrets from old Uncle Rebus, Brian. You forget, I can read your mind.'

'Well, you tell *me* then.'

'Could be they've not been paying their dues.'

'You mean protection?'

'Insurance, as people like to call it.'

'Well, maybe.'

'The dynamic duo at the Heartbreak Cafe seem to think maybe it's an unholy alliance of curry house owners disgruntled at the fall-off in trade.'

'I can't see that.'

'Neither can I. Maybe it was nobody, Brian. Maybe nobody was after Eddie and Pat. Maybe they were after *you*. Now why would that be?'

The pink in Holmes' cheeks grew slightly redder. 'You've seen the Black Book?'

'Of course I have. I was looking for clues, so I had a rifle through your stuff. And there it was, all in code, too. Or at least in shorthand, so nobody but another copper would know what you were on about. But I'm another copper, Brian. Now there were a lot of cases in there, but only one that stood out.'

'The Central Hotel.'

'Give the man a cigar. Yes, the Central. A poker game took place, and in attendance were Tam and Eck Robertson, neither of whom crop up in the list of punters at the Central that night. You've been trying to find them. No luck so far?' Holmes shook his head. 'But someone told you all this, didn't they? There's no mention in the files of any poker game. Now,' Rebus leaned closer, 'would I be right in thinking that the person who told you is the

116

mysterious El?' Holmes nodded. 'Then that's all you need to tell me, Brian. Who the hell is El?'

At that moment, a nurse pushed open the door and came in bearing medicine and a lunch tray for Holmes.

'I'm starving,' he explained to Rebus. 'This is my second meal since I woke up.' He lifted the metal cover from the plate. A pale pink slice of meat, watery mashed spuds, and sliced green beans.

'Yum yum,' said Rebus. But Holmes looked keen enough. He scooped some mash and gravy into his mouth and swallowed it down.

'I'd have thought,' he said, 'that since you've figured out the hard part, you wouldn't have had any trouble with El.'

'Sorry to disappoint you. Who is he?'

'It's Elvis,' said Brian Holmes. 'Elvis himself told me.' He lifted another forkful of mush to his lips and started to slurp it down.

12

Rebus studied the menu, finding little to his liking beyond the often painful puns. The Heartbreak Cafe was open all day, but he'd arrived just in time for the special luncheon menu. A foot-long sausage on a roll was predictably if unappetisingly a 'Hound Dog'. Rebus could only hope that there was no literal truth to the appelation. More obscure was the drinks list, with one wine called 'Mama Liked the Rosé'. Rebus decided that he wasn't so hungry after all. Instead, he nursed his 'Teddy' beer at the bar and handed the menu back to the teenage barman.

'Pat's not in then?' he asked casually.

'Doing some shopping. He'll be back later.'

Rebus nodded. 'But Eddie's around?'

'In the kitchen, yeah.' The barman glanced towards the restaurant area. He wore three gold studs in his left ear. 'He won't be much longer, unless he's making something special for tonight.'

'Right,' said Rebus. A few minutes later, he picked up his beer glass and wandered over to a huge jukebox near the toilets. Finding it to be ornamental only, he studied some of the Presley mementoes on the walls, including a signed photograph of the Vegas Elvis and what looked like a rare Sun Records pressing. Both were protected by thick framed glass, and both were picked out by spotlights from the surrounding gloom. Finding himself, as if by chance, at the door to the kitchen, Rebus pushed it open with his shoulder and let it swing shut behind him.

Eddie Ringan was creating. Sweat glistened on his face, thin strands of hair sticking to his brow, as he shook a small frying pan over a gas flame. The set-up was impressive: cleaner than Rebus had expected, with many more cookers and pots and work surfaces. A lot of money had been spent; the Cafe wasn't just a designer façade. Amusingly, it seemed to Rebus, there was different music here from the constant diet of Presley served at the bar. Eddie Ringan was listening to Miles Davis.

The chef hadn't noticed Rebus yet, and Rebus hadn't noticed a trainee chef who'd been fetching something from one of several fridges at the back of the kitchen.

Rebus watched as Eddie, pausing from his work, grabbed a bottle of Jim Beam by its neck and upended it into his mouth, taking it away again with a satisfied exhalation.

'Hey,' said the trainee chef, 'no one's allowed in here.' Eddie looked up from the pan and gave a whoop.

'You're just the man!' he cried. 'The very man! Come over here.'

If anything, he sounded drunker than at their first meeting. But then, at their first meeting there had been the civilising (or at least restricting) presence of Pat Calder, as well as the sobering fact of Brian Holmes's attack.

Rebus walked over to the cooker. He too was starting to sweat in the heat.

'This,' said Eddie Ringan, nodding towards the pan, 'is my latest dish. Pieces of Roquefort cheese *imprisoned* in breadcrumb and spice and fried. Either pan-fried or deep-fried, that's what I'm deciding.'

'Jailhouse Roquefort,' Rebus guessed. Ringan whooped again, losing his balance slightly and sliding back with one foot.

'*Your* idea, Inspector Rabies.'

'I'm flattered, but the name's Rebus.'

'Aye, well, you should be flattered. Maybe we'll gie you a wee mention on the menu. How about that, eh?' He studied the golden nuggets, turning them expertly with a fork. 'I'm giving this lot six minutes. Willie!'

'I'm right here.'

'How long's that been?'

The protégé checked his watch. 'Three and a half. I've put the butter down there next to the eggs.'

'Willie's my assistant, Inspector.'

The exasperation in Willie's voice and expressions made Rebus doubt he would be assisting for much longer. Though younger than Ringan, Willie was about the same size. You wouldn't call him slender. Rebus reckoned chefs were partial to too much R&D. 'Can we talk for a minute?'

'Two and a half minutes if you like.'

'I'd like to know about the Central Hotel.' Ringan didn't seem to hear this, his attention on the contents of the frying-pan. 'You were there the night it burned down.'

El was short for Elvis, and Elvis was code for Eddie Ringan. Holmes hadn't wanted the wrong people getting hold of the Black Book and being able to identify the person who'd been talking. That's why he'd gone an extra step in disguising Ringan's identity.

He'd also made Rebus promise that he wouldn't tell the chef Holmes had shared their secret. It *was* to have been a secret, a little tale spilt from a bottle of bourbon. But Ringan hadn't poured out nearly enough, he'd just given Holmes a taste.

'Did you hear me, Eddie?'

'A minute left, Inspector.'

'You never cropped up on the list of staff because you were moonlighting, working there some nights without the other place you worked at knowing anything about it. So you were able to give a false name, and nobody ever found out it was you there that night, the night of the poker game.'

'Nearly done.' There was more sweat on Eddie Ringan's

face now, and his mouth seemed stiff with suppressed anger.

'I'm nearly done too, Eddie. When did you start on the booze, eh? Just after that night, wasn't it? Because something happened in that hotel. I wonder what it was. Whatever it was, you saw it, and if you don't tell me about it, I'm going to find out anyway, and then I'm going to come back here for you.' To emphasise this, Rebus pushed a finger against the chef's arm.

Ringan snatched the frying-pan and swung it at Rebus, sending bits of Jailhouse Roquefort flying in arcs across the kitchen.

'Get the fuck away from me!'

Rebus dodged the frying-pan, but Ringan was still holding it in front of him, ready to lunge.

'Just you get the fuck out of here! Who told you, anyway?'

'Nobody needed to tell me, Eddie. I worked it out for myself.'

Willie meantime was down on one knee. A hot cube of cheese had caught him smack in the eye.

'I'm dying!' he called. 'Get an ambulance, get a lawyer! This is an industrial injury.'

Eddie Ringan glanced towards the trainee chef, then back at the frying-pan in his hand, then at Rebus, and he began to laugh, the laughter becoming uproarious, hysterical. But at least he put down the pan. He even picked up one of the cheese cubes and took a bite out of it.

'Tastes like shite,' he said, still laughing and spluttering bits of breadcrumb at Rebus.

'Are you going to tell me, Eddie?' Rebus asked calmly.

'I'm going to tell you this: get the fuck out.'

Rebus stood his ground, though Eddie had already turned his back. 'Tell me where I can find the Bru-Head Brothers.'

This brought more laughter.

'Just give me a start, Eddie. Then it'll be off your conscience.'

'I lost my conscience a long time ago, Inspector. Willie, let's get a fresh batch going.'

The young man was still checking for damage. He held one hand across his good eye like a patch. 'I cannae see a thing,' he complained. 'I think the retina's cracked.'

'And the cornea's melted,' added Ringan. 'Come on, I'm hoping to have this on the menu tonight.' He turned to Rebus, making a show of astonishment. 'Still here? A definite case of too many cooks.'

Rebus looked at him with sad, steady eyes. 'Just a start, Eddie.'

'Away tae fuck.'

Slowly, Rebus turned around and pushed open the door.

'Inspector!' He turned his head towards the chef. 'There's a pub in Cowdenbeath called The Midtown. The locals call it the Midden. I wouldn't eat the food there.'

Rebus nodded slowly. 'Thanks for the tip.'

'It's *you* that's supposed to give *me* the tip!' he heard Ringan roar as he exited from the kitchen. He placed his empty glass on the bartop.

'Kitchen's off limits,' the barman informed him.

'More like the outer bloody limits.'

But no, he knew that only now would he be going to the outer limits, back to the haunts of his youth.

13

He had only dropped into St Leonard's to pick up a few things from his desk, but the duty sergeant stopped him short.

'Gentleman here has been waiting to see you. He seems a bit anxious.'

The 'gentleman' in question had been standing in a corner, but was now directly in front of Rebus. 'You don't recognise me?'

Rebus studied the man for a moment longer, and felt an old loathing. 'Oh yes,' he said, 'I recognise you all right.'

'Didn't you get my message?'

This had been the other message relayed to him when he'd called in from Gorgie Road. He nodded.

'Well, what are you going to do?'

'What would you like me to do, Mr McPhail?'

'You've got to stop him!'

'Stop who exactly? And from what?'

'You said you got the message.'

'All I was told was that someone called Andrew McPhail had phoned wanting to speak to me.'

'What I want is bloody protection!'

'Calm down now.' Rebus saw that the desk sergeant was getting ready for action, but he didn't think there would be any need for that.

'What have I got to do?' McPhail was saying. 'You want me to hit you? That'd get me a night in the cells, wouldn't it? I'd be safe there.'

Rebus nodded. 'You'd be safe all right, until we told your cell mates about your past escapades.'

This seemed to calm McPhail down like a bucket of ice. Maybe he was remembering particular incidents during his spell in the Canadian prison. Or maybe it was a less localised fear. Whatever it was, it worked. His tone became quietly plaintive. 'But he'll kill me.'

'Who will?'

'Stop pretending! I know you set him on to me. It had to be you.'

'Humour me,' said Rebus.

'Maclean,' said McPhail. 'Alex Maclean.'

'And who is Alex Maclean?'

McPhail looked disgusted. He spoke in an undertone. 'The wee girl's stepfather. Melanie's stepfather.'

'Ah,' said Rebus, nodding now. He knew immediately what Jack Morton had done, bugger that he was. No wonder McPhail got in touch. And as Rebus had been round to see Mrs MacKenzie, he'd thought Rebus must be behind the whole scheme.

'Has he threatened you?'

McPhail nodded.

'In what way?'

'He came to the house. I wasn't there. He told Mrs MacKenzie he'd be back to get me. Poor woman's in a terrible state.'

'You could always move, get out of Edinburgh.'

'Christ, is that what you want? That's why you've set Maclean on me. Well, I'm staying put.'

'Heroic of you, Mr McPhail.'

'Look, I know what I've done, but that's behind me.'

Rebus nodded. 'And all you've got in front of you is the view from your bedroom.'

'Jesus, *I* didn't know Mrs MacKenzie lived across from a primary school!'

124

'Still, you could move. A location like that, it's bound to rile Maclean further.'

McPhail stared at Rebus. 'You're repulsive,' he said. 'Whatever I've done in my life, I'm willing to bet you've done worse. Never mind about me, I'll look after myself.' McPhail made show of pushing past Rebus towards the door.

'Ca' canny, Mr McPhail,' Rebus called after him.

'Christ,' said the desk sergeant, 'who was that?'

'That,' said Rebus, 'was someone finding out how it feels to be a victim.'

All the same, he felt a bit guilty. What if McPhail *had* been rehabilitated, and Maclean *did* do him some damage? Scared as he was, McPhail might even decide a first strike was his only form of defence. Well, Rebus had slightly more pressing concerns, hadn't he?

In the CID room, he studied the only available mug-shots of Tam and Eck Robertson, taken over five years ago. He got a DC to make him some photocopies, but then had a better idea. There was no police artist around, but that didn't bother Rebus. He knew where an artist could always be found.

It was five o'clock when he got to McShane's Bar near the bottom of the Royal Mile. McShane's was a haven for bearded folk fans and their woolly sweaters. Upstairs, there was always music, be it a professional performer or some punter who'd taken the stage to belt out 'Will Ye Go Lassie Go' or 'Both Sides O' The Tweed'.

Midgie McNair did good business in McShane's sketching flattering likenesses of acquiescent customers, who paid for the privilege and often bought the drinks as well.

At this early hour, Midgie was downstairs, reading a paperback at a corner table. His sketch-pad sat on the table beside him, along with half a dozen pencils. Rebus placed two pints on the table, then sat down and produced the photos of the Bru-Head Brothers.

'Not exactly Butch and Sundance, are they?' said Midgie McNair.

'Not exactly,' said Rebus.

14

John Rebus had once known Cowdenbeath very well indeed, having gone to school there. It was one of those Fife mining communities which had grown from a hamlet in the late nineteenth or early twentieth centuries when coal was in great demand, such demand that the cost of digging it out of the ground hardly entered the equation. But the coalfields of Fife didn't last long. There was still plenty of coal deep underground, but the thin warped strata were difficult (and therefore costly) to mine. He supposed some opencast mining might still be going on – at one time west central Fife had boasted Europe's biggest hole in the ground – but the deep pitshafts had all been filled in. In Rebus's youth there had been three obvious career choices for a fifteen-year-old boy: the pits, Rosyth Dockyard, or the Army. Rebus had chosen the last of these. Nowadays, it was probably the only choice on offer.

Like the towns and villages around it, Cowdenbeath looked and felt depressed: closed down shops and drab chainstore clothes. But he knew that the people were stronger than their situation might suggest. Hardship bred a bitter, quickfire humour and a resilience to all but the most terminal of life's tragedies. He didn't like to think about it too deeply, but inside he felt like he really was 'coming home'. Edinburgh might have been his base for twenty years, but he was a Fifer. 'Fly Fifers', some people called them. Rebus was ready to do battle with some very fly people indeed.

Monday night was the quietest of the week for pubs across the land. The pay packets or dole money had disappeared over the course of the weekend. Monday was for staying in. Not that you would know this from the scene that greeted Rebus as he pushed open the door to the Midden. Its name belittled it; its interior was no worse than many a bar in Edinburgh and elsewhere. Basic, yes, with a red linoleum floor spotted black from hundreds of cigarette dowps. The tables and chairs were functional, and though the bar was not large enough space had been found for a pool table and dartboard. A game of darts was in progress when Rebus entered, and one young man marched around the pool table, potting shot after shot as he squinted through the smoke which rose from the cigarette in his mouth. At a corner table three old men, all wearing flat bunnets, were playing a tense game of dominoes, groups of steady drinkers filling the other tables.

So Rebus had no choice but to stand at the bar. There was just room for one more, and he nodded a greeting to the pint drinkers either side of him. A greeting no one bothered to return.

'Pint of special, please,' he said to the slick-haired barman.

'Special, son, right you are.'

Rebus got the feeling this fiftyish bartender would call even the domino players 'son'. The drink was poured with the proper amount of care, like the ritual it was in this part of the world.

'Special, son, there you are.'

Rebus paid for the beer. It was the cheapest pint he'd bought in months. He started to think about how easy it would be to commute to work from Fife ...

'Pint of spesh, Dod.'

'Spesh, son, right you are.'

The pool player stood just behind Rebus, not quite menacingly. He placed his empty glass on the bartop and

128

waited for it to be refilled. Rebus knew the youth was interested, maybe waiting to see whether Rebus would speak. But Rebus didn't say anything. He just took photocopies of the two drawings out of his jacket pocket and unfolded them. He'd had ten copies of each made up at a newsagent's on the Royal Mile. The originals were safe in the glove compartment of his car; though how safe his car itself was, parked on the poorly lit street outside, was another matter.

He could feel the drinkers either side of him glance at the drawings, and didn't doubt that the youth was having a look too. Still nobody said anything.

'Spesh, son, there you are.' The pool player picked up the glass, spilling some beer onto the sheets of paper. Rebus turned his head towards him.

'Sorry about that.'

Rebus had seldom heard a less sincere tone of voice. 'That's all right,' he said, matching the tone. 'I've got plenty more copies.'

'Oh aye?' The youth took his change from the barman and went back to the pool table, crouching to load coins into the slot. The balls fell with a dull rumble and he started to rack them up, staring at Rebus.

'You do a bit of drawing, eh?'

Rebus, who had been wiping the drawings with his hand, turned to Dod the barman. 'Not me, no. Good though, aren't they?' He turned the drawings around slowly so Dod could get a better look.

'Oh aye, no' bad. I'm no' an expert, like. The only things anybody around here draws are the pension or the dole.' There was laughter at this.

'Or a bowl,' added one drinker. He made the word sound like 'bowel', but Rebus knew what he meant.

'Or a cigarette,' somebody else suggested, but the joke was by now history. The barman nodded towards the drawings. 'Anybody in particular, like?'

Rebus shrugged.

'Could be brothers, eh?'

Rebus turned to the drinker on his left, who had just spoken. 'What makes you say that?'

The drinker twitched and turned to stare at the row of optics behind the bar. 'They look similar.'

Rebus examined the two drawings. As requested, Midgie had aged the brothers five or six years. 'You could be right.'

'Or cousins maybe,' said the drinker on his right.

'Related, though,' Rebus mused.

'I cannae see it myself,' said Dod the barman.

'Look a bit closer,' Rebus advised. He ran his finger over the sheets of paper. 'Same chins, eyes look the same too. Maybe they *are* brothers.'

'Who are they, then?' asked the drinker on his right, a middle-aged man with square unshaven jaw and lively blue eyes.

But Rebus just shrugged again. One of the domino players came to the bar to order a round. He looked like he'd just won a rubber, and clapped his hands together.

'How's it going then, James?' he asked the drinker on Rebus's right.

'No' bad, Matt. Yourself?'

'Ach, just the same.' He smiled at Rebus. 'Havenae seen you in here afore, son.'

Rebus shook his head. 'I've been away.'

'Oh aye?' Three pints had appeared on a metal tray.

'There you go, Matt.'

'Thanks, Dod.' Matt handed over a ten-pound note. As he waited for change, he saw the drawings. 'Butch and Sundance, eh?' He laughed. Rebus smiled warmly. 'Or more like Steptoe and Son.'

'Steptoe and Brother,' Rebus suggested.

'Brothers?' Matt studied the drawings. He was still studying them when he asked, 'Are you the polis then, son?'

'Do I look like the polis?'

'No' exactly.'

'No' fat enough for a start,' said Dod. 'Eh, son?'

'You get skinny polis, though,' argued James. 'What about Stecky Jamieson?'

'Right enough,' said Dod. 'Thon bugger could hide behind a lamp post.'

Matt had picked up the tray of drinks. The other domino players at his table called out that they were 'gasping'. Matt nodded towards the drawings. 'I've seen yon buggers afore,' he said, before moving off.

Rebus drained his glass and ordered another. The drinker on his left finished and, fixing a bunnet to his head, started to make his goodbyes.

'Cheerio then, Dod.'

'Aye, cheerio.'

'Cheerio, James.'

This went on for minutes. The long cheerio. Rebus folded the drawings and put them in his pocket. He took his time over the second pint. There was some talk of football, extra-marital affairs, the nonexistent job market. Mind you, the amount of affairs that seemed to be going on, Rebus was surprised anyone found the time or energy for a job.

'You know what this part of Fife's become?' offered James. 'A giant DIY store. You either work in one, or you shop there. That's about it.'

'True enough,' said Dod, though there was little conviction in his voice.

Rebus finished the second pint and went to visit the gents'. The place stank to high heaven, and the graffiti was poor. Nobody came in for a quiet word, not that he'd been expecting it. On his way back from bathroom to bar he stopped at the dominoes game.

'Matt?' he asked. 'Sorry to interrupt. You didn't say where you thought you'd seen Butch and Sundance.'

'Maybe just the one o' them,' said Matt. The doms had been shuffled and he picked up seven, three in one hand and four in the other. 'It wasnae here, though. Maybe Lochgelly. For some reason, I think it was Lochgelly.' He put the dominoes face down on the tabletop and picked out the one he wished to play. The man next to him chapped.

'Bad sign that, Tam, this early on.'

Bad sign indeed. Rebus would have to go to Lochgelly. He returned to the bar and said his own brief cheerio.

'Or you could draw a fire,' someone at the bar was saying, poking the embers of that long-dead joke.

The drive from Cowdenbeath to Lochgelly took Rebus through Lumphinnans. His father had always made jokes about Lumphinnans; Rebus wasn't sure why, and certainly couldn't recall any of them. When he'd been young, the skies had been full of smoke, every house heated by a coal fire in the sitting room. The chimneys sent up a grey plume into the evening air, but not now. Now, central heating and gas had displaced Old King Coal.

It saddened Rebus, this silence of the lums.

It saddened him, too, that he would have to repeat his performance with the drawings. He'd hoped the Midden would be the start and finish of his quest. Of course, it was always possible Eddie had been setting a false trail in the first place. If so, Rebus would see he got his just deserts, and it wouldn't be Blue Suede Choux.

He did his act in three pubs nursing three half-pints, with no reaction save the usual bad jokes including the 'drawing the pension' line. But in the fourth bar, an understandably understated shack near the railway station, he drew the attention of a keen-eyed old man who had been cadging drinks all round the pub. At the time, Rebus was showing the drawings to a cluster of painters and decorators at the corner of the L-shaped bar.

He knew they were decorators because they'd asked him if he needed any work doing. 'On the fly, like. Cheaper that way.' Rebus shook his head and showed them the drawings.

The old man pushed his way into the group. He looked up at all the faces around him. 'All right, lads? Here, I was decorated in the war.' He cackled at his joke.

'So you keep telling us, Jock.'

'Every fuckin' night.'

'Without fuckin' fail.'

'Sorry, lads,' Jock apologised. He thrust a short thick finger at one of the drawings. 'Looks familiar.'

'Must be a bloody jockey then.' The decorator winked at Rebus. 'I'm no' joking, mister. Jock would recognise a racehorse's bahookey quicker than a human face.'

'Ach,' said Jock dismissively, 'away tae hell wi' you.' And to Rebus: 'Sure you dinnae owe me a drink fae last week ...?'

Five minutes after Rebus glumly left this last pub, a young man arrived. It had taken him some time, visiting all the bars between the Midden and here, asking whether a man had been in with some drawings. He was annoyed, too, at having to break off his pool practice so early. His screwball needed work. There was a competition on Sunday, and he had every intention of winning the £100 prize. If he didn't, there'd be trouble. But meantime, he knew he could do someone a favour by trailing this man who claimed not to be a copper. He knew it because he'd made a phone call from the Midden.

'You'd be doing me a favour,' the person on the other end of the line had said, when the pool player had finally been put through to him, having had to relate his story to two other people first.

It was useful to be owed a favour, so he'd taken off from the Midden, knowing that the man with the drawings

133

was on his way to Lochgelly. But now here he was at the far end of the town; there were no pubs after this until Lochore. And the man had gone. So the pool player made another call and gave his report. It wasn't much, he knew, but it had been time-consuming work all the same.

'I owe you one, Sharky,' the voice said.

Sharky felt elated as he got back into his rusty Datsun. And with luck, he'd still have time for a few games of pool before closing time.

John Rebus drove back to Edinburgh with just desserts on his mind. And Andrew McPhail, and Michael with his tranquillisers, and Patience, and Operation Moneybags, and many other things besides.

Michael was sound asleep when he arrived at the flat. He checked with the students, who were worried that his brother was maybe on some sort of drugs. He assured them the drugs were prescribed rather than proscribed. Then he telephoned Siobhan Clarke at home.

'How did it go today?'

'You had to be there, sir – I could write the book on boredom. Dougary had five visitors all day. He had pizza delivered lunch. Drove home at five-thirty.'

'Any of the visitors interesting?'

'I'll let you see the photographs. Customers, maybe. But they came out with as many limbs as they went in with. Will you be joining us tomorrow?'

'Probably.'

'Only I thought maybe we could talk about the Central Hotel.'

'Speaking of which, have you seen Brian?'

'I popped in after work. He looks great.' She paused. 'You sound tired. Have you been working?'

'Yes.'

'The Central?'

'Christ knows. I suppose so.' Rebus rubbed the back of

his neck. The hangover was starting already.

'You had to buy a few drinks?' Siobhan guessed.

'Yes.'

'And drink a few?'

'Right again, Sherlock.'

She laughed, then tutted. 'And afterwards you drove home. I'd be happy to chauffeur you if it would help.' She sounded like she meant it.

'Thanks, Clarke. I'll bear it in mind.' He paused. 'Know what I'd like for Christmas?'

'It's a long way off.'

'I'd like someone to *prove* that the corpse belongs to one of the Bru-Head Brothers.'

'The body had a broken –'

'I know, I've checked. The hospitals came up with spit.' He paused again. 'Not your problem,' he said. 'I'll see you tomorrow.'

'Good night, sir.'

Rebus sat in silence for a minute or two. Something about his conversation with Siobhan Clarke made him want to talk with Patience. He picked up the receiver again and rang her.

'Hello?'

Ye Gods, not an answering machine!

'Hello, Patience.'

'John.'

'I'd like to talk. Are you ready?'

There was silence, then: 'Yes, I think so. Let's talk.'

John Rebus lay down on the sofa, one hand behind his head. Nobody else used the phone that night.

15

John Rebus was in a good mood that Tuesday morning, for no other reason than that he'd spent what seemed like half the previous night on the phone with Patience. They were going to meet for a drink; he just had to wait for her to get back to him with a place and a time. He was still in a good mood when he opened the ground floor door and started up the stairs towards Operation Moneybags' Gorgie centre of operations.

He could hear voices; nothing unusual about that. But the voices grew in intensity as he climbed, and he opened the door just in time to see a man lunge at DC Petrie and butt him square on the nose. Petrie fell back against the window, knocking over the camera tripod. Blood gushed from his nostrils. Rebus only half took in that two small boys were watching, along with Siobhan Clarke and Elsa-Beth Jardine. The man was pulling Petrie upright when Rebus got an arm lock around him, pinning the man's arms to his side. He pulled Rebus to right and left, trying to throw him off, all the time yelling so loudly it was a wonder nobody on the street below could hear the commotion.

Rebus heaved the man backwards and turned him, so that he lost balance and fell to the floor, where Rebus sat on top of him. Petrie started forward, but the man lashed out with his legs and sent Petrie back into the window, where his elbow smashed the glass. Rebus did what he had to do. He punched the man in the throat.

'What the hell's going on here?' he asked. The man was gasping but still struggling. 'You, stop it!' Then something hit Rebus on the back of his head. It was the clenched fist of one of the boys, and it hit him right on his burnt patch of scalp. He screwed shut his eyes, fighting the stinging pain of the blow and a nausea in his gut, right where his muesli and tea with honey were sitting.

'Leave my dad alone!'

Siobhan Clarke grabbed the boy and dragged him off.

'Arrest that little bugger,' Rebus said. Then, to the boy's father: 'I mean it, too. If you don't calm down, I'm going to have *him* charged with assault. How would you like that?'

'He's too young,' gasped the man.

'Is he?' said Rebus. 'Are you sure?'

The man thought about it and calmed down.

'That's better.' Rebus rose from the man's chest. 'Now is *someone* going to explain all this to me?'

It was quickly explained, once Petrie had been sent off to find a doctor for his nose and the boys had been sent home. The man was called Bill Chilton, and Bill Chilton didn't like squatters.

'Squatters?'

'That's what Wee Neilly told me.'

'Squatters?' Rebus turned to Siobhan Clarke. She'd been downstairs to check no passers-by had been injured by falling glass, and more importantly to explain the 'accident'.

'The two boys,' she said now, 'came barging in. They said they sometimes played here.'

Rebus stopped her and turned to Chilton. 'Why isn't Neil at school?'

'He's been suspended for fighting.'

Rebus nodded. 'He's got a fair punch on him.' The

137

back of his head throbbed agreement. He turned back to Siobhan.

'They asked us what we were doing, and Ms Jardine' – at this Elsa-Beth Jardine lowered her head – 'told them we were squatters.'

'Just joking,' Jardine found it necessary to add. Rebus feigned surprise, and she lowered her eyes again, blushing furiously.

'DC Petrie joined in, the boys cleared out, and we all had a laugh about it.'

'A laugh?' Rebus said. 'It wasn't a laugh, it was a breach of security.' He sounded as furious as he looked, so that even Siobhan turned her eyes away from his. He now turned his gaze on Bill Chilton.

'Well,' Chilton continued, 'Neil came home and told me there were squatters here. We've had a lot of that going on this past year or two, deserted tenement flats being broken open and used for all sorts of things ... drug pushing and that. Some of us are doing something about it.'

'What are we talking about here, Mr Chilton? Vigilante tactics? Pickaxe handles at dawn?'

Chilton was unabashed. '*You* lot are doing bugger all!'

'So you came up here looking to scare the squatters off?'

'Before they got a toe-hold, aye.'

'And?'

Chilton said nothing.

'And,' Rebus said for him, 'you started shouting the odds at DC Petrie, who started shouting back that he was a police officer and you'd better bugger off. Only by that time you were too fired up to back off. Got a bit of a temper, Mr Chilton? Maybe it's rubbed off on Neilly, eh? Did *you* get into a lot of fights at school?'

'What the hell's that got to do with anything?' Chilton's anger was rising again. Rebus raised a pacifying hand.

'It's a serious offence, assaulting a police officer.'

'Mistaken identity,' said Chilton.

'Even after he'd identified himself?'

Chilton shrugged. 'He never showed me any ID.'

Rebus raised an eyebrow. 'You're very knowledgeable about procedure. Maybe you've been in this sort of trouble before, eh?' This shut Chilton's mouth. 'Maybe if I go down the station and look you up on the computer ... what would this be, second offence? Third? Might we be talking about a wee trip to Saughton jail?' Chilton was looking decidedly uncomfortable, which was exactly what Rebus wanted.

'Of course,' he said, 'we could always shut the book on this one.' Chilton looked interested. '*If*,' Rebus warned, 'you could keep your gob shut about it. *And* get Neil and his pal to forget they saw anything.'

Chilton nodded towards the camera. 'You're watching somebody, eh? A stake-out?'

'Best if you don't know, Mr Chilton. Do we have a deal?'

Chilton thought about it, then nodded.

'Good,' said Rebus, 'now get the fuck out of here.'

Chilton knew when he was being made an offer. He got the fuck out of there. Rebus shook his head.

'Sir —'

'Shut up and listen,' Rebus told Siobhan Clarke. 'This could've blown the whole thing. Maybe it has, we won't know for a day or two. Meanwhile, get that camera set up again and get back to work. Phone HQ and get someone in here to board up the window, leaving a big enough hole for the camera. Either that or we need a new pane of glass.

'And listen to me, the two of you.' He raised a warning finger. 'Nobody gets to know about this, *nobody*. It's forgotten as of now, understand?'

They understood. What they did not understand perhaps was exactly why Rebus wanted it kept quiet. It wasn't that he feared the early termination of Operation Moneybags – as far as he was concerned, the whole project was doomed to failure anyway. No, it was another fear altogether, the fear that Detective Inspector Alister Flower, safe and snug in the Firth Pub with his own surveillance crew, would find out. By God, that would mean trouble, more trouble than Rebus was willing to contemplate.

A pity then that he hadn't managed to say anything to DC Peter Petrie, who went back to St Leonard's for a change of shirt. The blood on his T-shirt might have been mistaken for tomato sauce or old tea, but there was no doubting the cause of the white gauze pad which had been taped across his nose and half his face. And when questioned, Peter Petrie quite gladly told his story, embellishing it only a little – as, for example, in exaggerating his assailant's size, skill, and speed of attack. There were sympathetic smiles and shakes of the head, and the same comment was uttered by more than one fellow officer.

'Wait till Flower hears about this.'

By lunchtime, Flower had heard from several sources about the giant who had wreaked such havoc to the Gorgie surveillance.

'Dearie me,' he said, sipping an orange juice laced with blue label vodka. 'That's terrible. I wonder if Chief Inspector Lauderdale knows? Ach, of course he does, Rebus wouldn't try to keep a thing like that from him, would he?' And he smiled so warmly at the DC seated beside him that the DC got quite worried, really quite worried about his boss . . .

Siobhan picked up the telephone.

'Hello?' She watched John Rebus staring out of the broken window. He'd been watching the taxi offices for half an hour, so deep in thought that neither she nor Jardine had uttered a word to one another above a whisper. 'It's for you, sir.'

Rebus took the receiver from her. It was CID with a message to relay.

'Go ahead.'

'From someone called Pat Calder. He says a Mr Ringan has disappeared.'

'Disappeared?'

'Yes, and he wanted you to know. Do you want us to do anything this end?'

'No thanks, I'll go have a word myself. Thanks for letting me know.' Rebus put down the phone.

'Who's disappeared?' Siobhan asked.

'Eddie Ringan.'

'The Heartbreak Cafe?'

Rebus nodded. 'I was only speaking to him yesterday. He threatened me with a panful of hot cheese.' Siobhan was looking interested, but Rebus shook his head. 'You stay here, at least until Petrie gets back.' The Heartbreak Cafe was only five minutes away. Rebus wondered if Calder would be there. A kitchen without a chef, after all, it was hardly worth opening for the day ...

But when Rebus arrived, the Cafe was doing a brisk trade in early lunches. Calder, acting as maitre d', waved to Rebus when he entered. Passing the same young barman as yesterday, Rebus gave him a wink. Calder was looking frantic.

'What the hell did you say to Eddie yesterday?'

'What do you mean?'

'Come off it, you had a stand-up row, didn't you? I knew something was wrong. He was edgy as hell all last night, and his cooking went to pot.' Calder saw no humour in this. 'You must have said *some*thing.'

'Who told you?'

Calder cocked his head towards the kitchen. 'Willie.'

Rebus nodded understanding. 'And today, Willie gets his chance for fame and fortune.'

'He's doing the lunches, if that's what you mean.'

'So when did Eddie go missing?'

'After we closed last night, he went off to look for some club or other. One of those moveable feasts that takes over a warehouse for one night a week.'

'You didn't fancy it yourself?'

Calder wrinkled his nose in distaste.

'Would this be a club for gentlemen, Mr Calder?'

'A gay club, yes. No secret there, Inspector. It's all quite legit.'

'I'm sure it is. And Mr Ringan didn't come home?'

'No.'

'So maybe he found someone else to go home with . . .?'

'Eddie's not that type.'

'Then what type is he?'

'The *faithful* type, believe me. He often goes out drinking, but he always comes back.'

'Until now.'

'Yes.'

Rebus considered. 'Bit early yet to start a missing person file. We usually give it at least forty-eight hours, if there's no other evidence.'

'What sort of evidence?'

'Well, a body, for example.'

Calder turned his head away. 'Christ,' he said.

'Look, I'm sure there's nothing to worry about.'

'I'm not,' said Pat Calder.

No, and neither was John Rebus.

Calder slapped a smile on his face as a couple entered the Cafe. He picked up two menus and asked them to follow him to a table. They were in their early twenties and dressed fashionably, the man looking like he'd walked out of a 1930s gangster flick, the woman like she'd put on her wee sister's skirt by mistake.

142

When Calder came back he spoke in an undertone. 'Someone should tell her you can't hide acne with pan-stick. You know, Eddie hasn't been the same since the night Brian was attacked.'

'Brian's okay now, by the way.'

'Yes, Eddie rang the hospital yesterday.'

'He didn't visit, though?'

'We hate hospitals, too many friends dying in them lately.'

'The news about Brian didn't cheer him up?'

Calder pursed his lips. 'I suppose it did for a little while.' He pulled a notebook and pen out of his pocket. 'Must go and see what they want to drink.'

Rebus nodded. 'I'll just have a word with Willie and your barman, see what they think.'

'Fine. Lunch is on the house.' Rebus shook his head. 'We won't poison you, Inspector.'

'It's not that,' said Rebus. 'It's all this Presley stuff on the walls. It fair takes away my appetite.'

Willie the trainee chef looked like he was enjoying his day as ruler of all he surveyed. Flustered as he was, with no one to help him, still he gave off an air of never wanting things to change.

'Remember me, Willie?'

Willie glanced up. 'Jailhouse Roquefort?' He went back to shimmying pans, then started to chop a bunch of fresh parsley. Rebus marvelled at how speedily he worked with the knife mere millimetres from his fingertips.

'You here about Eddie? He's a mad bastard that, but a brilliant chef.'

'Must be fun to be in charge though?'

'It would be if I got the credit, but those buggers out there probably think the great Eduardo's prepared each dish of the day. Like Pat says, if they knew he wisnae here, they'd go off for a tandoori businessman's lunch at half the price.'

Rebus smiled. 'Still, being in charge ...'

Willie stopped chopping. 'What? You think I've got Eddie stashed away in my coal bunker? Just so I can have a day of tearing around like a mad-arsed fly?' He waved his knife towards the kitchen door. 'Pat might lend a hand, but no, he's got to be out there buttering up the clientele. Butter Pat, that's his name. If I was going to do away with either one of them, it'd be the one right outside that door.'

'You're taking it very seriously, Willie. Eddie's only been missing overnight. Could be sleeping it off in the gutter somewhere.'

'That's not what Pat thinks.'

'And what do *you* think?'

Willie tasted from a steaming vat. 'I think I've put too much cream in the *potage*.'

'It's the way Elvis would have wanted it,' commented Rebus.

The barman, whose name was Toni ('with an i'), poured Rebus a murky half pint of Cask Conditioned.

'This looks as conditioned as my hair.'

'I know a good hairdresser if you're interested.'

Rebus ignored the remark, then decided to ignore the beer too. He waited while Toni chattily served two student types at the other end of the bar.

'How did Eddie seem after I left yesterday?'

'What's the name of that Scorsese film?'

'*Taxi Driver*?'

The barman shook his head. '*Raging Bull*. That was Eddie.'

'He was like that all evening?'

'I didn't see him much. By the time he comes out of the kitchen, I'm putting on my coat to go home.'

144

'Was there anyone ... *unusual* in the bar last night?'

'You get a mixed crowd in here. Any particular *type* of unusual?'

'Forget it.'

It looked like Toni-with-an-i already had.

16

It was beginning to look like the circle was now complete. Eddie told Holmes something about the body in the Central Hotel. Holmes tried to find out more, by going after the Bru-Head Brothers. Then Rebus came along to offer help. Now all three had been warned off in some way or other. Well, he *hoped* Eddie was just being warned off. He hoped it wasn't more drastic. Everyone knew the chef had trouble keeping his mouth shut after a drink, and 'after a drink' seemed to be his permanent state. Yes, Rebus was worried. They'd tried scaring him off and only made him more determined. So would they now pull another stunt? Or would they perhaps revert to more certain means of silence?

Rebus's face was as dark as the sky when he walked back into St Leonard's, only to be ordered immediately to Lauderdale's office. Lauderdale was pouring whisky into three glasses.

'Ah, there you are.'

Rebus could not deny it. 'Summoned by Bell's, sir.' He accepted the glass, trying not to look at Alister Flower's beaming face. The three men sat down.

'Cheers,' offered Lauderdale.

'Here's tae us,' said Flower.

Rebus just drank.

'Been having a bit of bother, John?' Lauderdale was positioning his half-empty glass on the desk. When he used Rebus's first name, Rebus knew he was in trouble.

146

'I don't know about that, sir. There was a minor hiccup this morning, all taken care of.'

Lauderdale nodded, still seeming affable. Flower had crossed his legs, at ease with the world. When Lauderdale next spoke, he held up a finger to accompany each point.

'Two schoolkids barge in on you. Then DC Petrie gets into a punch-up with a complete stranger. A window is smashed, and so is Petrie's nose. DC Clarke's down at street level trying to brush away broken glass and curious passers-by.' He looked up from his full hand. 'Any possibility, John, that Operation Moneybags has been placed in jeopardy?'

'No possibility, sir.' Rebus held up one finger. 'The man won't talk, because if he does we'll charge him with assault.' A second finger. 'And the boys won't talk because the father will warn them not to.' He held his two fingers in the air, then lowered his hand.

'With all due respect, sir,' the Little Weed was saying, 'we've got a fight and a broken window in what was supposed to be a deserted building. People are nosy, it's human nature. They'll be looking up at that window tomorrow, and they'll be wondering. Any movement behind the window will be noticed.'

Lauderdale turned to Rebus. 'John?'

'What Inspector Flower says is true, sir, as far as it goes. But people are quick to forget. What they'll see tomorrow is a new window, end of story. Nobody saw anything from the taxi offices, and even if they heard the glass, it's not like it doesn't happen every day along Gorgie.'

'Even so, John ...'

'Even so, sir, it was a mistake. I've already made that clear to DC Clarke.' He could have told them that it was all the fault of the woman from Trading Standards, but making excuses made you seem weak. Rebus could take

147

this on the chin. He'd even take it on the back of his scalp if it would get him out of the office any faster. The aromas of whisky and body odour were making him slightly queasy.

'Alister?'

'Well, sir, you know my view on the subject.'

Lauderdale nodded. 'John,' he said, 'a lot of planning has gone into Operation Moneybags, and there's a lot at stake. If you're going to let a couple of kids wander into the middle of the surveillance, maybe it's time you rethought your priorities. For example, those files beside your desk. That stuff's five years old. Get your brain back to the here and now, understand?'

'Yes, sir.'

'We know you must have been affected by the attack on DS Holmes. What I'm asking is, are you up to helping run Operation Moneybags?'

Ah, here it was. The Little Weed wanted the surveillance for himself. He wanted to be the one to bring in Dougary.

'I'm up to it, sir.'

'No more fuck-ups then, understood?'

'Understood, sir.'

Rebus would have said anything to shorten the meeting; well, just about anything. But he was damned if he was going to hand *anything* to Flower, least of all a case like this, even if he *did* think it a waste of time. Get back to the here and now, Lauderdale had said. But when Rebus left the office, he knew exactly where his brain was heading: back to the there and then.

By late afternoon, he decided that he had only two options regarding the Central Hotel, only two people left who might help. He telephoned one, and after a little persuasion was able to arrange an immediate interview.

'There may be interruptions,' the secretary warned. 'We're very busy just now.'

'I can put up with interruptions.'

Twenty minutes later, he was ushered into a small wood-panelled office in a well-maintained old stone building. The windows looked out onto uglier new constructions of corrugated metal and shining steel. Steam billowed from pipes, but indoors you miraculously lost that strong brewery smell.

The door opened and a thirtyish man ambled into the room.

'Inspector Rebus?'

They shook hands. 'Good of you to see me at such short notice, sir.'

'Your call was intriguing. I still like a bit of intrigue.'

Close up, Rebus saw that Aengus Gibson was probably still in his twenties. The sober suit, the spectacles and short sleek hair made him seem older. He went to his desk, slipped off his jacket, and placed it carefully over the back of a large padded chair. Then he sat down and began rolling up his shirtsleeves.

'Sit yourself down, Inspector, please. Now, something to do with the Central Hotel, you said?'

There were papers laid out on the desk, and Gibson appeared to be browsing through them as Rebus spoke, but Rebus knew the man was taking in every word.

'As you know, Mr Gibson, the Central burnt down five years ago. The cause of the fire was never satisfactorily explained, but more disturbing still was the finding of a body, a body with a bullet-hole through the heart. The body has never been identified.'

Rebus paused. Gibson took off his glasses and laid them on top of the papers. 'I knew the Central quite well, Inspector. I'm sure my reputation precedes you into this office.'

'Past and present reputations, sir.'

Gibson made no show of hearing this. 'I was a bit wild in my youth, and a wilder crowd you'd be hard pressed to find than that congregating in the Central Hotel in *those* days.'

'You'd be in your early twenties, sir, hardly a "youth".'

'Some of us take longer to grow up than others.'

'Why did you arrange to meet Matthew Vanderhyde there?'

Gibson sat back in his chair. 'Ah, now I see why you're here. Well, I thought Uncle Matthew might appreciate the seedy glory of the Central. He was wild himself in years past.'

'And maybe also you thought it might shock him?'

'Nobody could shock Matthew Vanderhyde, Inspector.' He smiled. 'But perhaps you're right. Yes, I'm sure there was an element of that. I knew damned fine that my father had asked him to talk to me. So I arranged to meet in the worst place I could think of.'

'I could probably have helped find a few worse places than the Central.'

'Me too, really. But the Central was ... well, *central*.'

'And the two of you talked?'

'He talked. I was supposed to listen. But when you're with a blind man, Inspector, you don't need to put up any pretence. No need for glazed eyes and all that. I think I read the paper, tried the crossword, watched the TV. It didn't seem to matter to him. He was doing my father a favour, that was all.'

'But pretty soon afterwards you put your "Black Aengus" days behind you.'

'That's true, yes. Maybe Uncle Matthew's words had an effect after all.'

'And after the meeting?'

'We thought of having dinner together – not, I might add, in the Central. Filthiest kitchens I've ever seen. But I think I had a prior appointment with a young lady. Well, not that young, actually. Married, I seem to recall. Sometimes I miss those days. The media call me a reformed character. It's an easy cliché, but damned hard to live up to.'

'Your name never appeared on the official list of the Central's customers that night.'

'An oversight.'

'One you could have corrected by coming forward.'

'Giving yet more fuel to the newspapers.'

'What if they found out now that you *were* there?'

'Well, Inspector, that wouldn't be fuel.' Aengus Gibson's eyes were warm and clear. 'That would be an incendiary.'

'Is there anything you can tell me about that night, sir?'

'You seem to know all of it. I was in the bar with Matthew Vanderhyde. We left hours before the place caught fire.'

Rebus nodded. 'Have you ever been on the hotel's first floor, sir?'

'What an extraordinary question. It was *five years ago*.'

'A long time, certainly.'

'And now the case is being reopened?'

'In a way, sir, yes. We can't give too many details.'

'That's all right, I'll get my father to ask the Chief Constable. They're good friends, you know.'

Rebus kept silent. There was no case. Nothing he could present to his superiors would cause them to reopen it. He knew he was in this all on his own, and for not very good reasons. There was a brisk tap at the door, and an older man came into the office. His face strongly resembled Aengus Gibson's, but both face and body were much leaner. Ascetic was the word that came to mind. Broderick Gibson would rarely loosen his tight-knotted tie or undo the top button of his shirt. He wore a woollen V-neck below his suit jacket. Rebus had seen church elders like him. Their faces persuaded more guilt-money into the collection.

'Sorry to butt in,' Broderick Gibson said. 'These need a

look-over before tomorrow morning.' He placed a folder on the desk.

'Father, this is Inspector Rebus. Inspector, Broderick Gibson, my father.'

And the man who had started Gibson's Brewing from his garden shed back in the 1950s. Rebus shook the firm hand.

'No trouble I hope, Inspector?'

'None at all, sir,' replied Rebus.

Broderick Gibson turned to his son. 'You haven't forgotten that do tonight for the SSPCC?'

'No, father. Eight o'clock?'

'Damned if I can remember.'

'I think it's eight o'clock.'

'You're right, sir,' said Rebus.

'Oh?' Aengus Gibson looked surprised. 'Will you be there yourself?'

But Rebus shook his head. 'I read a piece about it in the paper.' He was so far below these people on the social ladder, he wondered if they could see him at all. As they'd climbed, they'd sawn off the rungs behind them. Rebus could only peer up into the clouds, catching a glimpse every now and then. But they *all* liked to be liked by the police. Which was probably why Broderick Gibson insisted on shaking Rebus's hand again before leaving.

With his father gone, Aengus Gibson seemed to relax. 'I'm sorry, I should have asked you before – would you like tea or coffee? I know you're on duty, so I won't ask if you'd like to try a beer.'

'Actually, sir,' said Rebus, glancing at the clock on the wall, 'I finished work five minutes ago.'

Aengus Gibson laughed and went to a large cupboard which, when opened, revealed three bar-pumps and a gathering of sparkling pint and half-pint glasses. 'The Dark is very good today,' he said.

152

'Dark's fine, but just a half.'

'A half of Dark it is.'

In fact, Rebus managed another half, this time of the pale ale. But it was the taste of the Dark that stayed with him as he drove back out through the brewery's wrought-iron gates. Gibson's Dark. The Gibsons, father and son, were dark, all right. You had to look beneath the surface to see it, but it was there. To the outside world, Aengus Gibson might be a changed man, but Rebus could see the young man was just barely in control of himself. He even wondered if Gibson might be on mood control drugs of some kind. He had spent some time in a private 'nursing' home – euphemism for psychiatric care. At least, that was the story Rebus had heard. He thought maybe he'd do a bit of digging, just to satisfy his curiosity. He was curious about one small detail in particular, one thing Aengus Gibson had said. He not only knew the kitchens of the Central Hotel were filthy – he'd *seen* them.

John Rebus found that very interesting indeed.

He returned to St Leonard's and was relieved to find no sign of Lauderdale or Little Weed. He'd forgotten to visit Holmes, so telephoned the hospital instead. He knew how it went at the Infirmary; they could wheel a payphone to your bed.

'Brian?'

'Hello there. I've just had a visit from Nell.' He sounded bright. Rebus hoped he wasn't just getting her sympathy vote.

'How is she?'

'She's okay. Any progress?'

Rebus thought about the past twenty-four hours. A lot of work. 'No,' he said, 'no progress.' He decided not to tell Holmes that Eddie Ringan was missing: he might worry himself back into relapse.

'Are you thinking of giving up?'

'I've got a lot on my plate, Brian, but no, I'm not giving up.'

"Thanks.'

Rebus almost blurted out, It's not just for you now, it's for my brother too. Instead, he told Holmes to take care, and promised him a visit soon.

'Better make it *very* soon, they're letting me out tomorrow or the day after.'

'That's good.'

'I don't know ... there's this nurse in here ...'

'Ach, away with ye!' But Rebus remembered a nurse who had treated his scalp, a nurse he'd become too friendly with. That had been the start of the trouble with Patience. 'Be careful,' he ordered, putting down the phone.

His next call was to the local newspaper. He spoke to someone there for a few minutes, after which he tried calling Siobhan Clarke in Gorgie. But there was no answer. Obviously Dougary had clocked off for the day, and with him her surveillance. Well, it was time for Inspector Rebus to clock off too. On his way out, he heard the unmistakable brag of Alister Flower's voice heading towards him. Rebus dodged into another office and waited for Flower and his underlings to pass. They hadn't been talking about him, which was something. He felt only a little ashamed at hiding. Every good soldier knew when to hide.

17

Michael was up and about that evening, doing a fair imitation of a telly addict. He held the remote control like it was a pacemaker, and stared deeply at anything on the screen. Rebus began to wonder about the dosages he'd been taking. But there still seemed to be a fair number of tablets in the bottle.

He went out and bought fish suppers from the local chip shop. It wasn't the best of stuff, but Rebus didn't feel like driving the distance to anywhere better. He remembered the chip shop in their home town, where the fryer would spit into the fat to check how hot it was. Michael smiled at the story, but his eyes never left the TV. He pushed chips into his mouth, chewing slowly, picking batter off the fish and eating that before attacking the fatty white flesh.

'Not bad chips,' Rebus commented, pouring Irn-Bru for both of them. He was waiting for Patience's phone call, giving the time and place for their meet. But whenever the phone did ring, it was for the students.

It rang for a fifth or sixth time, and Rebus picked up the receiver. 'Edinburgh University answering service?'

'It's me,' said Siobhan Clarke.

'Oh, hello there.'

'Don't sound *too* excited.'

'What can I do for you, Clarke?'

'I wanted to apologise for this morning.'

'Not entirely your fault.'

155

'I should have told those boys who we really were. I've been going over it again and again in my head, what I should have done.'

'Well, you won't do it again.'

'No, sir.' She paused. 'I heard you were carpeted.'

'You mean by the Chief Inspector?' Rebus smiled. 'More like a fireside rug than a length of Wilton. How's the window?'

'Boarded up. The glass'll be replaced overnight.'

'Anything of interest today?'

'You were there for it, sir. Petrie came back in the afternoon.'

'Oh yes, how was he?'

'Bandaged up like the Elephant Man.'

Rebus knew that if anyone had talked about the morning's incident – and someone had – it must be Petrie. He'd little sympathy. 'I'll see you tomorrow.'

'Yes, sir. Goodnight.'

'What was all that about?' asked Michael.

'Nothing.'

'I thought that's what you'd say. Is there any more Irn-Bru?'

Rebus passed him the bottle.

When Patience hadn't phoned by ten, he gave up and started to concentrate on the TV. He had half a mind to leave the receiver off its cradle. The next call came ten minutes later. There was tremendous background noise, a party or a pub. A bad song was being badly sung nearby.

'Turn that down a bit, Mickey.' Michael hit the mute button, silencing a politician on the news. 'Hello?'

'Is that you, Mr Rebus?'

'It's me.'

'Chick Muir here.' Chick was one of Rebus's contacts.

'What is it, Chick?' The song had come to an end, and Rebus heard clapping, laughter, and whistles.

'That fellow you were wanting to see, he's about twenty feet away from me with a treble whisky up at his nose.'

'Thanks, Chick. I'll be right there.'

'Wait a second, don't you want to know where I am?'

'Don't be stupid, Chick. I *know* where you are.'

Rebus put the receiver down and looked over at Mickey, who seemed to have fallen asleep. He switched off the television, and went to get his jacket.

It was a nap Chick Muir had been calling from the Bowery, a late-opening dive near the bottom of Easter Road. The pub had been called Finnegan's until a year ago, when a new owner had come up with the 'inspired' change of name, because, as he explained, he wanted to see loads of bums on seats.

He got bums all right, some of whom wouldn't have looked amiss in the original Bowery. He also got some students and perennial hard drinkers, partly because of the pub's location but mostly because of the late licence. There had never been any trouble though, well, none to speak of. Half the drinkers in the Bowery feared the other half, who meantime were busy fearing *them*. Besides which, it was rumoured Big Ger gave round-the-clock insurance – for a price.

Chick Muir often drank there, though he managed not to participate in what was reckoned to be Edinburgh's least musical karaoke. Eddie Ringan for one would have died on the spot at the various awful deaths suffered by 'Hound Dog' and 'Wooden Heart'. Off-key and out of condition, the singers could transform a simple word like 'crying' into a multi-syllabled meaningless drawl. Huh-kuh-rye-a-yeng was an approximation of the sound that greeted Rebus as he pulled at the double doors to the pub and slitted his eyes against the cigarette fug.

As 'Crying in the Chapel' came to its tearful end, Rebus felt a hand squeeze his arm.

'You made it then.'

'Hullo, Chick. What are you having?'

'A double Grouse would hit the spot, not that I believe they keep real Grouse in their Grouse bottles.' Chick Muir grinned, showing two rows of dull gold teeth. He was a foot and a half shorter than Rebus, and looked in this crowd like a wee boy lost in the woods. 'Still,' he said, 'it might not be Grouse, but it's a quarter gill.'

Well, there was logic in that somewhere. So Rebus pushed his way to the bar and shouted his order. There was applause all around as a favourite son of song took the stage. Rebus glanced along the bar and saw Deek Torrance, looking no more drunk or sober than the last time they'd met. As Rebus was paying for his drinks (he'd never to wait; they knew him in here) Torrance saw him, and gave a nod and a wave. Rebus indicated that he had to take the drinks but would be back, and Torrance nodded again.

The music had started up. Oh please, no, thought Rebus. Not 'Little Red Rooster'. On the video, a cockerel seemed to be taking an interest in the blonde farm-girl who had come out to collect the morning eggs.

'Here you are, Chick. Cheers.'

'Slainte.' Chick took a sip, savoured, then shook his head. 'I'm sure this isn't Grouse. Did you see him?'

'I saw him.'

'And it's the right chap?'

Rebus handed over a folded tenner, which Chick pocketed. 'It's him, all right.'

And indeed, Deek Torrance was squeezing his way towards them through the crush. But he stopped short and leaned over another drinker to tap Rebus's shoulder.

'John, just going –' He yanked his head towards the toilets at the side of the stage. 'Back in a min.' Rebus nodded his understanding and Torrance moved away again through the tide. Chick Muir sank his whisky. 'I'll make myself scarce,' he said.

'Aye, see you around, Chick.' Chick nodded and, placing his glass on a table, made for the exit. Rebus tried to shut out 'Little Red Rooster', and when this failed he followed Torrance to the toilets. He saw Deek having a word with the DJ on the stage, then pushing open the door of the gents'. Rebus glared at the singer as he passed, but the crowd was whipping the middle-aged man to greater and greater depths.

Deek was at the communal urinal, laughing at a cartoon on the wall. It showed two football players in Hearts strips involved in an act of buggery, and above it was the caption 'Jam Tarts – Well Stuffed!' It was the sort of thing you had to expect on Easter Road. In a pub somewhere in Gorgie there would be a similar cartoon portraying two Hibernian players. Rebus checked that no one else was in the gents'. Deek, looking over his shoulder, spotted him.

'John, I thought for a minute you were a willie-watcher.'

But Rebus was in serious mood. 'I need you to get me something, Deek.'

Torrance grunted.

'Remember when you said you could lay your hands on anything?'

'Anything from a shag to a shooter,' quoted Deek.

'The latter,' Rebus said simply. Deek Torrance looked like he might be about to comment. Instead, he grunted, zipped his fly, and went over to the washbasin.

'You could get into trouble.'

'I could.'

Torrance dried his hands on the filthy roller-towel. 'When would you need it?'

'ASAP.'

'Any particular model?' They were both serious now, talking in quiet, level tones.

'Whatever you can get will be fine. How much?'

'Anything up to a couple of hundred. You sure you want to do this?'

'I'm sure.'

'You could get a licence, make it legit.'

'I could.'

'But you probably won't.'

'You don't want to know, Deek.'

Deek grunted again. The door swung open and a young man, grinning from one side of his mouth while holding a cigarette in the other, breezed in. He ignored the two men and made for the urinal.

'Give me a phone number.' The youth half-glanced over his shoulder at them. 'Eyes front, son!' Torrance snarled at him. 'Guide dogs are gey expensive these days!'

Rebus tore a sheet from his notepad. 'Two numbers,' he said. 'Home and work.'

'I'll be in touch.'

Rebus pulled open the door. 'Buy you a drink?'

Torrance shook his head. 'I'm heading off.' He paused. 'You're sure about this?'

John Rebus nodded.

When Deek had gone, he bought himself another drink. He was shaking, his heart racing. A good-looking woman had been singing 'Band of Gold', and adequately too. She got the biggest cheer of the night. The DJ came to the microphone and repeated her name. There were more cheers as her boyfriend helped her down from the stage. His fingers were covered with gold rings. Now the DJ was introducing the next act.

'He's chosen to sing for us that great old number "King of the Road". So let's have a big hand for John Rebus!'

There was some applause, and the people who knew him lowered their drinks and looked towards where Rebus stood at the bar.

'You bastard, Deek!' he hissed. The DJ was looking out over the crowd.

'John, are you still with us?' The audience were looking around too. Someone, Rebus realised later, must have pointed him out, for suddenly the DJ was announcing that John was a shy one but he was standing at the bar with the black padded jacket on and his head buried in his glass. 'So let's coax him up here with an extra big hand.'

There was an extra big hand for John Rebus as he turned to face the crowd. It was fortunate indeed, he later decided, that Deek hadn't given him a gun then and there. Just the one bullet would have done.

Deek Torrance hated himself, but he made the phone call anyway. He made it from a public box beside a patch of waste ground. Despite the late hour, some children were riding their bikes noisily across the churned-up tarmac. They had set up a ramp from two planks and a milk crate, and launched themselves into darkness, landing heavily on their suffering tyres.

'It's Deek Torrance,' he said when the telephone was answered. He knew he would have to wait while his name was passed along. He rested his forehead against the side of the call-box. The plastic was cool. We all grow up, he said to himself. It's not much fun, but we all do it. No Peter Pans around these days.

Someone was on the line now. The telephone had been picked up at the other end.

'It's Deek Torrance,' he repeated, quite unnecessarily. 'I've got a bit of news ...'

18

Rebus was at work surprisingly early on Wednesday morning. He'd never been known as the earliest of arrivals, and his presence in the CID room made his more punctual colleagues look twice, just to be sure they weren't still warm and safe and dreaming in their beds.

They didn't get too close though, an early morning Rebus not being in the best of humours. But he'd wanted to get here before the day's swarm began: he didn't want too many people seeing just what information he was calling up on the computer.

Not that there was much on Aengus Grahame Fairmile Gibson. Public drunkenness mostly, usually with associated high jinks. Knocking the policeman's helmet off seemed to be a game enjoyed by youthful Gibson and his cronies. Other indiscretions included kerb-crawling in a part of town not renowned for its prostitutes, and an attempt to enter a friend's flat by the window (the key having been lost) which landed him in the wrong flat.

But it all came to a stop five years ago. From then till now, Gibson had received not so much as a parking ticket or a speeding fine. So much for his police files. Rebus punched in Broderick Gibson, too, not expecting anything. His expectations were fulfilled. The elder Gibson's 'youthful indiscretions' would be the stuff of musty old files in an annexe somewhere – always supposing there were any to begin with. Rebus had the feeling that anyone associated with Scottish Sword & Shield would probably have been arrested for disorderly conduct or breach of the peace at *some* point in their career. The possible exception, perhaps, being Matthew Vanderhyde.

He made a phone call to check that the meeting he'd arranged yesterday was still on, then switched off the computer and headed out of the building, just as a bleary Chief Superintendent Watson was coming in.

He waited in the newspaper office's public area, flipping through the past week's editions. A few early punters came in with Spot the Ball coupons or the like, and a few more hopefuls were checking copy with the people on the classified ads desk.

'Inspector Rebus.' She'd come from behind the main desk, where a stern security man had been keeping a watchful eye on Rebus. She was already wearing her raincoat, so there was to be no tour of the premises today, though she'd been promising him for weeks.

Her name was Mairie Henderson and she was in her early twenties. Rebus had come up against her when she was compiling a postmortem feature on the Gregor Jack case. Rebus had just wanted to forget about the whole ugly episode, but she'd been persistent ... and persuasive. She was just out of college, where she'd won awards for her student journalism and for pieces she'd contributed to the daily and weekly press. She hadn't yet forgotten how to be hungry; Rebus liked that.

'Come on,' she said. 'I'm starving. I'll buy you breakfast.'

So they went to a little cafe/bakery on South Bridge, where there were difficult choices to be made. Was it too early for pies and bridies? Too early for a fruit scone? Well then, they'd be like everyone else and settle for sliced sausage, black pudding and fried eggs.

'No haggis or dumpling?' Mairie was so imploring, the woman at the counter went off to ask the chef. Which

163

made Rebus make a mental note to phone Pat Calder sometime today. But there was no haggis or dumpling, not even for ready money. So they took their trays to the cash till, where Mairie insisted on paying.

'After all, you're going to give me the story of the decade.'

'I don't know about that.'

'One of these days you will, trust me.'

They squeezed into a booth and she reached for the brown sauce, then for the ketchup. 'I can never decide between the two. Shame about the fried dumpling, that's my favourite.'

She was about five feet five inches and had about as much fat on her as a rabbit in a butcher's window. Rebus looked down at his fry-up and suddenly didn't feel very hungry. He sipped the weak coffee.

'So what's it all about?' she asked, having made a good start into the food on her plate.

'You tell me.'

She waved a no-no with her knife. 'Not till you tell me why you want to know.'

'That's not the way the game's played.'

'We'll change the rules, then.' She scooped up some egg-white with her fork. She had her coat wrapped tight around her, though it was steamy in the cafe. Good legs too; Rebus missed seeing her legs. He blew on the coffee, then sipped again. She'd be willing to wait all day for him to say something.

'Remember the fire at the Central Hotel?' he said at last.

'I was still at school.'

'A body turned up in the ruins.' She nodded encouragement. 'Well, maybe there's new evidence ... no, not new evidence. It's just that some things have been happening, and I think they've got something to do with that fire and that shooting.'

'This isn't an official investigation, then?'

'Not yet.'

'And there's no story?'

Rebus shook his head. 'Nothing that wouldn't get you pasted in a libel court.'

'I could live with that, if the story was good enough.'

'It isn't, not yet.'

She began mopping-up operations with a triangle of buttered bread. 'So let me get this straight: you're on your own looking into a fire from five years ago?'

A fire which turned one man to drink, he could have said, and led another to the path of self-righteousness. But all he did was nod.

'And what's Gibson got to do with it?'

'Strictly between us, he was there that night. Yet he was kept off the list of the hotel's customers.'

'His father pulled some strings?'

'Could be.'

'Well, that's already a story.'

'I've nothing to back it up.' This was a lie, there was always Vanderhyde; but he wasn't going to tell her that. He didn't want her getting ideas. The way she was staring, she was getting plenty of those anyway.

'Nothing?'

'Nothing,' he repeated.

'Well, I don't know that this will help.' She opened her coat and pulled out the file which she'd been hiding, tucked down the front of her fashion-cut denims. He accepted the file from her, looking around the cafe. Nobody seemed to be paying attention.

'A bit cloak and dagger,' he told her. She shrugged.

'So I've seen too many films.'

Rebus opened the file. It bore no title, but inside were cuttings and 'spiked' stories concerning Aengus Gibson.

'Those are only from five years ago to the present. There isn't much, mostly charity work, giving to good causes. A little bit about the brewery's rising image and ditto profits.'

He glanced through the stuff. It was worthless. 'I was hoping to find out something about him from just after the fire.'

Mairie nodded. 'So you said on the phone. That's why I talked to a few people, including our chief sub. He says Gibson went into a psychiatric hospital. Nervous breakdown was the word.'

'Were the words,' corrected Rebus.

'Depends,' she said cryptically. Then: 'He was there the best part of three months. There was never a story, the father kept it out of the papers. When Aengus reappeared, *that's* when he started working in the business, and that's when he started all the do-gooding.'

'Shouldn't that be good-doing?'

She smiled. 'Depends,' she said. Then, of the file, 'It's not much, is it?' Rebus shook his head. 'I thought not. Still, it's all there was.'

'What about your chief sub? Would he be able to say *exactly* when Gibson went into that hospital?'

'I don't know. No harm in asking. Do you want me to?'

'Yes, I do.'

'All right then. And one more question.'

'Yes?'

'Aren't you going to eat any of that?'

Rebus pushed his plate across to her and watched her take her fill.

When he got back to St Leonard's, there was a call from the Chief Super's office. Chief Superintendent Watson wanted to see him straight away, as in ten minutes ago. Rebus checked that there were no messages for him, and called Siobhan Clarke in Gorgie to make sure the new window had been fitted.

'It's perfect,' she told him. 'It's got white gunk on it, window polish or something. We just didn't bother wiping it off. We can take shots through it, but from the outside it just looks like a new window that's waiting to be cleaned.'

'Fine,' said Rebus. He wanted to make sure he was up to date. If Watson intended to carpet him over yesterday, it would be considerably more than Lauderdale's fireside rug.

But Rebus had got it way wrong.

'What the hell are you up to?' Watson looked like he'd run a half-marathon gobbling down chilli peppers all the way. His breathing was raspy, his cheeks a dark cherry colour. If he walked into a hospital, they'd have him whisked to emergency on a two-man stretcher.

No, better make that a four-man.

'I'm not sure what you mean, sir.'

Watson fairly pounded the desk with his fist. A pencil dropped onto the floor. 'You're not sure what I mean!'

Rebus moved forward to pick up the pencil.

'Leave it! Just sit down.' Rebus went to sit. 'No, better yet, keep standing.' Rebus stood up. 'Now, just tell me why.' Rebus remembered a science teacher at his secondary school, a man with an evil temper who had spoken to the teenage Rebus just like this. 'Just tell me why.'

'Yes, sir.'

'Go on then.'

'With respect, sir, why what?'

The words came out through gritted teeth. 'Why you've seen fit to start pestering Broderick Gibson.'

'With respect, sir –'

'Stop all that "with respect" shite! Just give me an answer.'

'I'm not pestering Broderick Gibson, sir.'

'Then what *are* you doing, wooing him? The Chief

Constable phoned me this morning in absolute fucking apoplexy!' Watson, being a Christian of no mean persuasion, didn't swear often. It was a bad sign.

Rebus saw it all. The bash for the SSPCC. Yes, and Broderick Gibson collaring his friend the Chief Constable. One of your minions has been on to me, what's it all about? The Chief Constable not knowing anything about it, stuttering and spluttering and saying he'd get to the bottom of it. Just give me the officer's name . . .

'It's his son I'm interested in, sir.'

'But you looked both of them up on the computer this morning.'

Ah, so *some*one had taken notice of his early shift. 'Yes, I did, but I was really only interested in Aengus.'

'You still haven't explained why.'

'No, sir, well, it's a bit . . . nebulous.'

Watson frowned. '*Nebulous?* When's the graduation party?' Rebus didn't get it. 'Since you've obviously,' Watson was happy to explain, 'just got your astronomy degree!' He poured himself coffee from the machine on the floor, offering none to Rebus who could just use a cup.

'It was the word that came to mind, sir,' he said.

'I can think of a few words too, Rebus. Your mother wouldn't like to hear them.'

No, thought Rebus, and yours would wash your mouth out with soap.

The Chief Super slurped his coffee. They didn't call him 'Farmer' for nothing; he had many ways and predilections that could only be described as agricultural.

'But before I say any of them,' he went on, 'I'm a generous enough man to say that I'll listen to your explanation. Just make it bloody convincing.'

'Yes, sir,' said Rebus. How could he make *any* of it sound convincing? He supposed he'd have to try.

So he tried, and halfway through Watson even told

him he could sit if he liked. At the end of fifteen minutes, Rebus placed his hands out in front of him, palms up, as if to say: that's all, folks.

Watson poured another cup of coffee and placed it on the desk in front of Rebus.

'Thank you, sir.' Rebus gulped it down black.

'John, have you ever thought you might be paranoid?'

'All the time, sir. Show me two men shaking hands and I'll show you a Masonic conspiracy.'

Watson almost smiled, before recalling that this was no joking matter. 'Look, let me put it like this. What you've got so far is ... well, it's ...'

'Nebulous, sir?'

'Piss and wind,' corrected Watson. 'Somebody died five years ago. Was it anyone important? Obviously not, or we'd know who they were by now. So we assume it was somebody the world had hardly known and was happy to forget. No grieving widow or weans, no family asking questions.'

'You're saying let it die, sir? Let somebody get away with murder?'

Watson looked exasperated. 'I'm saying we're stretched as it is.'

'All Brian Holmes did was ask a few questions. Somebody brained him for it. I take over, my flat's invaded and my brother half scared to death.'

'My point exactly, it's all become *personal*. You can't allow that to happen. Look at the other stuff on your plate. Operation Moneybags for a start, and I'm sure there's more besides.'

'You're asking me to drop it, sir? Might I ask if you're under any personal pressure?'

There was personal pressure aplenty as Watson's blood rose, his face purpling. 'Now wait just one second, that's not the sort of comment I can tolerate.'

'No, sir. Sorry, sir.' But Rebus had made his point. The

clever soldier knows when to duck. Rebus had taken his shot, and now he was ducking.

'I should think so,' said Watson, wriggling in his chair as though his trousers were lined with scouring-pads. 'Now here's what I think. I think that if you can bring me something concrete, the dead man's identity perhaps, within twenty-four hours, then we'll reopen the case. Otherwise, I want the whole thing dropped until such time as new evidence *does* come forward.'

'Fair enough, sir,' said Rebus. It wasn't much good arguing the point. Maybe twenty-four hours would be enough. And maybe Charlie Chan had a clan tartan. 'Thanks for the coffee, much appreciated.'

When Watson started to make his joke about feeling 'full of beans', Rebus made his excuses and left.

19

He was seated at his desk, glumly examining all the dead ends in the case, when he happened to catch word of an 'altercation' at a house in Broughton. He caught the address, but it took a few seconds for it to register with him. Minutes later, he was in his car heading into the east end of town. The traffic was its usual self, with agonisingly slow pockets at the major junctions. Rebus blamed the traffic lights. Why couldn't they just do away with them and let the pedestrians take their chances? No, there'd only be more hold-ups, what with all the ambulances they'd need to ferry away the injured and the dead.

Still, why was he hurrying? He thought he knew what he was going to find. He was wrong. (It was turning out to be one of those weeks.) A police car and an ambulance sat outside Mrs MacKenzie's two-storey house, and the neighbours were out in a show of conspicuous curiosity. Even the kids across the road were interested. It must be a break-time, and some of them pushed their heads between the vertical iron bars and stared open-mouthed at the brightly marked vehicles.

Rebus thought about those railings. Their intention was to keep the kids *in*, keep them safe. But could they keep anybody *out*?

Rebus flashed his ID at the constable on door duty and entered Mrs MacKenzie's house. She was wailing loudly, so that Rebus started to think of murder. A WPC comforted her, while trying to have a conversation with her own over-amplified shoulder radio. The WPC saw Rebus.

'Make her some tea, will you?' she pleaded.

'Sorry, hen, I'm only CID. Needs someone a bit more senior to mash a pot of Brooke Bond.' Rebus had his hands in his pockets, the casually informed observer, distanced from the mayhem into which he walked. He wandered over to the bird cage and peered in. On the sand floor, amidst feathers and husks and droppings, lay a mummified budgie.

'Away the crow road,' he muttered to himself, moving out of the living room. He saw the ambulancemen in the kitchen, and folowed them. There was a body on the floor, hands and face heavily bandaged. He couldn't see any blood, though. He nearly skited on wet linoleum, and steadied himself by gripping the edge of the antiquated gas cooker. It was warm to the touch. A police constable stood by the open back door, looking out to right and left. Rebus squeezed past the carers and their patient and joined the PC.

'Nice day, eh?'

'What?'

'I see you're admiring the weather.' Rebus showed his ID again.

'No, not that. Just seeing the way he went.'

Rebus nodded. 'How do you mean?'

'The neighbours say he climbed three fences, then ran down a close and away.' The PC pointed. 'That close there, just past the line full of washing.'

'Behind the clothes-pole?'

'Aye, that must be the one. Three fences ... one, two, three. It's got to be that close over there.'

'Well done, son, that really gets us a long way.'

The constable stared at him. 'My Inspector's a stickler for notes. You're from St Leonard's? Not quite your patch is it, sir?'

172

'Everywhere's my patch, son, and everybody's my constable. Now what happened here?'

'The gentleman on the floor was attacked. The attacker ran off.'

Rebus nodded. 'I can tell you the how and the who already.' The PC looked dubious. 'The attacker was a man called Alex Maclean, and he almost certainly punched or headbutted Mr McPhail there.'

The constable blinked, then shook his head. *'That's* Maclean lying there.' Rebus looked down, and for the first time took in the size of the man, a good forty pounds heavier than McPhail. 'And he wasn't punched or butted. He had a pot of boiling water thrown over him.'

Just a little abashed, Rebus listened without comment to the PC's version of events. McPhail, who had been steering well clear of the house, had at last telephoned to say he'd be popping over for some clothes and things. He'd fobbed Mrs MacKenzie off with some story about working long shifts in a supermarket. He'd arrived, and was in the kitchen chatting to his landlady while she put on the water for her boiled eggs (boiled eggs every Wednesday lunchtime; poached on Thursdays – this was one part of Mrs MacKenzie's statement she wanted to get absolutely clear). But Maclean had been watching the house, and saw McPhail go in. He opened the unlocked front door and ran into the kitchen. 'A terrifying sight,' according to Mrs MacKenzie. 'I'll never forget it if I live to be a hundred.'

It was at this point that McPhail lifted the pan and swung it at Maclean, showering him with boiling water. Then he'd opened the back door and fled. Over three fences and through a close. End of melodrama.

Rebus watched them lift Maclean into the back of the ambulance. They'd be taking him to the Infirmary. Soon everyone Rebus knew in Edinburgh would be lying in the

173

Infirmary. McPhail had been lucky this time. If he knew what was good for him, he would now take Rebus's advice and flee the city, dodging the police who would be looking for him.

Rebus wondered if McPhail really did know what was good for him. This, after all, was a man who thought little girls were good for him. He wondered this as he sat in heavy lunchtime traffic, slowly oozing towards St Leonard's. The route he'd taken to Broughton had been so slow, he saw little to lose by sticking to the bigger roads – Leith Street, The Bridges, and Nicolson Street. Something made him stay on this road till he came to the butcher's shop where Rory Kintoul had ended up, bleeding beneath the meat counter.

He registered only slight surprise at the wooden board which had been placed across the entire front window of the shop. Pinned to the board was a large white sheet of paper with thick felt-pen writing. The sign said simply 'Business as Usual'. Interesting, thought Rebus, parking his car. He noticed that rain or general wear underfoot had done away with the splashes of blood which had once left a crimson trail along the pavement.

Mr Bone the butcher was slicing corned beef with a manual machine whose circular blade hissed through the meat. He was smaller and thinner than most butchers Rebus had come across, his face all cheekbone and worry line, hair thinning and grey. There was no one else in the front of the shop, though Rebus could hear someone whistling as they worked in the back. Bone noticed that he had a customer.

'And what'll it be today, sir?'

Rebus noticed that the display cases just inside the front window were empty, doubtless waiting to be checked for slivers of glass before restocking. He nodded towards the wooden board. 'When did that happen?'

'Ach, last night.' Bone placed the sliced corned beef in

an unsullied section of the display case, then skewered the price marker into it. He wiped his hands on his white apron. 'Kids or drunks.'

'What was it, a brick?'

'Search me.'

'Well, if there was nothing lying in the shop it must have been a sledgehammer. I can't see a kick with a steel toecap doing that sort of damage.'

Now Bone looked at him properly, and recognised him. 'You were here when Rory ...'

'That's right, Mr Bone. They didn't use a sledgehammer on him though, did they?'

'I don't know what you mean.'

'Pound of beef links, by the way.'

Bone hesitated, then took out the string of sausages and cut a length from it.

'You could be right, of course,' Rebus continued. 'Could have been kids or drunks. Did anyone see anything?'

'I don't know.'

'You didn't report it?'

'Didn't have to. Police phoned me at two this morning to tell me about it.' He sounded disgruntled.

'All part of the service, Mr Bone.'

'That's just over the pound,' Bone said, looking at the weighing scales. He wrapped the sausages in white paper, then in brown, marking the price with a pencil on this outer wrapper. Rebus handed over a five-pound note.

'Insurance will take care of it, I suppose,' he said.

'Bloody hope so, the money they charge.'

Rebus accepted his change, and made sure to catch Bone's eye. 'But I meant the *real* insurance people, Mr Bone.' An elderly couple were coming into the shop.

'What happened, Mr Bone?' the woman asked, her husband shuffling along behind her.

'Just kids, Mrs Dowie,' said Bone in the voice he used with customers, a voice he hadn't been using with Rebus.

175

He was staring at Rebus, who gave him a wink, picked up his package, and left. Outside, he looked down at the brown paper parcel. It was chill in his hand. He was supposed to be cutting down on meat, wasn't he? Not that there was much meat in sausages anyway. Another passing shopper stopped to examine the boarded-up window, then went into the shop. Jim Bone would do good business today. Everyone would want to know what had happened. Rebus was different; he *knew* what had happened, though proving it wasn't going to be easy. Siobhan Clarke hadn't managed to talk to the stabbing victim yet. Maybe Rebus should push her along, especially now that she could tell Rory Kintoul all about his cousin's broken window.

Next to his car someone had parked a Land Rover-style 4×4, inside which a huge black dog was ravening to get out. Pedestrians were giving the car a wide berth, and quite right too: the whole vehicle rocked on its axle when the dog lunged at the back window. Rebus noticed that the considerate owner had left the window open an inch. Maybe it was a trap intended for a particularly stupid car thief.

Rebus stopped in front of the open window and unrolled the package of sausages into the car. They fell onto the seat where the dog sniffed them for a nanosecond before starting to dine.

The street was blessedly quiet as Rebus unlocked his own car.

'All part of the service,' he said to himself.

At the station, he telephoned the Heartbreak Cafe, where what sounded like a hastily recorded message told him the place would be shut 'due to convalescence'. In Brian Holmes' desk drawer, he found a print-out of names and phone numbers, those most often used by Holmes himself. Some numbers had been added at the bottom in blue biro, including one for Eddie Ringan marked (h).

Rebus returned to his desk and made the call. Pat Calder answered on the third ring.

'Mr Calder, it's DI Rebus.'

'Oh.' The hope left Calder's voice.

'No sign of him then?'

'None.'

'Right, let's make it official, then. He's a missing person. I'll have someone come over and –'

'Why can't you come?'

Rebus thought about it. 'No reason at all, sir.'

'Make it anytime you like, we're shut today.'

'What happened to wonderchef Willie?'

'We had a busy night, busier than usual.'

'He cracked up?'

'Came flying out of the kitchen yelling, "I'm the chef! I'm the chef!" Lifted some poor woman's entrée and started eating it himself with his face in the bowl. I think he'd been taking drugs.'

'Sounds like he was just doing a good impersonation of late-period Elvis. I'll be there in half an hour, if that's all right.'

Stockbridge's 'Colonies' had been constructed to house the working poor, but were now much desired by young professional types. They were designed as maisonettes, with steep flights of stone stairs leading to the first floor properties. Rebus found the proportions mean in comparison with his Marchmont tenement. No high ceilings here, and no huge rooms with splendid windows and original shutters.

But he could see miners and their families being cosy here a hundred years ago. His own father had been born in a miners' row in Fife. Rebus imagined it must have been very like this ... at least on the outside.

On the inside, Pat Calder had done incredible things. (Rebus didn't doubt that his was the designing and decorating hand.) There were wooden and brass ship's trunks, black anglepoise lamps, Japanese prints in ornate frames, a dinner table whose candelabra resembled some Jewish icon, and a huge TV/hi-fi centre. But of Elvis there was nary a jot. Rebus, seated in a black leather sofa, nodded towards one of the coffin-sized loudspeakers.

'Neighbours ever complain?'

'All the time,' admitted Calder. 'Eddie's proudest moment was when the guy from four doors down phoned to tell us he couldn't hear his TV.'

'Considerate, eh?'

Calder smiled. 'Eddie's never been exactly "politic".'

'Have you known one another long?'

Calder, lying stretched on the floor with his bum on a beanbag, blew nervous smoke from a black Sobranie cigarette. 'Two years casually. We moved in together about the time we had the idea for the Heartbreak.'

'What's he like? I mean, outside the restaurant?'

'Brilliant one minute, a spoilt brat the next.'

'Do you spoil him?'

'I buffer him from the world. At least, I used to.'

'So what was he like when you met?'

'Drinking more than he does now, if you can believe that.'

'Ever tell you why he started?' Rebus had refused a cigarette, but the smoke was getting to him. Maybe he'd have to change his mind.

'He said he drank to forget. Now you're going to ask, Forget what? And I'm going to say that he never told me.'

'He never even hinted?'

'I think he told Brian Holmes more than he told me.'

Jesus, was there a hint of jealousy there? Rebus had a sudden vision of Calder bashing Holmes on the napper ... and maybe even doing away with Fast Eddie too ...?

Calder laughed. 'I couldn't hurt him, Inspector. I know what you're thinking.'

'It must be frustrating, though? This genius, you call him, wasting it all for booze. People like that take a lot of looking after.'

'And you're right, it *can* become frustrating.'

'Especially when they're gassed all the time.'

Calder frowned, peering through the smoke from his nostrils. 'Why do you say "gassed"?'

'It means drunk.'

'I know it does. So do a lot of other words. It's just that Eddie used to have these nightmares. About being gassed or gassing people. You know, with *real* gas, like in the concentration camps.'

'He told you about these dreams?'

'Oh no, but he used to shout out in his sleep. A lot of gays went to the gas chambers, Inspector.'

'You think that's what he meant?'

Calder stubbed out the cigarette into a porcelain bedpan beside the fireplace. He got up awkwardly from the floor. 'Come on, I want to show you something.'

Rebus had already seen the kitchen and the bathroom, and so realised that the door Calder was leading him towards must be to the only bedroom. He didn't know quite what to expect.

'I know what you've been thinking,' Calder said, swinging the door wide open. 'This is all Eddie's work.'

And what a work it was. A huge double bed covered with what looked like several zebra-skins. And on the walls, several large paintings of the rhinestone Elvis at work, the face an intentional blur of pink and sheen. Rebus looked up. There was a mirror on the ceiling. He guessed that pretty much any position you took on that bed, you'd be able to watch a white one-piece suit at work with a microphone-hand raised high.

'Whatever turns you on,' he commented.

He visited Clarke and Petrie for a couple of hours, just to

show willing. Unsurprisingly, Jardine had been replaced by a young man called Madden with a stock of puns not heard since the days of valve radio.

'Madden by name,' the Trading Standards officer said by way of introduction, 'mad 'un by nature.'

Make that *steam* radio. Rebus began to wonder if it had been such a good idea, phoning Jardine's boss and swearing exotically at him for twenty minutes.

'I make the jokes around here, son,' he warned.

Rebus had spent more exciting afternoons in his life. For example, being taken by his father to watch Cowdenbeath reserves at home to Dundee. He managed to break the monotony only by stepping out to buy buns at a nearby bakery, though this sort of activity was supposed to be *verboten*. He kept the custard slice for himself, peeling away and discarding the icing. Madden asked if he could have it, and Rebus nodded.

Siobhan Clarke looked like she'd stepped under a gardyloo bucket. She tried not to show it, and smiled whenever she saw him looking in her direction, but there was definitely something up with her. Rebus couldn't be bothered asking what. He got the idea it was to do with Brian ... maybe Brian and Nell. He told her about Bone's window.

'Make some time,' he said. 'Track down Kintoul, if not at home then at the Infirmary. He works in the labs there, right?'

'Right.' Definitely something up with her.

As was his prerogative, Rebus eventually made his excuses and left. Back at St Leonard's, there was a message for him to call Mairie Henderson at work.

'Mairie?'

'Inspector, that didn't take long.'

'You're about the only lead I've got.'

'It's nice to feel wanted.' She had one of those accents that could sound sarcastic without really flexing any muscle. 'Don't get too excited, though.'

'Your Chief Sub didn't remember?'

'Only that it was around August, making it three months after the Central burnt down.'

'Could mean something or nothing.'

'I did my best.'

'Yes, thanks, Mairie.'

'Hold on, don't hang up!' Rebus wasn't about to. 'He did tell me something. Apparently some snippet that's stuck with him.' She paused.

'In your own time, Mairie.'

'This *is* my time, Inspector.' She paused again.

'Are you drawing on a fag?'

'What if I am?'

'Since when did you start smoking?'

'It beats chewing the ends off pencils.'

'You'll stunt your growth.'

'You sound like my dad.'

Well, that brought him back to earth. Here he'd thought they were ... what? Chatting away? Chatting one another *up*? Aye, in your dreams, John Rebus. Now she'd reminded him of the not insignificant age gap between them.

'Are you still there, Inspector?'

'Sorry, my hearing aid slipped out. What did the Chief Sub say?'

'Remember that story about Aengus Gibson entering the wrong flat?'

'I remember.'

'Well, the woman whose flat he broke into was called Mo Johnson.'

Rebus smiled. But then the smile faded. 'That name almost rings a bell.'

'He's a football player.'

'I *know* he's a football player. But a female Mo Johnson, *that's* what rings bells.' But they were faint, too faint.

'Let me know if you come up with anything.'

'I will, Mairie. And Mairie?'

'What?'

'Don't stay out too late.' Rebus terminated the call.

Mo Johnson. He supposed it must be short for Maureen. Where had he come across that name? He knew how he might check. But if Watson found out, it would mean more trouble. Ach, to hell with Watson anyway. He wasn't much more than slave to a coffee bean. Rebus went to the computer console and punched in the details, bringing up Aengus Gibson's record. The anecdote was there, but no charges had ever been pressed. The woman was not mentioned by name, and there was no sign of her address. But, since Gibson was involved, CID had taken an interest. You couldn't always depend on the lower ranks to hush things up properly.

And look who the investigating officer was: DS Jack Morton. Rebus closed the file and got back on the phone. The receiver was still warm.

'You're in luck, he got back from the pub five minutes ago.'

'Away, ya gobshite,' Rebus heard Morton say as he grabbed at the receiver. 'Hello?' Two minutes later, thanks to what was left of Jack Morton's memory, Rebus had an address for Mo Johnson.

A day of contrasts. From bakery to butchery, from The Colonies to Gorgie Road. And now to the edge of Dean Village. Rebus hadn't been down this way since the Water of Leith drowning. He had forgotten how beautiful it was. Tucked down a steep hill from Dean Bridge, the Village gave a good impression of rural peace. Yet it was a five-minute walk from the West End and Princes Street.

They were spoiling it, of course. The developers had squeezed their hands around vacant lots and decaying buildings and choked them into submission. The prices asked for the resultant 'apartments', prices as steep as Bell's Brae, boggled Rebus's mind. Not that Mo Johnson lived in one of the new buildings. No, her flat was a chunk of an older property at the bottom of the brae, with a view of the Water of Leith and Dean Bridge. But she no longer lived there, and the people who did were reluctant to allow Rebus in. They didn't think they had a new address for her. There had been another owner between her moving out and their moving in. They might still have *that* owner's new address, though it would go back a couple of years.

Did they know when Ms Johnson herself moved out?

Four years ago, maybe five.

Which brought Rebus back to the fire at the Central Hotel. Everything he did in this case seemed to bounce straight back to a period five years ago, when something had happened which had changed a lot of people's lives, and taken away at least one life too. He sat in his car wondering what to do next. He knew what to do, but had been putting it off. If tangling with the Gibsons could earn him minus points, he dreaded to think what he might earn by talking with the only other person he could think of who might be able to help.

Help? That was a laugh. But Rebus wanted to meet him all the same. Christ, Flower would have a field day if he found out. He'd hire tents and food and drink and invite everyone to the biggest party in town. Right up from Lauderdale to the Chief Constable, they'd be blowing fuses that could have run hydro stations.

Yes, the more Rebus thought about it, the more he knew it was the right thing to do. The right thing? He had so few openings left, it was the *only* thing. And looking on the bright side, if he did get caught, at least the celebration would bankrupt Little Weed ...

20

He telephoned first, Morris Cafferty not being a man you just dropped in on.

'Will I need my lawyer?' Cafferty growled, sounding amused. 'I'll answer that for you, Strawman, no I fucking won't. Because I've got something better than a lawyer here, better than a fucking judge in my pocket. I've got a dog that'll rip your oesophagus out if I tell it to lick your chops. Be here at six.' The phone went dead, leaving Rebus dry-mouthed and persuading himself all over again that this jumped-up bastard didn't scare him.

What scared him more was the realisation that someone somewhere in the ranks of the Lothian and Borders Police was probably listening in to Cafferty's telephone conversations. Rebus felt like he was in a corridor with doors locking behind him all the time. He saw a gas chamber in his mind and shivered, changing the picture.

Six o'clock wasn't very far away. And at least in dentists' waiting rooms they gave you magazines to pass the time.

Morris Gerald Cafferty lived in a mansion house in the expensive suburb of Duddingston. Duddingston was a 'suburb' by dint of having Arthur's Seat and Salisbury Crags between it and central Edinburgh. Cafferty liked living in Duddingston because it annoyed his neighbours, most of whom were lawyers, doctors and bankers, and also because it wasn't far from his actual and spiritual birthplace, Craigmillar. Craigmillar was one of the tougher

Edinburgh housing schemes. Cafferty grew up there, seeing his first trouble there and in neighbouring Niddrie. He'd led a gang of Craigmillar youths into Niddrie to sort out their rivals. There was a stabbing ... with an uprooted iron railing. Police discovered that the teenage Cafferty had already been in trouble at school for 'accidentally' jamming a ballpoint pen into the corner of a fellow pupil's eye.

It was the quiet start to a long career.

The wrought iron gates at the bottom of the driveway opened automatically as Rebus approached. He drove his car along a well-gritted private road with mature trees either side. You caught a glimpse of the house from the main road, nothing more. But Rebus had been here before; to ask questions, to make an arrest. He knew there was another smaller house behind the main house, linked by a covered walkway. This smaller house had been staff quarters in the days when a city merchant might have lived here. The gravel road forked to the front and back of the main house. A man directed Rebus towards the back: the servants' entrance. The man was very big with a biker helmet haircut, cut high at the fringe but falling over the ears. Where did Cafferty get them, these throwbacks?

The man followed him to the back of the house. Rebus knew where to park. There were three spaces, two vacant and one taken up by a Volvo estate. Rebus thought he recognised the Volvo, though it wasn't Cafferty's. Cafferty's collection of cars was kept in the vast garage. He had a Bentley and a cherry-red '63 T-Bird, neither of which he ever drove. For daily use, there was always the Jag, an XJS-HE. And for weekends there was a dependable Roller which Cafferty had owned for at least fifteen years.

The man opened Rebus's door for him, and pointed towards the small house. Rebus got out.

'Vidal Sassoon was booked up then,' he said.

'Uh?' The man turned his head right-side towards Rebus.

'Never mind.' He was about to walk away, but paused. 'Ever been in a fight with a man called Dougary?'

'Nane i' your business.'

Rebus shrugged. The big man closed the car door and stood watching Rebus walk away. So there was no chance to check the tax disc or anything else about the Volvo; nothing to do except memorise the number plate.

Rebus pulled open the door to the small house and was greeted by a wave of heat and steam. The whole structure had been gutted, so that a swimming pool and gymnasium could be installed. The pool was kidney-shaped, with a small circular pool off it – a jacuzzi, presumably. Rebus had always hated kidney pools: it was impossible to do laps in them. Not that he was much of a swimmer.

'Strawman! About bastardin' time!'

He didn't see Cafferty at first, though he had no trouble seeing who was standing over him. Cafferty lay on a massage table, head resting on a pile of towels. His back was being kneaded by none other than the Organ Grinder, who just happened to own a Volvo estate. The Organ Grinder sensibly pretended not to know Rebus; and when Cafferty wasn't looking, Rebus nodded almost imperceptibly his agreement with the pretence.

Cafferty had spun around on his backside and was now easing himself into a standing position. He tested his back and shoulders. 'That's magic,' he said. He removed the towel from around his loins and padded towards Rebus on bare feet.

'See, Strawman, no concealed weapons.' His laughter was like an apprentice with a rasp-file.

Rebus looked around. 'I don't see the –'

But suddenly there it was, pulling itself massively out of the swimming pool. Rebus hadn't even noticed it in there, retrieving a bone. Not a plastic bone either. The black beast dropped the bone at Cafferty's feet, sniffed at Rebus's legs, then shook itself dry onto him.

'Good boy, Kaiser,' said Cafferty. The parking attendant had joined them in the sticky heat. Rebus nodded nowhere in particular.

'I hope you got planning permission for this.'

'All above board, Strawman. Come on, you'd better get changed.'

'Changed for what?'

Laughter again. 'Don't worry, you're not staying to dinner. I'm going for a run, and so are you – if you want to talk to me.'

A run, Jesus! Cafferty turned and walked away towards what looked like a changing cubicle. He slapped the Organ Grinder as he passed him.

'Magic. Same time next week?'

He was hairily muscular, with a chest a borders farmer would be proud to own. There was flab, of course, but not as much as Rebus would have guessed. There was no doubt: Big Ger had got himself in shape. The backside and upper thighs were pockmarked, but the gut had been tightened. Rebus tried to remember when he'd last seen Cafferty. Probably in court ...

Rebus would have enjoyed a quiet word with the Organ Grinder, but now that the parking attendant gorilla was in spying distance, it just wasn't feasible. You couldn't be sure how much the one-eared man could hear.

'There's some stuff here, it should fit.'

The 'stuff' consisted of sweatshirt, running shorts, socks and trainers ... and a headband. There was no way Rebus was going to wear a headband. But when Cafferty emerged from his cubicle, *he* was wearing one, along with a white running vest and immaculate white shorts. He started to limber up while Rebus entered the cubicle to change.

What the hell am I doing? he asked himself. He had imagined a lot of things, but not this. Some things might be painful in life, but this, he had no doubt, was going to be torture.

'Where to?' he asked when they emerged from the overheated gym into the cool twilit evening. He wasn't wearing the headband. And he had put the sweatshirt on inside out. The legend across its front had read 'Kick me if I stop'. He supposed it represented Cafferty's idea of a joke.

'Sometimes I run to Duddingston Loch, sometimes up to the top of the Seat. You choose.' Big Ger was bouncing on the spot.

'The loch.'

'Right,' said Big Ger, and off they set.

Rebus spent the first few minutes checking that his body could take this sort of thing, which was why he was slow to spot the car following them. It was the Jag, driven by the parking attendant at a steady 0–5 mph.

'Remember the last time you gave evidence against me?' Big Ger said. As a conversational opening, it had its merits. Rebus merely nodded. They were running side by side, the pavements being all but deserted. He wondered if any undercover officers would be snapping photographs of this. 'Over in Glasgow, it was.'

'I remember.'

'Not guilty, of course.' Big Ger grinned. He looked like he'd had his teeth seen to as well. Rebus remembered them being greyish-green. Now they were a brilliantly capped white. And his hair ... was it thicker? One of those hair-weaves, maybe? 'Anyway, I heard afterwards you went back down to London and had a bit of a time.'

'You could say that.'

They ran another minute in silence. The pace wasn't exactly taxing, but then neither was Rebus in condition. His lungs were already passing him warnings of the red hot and burning varieties.

'You're getting thin at the back,' Cafferty noticed. 'A hair weave would sort that out.'

It was Rebus's turn to smile. 'You know damned fine I got burned.'

'Aye, and I know who burned you, too.'

Still, Rebus reckoned his own guess about the hair weave had been confirmed.

'Actually,' he said, 'I wanted to talk to you about another fire.'

'Oh aye?'

'At the Central.'

'The Central Hotel?' Rebus was pleased to notice that the words weren't coming so easily from Big Ger either now. 'That's prehistory.'

'Not as far as I'm concerned.'

'But what's it to do with me?'

'Two of your men were there that night, playing in a poker game.'

Cafferty shook his head. 'That can't be right. I won't have gamblers working for me. It's against the Bible.'

'Everything you do from waking till sleeping is against *somebody's* Bible, Cafferty.'

'Please, Strawman, call me *Mr* Cafferty.'

'I'll call you what I like.'

'And I'll call you the Strawman.'

The name jarred ... every time. It had been at the Glasgow trial, a sheet of notes wrongly glanced at by the prosecution, mistaking Rebus for the only other witness, a pub landlord called Stroman.

'Now then, Inspector Stroman ...' Oh, Cafferty had laughed at that, laughed from the dock so hard that he was in danger of contempt. His eyes had bored into Rebus like fat woodworm, and he'd mouthed the word one final time the way he'd heard it – Strawman.

'Like I say,' Rebus went on, 'two of your hired heid-the-ba's. Eck and Tam Robertson.'

189

They had just passed the Sheep's Heid pub, Rebus sorely tempted to veer inside, Cafferty knowing it.

'There'll be herbal tea when we get back. Watch out there!' His warning saved Rebus from stepping in a discreet dog turd.

'Thanks,' Rebus said grudgingly.

'I was thinking of the shoes,' Cafferty replied. 'Know what "flowers of Edinburgh" are?'

'A rock band?'

'Keech. They used to chuck all their keech out of the windows and onto the street. There was so much of it lying around, the locals called it the flowers of Edinburgh. I read that in a book.'

Rebus thought of Alister Flower and smiled. 'Makes you glad you're living in a decent society.'

'So it does,' said Cafferty, with no trace of irony. 'Eck and Tam Robertson, eh? The Bru-Heid Brothers. I won't lie to you, they used to work for me. Tam for just a few weeks, Eck for longer.'

'I won't ask what they did.'

Cafferty shrugged. 'They were general employees.'

'Covers a multitude of sins.'

'Look, I didn't ask you to come out here. But now that you are, I'm answering your questions, all right?'

'I appreciate it, really. You say you didn't know they were at the Central that night?'

'No.'

'Do you know what happened to them afterwards?'

'They stopped working for me. Not at the same time, Tam left first, I think. Tam then Eck. Tam was a dunderheid, Strawman, a real loser. I can't abide losers. I only hired him because Eck asked me to. Eck was a good worker.' He seemed lost in thought for a minute. 'You're looking for them?'

'That's it.'

'Sorry, I can't help.' Rebus wondered if Cafferty's cheeks

190

were half as red as his felt. He had a piercing stitch in his side, and didn't know how he was going to make the run back. 'You think they had something to do with the body?'

Rebus merely nodded.

'What makes you so sure?'

'I'm not sure. But if they *did* have something to do with it, I'm willing to bet you weren't a hundred miles behind.'

'Me?' Cafferty laughed again, but the laugh was strained. 'As I recall, I was on holiday in Malta with some friends.'

'You always seem to be with friends when anything happens.'

'I'm a gregarious man, I can't help it if I'm popular. Know something else I read about Scotland? The Pope called it "the arse of Europe".' Cafferty slowed to a stop. They'd come to near the top of Duddingston Loch, the city just visible down below them. 'Hard to believe, isn't it? The arse of Europe, it doesn't look like one to me.'

'Oh, I don't know,' said Rebus, bent over with hands on knees. 'If this is the arse ...' he looked up, 'I'd know where to stick the enema.'

Cafferty's laughter roared out all around. He was breathing deeply, trying to slow things down. When he spoke, it was in an undertone, though there was no one around to hear them. 'But we're a cruel people, Strawman. All of us, you and me. And we're ghouls.' His face was very close to Rebus's, both of them bent over. Rebus kept his eyes on the grass below him. 'When they killed the grave-robber Burke, they made souvenirs from his skin. I've got one in the house, I'll show it to you.' The voice might have been inside Rebus's own head. 'We *like* to watch, and that's the truth. I bet even you've got a taste for pain, Strawman. You're hurting all over, but you ran with me, you didn't give up. Why? Because you *like* the pain. It's what makes you a Calvinist.'

'It's what makes *you* a public menace.'

'Me? A simple businessman who has managed to survive this disease called recession.'

'No, you're more than that,' said Rebus, straightening up. 'You're the disease.'

Cafferty looked like he might throw a punch, but instead he pounded Rebus on the back. 'Come on, time to go.'

Rebus was about to plead another minute's rest, but saw Cafferty walking to the Jag. 'What?' Cafferty said. 'You think I'd run it *both ways*? Come on now, your herbal tea is waiting.'

And herbal tea it was, served up poolside after Rebus had showered and changed back into his clothes. He had the feeling someone had been through his wallet and diary in his absence, but knew they wouldn't have found much there. For one thing, he'd tucked his ID and credit cards into the front of his running shorts; for another, he'd about as much cash as would buy an evening paper and a packet of mints.

'Sorry I couldn't be more help,' said Cafferty after Rebus had sat himself down.

'You could if you tried,' Rebus replied. He was trying to stop his legs from shaking. They hadn't had this much exercise since the last time he'd flitted.

Cafferty just shrugged. He was now wearing baggy and wildly coloured swimming trunks, and had just had a dip. As he dried himself off, he showed enough anal cleavage to qualify as a construction worker.

The devil dog meantime sat by the pool licking its chops. Of the bone it had been chewing, there was not the slightest trace. Rebus suddenly placed the dog.

'Do you own a 4x4?' Cafferty nodded. 'I saw it parked across from Bone's the Butcher on South Clerk Street. This mutt was in the back.'

Cafferty shrugged. 'It's my wife's car.'

'And she often takes the dog into town?'

'She gets Kaiser's bones there. Besides, he's cheaper than a car alarm.' Cafferty smiled fondly at the dog. 'And I've never known anyone bypass him.'

'Maybe sausages would do it.' But this was lost on Cafferty. Rebus decided he was getting nowhere. It was time to try one final tactic. He finished the brew. It tasted like spearmint chewing gum. 'A colleague of mine was trying to track down the Robertson brothers. Someone put him in hospital.'

'Really?' Cafferty looked genuinely surprised. 'What happened?'

'He was attacked behind a restaurant called the Heart-break Cafe.'

'Dear me. Did he find them, Tam and Eck?'

'If he'd found them, I wouldn't have had to come here.'

'I thought maybe it was just an excuse for a blether about the good old days.'

'What good old days?'

'True enough, you look about as bad as ever. Not me, though. My wild days are behind me.' He sipped his tea to prove the point. 'I'm a changed man.'

Rebus nearly laughed. 'You tell that line so often in court, you're beginning to believe it.'

'No, it's true.'

'Then you wouldn't be trying to put the frighteners on me?'

Cafferty shook his head. He was crouching beside the dog, rubbing its head briskly. 'Oh no, Strawman, the day's long past when I'd take a set of six-inch carpentry nails and fix you to the floorboards in some derelict house. Or tickle your tonsils with jump-leads connected to a generator.' He was warming to his subject, looking almost as ready to pounce as his dog.

Rebus stayed nonchalant. Indeed, he had one to add to the list. 'Or hang me over the Forth Rail Bridge?' There

193

was silence, except for the hum of the jacuzzi and the snuffling of the dog. Then the door swung open and a woman's head smiled heedlessly towards them.

'Morris, dinner in ten minutes.'

'Thanks, Mo.'

The door closed again, and Cafferty got up. So did the dog. 'Well, Strawman, it's been lovely chatting away like this, but I better take a shower before I eat. Mo's always complaining I smell like chlorine. I keep telling her, we wouldn't have to put chlorine in the pool if the visitors didn't piss in it, but she blames Kaiser!'

'She's your ... er ...?'

'My wife. As of four years and three months.'

Rebus was nodding. He knew Cafferty was married, of course. He'd just forgotten the name of the lucky bride.

'She's the one who's changed me if anyone has,' Cafferty was saying. 'She makes me read all these books.'

Rebus knew the Nazis had read books too. 'Just one thing, Cafferty.'

'*Mr* Cafferty. Go on, indulge me.'

Rebus swallowed hard. 'Mr Cafferty. What's your wife's maiden name?'

'Morag,' said Cafferty, puzzled by the question. 'Morag Johnson.' Then he padded away towards the shower, kicking off his trunks, mooning mightily at Rebus as he did so.

Morag Johnson. Yes, of course. Rebus would bet that not many people tried the 'Mo Johnson' gag in front of Big Ger. But that's where he'd heard the name before. The woman into whose flat Aengus Gibson had trespassed had soon afterwards married Big Ger Cafferty. So soon after, in fact, that they *must* have been going out together at the time the break-in had occurred.

Rebus had his link between Aengus Gibson, the Bru-Head Brothers and Big Ger.

194

Now all he had to do was figure out what the hell it meant.

He rose from his chair, eliciting a low growl from the devil dog. Slowly and quietly he made for the door, knowing all Big Ger had to do was call from the shower, and Kaiser would be on Rebus faster than piss on a lamp post. As he made his exit, he was remembering those scenarios for his painful execution, so lovingly described by Big Ger.

John Rebus was once again grateful he didn't yet have the gun.

But there was something else. The way Big Ger had seemed surprised when told about Holmes. As if he *really* hadn't known about it. Added to which how keen he'd been to find out if Holmes had had any success tracking down Tam and Eck Roberston.

Rebus drove away with more mysteries than answers. But one question he was sure had been answered: Cafferty had been behind Michael's abduction. He was certain of it now.

21

'You can't have,' said Siobhan Clarke.

'And yet I have,' said Peter Petrie. He had run out of film. Plenty of spare batteries. Of batteries there were plenty. But film was there none. It was first thing Thursday morning, and the last thing Clarke needed. 'So you'd better go and fetch some pronto.'

'Why me?'

'Because *I* am in pain.' This was true. He was on painkillers for his nose, and had complained about nothing else all day yesterday. So much so that the maddening Madden had lost all sense of good fun and bad puns and had told Petrie to 'shut the fuck up'. Now they weren't talking. Siobhan wondered if it was a good idea to leave them alone.

'It's special film,' Petrie was telling her. He rummaged in the camera case and came out with an empty film-box, the flap of which he tore off and handed to her. 'This is the stuff.'

'This,' she said to him, grabbing the scrap of card, 'is a pain in the arse.'

'Try Pyle's,' said Madden.

She turned on him. 'Are you being funny?'

'It's the name of a camera shop on Morrison Street.'

'That's miles away!'

'Take your car,' Petrie suggested.

Siobhan grabbed her bag. 'Stuff that, I'll find somewhere before Morrison Street.'

However, after ten filmless minutes she began to realise that there was no great demand for special high-speed film in Gorgie Road. It wasn't as if you needed high-speed to take a photo of Hearts in action. She consoled herself with this thought and resigned herself to the walk to Morrison Street. Maybe she could catch a bus back.

She saw that she was nearing the Heartbreak Cafe, and crossed the road to look at it. It had looked closed yesterday when she drove past, and there was a sign in the window. She read now that the place was closed 'due to convalescence'. Strange, though, the door was open a couple of inches. And was there a funny smell, a smell like gas? She pushed the door open and peered in.

'Hello?'

Yes, definitely gas, and there was no one around. A woman on the street stopped to watch.

'Awfy smell o' gas, hen.'

Siobhan nodded and walked into the Heartbreak Cafe.

Without its lights on, and with little natural light, the place was all darkness and shadows. But the last thing she planned to do was flick an electric switch. She could see chinks of light through the kitchen door, and made towards it. Yes, there were windows in the kitchen, and the smell was much stronger here. She could hear the unmistakable hiss of escaping gas. With a hankie stuffed to her nose, she made for the emergency exit, and pushed at the bar which should release it. But the thing was sticking, or else ... She gave a mighty heave and the door grunted open an inch. Dustbins were being stored right against it on the outside. Fresh air started trickling in, the welcome smells of traffic exhaust and beer hops.

Now she had to find whichever cooker had been left on. Only as she turned did she see the legs and body which were lying on the floor, the head hidden inside a huge oven. She walked over and turned off the gas, then peered down. The body lay on its side, dressed in black and white check trousers and a white chef's jacket. She didn't recognise the man from his face, but the elaborately stitched name on his left breast made identification easy.

It was Eddie Ringan.

The place was still choking with gas, so she walked back to the emergency door and gave it another heave. This time it opened most of the way, scattering clanking dustbins onto the ground outside. It was then that a curious passer-by pushed open the door from the restaurant to the kitchen. His hand went to the light-switch.

'Don't touch tha –!'

There was a tremendous blast and fireball. The shock sent Siobhan Clarke flying backwards into the parking lot, where her landing was softened by the rubbish she'd scattered only seconds earlier. She didn't even suffer the same minor burns as the hapless passer-by, who went crashing back into the restaurant pursued by a blue ball of flame. But Eddie Ringan, well, he looked like he'd been done to a turn inside an oven which wasn't even hot.

By the time Rebus got there, aching after last night's exertions, the scene was one of immaculate chaos. Pat Calder had arrived in time to see his lover being carted away in a blue plastic bag. The bag was deemed necessary to stop bits of charred face breaking off and messing up the floor. The bagging itself had been overseen by a police doctor, but Rebus knew where Eddie would eventually end up: under the all-seeing scalpel of Dr Curt.

'All right, Clarke?'

Rebus affected the usual inspectorial nonchalance, hands in pockets and an air of having seen it all before.

'Apart from my coccyx, sir.' And she gave the bone a rub for luck.

'What happened?'

So she filled in the details, all the way from having no film (yes, why not drop Petrie in it?) to the passer-by who had nearly killed her. He had been seen to by the doctor too: frizzled eyebrows and lashes, some bruising from the fall. Rebus's scalp tingled at the thought. There was no smell of gas in the kitchen now. But there was a smell of cooked meat, almost inviting till you remembered its source.

Calder was seated at the bar, watching the world move past him in and out of the dream he had built with Eddie Ringan. Rebus sat down beside him, glad to take the weight off his legs.

'Those nightmares,' Calder said immediately, 'looks like he made them come true, eh?'

'Looks like it. Any idea why he'd kill himself?'

Calder shook his head. He was bearing up, but only just. 'I suppose it all got too much for him.'

'All what?'

Calder continued shaking his head. 'Perhaps we'll never know.'

'Don't you believe it,' Rebus said, trying not to make it sound like a threat. He must have failed, for suddenly Calder turned towards him.

'Can't you let it rest?' The pale eyes were glistening.

'No rest for the wicked, Mr Calder,' said Rebus. He slid off the barstool and went back into the kitchen. Siobhan was standing beside a shelf filled with basic cookery books.

'Most chefs,' she said, 'would rather die than keep this lot out on display.'

'He wasn't any ordinary chef.'

'Look at this one.' It was a school jotter, with ruled red lines about half an inch apart and an inch-wide margin. The margins were full of doodles and sketches, mostly of food and men with large quiffs. Neatly written in a large hand inside the margins were recipes. 'His own creations.' She flipped to the end. 'Oh look, here's Jailhouse Roquefort.' She quoted from the recipe. ' "With thanks to Inspector John Rebus for the idea." Well, well.' She was about to put the book back, but Rebus took it from her. He opened it at the inside cover, where he'd spotted a copious collection of doodles. Something had been written in the midst of the drawings (some of them gayly rude). But it had been scored out again with a darker pen.

'Can you make that out?'

They took the jotter to the back door and stood in the parking lot, where so recently someone had thumped Brian Holmes on the head. Siobhan started things off. 'Looks like the first word's "All".'

'And that's "turn",' said Rebus of a later word. 'Or maybe "tum".' But the rest remained beyond them. Rebus pocketed the recipe book.

'Thinking of a new career, sir?' Siobhan asked.

Rebus pondered a suitable comeback line. 'Shut up, Clarke,' he said.

Rebus dropped the jotter off at Fettes HQ, where they had people whose job it was to recover legibility from defaced and damaged writing. They were known as 'pen pals', the sort of boffins who liked to do really difficult crosswords.

'This won't take long,' one of them told Rebus. 'We'll just put it on the machine.'

'Great,' said Rebus. 'I'll come back in quarter of an hour.'

'Make it twenty minutes.'

Twenty minutes was fine by Rebus. While he was here and at a loose end, he might as well pay his respects to DI Gill Templer.

'Hello, Gill.' Her office smelt of expensive perfume. He'd forgotten what kind she wore. Chanel, was it? She slipped off her glasses and blinked at him.

'John, long time no see. Sit down.'

Rebus shook his head. 'I can't stay, the lab's going to have something for me in a minute. Just thought I'd see how you're doing.'

She nodded her answer. 'I'm doing fine. How about you?'

'Aw, not bad. You know how it is.'

'How's the doctor?'

'She's fine, aye.' He shuffled his feet. He hadn't expected this to be so awkward.

'It's not true she kicked you out, then?'

'How the hell do you know about that?'

Gill was smiling her lipsticked smile; a thin mouth, made for irony. 'Come on, John, this is *Edinburgh*. You want to keep secrets, move somewhere bigger than a village.'

'Who told you, though? How many people know?'

'Well, if they know here at Fettes, they're bound to know at St Leonard's.'

Christ. That meant Watson knew, Lauderdale knew, Flower knew. And none of them had said anything.

'It's only a temporary thing,' he muttered, shuffling his feet again. 'Patience has her nieces staying, so I moved back into my flat. Plus Michael's there just now.'

It was Gill Templer's turn to look surprised. 'Since when?'

'Ten days or so.'

'Is he back for good?'

Rebus shrugged. 'Depends, I suppose. Gill, I wouldn't want word getting round ...'

'Of course not! I can keep a secret.' She smiled again. 'Remember, I'm not *from* Edinburgh.'

'Me neither,' said Rebus. 'I just get screwed around here.' He checked his watch.

'Are my five minutes up?'

'Sorry.'

'Don't be, I've got plenty of work to be getting on with.' He turned to leave.

'John? Come up and see me again sometime.'

Rebus nodded. 'Mae West, right?'

'Right.'

'Bye, Gill.'

Halfway along her corridor, Rebus recalled that a Mae West was also the name for a life-jacket. He considered this, but shook his head. 'My life's complicated enough.'

He returned to the lab.

'You're a bit early,' he was told.

'Keen's the word you're looking for.'

'Well, speaking of words we're looking for, come and have a peek.' He was led to a computer console. The scribble had been OCR'd and fed into the computer, where it was now displayed on the large colour monitor. A lot of the overpenning had been 'erased', leaving the original message hopefully intact. The pen pal picked up a sheet of paper. 'Here are my ideas so far.' As he read them off, Rebus tried to see them in the message on the screen.

' "Ale I did, tum on the gum", "Ole I did man, term on the gam" ...' Rebus gazed up at him, and the pen pal grinned. 'Or maybe this,' he said. ' "All I did was turn on the gas".'

'What?'

' "All I did was turn on the gas".'

Rebus stared at the message on the screen. Yes, he could see it ... well, most of it. The pen pal was talking again.

'It helped that you told me he'd gassed himself. I still had that half in mind when I started working, and spotted "gas" straight off. A suicide note, maybe?'

Rebus looked disbelieving. 'What, scored out and sur-rounded by doodles on the inside cover of a jotter he tucked away on a shelf? Stick to what you know and you'll do fine.'

What Rebus knew was that Eddie Ringan had suffered nightmares during which he cried out the word 'gas'. Was this scribble the remnant from one of his bad nights? But then why score it out so heavily? Rebus picked up

202

the jotter from the OCR machine. The inside cover looked old, the stuff there going back a year or more. Some of the doodles looked more recent than the defaced message. Whenever Eddie had written this, it wasn't last night. Which meant, presumably, that it had no direct connection to his gassing himself. Making it ... a coincidence? Rebus didn't believe in coincidence, but he did believe in serendipity. He turned to the pen pal, who was looking not happy at Rebus's put-down.

'Thanks,' he said.

'You're welcome.'

Each was sure the other was being less than sincere.

Brian Holmes was waiting for him at St Leonard's, waiting to be welcomed back into the world.

'What the hell are you doing here?'

'Don't worry,' said Holmes, 'I'm just visiting. I've got another week on the sick.'

'How are you feeling?' Rebus was glancing nervously around, wondering if anyone had told Holmes about Eddie. He knew in his heart they hadn't, of course; if they had, Brian wouldn't be half as chipper.

'I get thumping headaches, but that apart I feel like I've had a holiday.' He patted his pocket. 'And DI Flower got up a collection. Nearly fifty quid.'

'The man's a saint,' said Rebus. 'I had a present I was going to bring you.'

'What?'

'A tape, the Stones' *Let it Bleed*.'

'Thanks a lot.'

'Something to cheer you up after Patsy De-Cline.'

'At least she can sing.'

Rebus smiled. 'You're fired. Are you at your aunt's?'

This quietened Holmes, as Rebus had hoped it would. Bring him down slowly, then drop the real news into his lap. 'For the meantime. Nell's ... well, she says she's not quite ready yet.'

Rebus knew the feeling; he wondered when Patience would be ready for that drink. 'Still,' he offered, 'things sound a bit brighter between the two of you.'

'Ach.' Holmes sat down opposite his superior. 'She wants me to leave the police.'

'That's a bit drastic.'

'So is separation.'

Rebus exhaled. 'I suppose so, but all the same ... What are you going to do?'

'Think it over, what else can I do?' He got back to his feet. 'Listen, I'd better get going. I only came in to –'

'Brian, sit down.' Holmes, recognising Rebus's tone, sat. 'I've got some bad news about Eddie.'

'Chef Eddie?' Rebus nodded. 'What about him?'

'There's been an accident. Well, sort of. Eddie was involved.'

There was no mistaking Rebus's meaning. He'd become good at this sort of speech through repetition over the years to the families of car crash victims, accidents at work, murders ...

'He's dead?' Holmes asked quietly. Rebus, lips pursed, nodded. 'Christ, I was going to drop in and see him. What happened?'

'We're not sure yet. The post-mortem will probably be this afternoon.'

Holmes was no fool; again he caught the gist. 'Accident, suicide or murder?'

'One of those last two.'

'And your money'd be on murder?'

'My money stays in my pocket till I've spoken to the tipster.'

'Meaning Dr Curt?'

Rebus nodded. 'Till then, there's not much we can do. Listen, let me get a car to take you home ...'

204

'No, no, I'll be all right.' He rose to his feet slowly, as though checking his bones for solidity. 'I'll be fine really. It's just ... poor Eddie. He was a friend of mine, you know?'

'I know,' said Rebus.

After Holmes had gone, Rebus was able to reflect that he'd gotten off lightly. Brian still wasn't operating at full throttle; partly the convalescence, partly the shock. So he hadn't asked Rebus any difficult questions. Questions like, does Eddie's death have anything to do with the person who nearly killed *me*? It was something Rebus had been wondering himself. Last night Eddie was missing, and Rebus had gone to see Cafferty. Today, first thing, Eddie was dead. Meaning one less person who could say anything about the night the Central burnt down; one less person who'd been there. But Rebus still had the gut feeling Cafferty had been surprised to learn of Holmes' attack. So what was the answer?

'I'm buggered if I know,' John Rebus said quietly to himself. His phone rang. He picked it up and heard pub noises, then Flower's voice.

'That's some team you've got there, Inspector. One gets his face mashed in, and now the other falls on her arse.' The connection was briskly severed.

'And bugger you, too, Flower,' Rebus said, all too aware that no one was listening.

22

Edinburgh's public mortuary was sited on the Cowgate, named for the route cattle would take when being brought into the city to be sold. It was a narrow canyon of a street with few businesses and only passing traffic. Way up above it were much busier streets, South Bridge for instance. They seemed so far from the Cowgate, it might as well have been underground.

Rebus wasn't sure the area had ever been anything other than a desperate meeting place for Edinburgh's poorest denizens, who often seemed like cattle themselves, dull-witted from lack of sunlight and grazing on begged handouts from passers-by. The Cowgate was ripe for redevelopment these days, but who would slaughter the cattle?

A fine setting for the understated mortuary where, when he wasn't teaching at the University, Dr Curt plied his trade.

'Look on the bright side,' he told Rebus. 'The Cowgate's got a couple of fine pubs.'

'And a few more you could shave a dead man with.'

Curt chuckled. 'Colourful, though I'm not sure the image conjured actually *means* anything.'

'I bow to your superior knowledge. Now, what have you got on Mr Ringan?'

'Ah, poor Orphan Eddie.' Curt liked to find names for all his cadavers. Rebus got the feeling the 'Orphan' prefix had been used many a time before. In Eddie Ringan's case, though, it was accurate. He had no living relations that anyone knew of, and so had been identified by Patrick Calder, and by Siobhan Clarke, since she'd been the one to find the body.

'Yes, that's the man I found,' she had said.

'Yes, that's Edward Ringan,' Pat Calder had said, before being led away by Toni the barman.

Rebus now stood with Curt beside the slab on which what was left of the corpse was being tidied up by an assistant. The assistant was whistling 'Those Were the Days' as he scraped miscellany into a bucket of offal. Rebus was reading through a list. He'd been through it three times already, trying to take his mind off the scene around him. Curt was smoking a cigarette. At the age of fifty-five, he'd decided he might as well start, since nothing else had so far managed to kill him. Rebus might have taken a cigarette from him, but they were Player's untipped, the smoking equivalent of paint stripper.

Maybe because he'd perused the list so often, something clicked at last. 'You know,' he said, 'we never found a suicide note.'

'They don't always leave them.'

'Eddie would have. *And* he'd have had Elvis singing *Heartbreak Hotel* on a tape player beside the oven.'

'Now that's style,' Curt said disingenuously.

'And now,' Rebus went on, 'from this list of the contents of his pockets, I see he didn't have any keys on him.'

'No keys, eh.' Curt was enjoying his break too much to bother trying to work it out. He knew Rebus would tell him anyway.

'So,' Rebus obliged, 'how did he get in? Or if he *did* use his keys to get in, where are they now?'

'Where indeed.' The attendant frowned as Curt stubbed his cigarette into the floor.

Rebus knew when he'd lost an audience. He put the list away. 'So what have you got for me?'

207

'Well, the usual tests will have to be carried out, of course.'

'Of course, but in the meantime ...?'

'In the meantime, a few points of interest.' Curt turned to the cadaver, forcing Rebus to do the same. There was a cover over the charred face, and the attendant had roughly sewn up the chest and stomach, now empty of their major organs, with thick black thread. The face had been badly burnt, but the rest of the body remained unaffected. The plump flesh was pale and shiny.

'Well,' Curt began, 'the burns were superficial merely. The internal organs were untouched by the blast. That made things easier. I would say he probably asphyxiated through inhalation of North Sea gas.' He turned to Rebus. 'That "North Sea" is pure conjecture.' Then he grinned again, a lopsided grin that meant one side of his mouth stayed closed. 'There was evidence of alcoholic intake. We'll have to wait for the test results to determine how much. A lot, I'd guess.'

'I'll bet his liver was a treat. He's been putting the stuff away for years.'

Curt seemed doubtful. He went to another table and returned with the organ itself, which had already been cross-sectioned. 'It's actually in pretty good shape. You said he was a spirits drinker?'

Rebus kept his eyes out of focus. It was something you learned. 'A bottle a day easy.'

'Well, it doesn't show from this.' Curt tossed the liver a few inches into the air. It slapped back down into his palm. He reminded Rebus of a butcher showing off to a potential buyer. 'There was also a bump to the head and bruising and minor burns to the arms.'

'Oh?'

'I'd imagine these are injuries often incurred by chefs in their daily duties. Hot fat spitting, pots and pans everywhere ...'

'Maybe,' said Rebus.

'And now we come to the section of the programme Hamish has been waiting for.' Curt nodded towards his assistant, who straightened his back in anticipation. 'I call him Hamish,' Curt confided, 'because he comes from the Hebrides. Hamish here spotted something *I* didn't. I've been putting off talking about it lest he become encephalitic.' He looked at Rebus. 'A little pathologist's joke.'

'You're not so small,' said Rebus.

'You need to know, Inspector, that Hamish has a fascination with teeth. Probably because his own as a child were terribly bad and he has memories of long days spent under the dentist's drill.'

Hamish looked as though this might actually be true.

'As a result, Hamish always looks in people's mouths, and this time he saw fit to inform me that there was some damage.'

'What sort of damage?'

'Scarring of the tissues lining the throat. Recent damage, too.'

'Like he'd been singing too loud?'

'Or screaming. But much more likely that something has been forced down his throat.'

Rebus's mind boggled. Curt always seemed able to do this to him. He swallowed, feeling how dry his own throat was. 'What sort of thing?'

Curt shrugged. 'Hamish suggested ... You understand, this is entirely conjecture – usually *your* field of expertise. Hamish suggested a pipe of some kind, something solid. I myself would add the possibility of a rubber or plastic tube.'

Rebus coughed. 'Not anything ... er, organic then?'

'You mean like a courgette? A banana?'

'You know damned well what I mean.'

Curt smiled and bowed his head. 'Of course I do, I'm sorry.' Then he shrugged. 'I wouldn't rule anything out.

209

But if you're suggesting a penis, it must have been sheathed in sandpaper.'

Behind them, Rebus heard Hamish stifle a laugh.

Rebus telephoned Pat Calder and asked if they might meet. Calder thought it over before agreeing.

'At the Colonies?' Rebus asked.

'Make it the Cafe, I'm heading over there anyway.'

So the Cafe it was. When Rebus arrived, the 'convalescence' sign had been replaced with one stating, 'Due to bereavement, this establishment has ceased trading.' It was signed Pat Calder.

As Rebus entered, he heard Calder roar, 'Do fuck off!' It was not, however, aimed at Rebus but at a young woman in a raincoat.

'Trouble, Mr Calder?'. Rebus walked into the restaurant. Calder was busy taking the mementoes down off the walls and packing them in newspaper. Rebus noticed three tea chests on the floor between the tables.

'This bloody reporter wants some blood and grief for her newspaper.'

'Is that right, miss?' Rebus gave Mairie Henderson a disapproving but, yes, almost *fatherly* look. The kind that let her know she should be ashamed.

'Mr Ringan was a popular figure in the city,' she told Rebus. 'I'm sure he'd have wanted our readers to know –'

Calder interrupted. 'He'd have wanted them to stuff their faces here, leave a fat cheque, then get the fuck out. Print *that!*'

'Quite an epitaph,' Mairie commented.

Calder looked like he'd brain her with the Elvis clock, the one with the King's arms replacing the usual clock hands. He thought better of it, and lifted the Elvis mirror (one of several) off the wall instead. He wouldn't dare smash that: seven years' bad junk food.

'I think you'd better go, miss,' Rebus said calmly.

'All right, I'm going.' She slung her bag over her shoulder and stalked past Rebus. She was wearing a skirt today, a short one too. But a good soldier knew when to keep eyes front. He smiled at Pat Calder, whose anguish was all too evident.

'Bit soon for all this, isn't it?'

'You can cook, can you, Inspector? Without Eddie, this place is ... it's nothing.'

'Looks like the local restaurants can sleep easy, then.'

'How do you mean?'

'Remember, Eddie thought the attack on Brian was a warning.'

'Yes, but what's that ...' Calder froze. 'You think someone ...? It was suicide, wasn't it?'

'Looked that way, certainly.'

'You mean you're not sure?'

'Did he seem the type who would kill himself?'

Calder's reply was cold. 'He was killing himself every day with drink. Maybe it all got too much. Like I said, Inspector, the attack on Brian affected Eddie. Maybe more than we knew.' He paused, still with the mirror gripped in both hands. 'You think it was murder?'

'I didn't say that, Mr Calder.'

'Who would do it?'

'Maybe you were behind with your payments.'

'What payments?'

'Protection payments, sir. Don't tell me it doesn't go on.'

Calder stared at him unblinking. 'You forget, I was in charge of finances, and we always paid our bills on time. All of them.'

Rebus took this information in, wondering exactly what it meant. 'If you think you know who might have wanted Eddie dead, best tell me, all right? Don't go doing anything rash.'

'Like what?'

Like buying a gun, Rebus thought, but he said nothing. Calder started to wrap the mirror. 'This is about all a newspaper's worth,' he said.

'She was only doing her job. You wouldn't have turned down a good review, would you?'

Calder smiled. 'We got plenty.'

'What will you do now?'

'I haven't thought about it. I'll go away, that's all I know.'

Rebus nodded towards the tea chests. 'And you'll keep all that stuff?'

'I couldn't throw it away, Inspector. It's all there is.'

Well, thought Rebus, there's the bedroom too. But he didn't say anything. He just watched Pat Calder pack everything away.

Hamish, real name Alasdair McDougall, had more or less been chased from his native Barra by his contemporaries, one of whom tried to drown him during a midnight boat crossing from South Uist after a party. Two minutes in the freezing waters of the Sound of Barra and he'd have been fit for nothing but fish-food, but they'd hauled him back into the boat and explained the whole thing away as an accident. Which is also what it would have been had he actually drowned.

He went to Oban first, then south to Glasgow before crossing to the east coast. Glasgow suited him in some respects, but not in others. Edinburgh suited him better. His parents had always denied to themselves that their son was homosexual, even when he'd stood there in front of them and said it. His father had quoted the Bible at him, the same way he'd been quoting it for seventeen years, a believer's righteous tremble in his voice. It had once been a powerful and persuasive performance; but now it seemed laughable.

'Just because it's in the Bible,' he'd told his father, 'doesn't mean you should take it as gospel.'

But to his father it was and always would be the literal truth. The Bible had been in the old man's hand as he'd shooed his youngest son out of the door of the croft house. 'Never dare to blacken our name!' he'd called. And Alasdair reckoned he'd lived up to this through introducing himself as Dougall and almost never passing on a last name. He had been Dougall to the gay community in Glasgow, and he was Dougall here in Edinburgh. He liked the life he'd made for himself (there was never a dull night), and he'd only been kicked-in twice. He had his clubs and pubs, his bunch of friends and a wider circle of acquaintances. He was even beginning to think of writing to his parents. He would tell them, By the time my boss gets through with a body, believe me there isn't very much left for Heaven to take.

He thought again of the plump young man who'd been gassed, and he laughed. He should have said something at the time, but hadn't. Why not? Was it because he still had one foot in the closet? He'd been accused of it before, when he'd refused to wear a pink triangle on his lapel. Certainly, he wasn't sure he wanted a policeman to know he was gay. And what would Dr Curt do? There was all sorts of homophobia about, an almost medieval fear of AIDS and its transmission. It wasn't that he couldn't live without the job, but he liked it well enough. He'd seen plenty of sheep and cattle slaughtered and quartered in his time on the island. This wasn't so very different.

No, he would keep his secret to himself. He wouldn't let on that he *knew* Eddie Ringan. He remembered the evening a week or so back. They went to Dougall's place and Eddie cooked up a chilli from stuff he found in the cupboards. Hot stuff. It really made you sweat. He wouldn't stay the night, though, wasn't that type. There'd

213

been a long kiss before parting, and half-promises of further trysts.

Yes, he knew Eddie, knew him well enough to be sure of one thing.

Whoever it was on the slab, it wasn't the guy who'd shared chilli in Dougall's bed.

Siobhan Clarke felt unnaturally calm and in control the rest of the day. She'd been given the day off from Operation Moneybags to get over the shock of her experience at the Heartbreak Cafe, but by late afternoon was itching to do *some*thing. So she drove out to Rory Kintoul's house on the half-chance. It was a neat and quite recent council semi in a cul-de-sac. The front garden was the size of a beer-mat but probably more hygienic; she reckoned she could eat her dinner off the trimmed weedless lawn without fear of food poisoning. She couldn't even say that of the plates in most police canteens. One gate led her down the path, and another brought her to Kintoul's front door. It was painted dark blue. Every fourth door in the street was dark blue. The others were plum-red, custard yellow, and battleship grey. Not exactly a riot of colour, but somehow in keeping with the pebbledash and tarmac. Some kids had chalked a complex hopscotch grid on the pavement and were now playing noisily. She'd smiled towards them, but they hadn't looked up from their game. A dog barked in a back garden a few doors down, but otherwise the street was quiet.

She rang the doorbell and waited. Nobody, it seemed, was home. She thought of the phrase 'gallus besom' as she took the liberty of peering in through the front window. A living room stretched to the back of the house. The dog was barking louder now, and through the far window she caught sight of a figure. She opened the garden gate and turned right, running through the close separating Kintoul's house from its neighbour. This led to

214

the back gardens. Kintoul had left his kitchen door open so as not to make a noise. He had one leg over his neighbour's fence, and was trying to shush the leashed mongrel.

'Mr Kintoul!' Siobhan called. When he looked up, she waved her hand. 'Sitting on the fence, I see. How about the two of us going inside for a word?'

She wasn't about to spare him any blushes. As he slouched towards her across the back green, she grinned. 'Running away from the police, eh? What've you got to hide?'

'Nuthin'.'

'You should be careful,' she warned. 'A stunt like that could open those stitches in your side.'

'Do you want everyone to hear? Get inside.' He almost pushed her through the kitchen door. It was exactly the invitation Siobhan wanted.

Rebus got the call at six-fifteen and arranged the meeting for ten. At eight, Patience called him. He knew he wouldn't sound right to her, would sound like his thoughts were elsewhere (which they were), but he wanted to keep her talking. He was filling the time till ten o'clock and didn't want any of it left vacant. He might start to think about it otherwise, might change his mind.

Eventually, for want of other topics, he told Patience all about Michael (who was asleep in the box room). At last they were on the same wavelength. Patience suggested counselling, and was amazed no one at the hospital had mentioned the possibility. She would look into it and get back to Rebus. Meantime, he'd have to watch Michael didn't go into clinical depression. The problem with those drugs was that they not only killed your fears, they could kill your emotions stone dead.

'He was so lively when he moved in,' Rebus said. 'The

students are wondering what the hell's happened to him. I think they're as worried as I am.'

Michael's self-proclaimed 'girlfriend' had spent time trying to talk to him, coaxing him out to pubs and clubs. But Michael had fought against it, and she hadn't shown her face for at least a day. One of the male students had approached Rebus in the kitchen and asked, in tones of deepest sympathy, if a bit of 'blaw' might help Mickey. Rebus had shaken his head. Christ, it might not be a bad idea, though.

But Patience was against it. 'Mix the stuff he's on with cannabis and God knows what sort of reaction you'd get: paranoia or a complete downer would be my guess.'

She was anti-drugs anyway, and not just the proscribed kinds. She knew that the easy way out for doctors was to fill out a form for the pharmacy. Valium, moggies, whatever it took. People all over Scotland, and especially the people who needed most help, were eating tablets like they were nourishment. And the doctors pointed to their workloads and said, What else can we do?

'Want me to come over?' she was asking now. It was a big step. Yes, Rebus wanted her to come over, but it was nearly nine.

'No, but I appreciate the thought.'

'Well, try not to leave him too long on his own. He's sleeping to escape something he needs to confront.'

'Bye, Patience.' Rebus put down the phone and made ready to leave the flat.

Why had he chosen the waterfront at North Queensferry for the meeting? Well, wasn't it obvious? He stood near the same hut they'd taken Michael to, and he got cold. He'd arrived early, and Deek naturally was late. Rebus didn't really mind. It gave him time to stare up at the rail bridge, wondering how it would feel to be lowered over the side at the dead of night. Screaming dumbly into your gag as they took the bag from your face. Looking all the way down. That's where Rebus was now, though he was at sea level. He was looking all the way down.

'Cold though, eh?' Deek Torrance rubbed his hands together.

'Thanks for setting me up the other night.'

'Eh?'

'"Sailor for trade or rent".'

'Oh aye, that.' Torrance grinned. '"King of the Road". That's not the way it goes, though ...'

'You've got it?'

Deek patted his coat pocket. He was jittery, with good cause. It wasn't every day you sold an illegal firearm to a policeman.

'Let's see it, then.'

'What? Out here?'

Rebus looked around. 'There's nobody here.'

Deek bit his lip, then resigned himself to lifting the handgun out of his pocket and placing it in John Rebus's palm.

The thing was a lifeless weight, but comfortable to hold. Rebus placed it in his own capacious pocket. 'Ammo?'

The bullets shook in their box like a baby's toy. Rebus pocketed them too, then reached into the back pocket of his trousers for the cash.

'Want to count it?'

Deek shook his head, then nodded across the road. 'I'll buy you a drink though, if you like.'

A drink sounded good to Rebus. 'I'll just get rid of this first.' He unlocked his car and slipped the gun and ammo underneath the driver's seat. He noticed he was trembling and a little dizzy as he stood back up. A drink would be good. He was hungry, too, but the thought of food made him want to boak. He looked again at the bridge. 'Come on, then,' he said to Deek Torrance.

Minus gun and with money in its place, Torrance was

217

more relaxed and loquacious. They sat in the Hawes Inn with their drinks. Torrance was explaining how the guns came into the country.

'See, it's easy to buy a gun in France. They even come around the towns in vans and flog them off the back. Stick a catalogue through your door to let you know what they'll have. I got to meet this French guy, not bad to say he's French. He's back and forth over the Channel, some sort of business he's in. He brings the guns with him, and I buy them. He brings Mace too, if you're interested.'

'Why didn't you say?' Rebus muttered into his pint. 'I wouldn't have needed the gun.'

'Eh?' Deek saw he was making a joke and laughed.

'So what have I got?' asked Rebus. 'It was a bit dark out there to see.'

'Well, they're all copies. Don't worry, I file off any identifiers myself. Yours is a Colt 45. It'll take ten rounds.'

'Eight millimetre?'

Deek nodded. 'There are twenty in the box. It's not the most lethal weapon around. I can get replica Uzis too.'

'Christ.' Rebus finished his pint. He suddenly wanted to be out of there.

'It's a living,' said Deek Torrance.

'Aye, right, a living,' said Rebus, getting up to go.

23

Next morning Rebus forced himself into the usual routine. He checked to see if there had been any sign of Andrew McPhail. There had not. Maclean hadn't been too badly hurt by the boiled water, most of which he'd deflected with his arms. Nobody was yet treating McPhail like a dangerous criminal. His description had been issued to bus and train stations, motorway service areas, and the like. If the manpower were available, Rebus knew *exactly* where he would start looking for him.

A shadow fell over his desk. It was the Little Weed.

'So,' Flower said, 'you lose a DS to a blow on the napper, and a DC to a gas explosion. What's for an encore?'

Rebus saw that they had an audience. Half the station had been waiting for a confrontation between the two inspectors. Now more detectives than usual seemed interested in the filing cabinets near Rebus's desk.

'It's easier if you do a handstand,' commented Rebus.

'What is?'

'Talking out of your arse.'

There were a few covering coughs from the filing cabinets. 'I've got some throat pastilles if you want them,' Rebus called. The cabinet doors slid shut. The audience moved away.

'You think you're God's gift, don't you?' Flower said. 'You think you're all it takes.'

'I'm better than some.'

'And a lot worse than others.'

Rebus picked up the previous evening's arrest sheet and started to read it. 'If you're finished . . .?'

Flower smiled. 'Rebus, I thought your kind went out with the dinosaurs.'

'Aye, but only because they turned *you* down when you asked them.'

Which made it two-nil as Alister Flower walked off the field. But Rebus knew there'd be another leg to the match, and another after that.

He looked again at the arrest sheet, checking he'd seen the name right, then sighed and went down to the cells. A cluster of young constables stood outside cell one, taking turns at the peephole.

'It's that guy with the tattoos,' one of them explained to Rebus.

'The Pincushion?'

The constable nodded. The Pincushion was tattooed from head to foot, not an inch unblemished. 'He's been brought in for questioning.'

Rebus nodded. Whenever they had reason to bring the Pincushion into a station, he always ended up naked.

'It's a good name, isn't it, sir?'

'What, Pincushion? It's better than my name for him, I suppose.'

'What's that.'

'Just another prick,' said Rebus, unlocking cell number two. He closed the door behind him. A young man was sitting on the bunk, unshaven and sorry-eyed.

'What happened to you, then?'

Andy Steele looked up at him, then away. The city of Edinburgh had not been kind to him during his visit. He ran a handful of fingers through his tousled hair.

'Did you go see your Auntie Ena?' he asked.

Rebus nodded. 'I didn't see your mum and dad, though.'

'Ach well, at least I managed that, eh? I managed to

track you down and put you in touch with her.'

'So what have you been up to since?'

Flakes of scalp were being clawed to the surface of Andy Steele's head. They floated down onto his trousers. 'Well, I did a bit of sightseeing.'

'They don't arrest you for that these days, though.'

Steele sighed and stopped scratching. 'Depends what sights you see. I told a man in a pub I was a private detective. He said he had a case for me.'

'Oh aye?' Rebus's attention was momentarily drawn to a crude game of noughts and crosses on the cell wall.

'His wife was cheating him. He told me where he thought I could find her, and he gave me a description. I got ten quid, with more when I reported back.'

'Go on.'

Andy Steele stared up at the ceiling. He knew he wasn't making himself look good, but it was a bit late for that anyway. 'It was a ground floor flat. I watched all evening. I saw the woman, she was there, all right. But no man. So I went round the back to get a better look. Someone must have spotted me and phoned the police.'

'You told them your story?'

Steele nodded. 'They even took me back to the bar. He wasn't there, of course, and nobody knew him. I didn't even know his name.'

'But his description of the woman was accurate?'

'Oh aye.'

'Probably an ex-wife or some old flame. He wanted to give them a scare, and it was worth ten notes to do it.'

'Except now the woman's pressing charges. Not a very good start to my career, is it, Inspector?'

'Depends,' said Rebus. 'Your career as a private dick may not be much cop, but as a peeping-tom your star is definitely in the ascendant.' Seeing Steele's misery, Rebus winked. 'Cheer up, I'll see what I can do.'

In fact, before he could do anything, Siobhan Clarke

was on the telephone from Gorgie to tell him about her meeting with Rory Kintoul.

'I asked him if he knew anything about his cousin's heavy betting. He wouldn't say, but I get the feeling they're a close-knit family. There were hundreds of photos in the living room: aunties and uncles, brothers and sisters, nieces, cousins, grannies ...'

'I get the idea. Did you mention the broken window?'

'Oh yes. He was so interested, he had to clamp himself to the chair to stop from jumping out of it. Not a great talker, though. He reckoned it must have been a drunk.'

'The same drunk who took a knife to his gut?'

'I didn't put it quite like that, and neither did he. I don't know whether it's relevant or not, but he did say he'd driven the butcher's van for his cousin.'

'What, full time?'

'Yes. Up until about a year ago.'

'I didn't know Bone's had a van. That'll be the next to go.'

'Sir?'

'The van. Smash the shop window, and if that doesn't work, torch the van.'

'You're saying it's all about protection?'

'Maybe protection, more likely money owing on bad bets. What do you think?'

'Well, I did raise that possibility with Kintoul.'

'And?'

'He laughed.'

'That's strong language coming from him.'

'Agreed, he's not exactly the emotional type.'

'So it's not betting money. I'll have another think.'

'His son came in while we were talking.'

'Refresh my memory.'

'Seventeen and unemployed, name's Jason. When Kintoul told him I was CID, the son looked worried.'

222

'A natural reaction in a teenager on the dole. They think we're press-ganging these days.'

'There was more to it than that.'

'How much more?'

'I don't know. Could be the usual, drugs and gangs.'

'We'll see if he's got a record. How's Moneybags?'

'Frankly, I'd rather be sewing mailbags.'

Rebus smiled. 'All part of the learning curve, Clarke,' he said, putting down the phone.

Somehow yesterday he'd forgotten to ask Pat Calder about the message on the inside of the recipe book. He didn't like to think it had been jostled from his mind by Mairie's legs or the sight of all those Elvises. Rebus had checked before leaving the station. Jason Kintoul was not on the files. Somehow the gun beneath the driver's seat helped keep Rebus's mind sharp. The drive to the Colonies didn't take long.

Pat Calder seemed quite shocked to see him.

'Morning,' said Rebus. 'Thought I'd find you at home.'

'Come in, Inspector.'

Rebus went in. The living room was much less tidy than on his previous visit, and he began to wonder which of the couple had been the tidier. Certainly, Eddie Ringan looked and acted like a slob, but you couldn't always tell.

'Sorry for the mess.'

'Well, you've got a lot on your mind just now.' The place was stuffy, with that heavy male smell you got sometimes in shared flats and locker-rooms. But usually it took more than one person to create it. Rebus began to wonder about the lean young bartender who'd accompanied Calder to the mortuary ...

'I've just been arranging the funeral,' Pat Calder was saying. 'It's on Monday. They asked if it would be family and friends. I had to tell them Eddie didn't have any family.'

'He had good friends, though.'

Calder smiled. 'Thank you, Inspector. Thank you for that. Was there something in particular ...?'

'It was just something we found at the scene.'

'Oh?'

'A sort of a message. It said, "I only turned on the gas".'

Calder froze. 'Christ, it *was* suicide, then?'

Rebus shrugged. 'It wasn't that kind of note. We found it on the inside of a school jotter.'

'Eddie's recipe book?'

'Yes.'

'I wondered where that had got to.'

'The message had been heavily scored out. I took it away for analysis.'

'Maybe it's something to do with the nightmares.'

'That's just what I was thinking. Depends what he was dreaming *about*, though, doesn't it? Nightmares can be about things you fear, *or* things you've done.'

'I'm no psychologist.'

'Me neither,' Rebus admitted. 'I take it Eddie had keys to the restaurant?'

'Yes.'

'We didn't find any on his body. Did you come across them when you were packing things up?'

'I don't think so. But how did he get in without keys?'

'You should be in CID, Mr Calder. That's what I've been wondering.' Rebus got up from the sofa. 'Well, sorry I had to come by.'

'Oh, that's all right. Can you tell Brian about the funeral arrangements? Warriston Cemetery at two o'clock.'

'Monday at two, I'll tell him. Oh, one last thing. You keep a record of table bookings, don't you?'

Calder seemed puzzled. 'Of course.'

'Only, I'd like to take a look. There might be some

names there that don't mean anything to you but might mean something to a policeman.'

Calder nodded. 'I see what you're getting at. I'll drop it into the station. I'm going to the Heartbreak at lunchtime, I'll pick it up then.'

'Still clearing stuff away?'

'No, it's a potential buyer. One of the pizza restaurants is looking to expand ...'

Whatever it was Pat Calder was hiding, he was doing only a fair job. But Rebus really didn't have the heart to start digging. There was way too much for him to worry about as it was. Starting with the gun. He'd sat with it in his car last night, his finger on the trigger. Just the way his instructor had taught him back in the Army: firm, but not tense. Like it was an erection, one you wanted to sustain.

He had been thinking too of goodies and baddies. If you thought bad things – dreams of cruelty and lust – that didn't make you bad. But if your head was full of civilised thoughts and you spent all day as a torturer ... It came down to the fact that you were judged by your actions in society, not by the inside of your head. So he'd no reason to feel bad about thinking grim and bloody thoughts. Not unless he turned thoughts into deeds. Yet going beyond thought would feel so good. More than that, it would feel *right*.

He stopped his car at the first church he came to. He hadn't attended any kind of worship for several months, always managing to make excuses and promises to himself that he'd try harder. It was just that Patience had made Sunday mornings so good.

Someone had been busy with a marker-pen on the wooden signboard in the churchyard, turning 'Our Lady of Perpetual Help' into 'Our Lady of Perpetual Hell'. Not the greatest of omens, but Rebus went inside anyway. He sat in a pew for a while. There weren't many souls in there with him. He had picked up a prayer book on the way in, and stared long and hard at its unjudgmental black cover, wondering why it made him feel so guilty. Eventually, a woman left the confessional, pulling up her headscarf. Rebus stood up and made himself enter the small box. He sat there in silence for a minute, trying to think what it was you were supposed to say.

'Forgive me, father, I'm about to sin.'

'We'll see about that, son,' came a gruff Irish voice from the other side of the grille. There was such assurance in the voice, Rebus almost smiled.

Instead he said, 'I'm not even a Catholic.'

'I'm sure that's true. But you're a Christian?'

'I suppose so. I used to go to church.'

'Do you believe?'

'I can't not believe.' He didn't add how hard he'd tried.

'Then tell me your problem.'

'Someone's been threatening me, my friends and family.'

'Have you gone to the police?'

'I am the police.'

'Ah. And now you're thinking of taking the law into your own hands, as they say in the films.'

'How did you know?'

'You're not the first bobby I've had in this confessional. There are a *few* Catholics in the police force.' This time Rebus did smile. 'So what is it you're going to do?'

'I've got a gun.'

There was an intake of breath. 'Now that's serious. Oh yes, that's serious. But you must see that if you use a gun, you turn into that which you despise so much. You turn into *them*.' The priest managed to hiss this last word.

'So what?' Rebus asked.

'So, ask yourself this. Can you live the rest of your life with the memories and the guilt?' The voice paused. 'I know what you Calvinists think. You think you're doomed from the start, so why not raise some hell before you get there? But I'm talking about *this* life, not the next. Do you want to live in Purgatory *before* you die?'

'No.'

'You'd be a bloody eejit to say anything else. Tie that gun to a rock and chuck it in the Forth, that's where it belongs.'

'Thank you, father.'

'You're more than welcome. And son?'

'Yes, father?'

'Come back and talk to me again. I like to know what madness you Prods are thinking. It gives me something to chew on when there's nothing good on the telly.'

Rebus didn't spend long at Gorgie Road. They weren't getting anywhere. The photos taken so far had been developed, and some of the faces identified. Those identified were all small-timers, old cons, or up-and-comers. They weren't so much small fish as spawn in a corner of the pond. It wasn't as if Flower was having better luck, which was just as well for Rebus. He couldn't wait for the Little Weed to put in his reimbursement claim. All those rounds of drinks ...

He felt revived by his talk with the priest, whose name he now realised he didn't even know. But then that was part of the deal, wasn't it? Sinners Anonymous. He might even grant the priest's wish and go back sometime. And tonight he'd drive out to the coast and get rid of the gun. It had been madness all along. In a sense, buying it had been enough. He'd never have used it, would he?

He parked at St Leonard's and went inside. There was a package for him at the front desk – the reservations book for the Heartbreak Cafe. Calder had put a note in with it.

'Well, Elvis ate pizza, didn't he?' So it looked like the Heartbreak was about to go Italian.

227

While he'd been reading the note, the desk officer had been phoning upstairs, keeping his voice low.

'What's all that about?' Rebus asked. He thought he'd overheard the distinct words 'He's here'.

'Nothing, sir,' said the desk officer. Rebus tried to stare an answer out of him, then turned away, just as the inner doors were pushed open in businesslike fashion by the Uglybug Sisters, Lauderdale and Flower.

'Can I have your car-keys?' Lauderdale demanded.

'What's going on?' Rebus looked to Flower, who resembled a preacher at a burning.

'The keys, please.' Lauderdale's hand was so steady, Rebus thought if he walked away and left the two men standing there, it would stay stretched out for hours. He handed over his keys.

'It's a pile of junk. If you don't kick it in the right place, you won't even get it to start.' He was following the two men through the doors and into the car park.

'I don't want to drive it,' Lauderdale said. He sounded threatening, but it was Flower's serene silence that most worried Rebus. Then it hit him: the gun! They knew about the gun. And yes, it was still under his driver's seat. Where else was he going to hide it – in the flat, where Michael might find it? In his trousers, where it would raise eyebrows? No, he'd left it in the car.

The door of which Lauderdale was now opening. Lauderdale turned towards him, his hand out again. 'The gun, Inspector Rebus.' And when Rebus didn't move: 'Give me the gun.'

24

He raised the gun and fired it – one, two, three shots. Then lowered it again.

They all took off their ear-protectors. The forensics man had fired the gun into what looked like a simple wooden crate. The bullets would be retrieved from its interior and could then be analysed. The scientist had been holding the gun's butt with a polythene glove over his hand. He dropped the gun into a polythene bag of its own before slipping off the glove.

'We'll let you know as soon as we can,' he told Chief Superintendent Watson, who nodded the man's dismissal. After he'd left the room, Watson turned to Lauderdale.

'Give it to me again, Frank.'

Lauderdale took a deep breath. This was the third time he'd told Watson the story, but he didn't mind. He didn't mind at all. 'Inspector Flower came to me late this morning and told me he'd received information –'

'What sort of information?'

'A phone call.'

'Anonymous, naturally.'

'Naturally.' Lauderdale took another breath. 'The caller told him the gun that had been used in the Central Hotel shooting five years ago was in Inspector Rebus's possession. Then he rang off.'

'And we're supposed to believe Rebus shot that man five years ago?'

Lauderdale didn't know. 'All I know is, there *was* a gun

in Rebus's car. And he says himself, it'll have his prints all over it. Whether it's the same gun or not, we'll know by the end of play today.'

'Don't sound so fucking cheerful! We both know this is a stitch-up.'

'What we know, sir,' said Lauderdale, ignoring Watson's outburst, 'is that Inspector Rebus has been carrying on a little private investigation of his own into the Central Hotel. The files are by the side of his desk. He wouldn't tell anyone why.'

'So he found something out and now somebody's worried. That's why they've planted the –'

'With respect, sir,' Lauderdale paused, 'nobody planted anything. Rebus has admitted he bought the gun from someone he calls "a stranger". He specifically *asked* this "stranger" to get a gun for him.'

'What for?'

'He says he was being threatened. Of course, he could be lying.'

'How do you mean?'

'Maybe the gun was the clue he found, the one that started him back into the Central files. Now he's spinning this story because at least then we can't accuse him of withholding evidence.'

Watson took this in. 'What do you think?'

'Without prejudice, sir –'

'Come on, Frank, we all know you hate Rebus's guts. When he saw you and Flower coming for him, he must have thought the lynch-mob had arrived.'

Lauderdale tried an easy laugh. 'Personalities aside, sir, even if we stick to the bare *facts*, Inspector Rebus is in serious trouble. Even supposing he did buy the gun, it's obviously a nasty piece of goods – it's had a file taken to it in the past.'

'He's worse than ever,' Watson mused, 'now that his girlfriend's kicked him out. I had high hopes there.'

'Sir?'

'She'd got him wearing decent clothes. Rebus was beginning to look ... promotable.'

Lauderdale nearly swallowed his tongue.

'Stupid bugger,' Watson went on. Lauderdale decided he was talking about Rebus. 'I suppose I'd better talk to him.'

'Do you want me to ...?'

'I want you to stay here and wait for those results. Where's Flower?'

'Back on duty, sir.'

'You mean back in the pub. I'll want to talk to him too. Funny how this anonymous Deep Throat just manages to talk to the one person in St Leonard's who loves Rebus as much as you do.'

'Loves, sir?'

'I said "loathes".'

But actually, as Rebus already knew, the call had been taken not by Flower himself but by a DC who just happened to know how Flower felt about Inspector John Rebus. He'd called Flower at the pub, and Flower had raced Jackie Stewart-style back to St Leonard's to tell Lauderdale.

Rebus knew this because he had time to kill at St Leonard's while everyone else was up at the forensic lab in Fettes. And he knew he had to be quick, because Watson would suspend him as soon as he came back. He found some carrier bags and put the Central Hotel files in them, along with the reservations book from the Heartbreak Cafe. Then he took the whole lot down to his car and threw them in the boot ... probably the first place Watson would want to look.

Christ, he'd been planning to get rid of that gun tonight.

Lauderdale had said it was 'suspected' of being the gun used in the Central Hotel murder. Well, that would be easy enough to prove or disprove. They still had the original bullet. Rebus wished he'd given the gun closer scrutiny. It had looked shiny new, but then maybe it had only ever been fired that one fatal time.

He didn't doubt that it *was* the gun. He just wondered how the hell they'd managed to set him up. The only answer was to work backwards. Deek had handed him the gun. So somehow they'd gotten to Deek. Well, Rebus himself had put word out that he was looking for Deek Torrance. And word got around. Someone had heard and been interested enough to track down Deek too. They'd asked him what his connection was with John Rebus. And when Rebus had then asked Deek for a gun, Deek had reported back to them.

Oh yes, that was it, all right. Rebus had set *himself* up by asking for the gun in the first place. Because then they'd known exactly what to do with him. Planting the gun was a bit *too* obvious, wasn't it? No one was going to be taken in. But it would have to be investigated, and investigations like that could take months, during which time he'd be suspended. They wanted him out of the way, that was all. Because he was getting close.

Rebus smiled to himself. He was no closer than Alaska ... unless he'd stumbled upon something without realising it. He needed to go over everything again, down to the last detail. But this would take time: time he was sure Watson would unwittingly be about to offer him.

So, when he walked into the Chief Superintendent's office, he surprised even Watson with his ease.

'John,' said Watson, after motioning for Rebus to sit, 'how come you always seem to have a banana skin up your sleeve?'

'Because I say the magic word, sir?' Rebus offered.

'And what is the magic word?'

Rebus looked surprised Watson didn't know. 'Abracadabra, sir.'

'John,' said Watson, 'I'm suspending you.'

'Thank you, sir,' said Rebus.

He spent that evening on the trail of Deek Torrance, even driving out to South Queensferry – the most forlorn hope of a forlorn night. Deek would have been paid plenty to get well away from the city. By now, he might not even be in the western hemisphere. Then again, maybe they'd have silenced him in some other more permanent way.

'Some pal you turned out to be,' Rebus muttered to himself more than once. And to complete the circle, he headed out to his favourite massage parlour. He always seemed to be the only customer, and had wondered how the Organ Grinder made his money. But now of course he knew: the Organ Grinder would come to your home. Always supposing you were wealthy enough ... or had reputation enough.

'How long have you been going out there?' Rebus asked. Prone on the table, he was aware that the Organ Grinder could break his neck or his back with consummate ease. But he didn't think he would. He hoped his instincts weren't wrong in this at least.

'Just a couple of months. Someone at a health club told his wife about me.'

'Know her, do you?'

'Not really. She thinks I'm too rough.'

'That's droll, coming from the wife of Big Ger Cafferty.'

'He's a villain, then?'

'Whatever gave you that idea?'

'You forget, I've not been up here that long.'

True, Rebus had forgotten the Organ Grinder's north London pedigree. When in the mood, he told wonderful stories of that city.

'Anything about him you want to tell me?' Rebus ventured, despite the thick hands on his neck.

233

'Nothing to tell,' said the Organ Grinder. 'Silence is a virtue, Inspector.'

'And there's too much of it around. You ever seen anyone out at his house?'

'Just his wife and the chauffeur.'

'Chauffeur? You mean the man mountain with the knob of gristle for a left ear?'

'That explains the haircut,' mused the Organ Grinder.

'Precious little else would,' said Rebus.

After the Organ Grinder had finished with him, Rebus went back to the flat. Michael was watching a late film, the glow from the TV set flicking across his rapt face. Rebus went over to the TV and switched it off. Michael still stared at the screen, not blinking. There was a cup of cold tea in his hand. Gently, Rebus took it from him.

'Mickey,' he said. 'I need someone to talk to.'

Michael blinked and looked up at him. 'You can always talk to me,' he said. 'You know that.'

'I know that,' said Rebus. 'We've got something else in common now.'

'What's that?'

Rebus sat down. 'We've both been recently suspended.'

25

Chief Superintendent Watson dreaded these Saturday mornings, when his wife would try to entice him to go shopping with her. Dreary hours in department stores and clothes shops, not to mention the supermarket, where he'd be guinea-pig for the latest microwavable Malaysian meal or some rude looking unpronounceable fruit. Worst of all, of course, he saw other men in exactly the same predicament. It was a wonder one of them didn't lose the rag and start screaming about how they used to be the hunters, fierce and proud.

But this morning he had the excuse of work. He always tried to have an excuse either for nipping into St Leonard's or else bringing work home with him. He sat in his study, listening to Radio Scotland and reading the newspaper, the house quiet and still around him. Then the telephone rang, annoying him until he remembered he was waiting for just this call. It was Ballistics at Fettes. After he took the call, he looked up a number in his card index and made another.

'I want you in my office Monday morning,' he told Rebus, 'for formal questioning.'

'From which I take it,' said Rebus, 'that I bought a lulu of a gun.'

'Lulu *and* her backing band.'

'They were called the Luvvers, sir. The bullets matched up?'

'Yes.'

'You knew they would,' said Rebus. 'And so did I.'

'It's awkward, John.'

'It's supposed to be.'

'For you as well as me.'

'With all respect, sir, I wasn't thinking of you ...'

When Siobhan Clarke woke up that morning, she glanced at the clock then shot out of bed. Christ, it was nearly nine! She had just run water for a bath, and was looking for clean underwear in the bathroom, when it hit her. It was the weekend! Nothing to rush for. In fact, quite the opposite. The relief team had taken over Moneybags, just for this first weekend, to see if there was any sign of life at Dougary's office. According to Trading Standards, Dougary's weekends were sacrosanct. He wouldn't go anywhere near Gorgie. But they had to be sure, so for this weekend only Operation Moneybags had a relief retinue, keeping an eye on the place. If nothing happened, next weekend they wouldn't bother. Dougary was blessedly fixed in his ways. She hadn't had to hang about too often on the surveillance past five-thirty, more often a bit earlier. Which suited Siobhan fine. It meant she'd managed a couple of useful trips to Dundee out of hours.

She'd arranged another trip for this morning, but didn't need to leave Edinburgh for an hour or so yet. And she was sure to be home before the Hibees kicked off.

Time now for some coffee. The living room was messy, but she didn't mind. She usually set aside Sunday morning for all the chores. That was the nice thing about living by yourself: your mess was your own. There was no one to comment on it or be disturbed by it. Crisp bags, pizza boxes, three-quarters-empty bottles of wine, old newspapers and magazines, CD cases, items of clothing, opened and unopened mail, plates and cutlery and every mug in the flat – these could all be found in her fourteen-by-twelve living room. Somewhere under the debris there was a futon and a cordless telephone.

The telephone was ringing. She reached under a pizza carton, picked up the receiver, and yanked up the aerial.

'Is that you, Clarke?'

'Yes, sir.' The last person she'd been expecting: John Rebus. She wandered through to the bathroom.

'Terrible interference,' said Rebus.

'I was just turning off the bath.'

'Christ, you're in the –'

'No, sir, not yet. Cordless phone.'

'I hate those things. You're talking for five minutes, then you hear the toilet flushing. Well, sorry to ... what time is it?'

'Just turned nine.'

'Really?' He sounded dead beat.

'Sir, I heard about your suspension.'

'That figures.'

'I know it's none of my business, but what were you doing with a gun in the first place?'

'Psychic protection.'

'Sorry?'

'That's what my brother calls it. He should know, he used to be a hypnotist.'

'Sir, are you all right?'

'I'm fine. Are you going to the game?'

'Not if you need me for anything else.'

'Well, I was wondering ... do you still have the Cafferty files?'

She had walked back into the living room. Oh, she still had the files, all right. Their contents were spread across her coffee table, her desk, and half the breakfast bar.

'Yes, sir.'

'Any chance you could bring them over to my flat? Only I've got the Central Hotel files here. Somewhere in them there's a clue I'm missing.'

'You want to cross-reference with the Cafferty files? That's a big job.'

'Not if two people are working on it.'

'What time do you want me there?'

Saturday at Brian Holmes' aunt's house in Barnton was a bit like Sunday, except that on Saturday he didn't have to deny her his company at the local presbyterian kirk. Was it any wonder that, having found the Heartbreak Cafe such a welcoming spot, he should have spent so long there? But those days were over. He tried to accept the fact that 'Elvis' was dead, but it was difficult. No more King Shrimp Creole or Blue Suede Choux or In the Gateau, no more Blue Hawaii cocktails. No more late nights of tequila slammers (with Jose Cuervo Gold, naturally) or Jim Beam (Eddie's preferred bourbon).

' "Keep on the Beam," he used to say.'

'There there, pet.' Oh great, now his aunt had caught him talking to himself. She'd brought him a cup of Ovaltine.

'This stuff's for bedtime,' he told her. 'It's not even noon.'

'It'll calm you down, Brian.'

He took a sip. Ach, it didn't taste bad anyway. Pat had dropped round to ask if he'd be a pall-bearer on Monday.

'It'd be an honour,' Holmes had told him, meaning it. Pat hadn't wanted to meet his eyes. Maybe he too was thinking of the nights they'd all spent slurring after-hours gossip at the bar. On one of those nights, when they'd been talking about great Scottish disasters, Eddie had suddenly announced that he'd been there when the Central Hotel caught fire.

'I was filling in for a guy, cash in the hand and no questions. Dead on my feet after the day-shift at the Eyrie.'

'I didn't know you'd worked at the Eyrie.'

'Assistant to the head man himself. If he doesn't get a

Michelin recommendation this year, he'd be as well giving up.'

'So what happened at the Central?' Holmes' head hadn't been entirely befuddled by spirits.

'Some poker game was going on, up in one of the rooms on the first floor.' He seemed to be losing it, drifting towards sleep. 'Tam and Eck were looking for players ...'

'Tam and Eck?'

'Tam and Eck Robertson ...'

'But what happened?'

'It's no good, Brian,' said Pat Calder, 'look at him.'

Though Eddie's eyes were open, head resting on his arms, arms spread across the bar, he was asleep.

'A cousin of mine was at Ibrox the day of the big crush,' Pat revealed, cleaning a pint glass.

'But do you remember where you were the night Jock Stein died?' Holmes asked. More stories had followed, Eddie sleeping through all of them.

Permanently asleep now. And Holmes was to be pall-bearer number four. He'd asked Pat a few questions.

'Funny,' Pat had said, 'your man Rebus asked me just the same.'

So Brian knew the case was in good hands.

Rebus drove around the lunchtime streets. On a Saturday, providing you steered clear of Princes Street, the city had a more relaxed feel. At least until about two-thirty, when either the east end or the west of the city (depending who was playing home) would fill with football fans. And on derby match days, best stay away from the centre altogether. But today wasn't a derby match, and Hibs were at home, so the town was quiet.

'You asked about him just the other week,' a barman told Rebus.

'And I'm asking again.'

He was again on the lookout for Deek Torrance; a seek

and destroy mission. He doubted Deek would be around, but sometimes money and alcohol did terrible things to a man, boosting his confidence, making him unwary of danger and vengeance. Rebus's hope was that Deek was still mingin' somewhere on the money he'd paid for the gun. As hopes went, it was more forlorn than most. But he did stumble upon Chick Muir in a Leith social club, and was able to tell him the news.

'That's just awfy,' Chick consoled. 'I'll keep my nose to the ground.'

Rebus appreciated the muddled sentiment. In Chick's case, it wouldn't be hard anyway. Informers were sometimes called snitches, and Chick's snitch was about as big as they came.

One-thirty found him leaving a dingy betting shop. He'd seen more hope and smiles in a hospice, and fewer tears too. Ten minutes later he was sitting down to microwaved haggis, neeps and tatties in the Sutherland Bar. Someone had left a newspaper on his chair, and he started to read it. By luck, it was open at a piece by Mairie Henderson.

'You're late,' he said as Mairie herself sat down. She nearly stood up again in anger.

'I was in here half an hour ago! Quarter past one, we arranged. I stayed till half past.'

'I thought half past was the agreement,' he said blithely.

'You weren't *here* at half past. You're lucky I came back.'

'Why did you?'

She tore the newspaper from him. 'I left my paper.'

'Not much in it anyway.' He scooped more haggis into his mouth.

'I thought you were buying me lunch.'

Rebus nodded towards the food counter. 'Help yourself. They'll add it to my tab.'

It took her a moment to decide that she was hungrier

than she was angry. She came back from the food counter with a plate of quiche and bean salad, and grabbed her purse. 'They don't *have* tabs here!' she informed him. Rebus winked.

'Just my little joke.' He tried to hand her some money, but she turned on her heels. Low heels, funny little shoes like children's Doc Marten's. And black tights. Rebus rolled the food around with his tongue. She sat down at last and took off her coat. It took her a moment to get comfortable.

'Anything to drink?' asked Rebus.

'I suppose it's my round?' she snapped.

He shook his head, so she asked for a gin and fresh orange. Rebus got the drinks, a half of Guinness for himself. There was probably more nutrition in the Guinness than in the meal he'd just consumed.

'So,' said Mairie, 'what's the big secret?'

Rebus used his little finger to draw his initials on the thick head of his drink, knowing they'd still be there when he reached the bottom. 'I've been shown the red card.'

That made her look up. 'What? Suspended?' She wasn't angry with him any more. She was a reporter, sniffing a story. He nodded. 'What happened?' Excitedly she forked up a mouthful of kidney bean and chickpea. Rebus had had a crash-course in pulses from his tenants. Never mind red kids and chicks, he could tell a borlotti from a pinto at fifty yards downwind.

'I came into possession of a handgun, a Colt 45. May or may not have been a copy.'

'And?' She nearly spattered him with pastry in her haste.

'And it was the gun used in the Central Hotel shooting.'

'No!' Her screech caused several drinkers to pause before their next swallow. The Sutherland was that kind of place. Riots in the streets would have merited a single measured comment. Rebus could see Mairie's head fairly filling to the brim with questions.

'Do you still write for the Sunday edition?' he asked her. She nodded, still busy trying to find an order for all the questions she had. 'What about doing me a favour, then? I've always wanted to be on the front page ...'

Not that he'd any intention of seeing his *own* name in the story. They went through it carefully together, back at the newspaper office. So Rebus got his tour of the building at last. It was a bit disappointing, all stairwell and open-plan and not much action. What action there was centred exclusively on Mairie's desk and its up-to-date word processor.

There was even a discussion with the editor of the Sunday. They needed to be sure of a few things. It was always like this with unattributed stories. In Scots law, there was no place for uncorroborated evidence. The press seemed to be following suit. But Rebus had a staunch defender in the woman whose byline would appear with the story. After a conference call with the paper's well-remunerated lawyer, the nod was given and Mairie started to hammer the keyboard into submission.

'I can't promise front page,' the editor warned. 'Beware the breaking story! As it is, you've just knocked a car crash and its three victims to the inside.'

Rebus stayed to watch the whole process. A series of commands on Mairie's computer sent the text to type-setting, which was done elsewhere in the building. Soon a laser printer was delivering a rough copy of how the front page might look tomorrow morning. And there along the bottom was the headline: GUN RECOVERED IN FIVE-YEAR-OLD MURDER MYSTERY.

'That'll change,' said Mairie. 'The sub will have a go at it once he's read the story.'

'Why?'

'Well, for one thing, it looks like the murder victim is a five-year-old.'

So it did. Rebus hadn't noticed. Mairie was staring at him.

'Isn't this going to get you in even *more* trouble?'

'Who's going to know it was me gave you the story?'

She smiled. 'Well, let's start with everyone in the City of Edinburgh Police.'

Rebus smiled too. He'd bought some caffeine pills this morning to keep him moving. They were working fine. 'If anyone asks,' he said, 'I'll just have to tell them the truth.'

'Which is what exactly?'

'That it wisnae me.'

26

Rebus dished out yet more money to the students that afternoon to get them out of the flat until midnight. He wondered if it were unique in Scottish social history for a landlord to be paying his own tenants. There were only two of them there, the other two (he'd now established that he had four permanent tenants, whose names he still had trouble with so never tried using) having headed home for purposes of cosseting and feeding-up.

Michael, however, stayed put. Rebus knew he wouldn't be any bother. He'd either be dozing in the box room or else watching the TV. He didn't seem to mind if the sound were turned off, just so long as there was a picture to stare at.

Rebus bought a bag of provisions: real coffee, milk, beer, soft drinks, and snacks. Back in the flat he remembered Siobhan was a vegetarian, and cursed himself for buying smoky bacon crisps. Bound to be artificial flavourings though, so maybe it didn't matter. She arrived at five-thirty.

'Come in, come in.' Rebus led her through the long dark hallway to the living room. 'This is my brother Michael.'

'Hello, Michael.'

'Mickey, this is DC Siobhan Clarke.' Michael nodded his head, blinking slowly. 'Here, let me take your jacket. How was the game, by the way?'

'Goalless.' Siobhan put down her two carrier-bags and

slipped off her black leather jacket. Rebus took the jacket into the hall and hung it up. When he came back, he noticed her studying the living room doubtfully.

'Bit of a tip,' he said, though he'd spent quarter of an hour tidying it.

'Big, though.' She didn't deny it was a tip. You could hardly see out of the huge sash window. And the carpet looked like it had moulted from a buffalo's back. As for the wallpaper ... she could well understand why the students had tried covering every inch with kd lang and Jesus & Mary Chain posters.

'Something to drink?'

She shook her head. 'Let's get on with it.' This wasn't quite what she'd imagined. The zombie brother didn't help, of course. But he wasn't much of a distraction either. They got down to work.

An hour later, they had scraped the surface of the files. Siobhan was lying on her side on the floor, legs curled up, one arm supporting her head. She was on her second can of cola. The file was on the floor in front of her. Rebus sat near her on the sofa, files on his lap and in a heap beside him. He had a pen behind his ear, just like a butcher or a turf accountant. Siobhan held her pen in her mouth, tapping it against her teeth when she was thinking. Some bad quiz show was playing to silent hysterics on the TV. For all the reaction on his face, Michael could have been watching a war trial.

He pulled himself out of the chair. 'I'm going to take forty winks,' he informed them. Siobhan tried not to look surprised when he made not for the living-room door but for the box room. He closed the door behind him.

'I'd like two things,' said Rebus. 'To identify the murder victim, once and for all.'

'And to identify the killer?' Siobhan guessed.

But Rebus shook his head. 'To place Big Ger at the scene.'

'There's no evidence he was anywhere near.'

'And maybe there never will be. But all the same ... We still don't know who was at the poker game. It can't just have been the Bru-Head Brothers.'

'We could talk to all the hotel's customers that night.'

'Yes, we could.' Rebus didn't sound enthusiastic.

'Or we could find the brothers – always supposing they're still alive – and ask them.'

'Their cousin might know where they are.'

'Who? Radiator McCallum?'

Rebus nodded. 'But then we don't know where he is either. Eddie Ringan was there, but he was never on the official list. Black Aengus wasn't on the list, and neither were the Bru-Head Brothers. I'm surprised we got any names at all.'

'We *are* talking about a long time ago.' Siobhan sounded more relaxed with Michael out of the room.

'We're also talking about long memories. Maybe I should have another go at Black Aengus.'

'Not if you know what's good for you.' Siobhan could have said something about Dundee, but she wanted it to be confirmed first, and she wanted it to be a surprise. She'd know by Monday.

The phone rang. Rebus picked it up.

'John? It's Patience.'

'Oh, hello there.'

'Hello yourself. I thought maybe we'd fix up that date.'

'Oh, right. For a drink?'

'Don't tell me you've forgotten? No, I know what it is: you're just playing hard to get. Don't push it *too* far, Rebus.'

'No, it's not that, I'm just a bit busy right this minute.' Siobhan seemed to take a hint, and got up, motioning that she'd make some coffee in the kitchen. Rebus nodded.

'Well, I'm sorry to interrupt whatever it is you're –'

'Don't take it the wrong way, Patience. I've just got things on my mind.'

'And I'm not included?'

Rebus made an exasperated sound. From the kitchen there came the louder sound of a sneeze. Aye, those Easter Road terraces could be snell.

'John,' said Patience, 'is there a woman in the flat?'

'Yes,' he said.

'One of the students?'

He seldom lied to her. 'No, a colleague. We're working through some case-notes.'

'I see.'

Christ, he should have tried lying. His head was too full of the Central Hotel to be able to cope with Patience's jousting. 'Look,' he said, 'have you got a time and place in mind for that drink?'

But Patience had rung off. Rebus stared at the receiver, shrugged, and placed it on the carpet. He didn't want any more interruptions.

'Coffee's on,' said Siobhan.

'Great.'

'Was it something I said?'

'What? No, no, just ... nothing.'

But Siobhan was canny. 'She heard me sneeze and thought you had another woman here.'

'I *do* have another woman here. It's just the way her mind works ... She doesn't exactly trust me.'

'And she should trust you?'

Rebus sighed. 'Tell me about the Robertson brothers again.'

Siobhan sat down on the floor and started to read from the file. From the sofa, Rebus looked down on her. The top of her head, the nape of her neck with its fine pale hairs disappearing into her collar. Small pierced ears ...

'We know they get on well. It was a close family, six kids in a one-bedroom cottage.'

'What happened to the other brothers and sisters?'

'Four sisters,' Siobhan read. 'Law-abiding wives and mothers these days. The boys were the only wild ones. Both like gambling, especially cards and the horses. Tam is the better card player of the two, but Eck has more luck on the horses ... Remember this stuff is six years old, and all hearsay in the first place.'

Rebus nodded. He was remembering the old man in that last pub in Lochgelly, the one who'd come cadging drinks from the painters and decorators. He'd said one of the drawings looked familiar. Then one of the painters had cut him short with a story about how he'd recognise a horse easier than a man. So the old guy was keen on the gee-gees, and so were Eck and Tam.

'Maybe he saw him in a bookie's,' Rebus wondered aloud.

'Sorry?'

So Rebus told her.

'It's worth a try,' she conceded. 'What else do we have to go on?'

Rebus had one good contact at Dunfermline CID, Detective Sergeant Hendry. It was rumoured that Hendry was too good at his job ever to merit promotion. Only the incompetent were promoted. It shuffled them out of the way. As a DI, Rebus didn't necessarily agree. But he knew Hendry should have been an Inspector long ago, and wondered what or who was blocking him. It couldn't be that Hendry was too abrasive: he was one of the calmest people Rebus had ever met. His hobby, bird-watching, reflected his nature. They'd exchanged home phone numbers once on a case. Yes, it was worth a try.

'Hello there, Hendry,' he said. 'It's Rebus here.'

'Rebus, trust you to disturb a working man's rest.'

'Been bird-watching?'

'I saw a spotted woodpecker this morning.'

'I saw a spotted dick once.'

'Ah, but I'm not a man of the world like you. So what do you want?'

'I want you to look in your local phone directory. I'm after bookie's shops.'

'Any one in particular?'

'No, I'm not picky. I need the names and addresses of all of them.'

'Which towns?'

Rebus thought. 'Dunfermline, Cowdenbeath, Lochgelly, Cardenden, Kelty, Ballingry. That'll do for starters.'

'This could take a bit of time. Can I phone you back?'

'Aye, sure. And ponder on two names for me. Tom and Eck Robertson. They're brothers.'

'Okay. You're at Arden Street, I hear.'

'What?'

'You got the heave from the doctor. What was it, your bedside manner?'

'Who told you?'

'Word gets around. Isn't it true then?'

'No, it's not. It's just that my brother's here for a ... ach, forget it.'

'Talk to you later.'

Rebus put down the phone. 'Would you credit that? Every bugger seems to know about Patience and me. Was there a notice in the papers, or something?'

Siobhan smiled. 'What now?'

'Hendry's going to get back with the details. Meantime, we could nip out and get a curry or something.'

'What if he phones while we're out?'

'He'll try again.'

'Haven't you got an answering machine?'

'I could never get it to work, so I chucked it out. Besides, there are that many bookie's shops in Fife, Hendry'd be on it for hours.'

They walked to Tollcross, Siobhan insistent that she could do with some fresh air.

'I thought you'd have had enough of that at the game.'

'Are you joking? *Fresh air?* Between the smoking and the smells of dead beer and pie-grease ...'

'You're putting me off my curry.'

'I bet you're the vindaloo type too.'

'Strictly Madras,' said Rebus.

During the meal, he reasoned that Siobhan might as well toddle off home afterwards. It wasn't as if they could do anything tonight with the list of betting shops. And tomorrow the shops would be closed. But Siobhan wanted to stick around at least until Hendry phoned.

'We haven't covered all the files yet,' she argued.

'True enough,' said Rebus. After the meal, while Siobhan drank a cup of coffee Rebus ordered some take-away for Michael.

'Is he all right?' Siobhan asked.

'He's getting better,' Rebus insisted. 'Those pills are nearly finished. He'll be fine once he's shot of them.'

As if to prove the point, when they got back to the flat Michael was in the kitchen, dunking a teabag in a mug of hot milky water. He looked like he'd just had a shower. He'd also shaved.

'I fetched you a curry,' Rebus said.

'You must be a mind reader.' Michael sniffed into the brown paper bag. 'Rogan Josh?' Rebus nodded and turned to Siobhan. 'Michael is the city's Rogan Josh expert.'

'There was a call while you were out.' Michael lifted the cardboard containers out of the bag.

'Hendry?'

'That was the name.'

'Did he leave a message?'

Michael unpeeled both cartons, meat and rice. 'He said you should get a pen and a lot of paper ready.'

Rebus smiled at Siobhan. 'Come on,' he said, 'let's save Hendry's phone bill.'

'I'm glad you phoned back,' were Hendry's first words. 'For one thing, I'm due at an indoor bowls tourney in half an hour. For another, this is a big list.'

'So let's have it,' said Rebus.

'I could fax it to you at the station?'

'No you couldn't, I'm out of the game.'

'I hadn't heard.'

'Funny, that; you hear about my love life fast enough. Ready when you are.'

As Hendry reeled off the names, addresses and phone numbers, Rebus relayed them to Siobhan. She claimed to be a fast writer, so was given the job of transcribing. But after ten minutes they switched over, her hand being sore. The final list covered three sides of A4. As well as the basic information, Hendry dropped in snippets of his own, such as licensing wrangles, suspected handling of stolen goods, hangouts for ne'er-do-wells and the like. Rebus was grateful for all of it.

'A fine institution, the bookie's,' he commented, when Siobhan handed him the receiver.

'You bet,' said Hendry. 'Can I go now?'

'Sure, and thanks for everything.'

'So long as it helps you get back in the game. We need all the fly-halfs we can get. Those two names didn't click with me, by the way. And Rebus?'

'What?'

'She sounds a right wee smasher.'

Hendry severed the connection before Rebus could explain. When it came to gossip, Hendry was a regular sweetie-wife. Rebus dreaded to think what stories he'd be hearing about himself in the next week or two.

'What was he saying?' Siobhan asked.

'Nothing.'

She'd been running through the list for herself. 'Well,' she said, 'no names there that mean anything to me.' Rebus took the list from her.

'Me neither.'

'Next stop Fife?'

'For me, yes. On Monday, I suppose.' Except that on Monday he'd to report to Chief Superintendent Watson *and* attend Eddie Ringan's funeral. 'You,' he said, 'are going to be busy shoring up our side of Operation Moneybags.'

'Oh, I thought I might go to the funeral. That'd give us the excuse for a couple of hours' work in Fife.'

Rebus shook his head. 'I appreciate the thought, but *you're* still on the force. I'm the one with time for this sort of legwork.' She looked bitterly disappointed. 'And that's an order,' Rebus told her.

'Yes, sir,' said Siobhan.

27

The thought of another interminable Sunday bothered Rebus so much that, after attending Mass, he drove across the Forth Road Bridge back into Fife.

He'd been to Our Lady of Perpetual Hell, sitting at the back, watching and wondering if the priest who led the worship was *his* priest. The accent was Scots-Irish; hard to tell. His priest had spoken quietly, while this one belted everything out at the top of his voice. Maybe some of the congregation were deaf. But at least there were a fair number of young folk in attendance. He was almost alone in not accepting communion.

West-central Fife could use a spot of communion itself. It would drink the wine and pawn the chalice. He decided to leave Dunfermline till last; it was the biggest town with the most locations. He'd start small. He couldn't recall whether it was quicker to get to Ballingry by coming off the motorway at Kinross, but certainly it was a much bonnier drive. He was tempted to stop at Loch Leven, site of many a childhood picnic and game of football. He still had a lump below his knee where Michael had kicked him once. The narrow, meandering roads were busy with Sunday drivers, their cars polished like medals. There was half a chance Hendry would be at the Loch Leven bird sanctuary, but Rebus didn't stop. Soon enough he was in the glummer confines of Ballingry. He didn't loiter longer than he needed to.

He wasn't sure what this trip was supposed to

accomplish. All the betting shops would be tight shut. Maybe he'd find someone he could gossip with about this or that bookie's, but he doubted it. He knew what he was doing. He was killing time, and this was a good place for it. At least here there was the illusion that he was doing something constructive about the case. So he parked outside the closed shop and constructively marked a tick against the address on his three-page list.

Of course, there *was* one more reason for his early rise this morning and his early exit from the house. In the car with him he had the Sunday paper. The Central Hotel story had stuck tenaciously to the front page, now with the headline CENTRAL MURDER BLAZE: GUN FOUND. Once Watson and co. saw it, they'd be on the phone to each other and, naturally, to John Rebus. But for once the students would have to field *his* calls. He'd read the story through twice to himself, knowing every word by heart. He was hoping that somewhere *some*body was reading it and starting to panic ...

Next stops: Lochore, Lochgelly, Cardenden. Rebus had been born and raised in Cardenden. Well, Bowhill actually, back when there had been four parishes: Auchterderran, Bowhill, Cardenden, and Dundonald. The ABCD, people called it. Then the post office had termed it all the one town, Cardenden. It wasn't so very much changed from the place Rebus had known. He stopped the car at the cemetery and spent a few minutes by the grave of his father and mother. A woman in her forties placed some flowers against a headstone nearby and smiled at Rebus as she passed him. When Rebus got back to the cemetery gates, she was waiting there.

'Johnny Rebus?'

It was so unexpected he grinned, the grin dissolving years from his face.

'I went to school with you,' the woman stated. 'Heather Cranston.'

'Heather ...?' He stared at her face. *'Cranny?'*

She put a hand to her mouth, blocking laughter. 'Nobody's called me that in twenty-odd years.'

He remembered her now. The way she always stifled laughs with her hand, embarrassed because her laugh sounded so funny to her. Now she nodded into the cemetery.

'I walk past your mum and dad most weeks.'

'It's more than I do.'

'Aye, but you're in Edinburgh or someplace now, aren't you?'

'That's right.'

'Just visiting?'

'Passing through.' They had come out of the cemetery now, and were walking downhill into Bowhill. They passed by Rebus's car, but he'd no wish to break off the conversation. So they walked.

'Aye,' she said, 'plenty of folk pass through. Never many stay put. I used to ken everybody in the place, but not now ...'

A yistiken awb-di. Listening to her, Rebus realised how much of the accent and the dialect he'd lost over the years.

'Come round for a cup of tea,' she was saying now.. He'd looked in vain for an engagement or wedding ring on her hand. She was by no means an unlovely woman. Big, whereas at school she'd been tiny and shy. Or maybe Rebus wasn't remembering right. Her cheeks were shining and there was mascara round her eyes. She was wearing black shoes with inch and a half heels, and tea-coloured tights on muscular legs. Rebus, who hadn't had breakfast or lunch, would bet that she had a pantry full of cakes and biscuits.

'Aye, why not?' he said.

She lived in a house along Craigside Road. They'd passed one betting shop on the way from the cemetery. It was as dead as the rest of the street.

'Are you going to take a look at the old house?' She meant the house he'd grown up in. He shrugged and watched her unlock her door. In the lobby, she listened for a second then yelled, 'Shug! Are you up there?' But there was no sound from upstairs. 'It's a miracle,' she said. 'Out of his bed before four o'clock. He must've gone out somewhere.' She saw the look on Rebus's face, and her hand went to her mouth. 'Don't worry, it's not a husband or boyfriend or anything. Hugh's my son.'

'Oh?'

She took off her coat. 'Away through you go.' She opened the living room door for him. It was a small room, choked with a huge three-piece suite, dining-table and chairs, wall-unit and TV. She'd had the chimney blocked off and central heating installed.

Rebus sank into one of the fireside chairs. 'But you're not married?'

She had slung her coat over the banister. 'Never really saw the point,' she said, entering the room. She devoured space as she moved, first to the radiator to check it was warm, then to the mantelpiece for cigarettes and her lighter. She offered one to Rebus.

'I've stopped,' he said. 'Doctor's orders.' Which was, in a sense, the truth.

'I tried stopping once or twice, but the weight I put on, you wouldn't credit it.' She inhaled deeply.

'So, Hugh's father . . .?'

She blew the smoke out of her nostrils. 'Never knew him, really.' She saw the look on Rebus's face. 'Have I shocked you, Johnny?'

'Just a bit, Cranny. You used to be . . . well . . .'

'Quiet? That was a lifetime ago. What do you fancy, coffee, tea or me?' And she laughed behind her cigarette hand.

'Coffee's fine,' said John Rebus, shifting in his chair.

She brought in two mugs of bitter instant. 'No biscuits, sorry, I'm all out.' She handed him his mug. 'I've already sugared it, hope that's all right.'

'Fine,' said Rebus, who did not take sugar. The mug was a souvenir of Blackpool. They talked about people they'd known at school. Sitting opposite him, she decided at one point to cross one leg over the other. But her skirt was too tight, so she gave up and tugged at the hem of the garment.

'So what brings you here? Passing through, you said?'

'Well, sort of. I'm actually looking for a bookie's shop.'

'We passed one on the –'

'This is a particular business. It's probably either new in the past five or so years, or else has been taken over by a new operator during that time.'

'Then you're after Hutchy's.' She said this nonchalantly, sucking on her cigarette afterwards.

'Hutchy's? But that place was around when *we* were growing up.'

She nodded. 'Named after Joe Hutchinson, he started it. Then he died and his son Howie took over. Tried changing the name of the place, but everybody kept calling it Hutchy's, so he gave up. About, oh, five years ago, maybe a bit less, he sold up and buggered off to Spain. Imagine, same age as us and he's made his pile. Retired to the sun. Nearest we get to the sun here is when the toaster's on.'

'So who did he sell the business to?'

She had to think about this. 'Greenwood, I think his name is. But the place is still called Hutchy's. That's what the sign says above the door. Aye, Tommy Greenwood.'

'Tommy? You're sure of that. Not Tom or Tam?'

She shook her permed head. She'd had a salt-and-pepper dye done quite recently. Rebus supposed it was to hide some authentic grey. The style itself could only be termed Bouffant Junior. It took Rebus back in time ...

'Tommy Greenwood,' she said. 'Friend of mine used to go out with him.'

'Had he been around Cardenden for long before he bought Hutchy's?'

'No time at all. We didn't know him from Adam. Then in short order he'd bought Hutchy's *and* the old doctor's house down near the river. The story goes, he paid Howie from a suitcase stacked with cash. The story goes, he *still* doesn't have a bank account.'

'So where did the money come from?'

'Aye, now you're asking a good question.' She nodded her head slowly. 'A few folk would like to know the answer to *that* one.'

He asked a few more questions about Greenwood, but there wasn't more she could tell. He kept himself to himself, walked between his house and the bookie's every day. Didn't own a flash car. No wife, no kids. Didn't do much in the way of socialising or drinking.

'He'd be quite a catch for some woman,' she said, in tones that let Rebus know she'd tried with the rod and line. 'Oh aye, quite a catch.'

Rebus escaped twenty minutes later, but not without an exchange of addresses and phone numbers and promises to keep in touch. He walked back slowly past Hutchy's – an uninspiring little double-front with peeling paint and smoky windows – and then briskly up the brae to the cemetery. At the cemetery, he saw that another car had been parked tight in behind his. A cherry-red Renault 5. He passed his own car and tapped on the window of the Renault. Siobhan Clarke put down her newspaper and wound open the window.

'What the hell are you doing here?' Rebus demanded.

'Following a hunch.'

'I don't have a hunch.'

258

'Took me a while. Did you start with Ballingry?' He nodded. 'That's what threw me. I came off the motorway at Kelty.'

'Listen,' Rebus said, 'I've found a contender.'

She didn't seem interested. 'Have you seen this morning's paper?'

'Oh that, I meant to tell you about it.'

'No, not the front page, the inside.'

'Inside?'

She tapped a headline and handed the paper through the window to him. THREE INJURED IN M8 SMASH. The story told how on Saturday morning a BMW left the motorway heading towards Glasgow and ended up in a field. The family in the car had all been hospitalised – wife, teenage son, and 'Edinburgh businessman David Dougary, 41'.

'Christ,' gasped Rebus, 'I knocked that off the front page.'

'Pity you didn't read it at the time. What'll happen now?'

Rebus read the story through again. 'I don't know. It'll depend. If they shut down or transfer the Gorgie operation, either we shut down or we follow it.'

'"We"? You're suspended, remember.'

'Or else Cafferty brings someone else in to take over while Dougary's on the mend.'

'It would be short notice.'

'Which means he'll hand pick someone.'

'Or fill in for Dougary himself?'

'I doubt it,' said Rebus, 'but wouldn't it be just magic if he did? The only way of knowing is to keep the surveillance going till *something* happens one way or the other.'

'And meantime?'

'Meantime, we've got a ton more bookie's shops to check.' Rebus turned and gave Bowhill a smiling glance.

'But something tells me we've already had a yankee come up.'

'What's a yankee?' Siobhan asked, as Rebus unlocked and got into his car.

When they stopped for a bite to eat and some tea in Dunfermline, Rebus told her the story of Hutchy's and the man with the case full of cash. Her face twitched a little, as though her tea were too hot or the egg mayonnaise sandwich too strong.

'What was that name again?' she asked.

'Tommy Greenwood.'

'But he's in the Cafferty file.'

'What?' It was Rebus's turn to twitch.

'Tommy Greenwood, I'm sure it is. He's ... he *was* one of Cafferty's associates years ago. Then he disappeared from the scene, like so many others. They'd quarrelled about equal shares, or something.'

'Sounds like a boulder round the balls and the old heave-ho off a bridge.'

'As you say, it's a mobile profession.'

'Glub, glub, glub, all the way to the bottom.'

Siobhan smiled. 'So is it the real Tommy Greenwood or not?'

Rebus shrugged. 'If the bugger's had plastic surgery, it could be hard to tell. All the same, there are ways.' He was nodding to himself. 'Oh yes, there are ways.'

Ways which started with a friendly taxman ...

More than one person that Sunday read the story on the front page of their morning paper with a mixture of anguish, fear, guilt, and fury. Telephone calls were made. Words were exchanged like bullets. But being Sunday, there wasn't much anyone could do about the situation except, if they were of a mind, pray. If the off-licences had been open, or the supermarkets and grocer's shops allowed to sell alcohol, they might have drowned their sorrows or assuaged their anger. As it was, the anger just built, and so did the anguish. Block by block, the structure neared completion. A roof, that was all it lacked. Something to keep the pressure in, or nature's forces out.

And it was all because of John Rebus. This was more or less agreed. John Rebus was out there with a battering ram, and more than one person was of a mind to unlock the door and let him in – let him into *their* lair. And then lock the door after him.

28

The meeting in Farmer Watson's office had been arranged for nine in the morning. Presumably, they wanted Rebus at his groggiest and most supine. He might growl loudly in the morning, but he didn't normally start biting till afternoon. That everyone from Watson to the canteen staff knew he was being fitted up didn't make things any less awkward. For a start, the investigation into the Central Hotel murder wasn't official, and Watson still wasn't keen to sanction it. So Rebus had been working rogue anyway. Give the Farmer his due, he looked after his team. They managed between them to concoct a story whereby Rebus had been given permission to do some digging into the files on his own time.

'With a view towards the case perhaps being reopened at a later date as fresh evidence allowed,' said the Farmer. His secretary, a smart woman with a scary taste in hair colourants, copied down these closing words. 'And date it a couple of weeks ago.'

'Yes, sir,' she said.

When she'd left the room, Rebus said, 'Thank you, sir.' He'd been standing throughout the proceedings, there being space for just the one chair, the one the secretary had been seated on. He now stepped gingerly over piles of files and placed his bum where hers had latterly been.

'I'm covering *my* hide as well as yours, John. And not a word to anyone, understand?'

'Yes, sir. What about Inspector Flower, won't he suspect? He's bound to complain to Chief Inspector Lauderdale at least.'

'Good. Him and Lauderdale can have a chinwag. There's something you've got to understand, John.' Watson clasped his hands together on the desk, his head sinking into huge rounded shoulders. He spoke softly. 'I *know* Lauderdale's after my job. I know I can trust him as far as I'd trust an Irish scoor-oot.' He paused. 'Do *you* want my job, Inspector?'

'No fear.'

Watson nodded. 'That's what I mean. Now, I know you're not going to be sitting on your hands for the next week or two, so take some advice. The law can't be tinkered with the way you tinker with an old car. *Think* before you do anything. And remember, stunts like buying a gun can get you thrown off the force.'

'But I didn't buy it, sir,' said Rebus, reciting the story they'd thought up, 'it came into my possession as a potential piece of evidence.'

Watson nodded. 'Quite a mouthful, eh? But it might just save your bacon.'

'I'm vegetarian, sir,' Rebus said. A statement which caused Watson to laugh very loudly indeed.

They were both more than a little interested in what was happening in Gorgie. The initial news had not seemed promising. Nobody had turned up at the office, nobody at all. An extra detail was now keeping a watch on the hospital where Dougary lay in traction. If nothing happened at the Gorgie end, they'd switch to the hospital until Dougary was up and about. Maybe he'd keep working from his bedside. Stranger things had happened.

But at eleven-thirty, a brightly polished Jag pulled into the taxi lot. The chauffeur, a huge man with long straight hair, got out, and when he opened the back door, out stepped Morris Gerald Cafferty.

'Got you, you bastard,' hissed DS Petrie, firing off a whole roll of film in the excitement. Siobhan was already telephoning St Leonard's. And after talking with CI Lauderdale, as instructed (though *not* by Lauderdale) she phoned Arden Street. Rebus picked up the phone on its second ring.

'Bingo,' she said. 'Cafferty's come calling.'

'Make sure the photographs are dated and timed.'

'Yes, sir. How did the meeting go?'

'I think the Farmer's in love with me.'

'They're both going in,' said Petrie, at last lifting his finger from the shutter release. The camera motor stopped. Madden, who had come over to the window to watch, asked who they were.

At the same time, Rebus was asking a similar question. 'Who's with Big Ger?'

'His driver.'

'Man mountain with long hair?'

'That's him.'

'That's also the guy who got his ear eaten by Davey Dougary.'

'No love lost there, then?'

'Except now the man mountain's working for Big Ger.' He thought for a moment. 'Knowing Big Ger, I'd say he put him on the payroll just to piss off Dougary.'

'Why would he do that?'

'His idea of a joke. Let me know when they come out again.'

'Will do.'

She phoned him back half an hour later. 'Cafferty's taken off again.'

'He didn't stay long.'

'But listen, the chauffeur stayed put.'

'What?'

'Cafferty drove off alone.'

'Well, I'll be buggered. He's putting the man mountain in charge of Dougary's accounts!'

'He must trust him.'

'I suppose he must. But I can't see the big chap having much experience running a book. He's strictly a guard dog.'

'Meaning?'

'Meaning Big Ger will have to nurse him along. Meaning Big Ger will be down at that office practically every day. It couldn't be better!'

'We'd better get in some more film, then.'

'Aye, don't let that stupid bugger Petrie run out again. How's his face by the way?'

'Itchy, but it hurts when he scratches.' Petrie glanced over, so she told him, 'Inspector Rebus was just asking after you.'

'Was I buggery,' said Rebus. 'I hope his nose drops off and falls in his thermos.'

'I'll pass your good wishes on, sir,' said Siobhan.

'Do that,' replied Rebus. 'And don't be shy about it either. Right, I'm off to a funeral.'

'I was talking to Brian, he said he's a pall-bearer.'

'Good,' said Rebus. 'That means I'll have a shoulder to cry on.'

Warriston Cemetery is a sprawling mix of graves, from the ancient (and sometimes desecrated) to the brand new. There are stones there whose messages have been eroded away to faint indents only. On a sunny day, it can be an educational walk, but at nights the local Hell's Angels chapter have been known to party hard, recreating scenes more like New Orleans voodoo than Scottish country dancing.

Rebus felt Eddie would have approved. The ceremony itself was simple and dignified, if you ignored the wreath

265

in the shape of an electric guitar and the fact that he was to be buried with an Elvis LP cover inside the casket.

Rebus stood at a distance from proceedings, and had turned down an invitation by Pat Calder to attend the reception afterwards, which was to be held not in the hollow Heartbreak Cafe but in the upstairs room of a nearby hostelry. Rebus was tempted for a moment – the chosen pub served Gibson's – but shook his head the way he'd shaken Calder's hand: with regrets.

Poor Eddie. For all that Rebus hadn't really known him, for all that the chef had tried scalping him with a panful of appetisers, Rebus had liked the man. He saw them all the time, people who could have made so much of their lives, yet hadn't. He knew he belonged with them. The losers.

But at least I'm still alive, he thought. And God willing nobody will dispatch me by funneling alcohol down my throat before turning on the gas. It struck him again: why the need for the funnel? All you had to do was take Eddie to any bar and he'd willingly render himself unconscious on tequila and bourbon. You didn't *need* to force him. Yet Dr Curt had tossed his liver in the air and proclaimed it a fair specimen. That was difficult to accept, except that he'd seen it with his own eyes.

Or had he?

He peered across the distance to where Pat Calder was taking hold of rope number one, testing it for tensile strength. Brian was number four, which meant he stood across the casket from Calder and sandwiched between two men Rebus didn't know. The barman Toni was number six. But Rebus's eyes were on Calder. Oh Jesus, you bastard, he thought. You didn't, did you? Then again, maybe you did.

He turned and ran, back to where his car was parked out on the road outside the cemetery. His destination was Arden Street.

Arden Street and the reservations book for the Heart-break Cafe.

As he saw it, Rebus had two choices. He could kick the door down, or he could try to open it quietly. It was a snib lock, the kind a stiff piece of plastic could sometimes open. Of course, there was a mortice deadlock too, but probably not engaged. When he pushed and pulled the door, there was enough give in it to suggest this was probably true. Only the snib then. But the gap where door met jamb was covered by a long strip of ornamental wood. This normally wouldn't deter a burglar, who would take a crowbar to it until he had access to the gap.

But Rebus had forgotten to pack his crowbar.

A rap with the door-knocker wouldn't elicit a response, would it? But he didn't fancy his chances of shouldering or kicking the door down, snib-lock or not. So he crouched down, opened the letterbox with one hand, put his eyes level with it, and reached up his other hand to the black iron ring, giving it five loud raps: shave-and-a-haircut, some people called it. It signalled a friend; at least, that's what Rebus hoped. There was neither sound nor movement from the inside of the maisonette. The Colonies was daytime quiet. He could probably crowbar the door open without anyone noticing. Instead, he tried the knocker again. The door had a spy-hole, and he was hoping someone might be intrigued enough to want to creep to the spy-hole and take a look.

Movement now, a shadow moving slowly from the living area towards the hall. Moving stealthily. And then a head sticking out of the doorway. It was all Rebus needed.

'Hello, Eddie,' he called. 'I've got your wreath here.'

Eddie Ringan let him in.

He was dressed in a red silk kimono-style gown with a fierce dragon crawling all down its back. On the arms were symbols Rebus didn't understand. They didn't worry him. Eddie flopped onto the sofa, usually Rebus's perch, so Rebus made do with standing.

'I was lying about the wreath,' he said.

'It's the thought that counts. Nice suit, too.'

'I had to borrow the tie,' said Rebus.

'Black ties are cool.' Eddie looked like death warmed up. His eyes were dark-ringed and bloodshot, and his face resembled a prisoner's: sunless grey, lacking hope. He scratched himself under the armpit. 'So how did it go?'

'I left just as they were lowering you away.'

'They'll be at the reception now. Wish I could have done the catering myself, but you know how it is.'

Rebus nodded. 'It's not easy being a corpse. You'd have found that out.'

'Some people have managed quite nicely in the past.'

'Like Radiator McCallum and the Robertson brothers?'

Eddie produced a grim smile. 'One of those, yes.'

'You must be pretty desperate to stage your own death.'

'I'm not saying anything.'

'That's fine.' There was silence for a minute until Eddie broke it.

'How did you find out?'

Rebus absent-mindedly took a cigarette from the pack on the mantelpiece. 'It was Pat. He made up this unnecessarily exaggerated story.'

'That's Pat for you. Amateur fucking dramatics all the way.'

'He said Willie stormed out of the restaurant after sticking his face in some poor punter's plate. I checked with a couple of the people who ate there that night. A quick phone call was all it took. Nobody saw anything of the sort. Then there was the dead man's liver. It was in good nick, so it couldn't possibly have been yours.'

'You can say that again.'

Rebus was about to light up. He caught himself, lifted

the cigarette from his mouth, and placed it beside the packet.

'Then I checked missing persons. Seems Willie hasn't been back to his digs in a few days. The whole thing was amateurish, Eddie. If the poor bugger hadn't got his face blown away in the explosion, we'd've known straight away it wasn't you.'

'Would you? We wondered about that, we reckoned with Brian off the scene and Haymarket not your territory, it might just work.'

Rebus shook his head. 'For a start, we take photographs, and I'd have seen them sooner or later. I always do.' He paused. 'So why did you kill him?'

'It was an accident.'

'Let me guess, you came back late to the restaurant after a pretty good bender. You were angry as hell to see Willie had coped. You had a fight, he smashed his head. Then you had an idea.'

'Maybe.'

'There's only one rotten thing about the whole story,' said Rebus. Eddie shifted on the sofa. He looked ridiculous in the kimono, and had folded his arms protectively. He was staring at the fireplace, avoiding Rebus altogether.

'What?' he said finally.

'Pat said Willie ran out of the Cafe on *Tuesday* night. His body wasn't found until Thursday morning. If he'd died in a fight on Tuesday, lividity and rigor mortis would have told the pathologist the body was old. But it wasn't, it was fresh. Which means you didn't booze him up and gas him until early Thursday morning. You must've kept him alive all day Wednesday, knowing pretty well what you were going to do with him.'

'I'm not saying anything.'

'No, *I'm* saying it. Like I say, a desperate remedy, Eddie. About as desperate as they come. Now come on.'

'What?'

'We're taking a drive.'

'Where to?'

'Down to the station, of course. Get some clothes on.' Rebus watched him try to stand up. His legs took a while to lock upright. Yes, murder could do that to you. It was the opposite of rigor mortis. It was liquefaction, the jelly effect. It took him a long time to dress, Rebus watching throughout. There were tears in Eddie's eyes when he finished, and his lips were wet with saliva.

Rebus nodded. 'You'll do,' he said. He fully intended taking Eddie to St Leonard's.

But they'd be taking the scenic route.

'Where are we going?'

'A little drive. Nice day for it.'

Eddie looked out of the windscreen. It was a uniform grey outside, buildings and sky, with rain threatening and the breeze gaining force. He started to get the idea when they turned up Holyrood Park Road, heading straight for Arthur's Seat. And when Rebus took a right, away from Holyrood and in the direction of Duddingston, Eddie started to look very worried indeed.

'You know where we're going?' Rebus suggested.

'No.'

'Oh well.'

He kept driving, drove all the way up to the gates of the house and signalled with his indicator that he was turning into the drive.

'Christ, no!' yelped Eddie Ringan. He tucked his knees in front of him, wedging them against the dashboard like he thought they were about to crash. Instead of turning in at the gates, Rebus cruised past them and stopped kerbside. You caught a glimpse of Cafferty's mansion from here. Presumably, if someone up at the house were looking out of the right window, they could see the car.

'No, no.' Eddie was weeping.

'You *do* know where we are,' Rebus said, voicing surprise. 'You know Big Ger, then?' He waited till Eddie nodded. The chef had assumed a foetal position, feet on the seat beneath him, head tucked into his knees. 'Are you scared of him?' Eddie nodded again. 'Why?' Slowly, Eddie shook his head. 'Is it because of the Central Hotel?'

'Why did I have to tell Brian?' It was a loud yell, all the louder for being confined by the car. 'Why the fuck am I so stupid?'

'They've found the gun, you know.'

'I don't know anything about that.'

'You never saw the gun?'

Eddie shook his head. Damn, Rebus had been expecting more. 'So what did you see?'

'I was in the kitchens.'

'Yes?'

'This guy came running in, screaming at me to turn on the gas. He looked crazy, spots of blood on his face ... in his eyelashes.' Eddie was calming as the exorcism took effect. 'He started to turn on all the gas rings. Not lighting them. He looked so crazy, I helped him. I turned on the gas, just like he told me to.'

'And then?'

'I got out of there. I wasn't sticking around. I thought the same as everybody else: it was for the insurance money. Till they found the body. A week later, I got a visit from Big Ger. A *painful* visit. The message was: never say a word, not a word about what happened.'

'Was Big Ger there that night?'

Eddie shrugged. Damn him again! 'I was in the kitchens. I only saw the crazy guy.'

Well, Rebus knew who *that* was – someone who'd seen the state of the Central kitchens. 'Black Aengus?' he asked.

Eddie didn't say anything for a few minutes, just stared blearily out of the windscreen. Then: 'Big Ger's bound to find out I said something. Every now and then he sends

271

another warning. Nothing physical ... not to me, at least. Just to let me know he remembers. He'll kill me.' He turned his head to Rebus. 'He'll kill me, and all I did was turn on the gas.'

'The man with the blood, it was Aengus Gibson, wasn't it?'

Eddie nodded slowly, screwing shut his eyes and wringing out tears. Rebus started the car. As he was driving off, he saw the 4x4 coming towards him from the opposite direction. It was signalling to pull into the gates, and the gates themselves were opening compliantly. The car was driven by a thug whose face was new to Rebus. In the back seat sat Mo Cafferty.

It bothered him, during the short drive back to St Leonard's, with Eddie bawling and huddled in the passenger seat. It bothered him. Could Mo Cafferty drive at all? That would be easy enough to check: a quick chat with DVLC. If she couldn't, if she needed a chauffeur, then who was driving the 4x4 that day Rebus had seen it parked outside Bone's? And wasn't *that* quite a coincidence anyway? John Rebus didn't believe in coincidences.

'The Heartbreak Cafe didn't get its meat from Bone's, did it?' he asked Eddie, who misinterpreted the question. 'I mean Bone's the butcher's shop,' Rebus explained. But Eddie shook his head. 'Never mind,' said Rebus.

Back at St Leonard's, the very person he wanted to see was waiting for him.

'Why aren't you out at Gorgie?' he asked.

'Why aren't you on suspension?' Siobhan Clarke asked back.

'That's below the belt. Besides, I asked first.'

'I had to come and pick up these.' She waved a huge brown envelope at him.

'Well, listen, I've got a little job for you. Several, in fact.

272

First, we need to have Eddie Ringan's casket back up out of the ground.'

'What?'

'It's not Eddie inside, I've just put him in the cells. You'll need to interview and book him. I'll tell you all about it.'

'I'm going to need to write all this down.'

'No you won't, your memory's good enough.'

'Not when my brain's in shock. You mean that wasn't Eddie in the oven?'

'That's what I mean. Next, check and see if Mo Cafferty has a driving licence.'

'What for?'

'Just do it. And do you remember telling me that when Bone won his Merc, he put up *his share* of the business to cover the bet? Your words: his share.'

'I remember. His wife told me.'

Rebus nodded. 'I want to know who owns the other half.'

'Is that all, sir?'

Rebus thought. 'No, not quite. Check Bone's Merc. See if anyone owned it before him. That way, we'll know who he won it from.' He looked at her unblinking. 'Quick as you can, eh?'

'Quick as I can, sir. Now, do you want to know what's in the envelope? It's for the man who has everything.'

'Go on then, surprise me.'

So she did.

Rebus was so surprised, he bought her coffee and a dough-ring in the canteen. The X-rays lay on the table between them.

'I don't believe this,' he kept saying. 'I really don't believe this. I put out a search for these *ages* ago.'

'They were in the records office at Ninewells.'

'But I *asked* them!'

'But did you ask nicely?'

Siobhan had explained that she'd been able to take a few trips to Dundee, chatting up anyone who might be useful, and especially in the chaotic records department, which had been moved and reorganised a few years before, leaving older records an ignored shambles. It had taken time. More than that, she'd had to promise a date to the young man who'd finally come up with the goods.

Rebus held up one of the X-rays again.

'Broken right arm,' Siobhan confirmed. 'Twelve years ago. While he was living and working in Dundee.'

'Tam Roberston,' Rebus said simply. That was that then: the dead man, the man with the bullet wound through his heart, the bullet from Rebus's Colt 45, was Tam Robertson.

'Difficult to prove in a court of law,' Siobhan suggested. True enough, you'd need more than hearsay and an X-ray to prove identity to a jury.

'There are ways,' said Rebus. 'We can try dental records again, now we've got an idea who the corpse is. Then there's superimposition. For the moment, it's enough for me that *I'm* satisfied.' He nodded. 'Well done, Clarke.' He started to get up.

'Sir?'

'Yes?'

She was smiling. 'Merry Christmas, sir.'

29

He phoned Gibson's Brewery, only to be told that 'Mr Aengus' was attending an ale competition in Newcastle, due back later tonight. So he called the Inland Revenue and spoke for a while to the inspector in charge of his case. If he was going to confront Tommy Greenwood, he'd need all the ammo he could gather ... bad metaphor considering, but true all the same. He left his car at St Leonard's while he went for a walk, trying to clear his head. Everything was coming together now. Aengus Gibson had been playing cards with Tam Robertson, and had shot him. Then set fire to the hotel to cover up the murder. It should all be tied up, but Rebus's brain was posing more questions than answers. Was it likely Aengus carried a gun around with him, even in his wild days? Why didn't Eck, also present, seek revenge for his brother? Wouldn't Aengus have had to shut him up somehow? Was it likely that only three of them were involved in the poker game? And who had delivered the gun to Deek Torrance? So many questions.

As he came down onto South Clerk Street, he saw that a van was parked outside Bone's. A new plate-glass window was being installed in the shop itself, and the van door was open at the back. Rebus walked over to the van and looked in the back. It had been a proper butcher's van at one time, and nobody had bothered changing it. You climbed a step into the back, where there were counters and cupboards and a small fridge-freezer. The van would have had its usual rounds of the housing schemes in the city, housewives and retired folk queuing for meat rather than travelling to a shop. A man in a white apron came out of Bone's with an ex-pig hoisted on his shoulder.

'Excuse me,' he said, carrying the carcass into the van.

'You use this for deliveries?' Rebus asked.

The man nodded. 'Just to restaurants.'

'I remember when a butcher's van used to come by our way,' Rebus reminisced.

'Aye, it's not economic these days, though.'

'Everything changes,' said Rebus. The man nodded agreement. Rebus was examining the interior again. To get behind the counter, you climbed into the van, pulled a hinged section of the counter up, and pushed open a narrow little door. Narrow: that's what the back of the van was. He remembered Michael's description of the van he'd been shunted about in. A narrow van with a smell. As the man came out of the van, he disturbed something with his foot. It was a piece of straw. Straw in a butcher's van? None of the animals carried in here had seen straw for a while.

Rebus looked into the shop. A young assistant was watching the glass being installed.

'Open for business, sir,' he informed Rebus cheerily.

'I was looking for Mr Bone.'

'He's not in this afternoon.'

Rebus nodded towards the van. 'Do you still do runs?'

'What, house-to-house?' The young man shook his head. 'Just general deliveries, bulk stuff.'

Yes, Rebus would agree with that.

He walked back up to St Leonard's, and caught Siobhan again. 'I forgot to say ...'

'More work?'

'Not much more. Pat Calder, you'll need to bring him in for questioning too. He'll be back home by now and getting frantic wondering where Eddie's sloped off to. I'm just sorry I won't be around for the reunion. I suppose I can always catch it in court . . .'

It had been quite a day already, and it wasn't yet six o'clock. Back in the flat, the students were cooking a lentil curry while Michael sat in the living room reading another book on hypnotherapy. It had all become very settled in the flat, very ... well, the word that came to mind was *homely*. It was a strange word to use about a bunch of teenage students, a copper and an ex-con, yet it seemed just about right.

Michael had finished the tablets, and looked the better for it. He was supposed to arrange a check-up, but Rebus was dubious: they'd probably only stick him on more tablets. The scars would heal over naturally. All it took was time. He'd certainly regained his appetite: two helpings of curry.

After the meal they all sat around in the living room, the students drinking wine, Michael refusing it, Rebus supping beer from a can. There was music, the kind that never went away: the Stones and the Doors, Janis Joplin, very early Pink Floyd. It was one of those evenings. Rebus felt absolutely shattered, and blamed it on the caffeine tablets he'd been taking. Here he'd been worrying about Michael, and all the time he'd been swallowing down his own bad medicine. They'd seen him through the weekend, sleeping little and thinking lots. But you couldn't go on like that forever. And what with the music and the beer and the relaxed conversation, he'd almost certainly fall asleep here on the sofa . . .

'What was that?'

'Sounds like somebody smashed a bottle or something.'

The students got up to look out of the window. 'Can't see anything.'

'No, look, there's glass on the road.' They turned to

Rebus. 'Someone's broken your windshield.'

Someone had indeed broken his windshield, as he found when he wandered downstairs and into the street. Other neighbours had gathered at doors and windows to check the scene. But most of them were retreating now. There was a chunk of rock on the passenger seat, surrounded by jewels of shattered glass. Nearby a car was reversing lazily out of its parking spot. It stopped in the road beside him. The passenger side window went down.

'What happened?'

'Nothing. Just a rock through the windscreen.'

'What?' The passenger turned to his driver. 'Wait here a second.' He got out to examine the damage. 'Who the hell would want to do that?'

'How many names do you want?' Rebus reached into the car to pull out the rock, and felt something collide with the back of his head. It didn't make sense for a moment, but by then he was being dragged away from the car into the road. He heard a car reverse and stop. He tried to resist, clawing at the unyielding tarmac with his fingernails. Jesus, he was going to pass out. His head was trying to close all channels. Each thud of his heart brought intense new pain to his skull. Someone had opened a window and was shouting something, some warning or complaint. He was alone in the middle of the road now. The passenger had run back to the car and slammed the door shut. Rebus pushed himself onto all fours, a baby resisting gravity for the first time. He blinked, trying to see out of cloudy eyes. He saw headlights, and knew what they were going to do.

They were going to drive straight over him.

Sucker punch, and he'd fallen for it. The offer of help from your attacker routine. Older than Arthur's Seat itself. The car's engine roared, and the tyres squealed towards him, dragging the body of the car with them. Rebus wondered if he'd get the licence number before he died.

A hand grabbed the neck of his shirt and hauled, pulling him backwards out of the road. The car caught his legs, tossing one shoe up off his foot and into the air. The car didn't stop, or even slow down, just kept on up the slope to the top of the road, where it took a right and disappeared.

'Are you okay, John?'

It was Michael. 'You saved my life there, Mickey.' Adrenalin was mixing with pain in Rebus's body, making him feel sick. He threw up undigested lentil curry onto the pavement.

'Try to stand up,' said Michael. Rebus tried and failed.

'My legs hurt,' he said. 'Christ, do my legs hurt!'

The X-rays showed no breaks or fractures, not even a bone chipped. 'Just bad bruising, Inspector,' said the woman doctor at the Infirmary. 'You were lucky. A hit like that could have done a lot of damage.'

Rebus nodded. 'I suppose I should have known,' he said. 'I've been due a visit here as a patient. Christ knows I've been here enough recently as a visitor.'

'I'll just fetch you something,' said the doctor.

'Wait a second, doctor. Are your labs open in the evening?'

She shook her head. 'Why do you ask?'

'Nothing.'

She left the room. Michael came closer. 'How do you feel?'

'I don't know which hurts worse, my head or my left leg.'

'No great loss to association football.'

Rebus almost smiled, but grimaced instead. Any movement of his face muscles sent electric spurts through his brain. The doctor came back into the room. 'Here you are,' she said. 'This should help.'

Rebus had been expecting painkillers. But she was holding a walking stick.

It was an aluminium walking stick, hollow and therefore lightweight, with a large rubberised grip and adjustable height courtesy of a series of holes in its shaft, into which a locking-pin could be placed. It looked like some strange wind instrument, but Rebus was glad of it as he walked out of the hospital.

Back at the flat, however, one of the solicitous students said he had something better, and came back from his bedroom with a black wooden cane with a silver and bone handle. Rebus tried it. It was a good height for him.

'I bought it in a junk shop,' the student said, 'don't ask me why.'

'Looks like it should have a concealed sword,' said Rebus. He tried twisting and pulling at the handle, but nothing happened. 'So much for that.'

The police, who had talked to Rebus at the Infirmary, had also spoken to the students.

'This constable,' related the walking-stick owner, whose name Rebus was sure was Ed, 'I mean, he was looking at us like we were squatters, and he was asking, was Inspector Rebus in here with you? And we were nodding, yes he was. And the constable couldn't figure it out at all.' He started laughing. Even Michael smiled. Someone else made a pot of herbal tea.

Great, thought Rebus. Another story that would be doing the rounds: Rebus fills his flat with students, then sits around with them of an evening with wine and beer. At the Infirmary, they'd asked if he'd recognised either of the men. The answer was no. It was a mobile profession, after all ... One of the neighbours had caught the car's number plate. It was a Ford Escort, stolen only an hour or so before from a car park near the Sheraton on Lothian Road. They would find it abandoned quite soon, probably not far from Marchmont. There wouldn't be any finger-prints.

'They must've been crazy,' Michael said on the way home, Rebus having got them a lift in the back of a patrol car. 'Thinking they could pull a stunt like that.'

'It wasn't a stunt, Michael. Somebody's desperate. That story in yesterday's paper has really shaken them up.' After all, wasn't that exactly what he'd wanted? He'd sought a reaction, and here it was.

From the flat he telephoned an emergency windscreen replacement firm. It would cost the earth, but he needed the car first thing in the morning. He just prayed his leg wouldn't seize up in the night.

30

Which of course it did. He was up at five, practising walking across the living room, trying to unstiffen the joints and tendons. He looked at his left leg. A spectacular blood-filled bruise stretched across his calf, wrapping itself around most of the front of the leg too. If the bony front of his leg had taken the impact rather than the fleshy back, there would have been at the very least a clean break. He swallowed two paracetamol – recommended for the pain by the Infirmary doctor – and waited for morning proper to arrive. He'd needed sleep last night, but hadn't got much. Today he'd be living on his wits. He just hoped those wits would be sharp enough.

At six-thirty he managed the tenement stairs and hobbled to his car, now boasting a windscreen worth more than the rest of it put together. Traffic wasn't quite heavy yet coming into town, and non-existent heading out, so the drive itself was mercifully shortened. Pressing down on the clutch hurt all the way up into his groin. He took the coast road out to North Berwick, letting the engine labour rather than changing gears too often. Just the other side of the town, he found the house he was looking for. Well, an estate, actually, and not a housing estate. It must have been about thirty or forty acres, with an uninterrupted view across the mouth of the Forth to the dark lump of Bass Rock. Rebus wasn't much good at architecture; Georgian, he'd guess. It looked like a lot of the houses in Edinburgh's New Town, with fluted stone columns either side of the doorway and large sash windows, nine panes of glass to each half.

Broderick Gibson had come a long way since those days in his garden shed, pottering with homebrew recipes. Rebus parked outside the front door and rang the bell. The door was opened by Mrs Gibson. Rebus introduced himself.

'It's a bit early, Inspector. Is anything wrong?'

'If I could just speak to your son, please.'

'He's eating breakfast. Why don't you wait in the sitting-room and I'll bring you –'

'It's all right, mother.' Aengus Gibson was still chewing and wiping his chin with a cloth napkin. He stood in the dining-room doorway. 'Come in here, Inspector.'

Rebus smiled at the defeated Mrs Gibson as he passed her.

'What's happened to your leg?' Gibson asked.

'I thought you might know, sir.'

'Oh? Why?' Aengus had seated himself at the table. Rebus had been entertaining an image of silver service – tureens and hot-plates, kedgeree or kippers, Wedgewood plates, and tea poured by a manservant. But all he saw was a plain white plate with greasy sausage and eggs on it. Buttered toast on the side and a mug of coffee. There were two newspapers folded beside Aengus – Mairie's paper and the *Financial Times* – and enough crumbs around the table to suggest that mother and father had eaten already.

Mrs Gibson put her head round the door. 'A cup of coffee, Inspector?'

'No, thank you, Mrs Gibson.' She smiled and retreated.

'I just thought,' Rebus said to Aengus, 'you might have arranged it.'

'I don't understand.'

'Trying to shut me up before I can ask a few questions about the Central Hotel.'

'That again!' Aengus bit into a piece of toast.

'Yes, that again.' Rebus sat down at the table, stretching his left leg out in front of him. 'You see, I *know* you were there that night, long after Mr Vanderhyde left. I know you were at a poker game set up by two villains called Tam and Eck Robertson. I know someone shot and killed Tam, and I know you ran into the kitchens covered in blood and screaming for all the gas rings to be turned on. That, Mr Gibson, is what I know.'

Gibson seemed to have trouble swallowing the chewed toast. He gulped coffee, and wiped his mouth again.

'Well, Inspector,' he said, 'if that's what you know, I suggest you don't know very much.'

'Maybe you'd like to tell me the rest, sir?'

They sat in silence. Aengus toyed with the empty mug, Rebus waiting for him to speak. The door burst open.

'Get out of here!' roared Broderick Gibson. He was wearing trousers and an open-necked shirt, whose cuffs flapped for want of their links. Obviously, his wife had disturbed him halfway through dressing. 'I could have you arrested right this minute!' he said. 'The Chief Constable tells me you've been suspended.'

Rebus stood up slowly, making much of his injured leg. But there was no charity in Broderick Gibson.

'And stay away from us, unless you have the authority! I'll be talking to my solicitor this morning.'

Rebus was at the door now. He stopped and looked into Broderick Gibson's eyes. 'I suggest you do that, sir. And you might care to tell him where *you* were the night the Central Hotel burnt down. Your son's in serious trouble, Mr Gibson. You can't hide him from the fact forever.'

'Just get out,' Gibson hissed.

'You haven't asked about my leg.'

'What?'

'Nothing, sir, just wondering aloud ...'

As Rebus walked back across the large hallway, with

its paintings and candelabra and fine curving stairwell, he felt how cold the house was. It wasn't just its age or the tiled floor either; the place was cold at its heart.

He arrived in Gorgie just as Siobhan was pouring her first cup of decaf of the day.

'What happened to your leg?' she asked.

Rebus pointed with his stick to the man stationed behind the camera.

'What the hell are you doing here?'

'I'm relieving Petrie,' said Brian Holmes.

'I wonder what any of us is doing here,' said Siobhan. Rebus ignored her.

'You're off sick.'

'I was bored, I came back early. I spoke to the Chief Super yesterday and he okayed it. So here I am.' Holmes looked fine but sounded dour. 'There was an ulterior motive, though,' he said. 'I wanted to hear from Siobhan herself the story of Eddie and Pat. It all sounds so ... incredible. I mean, I *cried* at that cemetery yesterday, and the bastard I was crying for was sitting at home playing with himself.'

'He'll be playing with himself in jail soon,' said Rebus. Then, to Siobhan: 'Give me some of that coffee.' He drank two scalding swallows before passing the plastic cup back. 'Thanks. Any progress?'

'No one's arrived yet. Not even our Trading Standards companion.'

'I meant those other things.'

'What *did* happen to your leg?' Holmes asked. So Rebus told them all about it.

'It's my fault,' Holmes said, 'for getting you into this in the first place.'

'That's right, it is,' said Rebus, 'and as penance you can keep your eyes glued to that window.' He turned to Siobhan. 'So?'

She took a deep breath. 'So I interviewed Ringan and Calder yesterday afternoon. They've both been charged. I also checked and Mrs Cafferty doesn't have a driving licence, not under her married or her maiden name. Bone's Mercedes belonged to –'

'Big Ger Cafferty.'

'You already knew?'

'I guessed,' said Rebus. 'What about the other half of Bone's business?'

'Owned by a company called Geronimo Holdings.'

'Which in turn is owned by Big Ger?'

'And sweetly, the word Geronimo includes both his and his wife's names. So what do you make of it?'

'Looks to me like Ger probably won his half of the business in a bet with Bone.'

'Either that,' added Holmes, 'or he got it in lieu of protection money Bone couldn't afford.'

'Maybe,' said Rebus. 'But the bet's more likely.'

'After all,' said Siobhan, 'Bone won the car in a bet with Cafferty. They've gambled together in the past.'

Rebus nodded. 'Well, it all adds up to a tight connection between the two of them. And there's a tighter connection too, though I can't prove it just yet.'

'Hang on,' said Siobhan, 'if the stabbing and the smashed window are to do with protection or gambling, then they're to do with Cafferty. Which means, since Cafferty owns half the business, that Cafferty smashed his *own* window.'

Rebus was shaking his head. 'I didn't say they were to do with protection or gambling.'

'And where does the cousin fit in?' Holmes interrupted.

'My my,' commented Rebus, 'you *are* keen to be back, aren't you? I'm not sure exactly where Kintoul fits in, but I'm getting a fair idea.'

'Hold on,' said Holmes, 'here we are.'

They all watched as a battered purple mini drove up to

the taxi offices. When the driver's door opened, the man mountain squeezed himself out.

'Like toothpaste from the tube,' said Rebus.

'Christ,' added Holmes, 'he must've taken out the front seats.'

'All alone today,' Siobhan noted.

'I'll bet Cafferty drops in sometime, though,' said Rebus, 'just to check. He's been ripped off badly in the past, he won't want it happening again.'

'Ripped off badly?' Siobhan echoed. 'How do you know that?'

Rebus winked at her. 'It's an odds-on bet,' he said.

He had to wait till after lunch for the information he needed. He had it faxed to him at a local newsagent's. During the long wait in Gorgie, he'd discussed the case with Holmes and Siobhan. They both were of the same mind in one particular: nobody would testify against Cafferty. And of like minds in another: they couldn't even be sure Cafferty had anything to do with it.

'I'll find out this afternoon,' Rebus told them, heading out to pick up the fax.

He was getting used to walking with the cane, and as long as he kept moving, the leg itself didn't stiffen up. But he knew the drive to Cardenden wouldn't do him much good. He considered the train, but ruled it out in short order. He might want to escape from Fife in a hurry; and Scotrail's timetables just didn't fit the bill.

It was just after two-thirty when he pushed open the door of Hutchy's betting shop. The place was airless, smelling old and undusted. The cigarette butts on the floor were probably last week's. There was a two-thirty-five race, and a few punters lined the walls waiting for the commentary. Rebus didn't let the look of the place put him off. Nobody wanted to bet in a plush establishment: it meant the bookie was making too much money. These tawdry surroundings were all psychology. You might not be winning, the bookmaker was saying, but look at me, I'm not doing any better.

Except that he was.

Rebus noticed a half-familiar face studying the form on one of the newspapers pinned to the wall. But then this town was full of half-familiar faces. He approached the glass-partitioned desk. 'I'd like a word with Mr Greenwood, please.'

'Do you have an appointment?'

But Rebus was no longer talking to the woman. His attention was on the man who'd looked up from a desk behind her. 'Mr Greenwood, I'm a police officer. Can we have a word?'

Greenwood thought about it, then got up, unlocked the door of the booth, and came out. 'Round here,' he said, leading Rebus to the rear of the shop. He unlocked another door, letting them into a much cosier and more private office.

'Any trouble?' he asked immediately, sitting down and reaching into his desk drawer for a bottle of whisky.

'Not for me, sir,' Rebus said. He sat down opposite Greenwood and stared at him. Christ, it was difficult after all these years. But Midge's portrait wasn't so far off the mark. A chess player would be making ready to play a pawn; Rebus decided to sacrifice his queen. 'So, Eck,' he said, getting comfortable, 'how've things been?'

Greenwood looked around. 'Are you talking to me?'

'I suppose I must be. My name's not Eck. Do you want to keep playing games? Fine then, let's play games.' Greenwood was pouring himself a large whisky. 'Your name is Eck Robertson. You fled from the Cafferty gang taking with you quite a lot of Big Ger's money. You also took another man's identity – Thomas Greenwood. You knew Tommy wouldn't complain because he was dead.

Another one of Big Ger's incredible disappearing acts. You took his name and his identity, and you set up for yourself in the arse-end of Fife, living out of a suitcase full of money till you got this place in profit.' Rebus paused. 'How am I doing?'

Greenwood, *aka* Eck Robertson, swallowed loudly and refilled his glass.

'You took too much of Greenwood's identity, though. When you set up here, Inland Revenue got onto you for an unpaid income tax bill. You wrote to them, and eventually you paid up.' Rebus brought the faxed sheets from his pocket. 'I've got a copy of your letter here, along with some earlier stuff from the *real* Thomas Greenwood. Wait till a handwriting expert gets hold of them in court. Have you ever seen those guys work on a jury? It's like Perry Mason. Even I can see the signatures aren't the same.'

'I changed my writing style.'

Rebus smiled. 'Changed your face too. Dyed hair, shaved off your moustache, contact lenses ... tinted. Your eyes used to be hazel, didn't they, Eck?'

'I keep telling you, my name's –'

Rebus got up. 'Whatever you say. I'm sure Big Ger will recognise you quick enough.'

'Wait a minute, sit down.' Rebus sat and waited. Eck Robertson tried to smile. He flicked on his radio for a moment and listened to the race, then flicked it off again. A six-to-one shot had romped home.

'Another win for the bookies,' Rebus said. 'Always liked the horses, didn't you? Not as much as Tam, though, Tam just loved betting. He bet you he could screw money out of Big Ger without Ger noticing. Creaming it off just a little at a time, but it all mounted up. Here.' Rebus tossed the drawing of Tam Robertson onto the desk. 'Here's what he might look like these days if Big Ger hadn't found out.'

Eck Robertson stared at the drawing, tracing a finger over it.

'You had to do a runner before Big Ger caught you, so you took the money. Then Radiator ran too. After all, he'd introduced the two of you into the gang. He'd be in for punishment too.' Rebus paused again. 'Or did Big Ger catch up with him?'

Robertson, eyes still on the drawing, shrugged.

'Well, whatever,' said Rebus. 'I think I'll have that whisky now.' His leg was hurting like blazes, his knuckles white on the handle of the cane. It took Robertson a while to pour the drink. 'So,' Rebus asked him, 'anything you want to add?'

'How did you find me?'

'Somebody spotted you.'

Robertson nodded. 'The chef, what's his name? Ringan? I saw him in some pub in Cowdenbeath. He looked like he was on a bender, so I got out fast. I didn't think he'd seen me, and if he had I didn't think he'd recognise me. I was wrong, eh?'

'You were wrong.' Rebus sipped the whisky like it was medicine on a spoon.

'It was Aengus Gibson,' Robertson said suddenly. 'Aengus Gibson had the gun.'

And then he told the rest of the story. Tam had been cheating at poker, as usual. But Aengus was on to him, and drew the gun. Shot Tam dead.

'We scarpered.'

'What?' Rebus was disbelieving. 'No thoughts of revenge? That young drunk had just killed your brother!'

'Nobody touched Black Aengus. He was Big Ger's pal. They got friendly after some misunderstanding, a break-in at Mo's flat. Big Ger had plans for him.'

'What sort of plans?'

Robertson shrugged. 'Just plans. You're right about the money. I knew I had to run while I could.'

290

'Why here, though?'

Robertson blinked. 'It was the last station on the line. Big Ger's never had much interest in Fife. It would mean tackling the Italians and the Orangemen.'

Rebus was doing some quick thinking. 'So what did Ger do when Aengus shot Tam?'

'How do you mean?'

'Eck, I *know* Big Ger was at the poker game. So what did he do?'

'He scarpered the same as the rest of us.'

So Big Ger *had* been there! Robertson's eyes were on his brother's portrait again. Rebus had a very good idea, too, what Cafferty's 'plans' for Aengus must have been. Imagine, having such a hold over someone who'd one day control the Gibson Brewing business. Such a hold all these years ...

'Who took away the gun, Eck?'

Eck shrugged again. Rebus got the idea he'd stopped listening. He rapped the edge of the desk with his cane. 'You went to a lot of trouble, Eck. Eddie Ringan appreciated that. He learned from you that it's possible to disappear. A handy lesson when Big Ger's after you. He *really* makes people disappear, doesn't he? Dumping them at sea like that. That's what he does, isn't it?'

'After a while, aye.'

Rebus frowned at this. But then Eck Robertson's next words hit him.

'Nobody notices a butcher's van.'

Rebus nodded, smiling. 'You're right about that.' He wet his lips. 'Eck, would you testify against him? In closed court, keep your new identity secret? Would you?'

But Eck Robertson was shaking his head. He was still shaking it when the door burst open. Ah, the half-remembered face from the form sheets. It was the pool player from the Midden.

'All right, Tommy?'

291

'Fine, Sharky, fine.' But 'Tommy Greenwood' didn't look it.

'Out you go, son,' said Rebus, 'Mr Greenwood and me have got business.'

Sharky ignored him. 'Want me to chuck him out, Tommy?'

Tommy Greenwood never got a chance to answer. Rebus pushed the handle of his cane hard up under Sharky's nose and then whipped it harder still against his knees. The young man crumpled. Rebus stood up. 'Handy thing, this,' he said. He pointed it at Eck Robertson. 'You can keep the picture as a reminder, Eck. Meantime, I'll be back. I want you to testify against Cafferty. Not now, not yet. Sometime after I've got him firm on a charge. And if you won't testify, I can always resurrect Eck Robertson. Think about it. One way or the other, Big Ger'll know.'

He was crossing the Forth Road Bridge when he heard the news on the radio.

'Aw Christ,' he said, stepping on the accelerator.

31

Rebus showed his ID as he drove through the brewery gates. There was only the one police car left at the scene, and no sign of an ambulance. Workers stood around in huddled, low-talking groups, passing round cigarettes and stories.

Rebus knew the detective sergeant. He worked out of Edinburgh West, and his unfortunate name was Robert Burns. This Burns was tall and bulky and red-haired, with freckles on his face. On Sunday afternoons, he could sometimes be found at the foot of the Mound, where he would lambast the strolling heathens. Rebus was glad to see Burns. You might get fire and brimstone with him, but you'd never get waffle.

Burns pointed to the huge aluminium tank. 'He climbed to the top.' Yes, Rebus could see all too clearly the metal stairwell which reached to the top of the tank, with walkways circling the tank every thirty feet or so. 'And when he got to the top, he jumped. A lot of the workers saw him, and they all said the same thing. He just climbed steadily till there were no more stairs, and then he threw himself off, arms stretched out. One of them said the dive was better than anything he'd seen in the Olympics.'

'That good, eh?' They weren't the only ones staring at the tank. Some of the workforce glanced up from time to time, then traced Aengus Gibson's descent. He'd hit the tarmac and crumpled like a concertina. There was a dent in the ground as though a boulder had been lifted from the spot.

'His father tried chasing after him,' Burns was saying. 'Didn't get very far. Old boy like that, it's a wonder his heart didn't give out. They had to help him down from the third circle.'

Rebus counted up three walkways. 'A bit of Dante, eh?' he said, winking at Burns.

'The old boy's saying it was an accident.'

'Of course he is.'

'It wasn't, though.'

'Of course it wasn't.'

'I've got a dozen witnesses who say he jumped.'

'A dozen witnesses,' Rebus corrected, 'who'll change their minds if their jobs are on the line.'

'Aye, right enough.'

Rebus breathed in. He'd always liked that smell of hops, but from now on he knew it would smell differently to him. It would smell like this moment, played over time and time again.

'The Lord giveth and the Lord taketh away,' said Burns. 'What happened to your leg, by the way?'

'Ingrown toenails,' said Rebus. 'The Lord gave them, the Infirmary took them away.'

Burns was shaking his head at this easy blasphemy when a window in the building behind them opened.

'You!' shouted Broderick Gibson. 'You killed him! You did it!' His crooked finger, a finger he seemed unable to straighten, was mostly pointed at Rebus. His eyes were like wet glass, his breathing strained. Someone was trying to coax him gently back into the office, hands on his shoulders. 'There'll be a reckoning!' he called to Rebus. 'Mark my words. There'll come a reckoning!'

The old man was finally pulled inside, the window falling shut after him. The workers were looking over towards the two policemen.

'He must be one of yours,' said Rebus, making for his car.

That was that then. Aengus Gibson had shot and killed Tam Robertson, and now Aengus was dead. End of story. Rebus could think of one person not in Aengus's family who was going to be very upset: Big Ger Cafferty. Cafferty had protected Black Aengus, maybe even blackmailed him, all the time waiting for the day when the young man would take over the brewery. With Aengus dead, the whole edifice fell, and good riddance to it.

Still, there was no comeback for Cafferty, no punishment.

Back at the flat, Michael had some news.

'The doc's been trying to get you.'

'Which one? I've seen so many recently.'

'Dr Patience Aitken. She seems to think you're avoiding her. Sounds like the ploy's working, too.'

'It's not a ploy. I've just had a lot on my plate.'

'And if you don't finish it, you won't get afters.' Michael smiled. 'She sounds nice, by the way.'

'She *is* nice. I'm the arsehole.'

'So go see her.'

Rebus flopped onto the sofa. 'Maybe I will. What are you reading?' Michael showed him the cover. 'Another book on hypnotherapy. You must have exhausted the field.'

'I've just been scratching the surface.' Michael paused. 'I'm going to take a course.'

'Oh?'

'I'm going to become a hypnotherapist. I mean, I know I can hypnotise people.'

'You can certainly get them to take their trousers off and bark like dogs.'

'Exactly, it's about time I put it to better use.'

'They say laughter is the best medicine.'

'Shut up, John, I'm trying to be serious. And I'm moving back in with Chrissie and the kids.'

'Oh?'

'I've talked with her. We've decided to try again.'

'Sounds romantic.'

'Well, one of us has got to have some romance in his soul.' Michael picked up the telephone and handed it to Rebus. 'Now phone the doctor.'

'Yes, sir,' said Rebus.

Broderick Gibson had clout, there was no denying it. On Wednesday morning the newspapers reported the 'tragic accident' at the Gibson Brewery near Fountainbridge, Edinburgh. There were photos of Aengus, some in his Black Aengus days, others showing the later model at charity events. There wasn't a whisper of suicide. It was another cover-up by Aengus's father, another distortion of the truth. It had become just something Broderick Gibson did, a part of the routine.

At ten-fifteen, Rebus received a phone call. It was Chief Superintendent Watson.

'There's someone here to see you,' he said. 'I told him you're under suspension, but he's bloody insistent.'

'Who is it?' asked Rebus.

'Some blind old duffer called Vanderhyde.'

Vanderhyde was still waiting when Rebus arrived. He looked quite at ease, concentrating on the sounds around him. Chatter and phone calls and the clacking of keyboards. He was seated on a chair facing Rebus's desk. Rebus tiptoed painfully around him and sat down. He watched Matthew Vanderhyde for a couple of minutes. He was dressed in a dark suit, white shirt and black tie: mourning clothes. He carried a blue cardboard folder, which he rested on his thighs. His walking-stick rested against the side of his chair.

'Well, Inspector,' said Vanderhyde suddenly, 'seen enough?'

Rebus gave a wry smile. 'Good morning, Mr Vanderhyde. What gave me away?'

'You're carrying a cane of some kind. It hit the corner of your desk.'

Rebus nodded. 'I was sorry to hear –'

'No sorrier than his parents. They've worked hard over the years with Aengus. He has *been* hard work. Devilish hard at times. Now it's all gone to waste.' Vanderhyde leaned forward in his chair. Had he been sighted, his eyes would have been boring into Rebus's. As it was, Rebus could see his own face reflected in the double mirror of Vanderhyde's glasses. 'Did he deserve to die, Inspector?'

'He had a choice.'

'Did he?'

Rebus was remembering the priest's words. *Can you live the rest of your life with the memories and the guilt?* Vanderhyde knew Rebus wasn't about to answer. He nodded slowly, and sat back a little in his chair.

'You were there that night, weren't you?' Rebus asked.

'Where?'

'At the card game.'

'Blind men make poor card-players, Inspector.'

'A sighted person could help them.' Rebus waited. Vanderhyde sat stiff and straight like the wax figure of a Victorian. 'Maybe someone like Broderick Gibson.'

Vanderhyde's fingers played over the blue folder, gripped it, and passed it over the desk.

'Broderick wanted you to have this.'

'What is it?'

'He wouldn't say. All he did say was, he hoped you'll think it was worth it, though he himself doubts it.' Vanderhyde paused. 'Of course, I was curious enough to study it in my own particular way. It's a book of some kind.' Rebus accepted the heavy folder, and Vanderhyde took his own hand away, finding his walking-stick and resting the hand there. 'Some keys were found on Aengus.

They didn't seem to match any known lock. Last night, Broderick found some bank statements detailing monthly payments to an estate office. He knows the head of the office, so he phoned him. Aengus, it seems, had been leasing a flat in Blair Street.'

Rebus knew it, a narrow passage between the High Street and the Cowgate, balanced precariously between respectability and low living. 'Nobody knew about it?'

Vanderhyde shook his head. 'It was his little den, Inspector. A real rat's nest, according to Broderick. Mouldering food and empty bottles, pornographic videos ...'

'A regular bachelor pad.'

Vanderhyde ignored his levity. 'This book was found there.'

Rebus had already opened the folder. Inside was a large ring-bound notebook. It bore no title, but its narrow lines were filled with writing. A few sentences told Rebus what it was: Aengus Gibson's journal.

32

Rebus sat at his desk reading. Nobody bothered him, despite the fact that he was supposed to be suspended. The day grew sunless, and the office emptied slowly. He might as well have been in solitary confinement for all the notice he took. His phone was off its hook and his head, bowed over the journal, was hidden by his hands; a clear sign that he did not want to be disturbed.

He read the journal quickly first time through. After all, only some of the pages were germane. The early entries were full of wild parties, illicit coitus in country mansions with married women who were still 'names' even today, and more often with the daughters of those women. Arguments with father and mother, usually over money. Money. There was a lot of money in these early entries, money spent on travel, cars, champagne, clothes. However, the journal itself opened quite strangely:

Sometimes, mostly when I'm alone, but occasionally in company, I catch a glimpse of someone from the corner of my eye. Or think I do. When I look properly, there's nobody there. There may be some shape there, some interesting, unconscious arrangement of the edge of an open door and the window frame beyond it, or whatever, which gives the hint of a human shape. I mention the door and the window frame because it is the most recent example.

I am becoming convinced, however, that I really am

seeing things. And what I am seeing – being shown, to be more accurate – is myself. That other part of me. I went to church when I was a child, and believed in ghosts. I still believe in ghosts ...

Rebus skipped to the start of the next entry:

I can write this journal safe in the knowledge that whoever is reading it – yes you, dear reader – does so after my death. Nobody knows it is here, and since I have no friends, no confidants or confidantes, it is unlikely that anyone will sneak a look at it. A burglar may carry it off, of course. If so, shame on you: it is the least valuable thing in this flat, though it may become more valuable the longer I write ...

There were huge gaps in the chronology. A single year might garner half a dozen dated entries. Black Aengus, it seemed, was no more regular in keeping a diary than he was in anything else. Five years ago, though, there had been a spate of entries. The accidental break-in at Mo Johnson's flat; Aengus becoming friendly with Mo and being introduced by her to a certain Morris Cafferty. After a while, Cafferty became simply 'Big Ger' as Aengus and he met at parties and in pubs and clubs.

By far the longest entry, however, belonged to the one day Rebus was really interested in:

This isn't a bad place really. The nursing staff are understanding and ready with jokes and stories. They carry me with all gentleness back to my room when I find I've wandered from it. The corridors are long and mazey. I thought I saw a tree once in one corridor, but it was a painting on the window. A nurse placed my hand on the cold glass so I could be sure in my mind.

Like the rest of them, she refused to smuggle in any vodka.

From my window I can see a squirrel – a red squirrel, I think – leaping between trees, and beyond that hills covered with stunted foliage, like a bad school haircut.

But I'm not really seeing this pastoral scene. I'm looking into a room, a room where I think I'll be spending a great deal of my time, even after I've left this hospital.

Why did I ever try to talk my father into going to the poker game? I know the answer now. Because Cafferty wanted him there. And father was keen enough – there's still a spark in him, a spark of the wildness that has been his legacy to me. But he couldn't come. Had he been there, I wonder if things would have turned out differently.

I met Uncle Matthew in the bar. God, what a bore. He thinks that because he has dabbled with demons and the hobgoblins of nationalism he has some import in the world. I could have told him, men like Cafferty have import. They are the hidden movers and shakers, the deal-makers. Simply, they get things done. And God, what things!

Tam Robertson suggested that I join the poker game which was happening upstairs. The stake money required was not high, and I knew I could always nip over to Blair Street for more cash if needed. Of course, I knew Tam Robertson's reputation. He dealt cards in a strange manner, elbow jutting out and up. Though I couldn't fathom how, some people reckoned he was able to see the underside of the cards as he dealt. His brother, Eck, explained it away by saying Tam had broken his arm as a young man. Well, I'm no card sharp, and I expected to lose a few quid, but I was sure I'd know if anyone tried to cheat me.

But then the other two players arrived, and I knew I would not be cheated. One was Cafferty. He was with a man called Jimmy Bone, a butcher by trade. He looked like a butcher, too – puffy-faced, red-cheeked, with fingers as fat as link sausages. He had a just-scrubbed look too. You often get that with butchers, surgeons, workers in the slaughterhouse. They like to look cleaner than clean.

Now that I think of it, Cafferty looked like that too. And Eck. And Tam. Tam was always rubbing his hands, giving off an aroma of lemon soap. Or he would examine his fingernails and pick beneath them. To look at his clothes, you would never guess, but he was pathologically hygienic. I realise now – blessed hindsight! – that the Robertson brothers were not pleased to see Cafferty. Nor did the butcher look happy at having been cajoled into playing. He kept complaining that he owed too much as it was, but Cafferty wouldn't hear of it.

The butcher was a dreadful poker player. He mimed dejection whenever he had a bad hand, and fidgeted, shuffling his feet, when he had a good one. As the game wore on, it was obvious there was an undercurrent between Cafferty and the Robertsons. Cafferty kept complaining about business. It was slow, money wasn't what it was. Then he turned to me abruptly and slapped his palm against the back of my hand.

'How many dead men have you seen?'

In Cafferty's company, I affected more bravado even than usual, an effect achieved in most part by seeming preternaturally relaxed.

'Not many,' I said (or something offhand like that).

'Any at all?' he persisted. He didn't wait for an answer. 'I've seen dozens. Yes, dozens. What's more, Black Aengus, I've killed my fair share of them.'

He lifted his hand away, sat back and said nothing. The next hand was dealt in silence. I wished Mo were around. She had a way of calming him down. He was drinking whisky from the bottle, sloshing it around in his mouth before swallowing noisily. Sober, he is unpredictable; drunk, he is dangerous. That's why I like him. I even admire him, in a strange sort of way. He gets what he wants by any means necessary. There is something magnetic about that singularity of mind. And of course, in his company I am someone to be respected, respected by people who would

302

normally call me a stuck-up snob and, as one person did, 'a pissed-up piece of shite'. Cafferty took exception when I told him I'd been called this. He paid the man responsible a visit.

What makes him want to spend time with me? Before that night, I'd thought maybe we saw fire in one another's eyes. But now I know differently. He spent time with me because I was going to be another means to an end. A final, bitter end.

I was drinking vodka, at first with orange, later neat – but always from a glass and always with ice. The Robertsons drank beer. They had a crate of bottles on the floor between them. The butcher drank whisky, whenever Cafferty deigned to pour him some, which wasn't often enough for the poor butcher. I was twenty quid down within a matter of minutes, and sixty quid down after a quarter of an hour. Cafferty placed his hand on mine again.

'If I'd not strayed along,' he said, 'they'd have had the shirt off your back and the breeks off your arse.'

'I never cheat,' said Tam Robertson. I got the feeling Cafferty had been wanting him to say something all along. Robertson acknowledged this by biting his lip.

Cafferty asked him if he was sure he didn't cheat. Robertson said nothing. His brother tried to calm things down, putting our minds back onto the game. But Cafferty grinned at Tam Robertson as he picked up his cards. Later, he started again.

'I've killed a lot of men,' he said, directing his eyes at me but his voice at the Robertsons. 'But not one of those killings wasn't justified. People who owed me, people who'd done me wrong, people who'd cheated. The way I look at it, everybody knows what he's getting into. Doesn't he?'

For want of any other answer, I agreed.

'And once you're into something, there are consequences to be faced, aren't there?' I nodded again. 'Black Aengus,' he said, 'have you ever *thought* about killing someone?'

303

'Many a time.'

This was true, though I wish now I'd held my tongue. I'd wanted to kill men wealthier than me, more handsome than me, men possessing beautiful women, and women who rejected my advances. I'd wanted to kill people who refused me service when drunk, people who didn't smile back when I smiled at them, people who were paged in hotels and made movies in Hollywood and owned ranches and castles and their own private armies. So my answer was accurate.

'Many a time.'

Cafferty was nodding. He'd almost finished the whisky. I thought something must be about to happen, some act of violence, and I was prepared for it – or thought I was. The Robertsons looked ready either to explode or implode. Tam had his hands on the edge of the table, ready to jump to his feet. And then the door opened. It was someone from the kitchens, bringing us up the sandwiches we'd ordered earlier. Smoked salmon and roast beef. The man waited to be paid.

'Go on, Tam,' said Cafferty quietly, 'you're the one with the luck tonight. Pay the man.'

Grudgingly, Tam counted out some notes and handed them over.

'And a tip,' said Cafferty. Another note was handed over. The waiter left the room. 'A very nice gesture,' said Cafferty. It was his turn to deal. 'How much are you down now, Black Aengus?'

'I'm not bad,' I said.

'I asked how much.'

'About forty.' I'd been a hundred down at one stage, but two decent hands had repaired some of the damage. Plus – there could be no doubt about it – the best card players around the table, by which I mean the Robertson brothers, were finding it hard to concentrate. The room was not warm, but there was sweat trickling down from Eck's sideburns. He kept rubbing the sweat away.

'You're letting them cheat you out of forty?' Cafferty said conversationally.

Tam Robertson leapt to his feet, his chair tipping over behind him.

'I've heard just about enough!'

But Eck righted the chair and pulled him down into it. Cafferty had finished dealing and was studying his cards, as though oblivious to the whole scene. The butcher got up suddenly, anouncing that he was going to be sick. He walked quickly out of the room.

'He won't be back,' Cafferty announced.

I said something lame to the effect that I was thinking of an early night myself. When Cafferty turned to me, he looked and sounded unlike any of his many personalities, the many I'd encountered so far.

'You wouldn't know an early night if it kicked you in the cunt.' He had started to gather up the cards for a redeal. I could feel blood tingling in my cheeks. He'd spoken with something close to revulsion. I told myself that he'd just drunk too much. People often said things ... etc. Look at me, I was one to be upset about the nasty things drunks could say!

He dealt the hand again. When it came time for him to make his initial bet, he threw a note into the pot, then laid his cards face down on the table. He reached into the waistband of his trousers. He'd worn a suit throughout; he always looks smart. He says the police are warier of picking up people wearing good clothes, and certainly more wary about punching or kicking them.

'They don't like to see good material ruined,' he told me. 'Canny Scots, you see.'

Now, when he withdrew his hand from the waistband, it was holding a pistol of some kind. The Robertsons started to object, while I just stared at the gun. I'd seen guns before, but never this close and in this kind of situation. Suddenly, the vodka, which had been having little or no effect all night, swam through me like waste through a sewer-pipe. I thought I was going to be sick, but swallowed it down. I even thought I might pass out. And all the time Cafferty was talking calm as you like about how Tam had been cheating him and where was the money.

'And you've been cheating Black Aengus too,' he said. I wanted to protest that this wasn't true, but still thought I might be sick if I opened my mouth, so I just shook my head, after which I felt even dizzier. You can't know the pain and frustration I'm feeling as I try to write this down candidly and exactly. Fourteen weeks have passed since that night, but every night it comes back to me, waking and sleeping. They're giving me drugs here, and strictly no alcohol. During the day I can walk in the grounds. There are 'encounter groups' where I'm supposed to talk my way out of my problem. Christ, if it were only that easy! The first thing my father did was get me out of the way. I am tempted to say *his* way. His answer was to send me on holiday. Mother chaperoned me around New England, where an aunt has a house in Bar Harbor. I tried talking to mother, but didn't seem to make much sense. She had that stupid sympathetic smile pasted onto her face.

I digress, not that it matters. Back to the poker game. You've perhaps guessed what happened next. I felt Cafferty's hand on mine, only this time he lifted my hand up in his. Then he placed the gun in my hand. I can feel it now, cold and hard. Half of me thought the gun was fake and he was just going to scare the Robertsons. The other half knew the gun was real, but didn't think he would use it.

Then I felt his fingers pushing mine until my index finger was around the trigger. His hand now fully enclosed mine, and aimed the gun. He squeezed his finger against mine, and there was an explosion in the room, and wisps of acrid powder. Blood freckled us all. It was warm for a moment, then cold against my skin. Eck was leaning over his brother, speaking to him. The gun clattered onto the table. Though I didn't take it in at the time, Cafferty proceeded to wrap the gun in a polythene bag. I know that any prints on it must be mine.

I flew up from the table, panicking, hysterical. Cafferty was seated still, and looking pacified. His calm had the opposite effect on me. I threw the vodka bottle against the wall, where it smashed, dousing wallpaper and curtains in alcohol. Seeing an idea, I grabbed a lighter from the table and ignited the vodka. Only now did Cafferty get up. He was swearing at me, and tried to douse the flames, but they were licking up the curtains out of our reach, scudding across the fabric wallcovering on the ceiling. He saw the fire was moving quicker than we could. I think Eck had already forsaken his brother and fled before I ran out of the room. I took the stairs three at a time and burst into the kitchens, demanding that all the gas be turned on. If the Central was going to burn, let it take the evidence with it.

I must have looked crazy enough, for the chef followed my instructions. I think he was the same person who served us the sandwiches, only he'd changed jackets. It was late, and he was alone in the kitchen, writing something down in a book. I told him to get out. He left by the back way, and I followed, keeping my head low as I jogged back to Blair Street.

I think that's everything. It doesn't feel any better for the writing down. There's no exorcism or catharsis. Maybe there never will be. You see, they've found the body. More than that, they know the man was shot. I don't see how the devil they can know, but they do. Maybe someone told them. Eck Robertson would have reason to. He's the only one who could tell. It's all my fault. I know that Cafferty started swearing at me because I'd mucked things up by setting fire to the room. If I hadn't, he would have seen to

307

it that Tam Robertson's body disappeared in the usual way. No one would have known. We would have gotten away with murder.

But 'getting away with it' isn't always getting away with it. The corpse haunts me. Last night I dreamt it came back to me, charred, smouldering. Pointing a finger towards me and squeezing the trigger. Oh Christ, this is agony. And they think I'm here for alcoholism. I still haven't told father all of it, not yet. He knows, though. He knows I was there. But he's not saying anything. Sometimes I wish he'd hit me more as a child and not let me misbehave. He *liked* me to misbehave! 'We'll make a man of you,' he used to say. Father, I am made.

That was that. Rebus sat back in his chair and stared at the ceiling. Eddie Ringan knew a little more than he'd been telling. He'd been a witness at the card game and could place Cafferty there. No wonder he'd been running scared. Cafferty probably hadn't known him back then, hadn't paid attention to a waiter who was moonlighting anyway and not one of the regular staff.

Rebus rubbed his eyes and returned to the journal. There was a bit about a holiday, then about the hospital again. And then a few months later:

I saw Cafferty today (Sunday). Not my idea. He must have been following me. He caught up on Blackford Hill. I'd come through the Hermitage, climbing the steep face of the hill. He must have thought I was trying to get away from him. He pulled on my arm, swinging me around. I think I nearly jumped out of my skin.

He told me I had to keep my nose clean from now on. He said it was a good idea, going into that hospital. I think he was trying to let me know that he knew everything I'd been up to. I think I know what he's doing. He's biding his time. Watching me as I take instructions in the business.

Waiting for the day when I take over from my father. I think he wants it all, body and soul.

Yes, body and soul.

There was a lot more, the style and substance of the entries changing as Aengus too tried to change. He'd found it hard work. The public face, the charity face, masked a yearning for some of that wild past. Rebus flipped to the final entry, undated:

You know, dear friend or foe, I liked the feel of that gun in my hand. And when Cafferty put my finger on the trigger ... he *did* squeeze it. I'm certain of that. But supposing he hadn't? Would I still have fired, with his strong unfailing hand on mine? After all these years, all the bad dreams, the cold sweats and sudden surges, something has happened. The case is being reopened. I've spoken with Cafferty who tells me not to worry. He says I should concentrate my energies on the brewery. He seems to know more about our finances than I do. Father is talking of retiring next year. The business will be all mine, and all Cafferty's. I've seen him at charity functions, accompanied by Mo, and at various public occasions. We've talked, but never since that night have we enjoyed one another's company. I lost my usefulness that night. Perhaps I just showed my weakness by smashing the bottle. Or perhaps that had been the plan all along. He always gives me a wink when he sees me. But then he winks at just about everyone. But when he winks at me, when he closes his eye for that second, it's as if he's taking aim, setting me in his sights. Christ, is there no end in sight? If I weren't so scared, I'd be praying the police would find me. But Cafferty won't let them. He never will let them, never.

Rebus closed the journal. His heart was beating fast, hands trembling. You poor bugger, Aengus. When you

309

read we'd got the gun, you thought we'd fingerprint it and then we'd come looking for you.

But instead, Cafferty had blown his trump trying to incriminate Rebus, just to keep him out of the picture for a while. And the irony of it all was, with the prints messed up, Black Aengus was in the clear – in the clear for a murder he didn't really commit.

Again, though, it was all uncorroborated. Rebus imagined the field day the defence would have if he walked into the Royal Mile courts with nothing more than the journal of a recovering dipsomaniac. The Edinburgh law courts were notoriously tough at the best of times. With the sort of advocate Cafferty could afford, it was a definite loser from the word go.

Yet Rebus *knew* he had to do something about Cafferty. The man deserved punishment, a million punishments. Let the punishment fit the crime, he thought. But he shook the notion away. No more guns.

He didn't go home, not right away. He walked out of the now-empty office and got into his car. And sat there, in the car park. The key was in the ignition, but he let it sit there. His hands rested lightly on the steering-wheel. After almost an hour, he started the engine, mostly because he was getting cold. He didn't go anywhere, except inside his head, and slowly but surely, with back-tracking and rerouting along the way, the idea came to him. Let the punishment fit the crime. Yes, but not Cafferty's punishment. No, not Cafferty's.

Andrew McPhail's.

33

Rebus didn't go near St Leonard's for a couple of days, though he did get a message from Farmer Watson that Broderick Gibson was considering bringing an action against him, for harrying his son.

'He's been harrying himself for years,' was Rebus's only comment.

But he was waiting in his car when they released Andy Steele. The fisherman cum private eye blinked into the sun. Rebus sounded his horn, and Steele approached warily. Rebus wound down his window.

'Oh, it's you,' said Steele. There was disappointment in his voice. Rebus had said he'd see what he could do for the young man, then had left him to languish, never coming near.

'They let you out, then,' said Rebus.

'Aye, on bail.'

'That's because someone put up the money for you.'

Steele nodded, then started. 'You?'

'Me,' said Rebus. 'Now get in, I've got a job for you.'

'What sort of job?'

'Get in and I'll tell you.'

There was a bit more life in Steele as he walked round to the passenger side and opened the door.

'You want to be a private eye,' stated Rebus. 'Fair enough. I've got a job for you.'

Steele seemed unable to take it in for a moment, then

cleared his head by shaking it briskly, rubbing his hands through his hair.

'Great,' he said. 'So long as it's not against the law.'

'Oh, it's nothing illicit. All I want you to do is talk to a few folk. They're good listeners too, shouldn't be any problem.'

'What am I going to tell them?'

Rebus started the car. 'That there's a contract out on a certain individual.'

'A contract?'

'Come on, Andy, you've seen the films. A contract.'

'A contract,' Andy Steele mouthed, as Rebus pulled into the traffic.

There was still no sign of Andrew McPhail. Alex Maclean, Rebus discovered, was back in circulation though not yet back at work. When Rebus visited Mrs Mackenzie, she said she hadn't seen a man with bandaged hands and face hanging around. But one of the neighbours had. Well, it didn't matter, McPhail wouldn't be coming back here again. He would probably write or telephone with a forwarding address, asking his landlady to send on his stuff. Rebus looked towards the school as he got back into his car. The children were in their own little world ... and safe.

He did a lot of driving, visiting schools and playparks. He knew McPhail must be sleeping rough. Maybe he was well away from Edinburgh by now. Rebus had a vision of him climbing up onto a coal train headed slowly south. A hand reached out and helped McPhail into the wagon. It was Deek Torrance. The opening credits began to roll ...

It didn't matter if he couldn't find McPhail; it would just be a nice touch. A nicely cruel touch.

Wester Hailes was a good place to get lost, meaning it was an easy place to get lost. Sited to the far west of the

312

city, visible from the bypass which gave Edinburgh such a wide berth, Wester Hailes was somewhere the city put people so it could forget about them. The architecture was unenthusiastic, the walls of the flat-blocks finished off with damp and cracks.

People might leave Wester Hailes, or stay there all their lives, surrounded by roads and industrial estates and empty green spaces. It had never before struck Rebus that it would make a good hiding place. You could walk the streets, or the Kingsknowe golf course, or the roads around Sighthill, and as long as you didn't look out of place you would be safe. There were places you could sleep without being discovered. And if you were of a mind, there was a school. A school and quite a few play-parks.

This was where, on the second day, he found Andrew McPhail. Never mind watching the bus and railway stations, Rebus had known where to look. He followed McPhail for three-quarters of an hour, at first in the car and then, when McPhail took a pedestrian shortcut, awkwardly on foot. McPhail kept moving, his gait brisk. A man out for a walk, that was all. A bit shabby maybe, but these days with unemployment what it was, you lost the will to shave every morning, didn't you?

McPhail was careful not to draw attention to himself. He didn't pause to stare at any children he saw. He just smiled towards them and went on his way. When Rebus had seen enough, he gained quickly and tapped him on the shoulder. He might as well have used a cattle-prod.

'Jesus, it's you!' McPhail's hand went to his chest. 'You nearly gave me a heart attack.'

'That would have saved Alex Maclean a job.'

'How is he?'

'Minor burns. He's up and about and on the warpath.'

'Christ's sake! We're talking about something that happened *years* ago!'

'And it's not going to happen again?'

313

'No!'

'And it was an accident you ended up living across from a primary school?'

'Yes.'

'And I was wrong to think I'd find you somewhere near a school or a playground . . .?'

McPhail opened his mouth, then closed it again. He shook his head. 'No, you weren't wrong. I still like kids. But I never . . . I'd never do anything to them. I won't even speak to them these days.' He looked up at Rebus. 'I'm *trying*, Inspector.'

Everyone wanted a second chance: Michael, McPhail, even Black Aengus. Sometimes, Rebus could help. 'Tell you what,' he said. 'There are programmes for past offenders. You could go into one of them, not in Edinburgh, somewhere else. You could sign on for social security and look for a job.' McPhail looked ready to say something. 'I know it takes money, a wee bit of cash to get you on your feet. But I can help with that too.'

McPhail blinked, one eye staying half closed. 'Why?'

'Because I want to. And afterwards, you'll be left alone, I promise. I won't tell anyone where you are or what's happened to you. Is it a deal?'

McPhail thought about it – for two seconds. 'A deal,' he said.

'Fine then.' Rebus put his hand on McPhail's shoulder again, drawing him a little closer. 'There's just one small thing I'd like you to do for me first . . .'

It had been quiet in the social club, and Chick Muir was thinking of heading home when the young chap at the bar asked if he could buy him a drink. Chick readily agreed.

'I don't like drinking on my own,' the young man explained.

'Who can blame you?' said Chick agreeably, handing

his empty glass to the barman. 'Not from round here?'

'Aberdeen,' said the young man.

'A long way from home. Is it still like Dallas up there?'

Chick meant the oil-boom, which had actually disappeared almost as quickly as it had begun, except in the mythology of those people not living in Aberdeen.

'Maybe it is,' said the young man, 'but that didn't stop them sacking me.'

'Sorry to hear it.' Chick really was too. He'd been hoping the young man was off the oil rigs with cash to burn. He was planning to tap him for a tenner, but now shrugged away the idea.

'I'm Andy Steele, by the way.'

'Chick Muir.' Chick placed his cigarette in his mouth so he could shake Andy Steele's hand. The grip was like a rubbish-crusher.

'The money didn't bring much luck to Aberdeen, you know,' Steele was reminiscing. 'Just a load of sharks and gangsters.'

'I'll believe it.' Muir was already halfway through his drink. He wished he'd been drinking a whisky instead of the half-pint when he'd been asked about another. It didn't look good exchanging a half-pint for a nip, so he was stuck with a half.

'That's mostly why I'm here,' said Steele.

'What? Gangsters?' Muir sounded amused.

'In a way. I'm visiting a friend, too, but I thought while I was here I might pick up a few bob.'

'How's that?' Chick was beginning to feel uncomfortable, but also distinctly curious.

Steele dropped his voice, though they were alone at the bar. 'There's word going around Aberdeen that someone's out to get a certain individual in Edinburgh.'

The barman had turned on the tape machine behind the bar. The low-ceilinged room was promptly filled with a folk duet. They'd played the club last week, and the barman had made a tape of them. It sounded worse now than it had then.

'In the name of Auld Nick, turn that down!' Chick didn't have a loud voice, but no one could say it lacked authority. The barman turned the sound down a bit, and when Chick still glared at him turned it even lower. 'What was that?' he asked Andy Steele. Andy Steele, who had been enjoying his drink, put down the glass and told Chick Muir again. And a little while later, mission accomplished, he bought Chick a final drink and then left.

Chick Muir didn't touch this fresh half pint. He stared past it at his own reflection in the mirror behind the row of optics. Then he made a few phone calls, again roaring at the barman to 'turn that shite off!' The third call he made was to St Leonard's, where he was informed, a bit too light-heartedly, he thought, that Inspector Rebus had been suspended from duty pending enquiries. He tried Rebus at his flat, but no joy there either. Ach well, it wasn't so important. What mattered was that he'd talked to the big man. Now the big man owed him, and that was quite enough for the penniless Chick Muir to be going on with.

Andy Steele gave the same performance in a meanly lit pub and a betting shop, and that evening was at Powderhall for the greyhound racing. He recited to himself the description Rebus had given him, and eventually spotted the man tucking into a meal of potato crisps at a window-seat in the bar.

'Are you Shuggie Oliphant?' he asked.

'That's me,' said the huge thirtyish man. He was poking a finger into the farthest corner of the crisp-bag in search of salt.

'Somebody told me you might be interested in a bit of information I've got.'

Oliphant still hadn't looked at him. The bag emptied,

he folded it into a thin strip, then tied it in a knot and placed it on the table. There were four other granny knots just like it in a row. 'You don't get paid till I do,' Oliphant informed him, sucking on a greasy finger and smacking his lips.

Andy Steele sat down across from him. 'That's okay by me,' he said.

On Sunday morning Rebus waited at the top of a blustery Calton Hill. He walked around the observatory, as the other Sunday strollers were doing. His leg was definitely improving. People were pointing out distant landmarks. Broken clouds were moving rapidly over a pale blue sky. Nowhere else in the world, he reckoned, had this geography of bumps and valleys and outcrops. The volcanic plug beneath Edinburgh Castle had been the start of it. Too good a place *not* to build a fortress. And the town had grown around it, grown out as far as Wester Hailes and beyond.

The observatory was an odd building, if functional. The folly, on the other hand, was just that, and served no function at all save as a thing to clamber over and a place to spraypaint your name. It was one side of a projected Greek temple (Edinburgh, after all, being 'the Athens of the north'). The all-too-eccentric brain behind the scheme had run out of money after completion of this first side. And there it stood, a series of pillars on a plinth so tall kids had to stand on each other's shoulders to climb aboard.

When Rebus looked towards it, he saw a woman there swinging her legs from the plinth and waving towards him. It was Siobhan Clarke. He walked over to her.

'How long have you been here?' he called up.

'Not long. Where's your stick?'

'I can manage fine without it.' This was true, though by 'fine' he meant that he could hobble along at a reasonable pace. 'I see Hibs got a result yesterday.'

'About time.'

'No sign of himself?'

But Siobhan pointed to the car park. 'Here he comes now.'

A Mini Metro had climbed the road to the top of the hill and was squeezing into a space between two shinier larger cars. 'Give me a hand down,' said Siobhan.

'Watch for my leg,' Rebus complained. But she felt almost weightless as he lifted her down.

'Thanks,' she said. Brian Holmes had watched the performance before locking his car and coming towards them.

'A regular Baryshnikov,' he commented.

'Bless you,' said Rebus.

'So what's this all about, sir?' Siobhan asked. 'Why the secrecy?'

'There's nothing secret,' Rebus said, starting to walk, 'about an Inspector wanting to talk with two of his junior colleagues. *Trusted* junior colleagues.'

Siobhan caught Holmes's eye. Holmes shook his head: he wants something from us. As if she didn't know.

They leaned against a railing, enjoying the view, Rebus doing most of the talking. Siobhan and Holmes added occasional questions, mostly rhetorical.

'So this would be off our own bats?'

'Of course,' Rebus answered. 'Just two keen coppers with a little bit of initiative.' He had a question of his own. 'Will the lighting be difficult?'

Holmes shrugged. 'I'll ask Jimmy Hutton about that. He's a professional photographer. Does calendars and that sort of thing.'

'It's not going to be wee kittens or a Highland glen,' replied Rebus.

'No, sir,' said Holmes.

'And you think this'll work?' asked Siobhan.

Rebus shrugged. 'Let's wait and see.'

'We haven't said we'll do it, sir.'

'No,' said Rebus, turning away, 'but you will.'

34

Off their own initiative then, Holmes and Siobhan decided
to spend Monday evening doing a surveillance shift on
Operation Moneybags. Without heating, the room they
crouched in was cold and damp, and dark enough to
attract the odd mouse. Holmes had set the camera up,
after taking advice from the calendar man. He'd even
borrowed a special lens for the occasion, telephoto and
night-sighted. He hadn't bothered with his Walkman and
his Patsy Cline tapes: in the past, there'd always been
more than enough to talk about with Siobhan. But tonight
she didn't seem in the mood. She kept gnawing on her
top and bottom lips, and got up every now and then to
do stretching exercises.

'Don't you get stiff?' she asked him.

'Not me,' said Holmes quietly. 'I've been in training for
this – years of being a couch potato.'

'I thought you kept pretty fit.'

He watched her bend forward and lay her arms down
the length of one leg. 'And you must be double-jointed.'

'Not quite. You should've seen me in my teens.' Holmes'
grin was illuminated by the street light's diffuse orange
glow. 'Down, Rover,' said Siobhan. There was a scuttling
overhead.

'A rat,' said Holmes. 'Ever cornered one?' She shook
her head. 'They can jump like a Tummel salmon.'

'My parents took me to the hydro dam when I was a
kid.'

'At Pitlochry?' She nodded. 'So you've seen the salmon leaping?' She nodded again. 'Well,' said Holmes, 'imagine one of those with hair and fangs and a long thick tail.'

'I'd rather not.' She watched from the window. 'Do you think he'll come.'

'I don't know. John Rebus isn't often wrong.'

'Is that why everyone hates him?'

Holmes seemed a little surprised. 'Who hates him?'

She shrugged. 'People I've talked to at St Leonard's ... and other places. They don't trust him.'

'He wouldn't have it any other way.'

'Why not?'

'Because he's thrawn.' He was remembering the first time Rebus had used him in a case. He'd spent a cold frustrating evening watching for a dog-fight that never took place. He was hoping tonight would be better.

The rat was moving again, to the back of the room now, over by the door.

'*Do* you think he'll come?' Siobhan asked again.

'He'll come, lass.' They both turned towards the shape in the doorway. It was Rebus. 'You two,' he said, 'blethering like sweetiewives. I could have climbed those stairs in pit boots and you'd not have heard me.' He came over to the window. 'Anything?'

'Nothing, sir.'

Rebus angled his watch towards the light. 'I make it five to.'

The display on Siobhan's digital watch was backlit. 'Ten to, sir.'

'Bloody watch,' muttered Rebus. 'Not long now. There'll be some action by the top of the hour. Unless that daft Aberdonian's put the kibosh on it.'

But the 'daft Aberdonian' wasn't so daft. Big Ger Cafferty paid for information. Even if it was information he already knew, he tended to pay: it was a cheap way of making sure *everything* got back to him. For example, even though he'd already heard from two sources that the teuchters were planning to muscle in on him, he still paid Shug Oliphant a few notes for his effort. And Oliphant, who liked to keep his own sources sweet, handed over ten quid to Andy Steele, this representing two-fifths of Oliphant's reward.

'There you go,' he said.

'Cheers,' said Andy Steele, genuinely pleased.

'Found anything you like?'

Oliphant was referring to the videotapes which surrounded them in the small rental shop which he operated. The area behind the narrow counter was so small, Oliphant only just squeezed in there. Every time he moved he seemed to knock something off a shelf onto the floor, where it remained, since there was also no room for him to bend over.

'I've got some bits and pieces under the counter,' he went on, 'if you're interested.'

'No, I don't want a video.'

Oliphant grinned unpleasantly. 'I'm not sure the gentleman really believed your story,' Oliphant told Andy. 'But I've heard the rumour a few times since, so maybe there's something in it.'

'There is,' said Andy Steele. Rebus was right, if you told a deaf man something on Monday, by Tuesday it was in the evening paper. 'They've got a watch on his hangouts, including the operation in Gorgie.'

Oliphant looked mightily suspicious. 'How do you know?'

'Luck, really. I bumped into one of them. I knew him in Aberdeen. He told me to get out if I didn't want to get mixed up in it.'

'But you're still here.'

'I'm on the mail train tomorrow morning.'

'So something's happening tonight?' Oliphant still

sounded highly sceptical, but then that was his way.

Steele shrugged. 'All I know is, they're keeping watch. I think maybe they just want to talk.'

Oliphant considered, running his fingers over a video-box. 'There were two pubs last night got their windows smashed.' Steele didn't blink. 'Pubs where the gentleman drank. Could be a connection?'

Steele shrugged. 'Could be.' If he were being honest, he'd have told how he acted as getaway driver while Rebus himself tossed the large rocks through the glass. One of the pubs had been the Firth at Tollcross, the other the Bowery at the bottom of Easter Road.

But instead he said, 'Loon called McPhail, he's the one watching Gorgie. He's in charge.'

Oliphant nodded. 'You know the way it works, come back in a day or two. There'll be money if the gen's on the nail.'

But Steele shook his head. 'I'm off up to Aberdeen.'

'So you are,' said Oliphant. 'Tell you what,' he tore a sheet from a pad, 'give me your address and I'll send on the cash.'

Andy Steele had fun inventing the address.

Cafferty was playing snooker when he got the message. He had a quarter share in an upmarket snooker hall and leisure complex in Leith. The intended market had been yuppies, working class lads scraping their way up the greasy pole. But the yuppies had vanished in a puff of smoke. So now the complex was shifting cannily down-market with video bingo, happy hour, an arcade full of electronic machines, and plans for a bowling alley. Teenagers always seemed to have money in their pockets. They would carve the bowling alley out of the little-used gymnasium, the restaurant next to it, and the aerobics room beyond that.

Staying in business, Cafferty had found, was all about

remaining flexible. If the wind changed, you didn't try to steer in the opposite direction. Mooted future plans included a soul club and a 1940s ballroom, the latter complete with tea dances and 'blackout nights'. Groping nights, Cafferty called them.

He knew he was crap at snooker, but he liked the game. His theory was fine; it was the practice that was lacking. Vanity prevented him taking lessons, and his renowned lack of patience would have dissuaded all but the most foolhardy from giving them. On Mo's advice, he'd tried a few other sports – tennis, squash, even skiing one time. The only one he'd enjoyed was golf. He loved thwacking that ball all over the place. Problem was, he didn't know when to hold back, he was always overshooting. If he hadn't split at least a couple of balls after nine holes, he wasn't happy.

Snooker suited him. It had everything. Tactics, ciggies, booze, and a few sidebets. So here he was again in the hall, overhead lights flooding the green tables, dusk everywhere else. Quiet, too, therapeutic; just the clack of the balls, the occasional comment or joke, a floor-stomp with the cue to signal a worthy shot. Then Jimmy the Ear was coming towards him.

'Phone call from the house,' he told Cafferty. Then he gave him Oliphant's message.

Andrew McPhail trusted Rebus about as far as he could toss a caber into a gale. He knew he should be running for cover right now, let the caber land where it might. There were several ways it could go. Rebus might be setting up a meeting between McPhail and Maclean. Well, McPhail could prepare himself against this. Or it might be some other kind of ruse, probably ending up with a beating and the clear message to get the fuck out of Edinburgh.

Or it could be straight. Aye, if the spirit-level was bent.

Rebus had asked McPhail to deliver a message, a letter. He'd even handed over the envelope. The message was for a man called Cafferty, who would be leaving the taxi office on Gorgie Road around ten.

'So what's the message?'

'Never you mind,' Rebus had said.

'Why me?'

'It can't come from me, that's all you need to know. Just make sure it's him, and give him the envelope.'

'This stinks.'

'I can't make it any simpler. We'll meet afterwards and fix up your new future. The ball's already rolling.'

'Aye,' said McPhail, 'but where the fuck's the net?'

Yet here he was, walking up Gorgie Road. A bit cold, threatening rain. Rebus had taken him to St Leonard's this afternoon, let him shower and shave, even provided some clean clothes which he'd picked up from Mrs Mackenzie's.

'I don't want a tramp delivering my post,' he'd explained. Ah, the letter. McPhail wasn't donnert; he'd torn the envelope open earlier this evening. Inside was a smaller brown envelope with some writing on the front: NO PEEKING NOW, McPHAIL!

He'd thought about opening it anyway. It didn't feel like there was much inside, a single sheet of paper. But something stopped him, a pale spark of hope, the hope that everything was going to be all right.

He didn't have a watch, but was a good judge of time. It felt like ten o'clock. And here he was in front of the taxi office. There were lights on inside, and cabs ready and waiting outside. Their busiest shift would be starting soon, the rides home after closing time. The night air smelt like ten o'clock. Diesel from the railway lines, rain close by. Andrew McPhail waited.

He saw the headlights, and when the car – a Jag – swerved and mounted the pavement his first thought was:

drunk driver. But the car braked smoothly, stopping beside him, almost pinning him to the wire fence. The driver got out. He was big. A gust of wind flapped his long hair, and McPhail saw that one ear was missing.

'You McPhail?' he demanded. The back door of the Jag was opening slowly, another man getting out. He wasn't as big as the driver, but he somehow *seemed* larger. He was smiling unkindly.

The letter was in McPhail's pocket. 'Cafferty?' he asked, forcing the word from his lungs.

The smiling man blinked lazily in acknowledgement. In McPhail's other pocket was the broken neck of a whisky bottle he'd found beside an overflowing bottle bank. It wasn't much of a weapon, but it was all he could afford. Even so, he didn't rate his chances. His bladder felt painfully full. He reached for the letter.

The driver pinned his arms to his side and swung him around, so he was face to face with Cafferty, who swung a kick into his groin. The butt of a three-section snooker cue slipped expertly from Cafferty's coat sleeve into his hand. As McPhail doubled over, the cue caught him on the side of the jaw, fracturing it, dislodging teeth. He fell further forwards and was rewarded with the cue on the back of his neck. His whole body went numb. Now the driver was pulling his head up by the hair and Cafferty was forcing his mouth open with the cue, working it past his tongue and into his throat.

'Hold it there!' Two of them, a man and a woman, running from across the street and holding open their IDs. 'Police officers.'

Cafferty lifted both hands away, raising them head high. He had left the cue in McPhail's mouth. The driver released the battered man, who remained upright on his knees. Shakily, Andrew McPhail started to pull the snooker cue out of his throat. There were sirens close by as a police car approached.

'It's nothing, officer,' Cafferty was saying, 'a misunderstanding.'

'Some misunderstanding,' said the male police officer. His sidekick slipped her hand into McPhail's pocket. She felt a broken bottle. Wrong pocket. From the other pocket she produced the letter, crumpled now. She handed it to Cafferty.

'Open this, please, sir,' she said.

Cafferty stared at it. 'Is this a set-up?' But he opened it anyway. Inside was a scrap of paper, which he unfolded. The note was unsigned. He knew who it was from anyway. 'Rebus!' he spat. 'That bastard Rebus!'

A few minutes later, as Cafferty and his driver were being taken away, and the ambulance was arriving for Andrew McPhail, Siobhan picked up the note which Cafferty had dropped. It said simply, 'I hope they sell your skin for souvenirs.' She frowned and looked up at the surveillance window, but couldn't see anyone there.

Had she seen anything, it would have been the outline of a man making the shape of a gun from his fist, lining up the thumb so Cafferty was in its sights, and pulling the imaginary trigger.

Bang!

35

Nobody at St Leonard's believed Holmes and Siobhan were there that night simply out of an exaggerated sense of duty. The more credible version had them meeting for a clandestine shag and just happening upon the beating. Lucky there was film in the surveillance camera. And didn't the photos come out well?

With Cafferty in custody, they got the chance to take away his things and have yet another look at them ... including the infamous coded diary. Watson and Lauderdale were poring over xeroxed sheets from it when there was a knock at the Chief Super's door.

'Come!' called Watson.

John Rebus walked in and looked around admiringly at the sudden floorspace. 'I see you got your cabinets, sir.'

Lauderdale pulled himself up straight. 'What the hell are you doing here? You're suspended from duty.'

'It's all right, Frank,' said Watson, 'I asked Inspector Rebus to come in.' He turned the xeroxed pages towards Rebus. 'Take a look.'

It didn't take long. The problem with the code in the past was that they hadn't known *what* to look for. But now Rebus had a more than fair idea. He stabbed one entry. 'There,' he said. '3TUB SCS.'

'Yes?'

'It means the butcher on South Clerk Street owes three thousand. He's abbreviated 'butcher' and written it backwards.'

Lauderdale looked disbelieving. 'Are you sure?'

Rebus shrugged. 'Put the experts at Fettes onto it. They should be able to find at least a few more late-payers.'

'Thank you, John,' said Watson. Rebus turned smartly and left the room. Lauderdale stared at his superior.

'I get the feeling,' he said, 'something's going on here I don't know about.'

'Well, Frank,' said Watson, 'why should today be different from any other?'

Which, as the saying went, put CI Lauderdale's gas at a very low peep.

It was Siobhan Clarke who came up with the most important piece of information in the whole case.

It *was* a case now. Rebus didn't mind that the machine was in operation without him. Holmes and Clarke reported back to him at the end of each day. The code-breakers had been hard at work, as a result of which detectives were talking to Cafferty's black book victims. It would only take one or two of them in court, and Cafferty would be going down. So far, though, no one was talking. Rebus had an idea of one person who, given enough persuasion, might.

Then Siobhan mentioned that Cafferty's company Geronimo Holdings held a seventy-nine per cent share in a large farm in the south-west Borders, not so very far from the coastline where the bodies had been washing up until recently. A party was sent to the farm. They found plenty for the forensic scientists to start working on ... especially the pigsties. The sties themselves were clean enough, but there was an enclosed area of storage space above each ramshackle sty. Most of the farm had turned itself over to the latest in high-tech agriculture, but not the sties. It was this which initially alerted the police. Above the pigsties, in the dark enclosures strewn with rank straw, there was a tangible reek of something unwholesome, something putrid. Strips of cloth were found; in one corner there lay a man's trouser-belt. The area was photographed and picked over for its least congruous particles. Upstairs in the farmhouse, meanwhile, a man who claimed initially to be an agricultural labourer eventually admitted to being Derek Torrance, better known as Deek.

At the same time, Rebus was driving out to Dalkeith, to Duncton Terrace, to be precise. It was early evening, and the Kintoul family was at home. Mother, father and son took up three sides of a fold-down table in the kitchen. The chip-pan was still smouldering and spitting on the greasy gas cooker. The vinyl wallpaper was slick with condensation. Most of the food on the plates was disguised by brown sauce. Rebus could smell vinegar and washing-up liquid. Rory Kintoul excused himself and went with Rebus into the living room. Kitchen and living room were connected by a serving hatch. Rebus wondered if wife and son would be listening at the hatch.

Rebus sat in one fireside chair, Kintoul opposite him.

'Sorry if it's a bad time,' Rebus began. There was a ritual to be followed, after all.

'What is it, Inspector?'

'You'll have heard, Mr Kintoul, we've arrested Morris Cafferty. He'll be going away for quite a while.' Rebus looked at the photos on the mantelpiece, snapshots of gap-toothed kids, nephews and nieces. He smiled at them. 'I just thought maybe it was time you got it off your chest.'

He kept silent for a moment, still examining the framed photos. Kintoul said nothing.

'Only,' said Rebus, 'I know you're a good man. I mean, a *good* man. You put family first, am I right?' Kintoul nodded uncertainly. 'Your wife and son, you'd do anything for them. Same goes for your other family, parents, sisters, brothers, cousins . . .' Rebus trailed off.

'I know Cafferty's going away,' said Kintoul.

'And?'

Kintoul shrugged.

'It's like this,' said Rebus. 'We know just about all there is to know. We just need a little corroboration.'

'That means testifying?'

Rebus nodded. Eddie Ringan would be testifying too, telling all he knew about the Central Hotel, in return for a good word from the police come his own trial. 'Mr Kintoul, you've got to accept something. You've got to accept that you've changed, you're not the same man you were a year or two ago. Why did you do it?' Rebus asked the way a friend would, just curious.

Kintoul wiped a smear of sauce from his chin. 'It was a favour. Jim always needed favours.'

'So you drove the van?'

'Yes, I did his rounds.'

'But you were a lab technician!'

Kintoul smiled. 'And I could earn more on the butcher's round.' He shrugged again. 'Like you say, Inspector, I put family first, especially where money's concerned.'

'Go on.'

'How much do you know?'

'We know the van was used to dump the bodies.'

'Nobody ever notices a butcher's van.'

'Except a poor constable in north-east Fife. He ended up with concussion.'

'That was after my time. I was shot of it by then.' He waited till Rebus nodded agreement, then went on. 'Only, when I wanted out Cafferty didn't want me out. He was putting pressure on.'

'That's how you got stabbed?'

'It was that bodyguard of his, Jimmy the Ear. He lost the head. Knifed me as I was getting out of the car. Crazy bastard.' Kintoul glanced towards the serving-hatch. 'You know what Cafferty did when I said I wanted to stop driving the van? He offered Jason a job "driving" for him. Jason's my son.'

Rebus nodded. 'But why all this fuss? Cafferty could get a hundred guys to drive a van for him.'

'I thought you knew him, Inspector. Cafferty's like that. He's ... particular about his flesh.'

'He's off his head,' commented Rebus. 'How did you get sucked in in the first place?'

'I was still driving full-time when Cafferty won half the business from Jimmy. One evening, one of Cafferty's men turned up all smarmy, told me we'd be taking a run to the coast early next morning. Via some farm in the Borders.'

'You went to the farm?' So that's why there was straw in the van.

The colour was seeping from Kintoul's face like blood from a cut of meat.

'Oh aye. There was something in the pigsties, tied up in fertiliser bags. Stank to high heaven. I'd been working in a butcher's long enough to know it had been rotting in that sty for a good few weeks, months, even.'

'A corpse?'

'Easy to tell, isn't it? I threw my guts up. Cafferty's man said what a waste, I should've done it into the trough.' Kintoul paused. He was still wiping at his chin, though the sauce mark had long ago been erased. 'Cafferty liked the bodies to be rotten, less chance of them washing ashore in any recognisable state.'

'Christ.'

'I haven't come to the worst part yet.' In the next room, Kintoul's wife and son were speaking in undertones. Rebus was in no hurry, and merely watched as Kintoul got up to stare from his back window. There was a patch of garden out there he could call his own. It was small, but it was his. He came back and stood in front of the gas fire, not looking at Rebus.

'I was there one day when he killed someone,' he said

332

baldly. Then he screwed shut his eyes. Rebus was trying to control his own breathing. This guy would make a gem of a witness.

'Killed them how?' Still not pressing; still the friend.

Kintoul tipped his head back, feeding tears back where they had come from. 'How? With his bare hands. We'd arrived late. The van had broken down in the middle of nowhere. It was about ten in the morning. Mist all around the farm, like driving into Brigadoon. They were both wearing business suits, that's what got me. And they were up to their ankles in glaur.'

Rebus frowned, not quite comprehending. 'They were *in* the pigsty?'

Kintoul nodded. 'There's a fenced run. Cafferty was in there with this man. There were other people watching through the fence.' He swallowed. 'I swear Cafferty looked like he was enjoying it. There with the mud lapping at him, and the pigs squealing in their boxes wondering what the hell was happening, and all the silent onlookers.' Kintoul tried to shake the memory away, probably a daily event.

'They were fighting?'

'The other man looked like he'd been roughed up beforehand. Nobody'd call it a fair fight. And eventually, after Cafferty'd beaten the living shite out of him, he grabbed him by the neck and forced him down into the muck. He stood on the man's back, balancing there, and holding the face down with his hands. He looked like it was nothing new. Then the man stopped struggling ...'

Rebus and Kintoul were silent, blood pounding through them, both trying to cope with the vision of an early morning pigsty ... 'Afterwards,' said Kintoul, his voice lower than ever, 'he beamed at us like it was his coronation.'

Then, in complete grimacing silence, he started to weep.

Rebus was visiting the Infirmary so often he was considering taking out a season ticket. But he hadn't expected to see Flower there.

'Checking in? The psychiatric section's down the hall.'

'Ha ha,' said Flower.

'What are you doing here anyway?'

'I could ask you the same question.'

'I live here, what about you?'

'I came to ask some questions.'

'Of Andrew McPhail?' Flower nodded. 'Did nobody tell you his jaw's wired shut?' Flower twitched, producing a good wide grin from Rebus. 'How come it's your business anyway?'

'It involves Cafferty,' Flower said.

'Oh aye, so it does, I'd forgotten.'

'Looks like we've got him this time.'

'Looks like it. But you never know with Cafferty.' Rebus stared unblinking at Flower as he spoke. 'The reason he's lasted so long is he's clever. He's clever, and he's got the best lawyers. Plus he's got people scared of him, and he's got people in his pocket ... maybe even a copper or three.'

Flower had stared out the gaze; now he blinked. 'You think I was in Cafferty's pocket?'

Rebus had been pondering this. He had Cafferty marked down for the attack on Michael and the scam with the gun. As for the clumsy hit-and-run attempt, that was so amateurish, he guessed at Broderick Gibson for its architect. Quite simply, Cafferty would have used better men.

He'd been silent long enough, so he shook his head. 'I don't think you're that smart. Cafferty likes smart people. But I *do* think you had a word with the Inland Revenue about me.'

'I don't know what you're talking about.'

Rebus grinned. 'I do like a cliché.' Then he walked on down the hall.

Andrew McPhail was easy to find. You just looked for the broken face. He was wired up like somebody's first

334

attempt at a junction box. Rebus thought he could see where they'd used two wires where one would have sufficed. But then he was no doctor. McPhail had his eyes closed.

'Hello there,' said Rebus. The eyes opened. There was anger there, but Rebus could cope with it. He held up a hand. 'No,' he said, 'don't bother to thank me.' Then he smiled. 'It's all set up for when they let you out. Up north for rehabilitation, maybe a job, and bracing coastal walks. Man, I envy you.' He looked around the ward. Every bed had a body in it. The nurses looked like they could use a holiday or at the very least a gin and lime with some dry-roast peanuts.

'I said I'd leave you alone,' Rebus went on, 'and I keep my word. But a piece of advice.' He rested his hands on the edge of the bed and leaned towards McPhail. 'Cafferty's the biggest villain in town. You're probably the only bugger in Edinburgh who didn't know that. Now his men know a guy called McPhail set their boss up. So don't ever think of coming back, will you?' McPhail still glared at him. 'Good,' said Rebus. He straightened up, turned, and walked away, then paused and turned. 'Oh,' he said, 'and I meant to say something.' He returned to the bed and stood at its foot, where charts showed McPhail's temperature and medicaments. Rebus waited till McPhail's wet eyes were on his, then he smiled sympathetically again.

'Sorry,' he said. This time, when he turned he kept on walking.

Andy Steele had been the necessary go-between. It was too dangerous for Rebus to put the story out first-hand. The source of the tale might have got back to Cafferty, and that would have ruined everything. McPhail hadn't been necessary, but he'd been useful. Rebus explained the ruse twice to Andy Steele, and even then the young fisherman didn't seem to take it all in. He had the look of a man with a dozen unaskable questions.

'So what are you going to do now?' Rebus asked. He'd been hoping in fact that Steele might already have left for home.

'Oh, I'm applying for a grant,' said Steele.

'You mean like university?'

But Steele hooted. 'Not likely! It's one of those schemes to get the unemployed into business.'

'Oh aye?'

Steele nodded. 'I'm eligible.'

'So what's the business?'

'A detective agency, of course!'

'Where exactly?'

'Edinburgh. I've made more money since I came here than I made in six months in Aberdeen.'

'You cannot be serious,' said Rebus. But Andy Steele was.

36

He had one last meeting planned, and wasn't looking forward to it. He walked from St Leonard's to the University library at George Square. The indifferent security man on the door glanced at his ID and nodded him towards the front desk, where Nell Stapleton, tall and broad-shouldered, was taking returned books from a duffel-coated student. She caught his eye and looked surprised. Pleased at first; but as she went through the books, Rebus saw her mind wasn't wholly on the job. At last, she came over to him.

'Hello, John.'

'Nell.'

'What brings you here?'

'Can we have a word?'

She checked with the other assistant that it was okay to take a five-minute break. They walked as far as a book-lined corridor.

'Brian tells me you've closed the case, the one he was so worried about.'

Rebus nodded.

'That's great news. Thanks for your help.'

Rebus shrugged.

She tilted her head slightly. 'Is something the matter?'

'I'm not sure,' said Rebus. 'Do you want to tell me?'

'Me?'

Rebus nodded again.

'I don't understand.'

'You've lived with a policeman, Nell. You know we deal in motives. Sometimes there isn't much else to go on. I've been thinking about motives recently.' He shut up as a female student pulled open a door, came out into the corridor, smiled briefly at Nell, and went on her way. Nell watched her go. Rebus thought she would like to swop bodies for a few minutes.

'Motives?' she said. She was leaning against the wall, but Rebus got no notion of calmness from her stance.

'Remember,' he said, 'that night in the hospital, the night Brian was attacked. You said something about an argument, and him going off to the Heartbreak Cafe?'

She nodded. 'That's right. We met that night to talk over a drink. But we argued. I don't see –'

'Only, I've been thinking about the motive behind the attack. There were too many at first, but I've narrowed them down. They're all motives *you'd* have, Nell.'

'What?'

'You told me you were scared for him, scared because *he* was scared. And he was scared because he was poking into something that could nail Big Ger Cafferty. Wouldn't it be better if there was *another* body on the case, someone else to attract the fire? Me, in other words. So you got me involved.'

'Now wait a minute –'

But Rebus held his hand up and closed his eyes, begging silence. 'Then,' he said, 'there was DC Clarke. They were getting along so famously together. Jealousy maybe? Always a good motive.'

'I don't believe this.'

Rebus ignored her. 'And of course the simplest motive. The two of you had been rowing about whether or not to have kids. That and the fact that he was overworking, not paying you enough attention.'

'Did he tell you that?'

Rebus did not sound unkind. 'You told me yourself

338

you'd had a row that evening. You knew where he was headed – same place as always. So why not wait near his car and brain him when he came out? A nice simple revenge.' Rebus paused. 'How many motives does that make? I've lost count. Enough to be going on with, eh?'

'I don't believe this.' Tears were rising into her eyes. Every time she blinked, more appeared. She ran a thumb and forefinger down her nose, clearing it, breathing in noisily. 'What are you going to do?' she asked at last.

'I'm going to lend you a hankie,' said Rebus.

'I don't want your fucking hankie!'

Rebus put a finger to his lips. 'This is a library, remember?'

She sniffed and wiped away tears.

'Nell,' he said quietly, 'I don't want you to say anything. I don't want to know. I just want *you* to know. All right?'

'You think you're so fucking smart.'

He shrugged. 'The offer of a hankie still stands.'

'Get stuffed.'

'Do you really want Brian to leave the force?'

But she was walking away from him, head held high, shoulders swinging just a little exaggeratedly. He watched her go behind the desk, where her co-worker saw something was wrong and put a comforting arm around her. Rebus examined the shelves of books in front of him in the corridor, but saw nothing to delay his leavetaking.

He sat on a bench in the Meadows, the back of the library rising up behind him. He had his hands in his pockets as he watched a hastily arranged game of football. Eight men against seven. They'd come over to him and asked if he fancied making up the numbers.

'You must be desperate,' he'd said, shaking his head. The goalposts comprised one orange and white traffic cone, one pile of coats, one pile of folders and books, and a branch stuck in the ground. Rebus glanced at his watch more often than necessary. No one on the field was worrying too much about the time taken to play the first half. Two of the players looked like brothers though they played on opposing sides. Mickey had left the flat that morning, taking the photo of their dad and Uncle Jimmy with him.

'To remind me,' he'd said.

A woman in a Burberry trenchcoat sat down on the bench beside him.

'Are they any good?' she asked.

'They'd give Hibs a run for their money.'

'How good does that make them?' she asked.

Rebus turned towards Dr Patience Aitken and smiled, reaching out to take her hand in his. 'What kept you so long?' he asked.

'Just the usual,' she said. 'Work.'

'I tried phoning you so often.'

'Put my mind at rest then,' she said.

'How?'

She moved closer. 'Tell me I'm not just a number in your little black book ...'